TRINE REVELATION

THE KINDERRA SAGA:
BOOK 3

By C.K. Donnelly

First hardcover edition 2022

PHOTO CREDIT: Mike Harvey/Peak Image Photo
KINDERRA MAP CREDIT: Emily Rakić/Emily's World of Design
COVER & LEARNING HALL CREDIT: Kim Dingwall

ISBN 978-1-7350518-8-8 (Hardcover)
ISBN 978-1-7350518-9-5 (Softcover)
ISBN 979-8-9863195-0-6 (Ebook)

Published in the United States by Kibbe Creative Media, LLC

www.ckdonnelly.com

TRINE RISING
The Kinderra Saga: Book 1

Not all gifts are blessings…

Sixteen-summer-old Mirana Pinal is one of the few to have ever possessed all three magical powers of the Aspects. She has terrifying visions, however, that if she wields her powers, her homeland of Kinderra will be destroyed—through her. Desperate to keep her dark fate from unfolding, she tells no one about her destructive destiny but her beloved Teague Beltran, a young apprentice herbsman born without powers.

When Mirana receives alarming premonitions of an enemy attack on Kinderra, she is forced to reveal to her people that she is a Trine to warn them of the impending assault.

As the Kinderrans fight to hold armies of a cunning and ruthless enemy warlord at bay, Mirana must decide if using her powers will aid her people—or will bring them more peril.

TRINE FALLACY
The Kinderra Saga: Book 2

Dark choices for good reasons...

As the Dark Trine's noose tightens around Kinderra, young Trine Mirana Pinal and her mentor, the Trine hero Tetric Garis, embark on a quest to learn how the enigmatic watchtower of Jasal's Keep once saved the land. Teague Beltran, Mirana's beloved and an Unaspected herbsman's apprentice, wants nothing more than to kill the Dark Trine himself. As one born without magical powers, however, he is forbidden to take up arms in battle. His confrontation with the Dark Trine's forces may force him to sacrifice his healing oath. Mirana fears using her Aspects with the Light from Within will not be enough to save her people. The strength of her Aspects through the Power from Without, however, will lead her down a path she must not follow. Both must answer their true calling, but each choice may leave them—and Kinderra—without hope.

ACKNOWLEDGMENTS

To Wayne, who kept this "unsuccessful quitter" from quitting!

Isaiah 49:4

"Though I thought I had toiled in vain, and for nothing, uselessly, spent my strength. Yet my reward is with the Lord, my recompense is with my God."

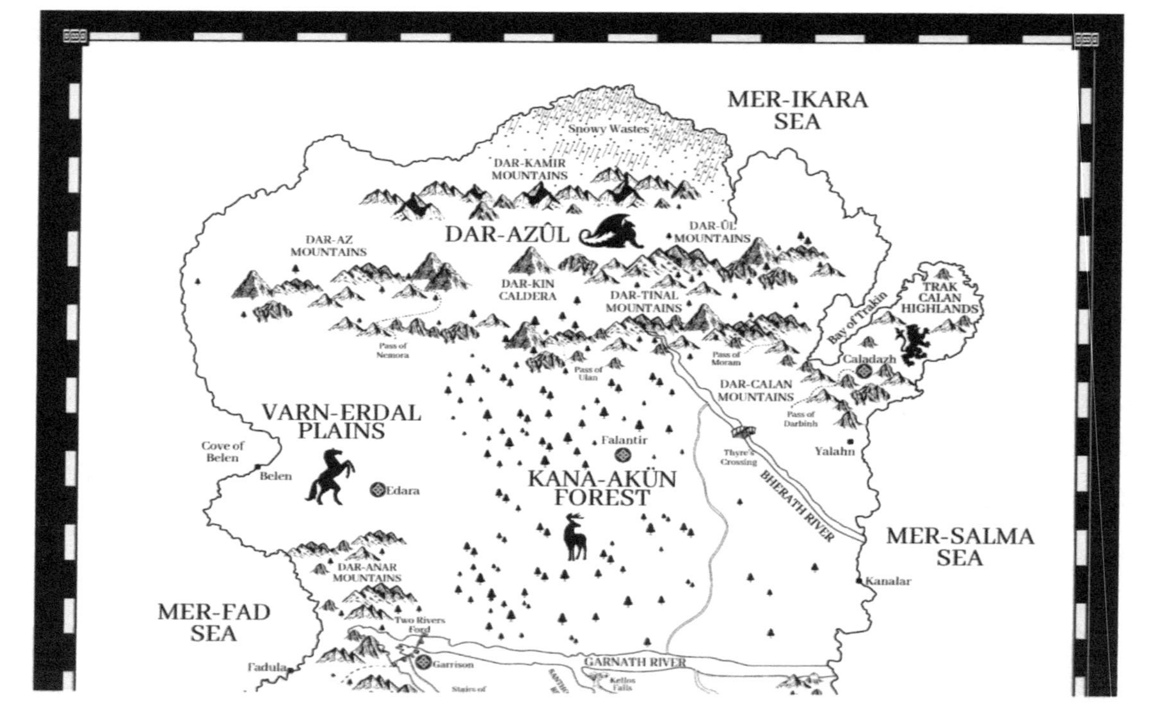

MER-IKARA SEA
Snowy Wastes
DAR-KAMIR MOUNTAINS
DAR-AZ MOUNTAINS
DAR-AZÛL
DAR-ÛL MOUNTAINS
DAR-KIN CALDERA
DAR-TINAL MOUNTAINS
TRAK CALAN HIGHLANDS
Bay of Trakin
Pass of Nemora
Pass of Ulan
Pass of Moram
Pass of Darbinh
Caladazh
DAR-CALAN MOUNTAINS
Yalahn
VARN-ERDAL PLAINS
Cove of Belen
Belen
Edara
Falantir
Thyre's Crossing
BHERATH RIVER
MER-SALMA SEA
KANA-AKÜN FOREST
DAR-ANAR MOUNTAINS
MER-FAD SEA
Two Rivers Ford
Kanalar
Fadula
Garrison
Staires of
GARNATH RIVER
Kellos Falls

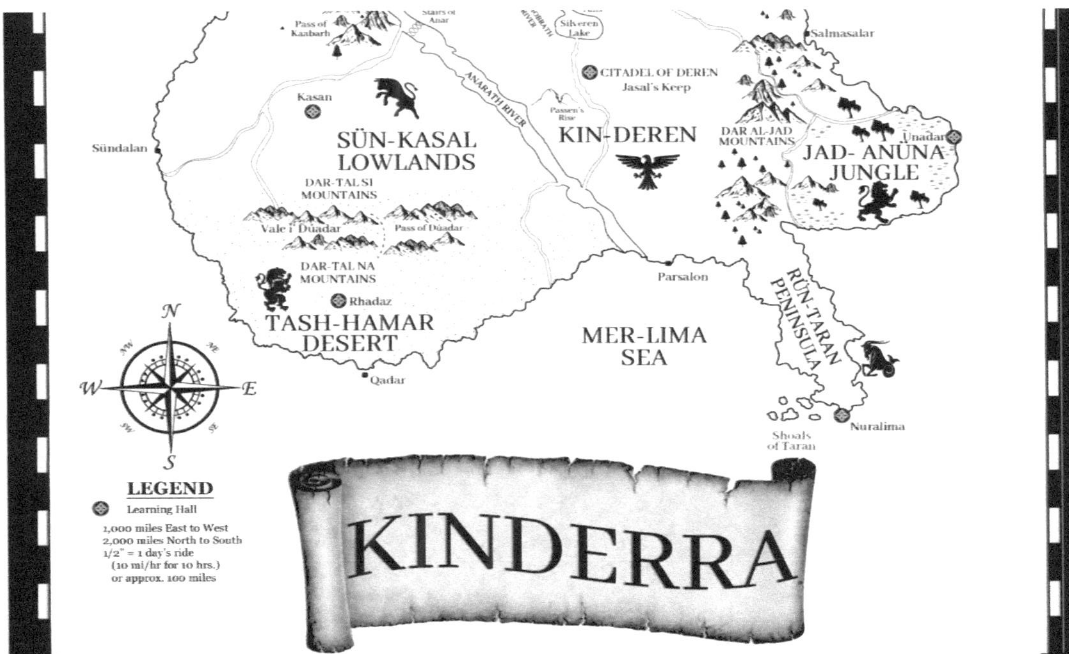

KINDERRA
SÜN-KASAL LOWLANDS
Pass of Kaabarh
Stairs of Anar
Kasan
Sündalan
DAR-TAL SI MOUNTAINS
Vale i Dúadar
Pass of Dúadar
DAR-TAL NA MOUNTAINS
Rhadaz
TASH-HAMAR DESERT
Qadar
ANARATH RIVER
GOBRATH RIVER
Silveren Lake
CITADEL OF DEREN
Jasal's Keep
Passen's Rise
KIN-DEREN
DAR AL-JAD MOUNTAINS
Salmasalar
JAD-ANUNA JUNGLE
Unadar
Parsalon
MER-LIMA SEA
RÚN-TARAN PENINSULA
Shoals of Taran
Nuralima
N
S
E
W
NW
NE
SW
SE
LEGEND
Learning Hall
1,000 miles East to West
2,000 miles North to South
1/2" = 1 day's ride
(10 mi/hr for 10 hrs.)
or approx. 100 miles

Kaarl and Deide's room
Miraná's room
Tetric Garit's Room
Training Rooms
Gathering Hall
Prime's Chambers
Kitchens,
Storerooms,
Dining Hall
Jasal's Keep
Healing Hostel
Stables
Well
Entrance Gates
Library
1/4 mile
N
Kin-Deren Learning Hall

The Trine Prophecy
—The Book of Kinderra

"And it shall come to pass that Kinderra will cry out in such agony as to deafen even her birth. The chosen shall be like a ship without a keel. Aspect will appear where there was none. Light will be dark; dark will be light. One will come forth, thrice-cursed, to destroy. One will come forth, thrice-blessed, to rebuild. End and beginning in one, in both. Only hope shall remain."

CHAPTER 1

The fragile mica sheets of the pendant glowed in Mirana Pinal's hand.

She had to warn her parents—all of Kinderra—that Trine Tetric Garis was a traitor. Thousands of miles lay between them though, an endless ocean of land. Would her father even acknowledge her call after she had left him? She had told them, her father and mother both, that she never wanted to see them again.

"Think."

Tetric would expect her to call her father. No, she needed to call someone else.

Mirana opened herself to her Aspects as best she could. Without a true amulet to focus her powers, it would be difficult, but maybe Teague's pendant would be strong enough.

Her Aspects wrapped themselves around the crystalline sheets. The delicate necklace would not be able to bear the full strength of her powers the way the flawless gemstone of a real amulet would, but it was all she had.

She searched for a living essence with her Aspects. Once, she had existed as only life's music, when she was a babe unborn within her mother's womb. Her mother was the melody, and she was the harmony. Her mother was the first life she had ever known. Separate, yet together as one. The same life music, in one, in both. Like her Trine Aspects.

She opened her heart to the world before her, heartbeats, the music of life. One of those notes was from her mother. She sought to deepen the connection, as she had contacted her father to warn him of the grynwen ambush. He had heard her.

But so had the Dark Trine.

Mirana abruptly dropped the connection to her mother.

A humid breeze drifted across the dry grass of Rün-Taran's coastal headlands and tugged at her hair. It carried the exotic, heavy, almost cloying odor of humus and leaf decay. The jungles of Jad-Anüna province loomed to the northeast.

With that seemingly miraculous warning call to her father, she had unwittingly given away his location and that of the men and women of the elite strike force of the il'Kin. The Dark Trine had indeed found her father, but the wolf had arrived in the guise of a lamb, with her father none the wiser. If she reached her mother now, Tetric would do the same, only this time the wolf might show his fangs. Thousands of them.

She screamed at the sky with fury and unrequited grief. "Damn you, Tetric Garis! Damn you to the Underworld for all eternity!"

She had trusted him as the continent's healer. Her healer. In the end, he had healed nothing. He had convinced her of the noble nature of the Power from Without. And she used that power to kill an innocent man. He had used her powers to murder two people. He had lied to her, corrupted her, betrayed her.

And she allowed it. All of it.

Her former *patrua* mentor had indeed guided her closer to her destiny. Only it was the one she had worked so hard to avoid. She had meant to save the ship on which they had traveled and its sailors from crashing into jagged shoals. Instead, she listened to her *patrua*'s lies and took the life force of a man in a fatal irony meant to save him. The Power from Without was not a different gift—no different lineage flowed in her veins to convey its bond. The Power from Without was a choice. A horrific, ruinous, addictive, murderous choice.

Instead of healing her from her fate of darkness, Tetric Garis had sealed it. She had allowed his beliefs to turn her traitorous against her own convictions. And so, her destiny of destroying all that she held dear was now that much closer.

Mirana knelt and covered her face with her hands. She could not cry. The hurt was too deep.

"You were supposed to save us. You were supposed to save me."

Tetric knew her mind, her presence, her Aspects. He could find her anywhere. If she tried to warn anyone of who he truly was, he might kill her. Or the person she was trying to warn.

She could ride west; she could go home to Deren and warn her parents and the Fal'kin directly. She could leave this quest, with its harrowing keep writings portending suicide and its utter betrayal, behind. She could go home!

But if she did, Tetric would win.

Her former mentor would find some way of locating the last keep passage himself. He would gain control of the keep in Deren and its power. He would end the war, not by the cessation of hostilities, but by subjugating those he could. And those he couldn't, he would kill. People like Teague.

Mirana held the pendant close to her heart. Three tiny, now-faded peda blossoms lay between whisper-thin sheets of mica encircled by a crude setting of tarnished gold. It was simply, beautifully made, so perfectly imperfect. It had been Teague's pledge to her, his commitment to join his life to hers. A commitment she had broken. Irrevocably. To save his life.

Teague would have followed her on the quest to find the missing journal entries regarding the construction of Jasal's Keep. But if he remained at her side, at some point, the Dark Trine would kill him. She had seen her beloved die in her recurring vision of Jasal's Keep exploding in white light. A vision she knew to be as true and real as the air she breathed. A vision Teague had never believed.

To drive him from her, she had told him his lack of the magical and miraculous powers of the Aspects meant he no longer had a place in her life. She had shattered him, killing his love for her. Once something died, calling it back was impossible. Asking for both Teague's love and Kinderra's peace was asking too much.

Mirana stroked her horse's coppery coat. Ashtar stood seventeen hands if he was an inch. His heart was the only thing greater than his strength. How long had she and Ashtar ridden after leaving Tetric? She could not recall the days.

She reached for the waterskin and poured water into the horse's mouth.

"Here, you beautiful beast."

The big chestnut eagerly lapped it up. She would drink after he had some. He couldn't shut away his needs the way she could.

"I swear to you, Ashtar, get me to Caladazh ahead of Tetric, and you will have an entire lake of sweet water to yourself."

When she found the last passage hidden somewhere in Trak-Calan, she would know what the keep was and how it saved Deren. She would know just what Jasal Pinal had done at his watchtower to stop the Ken'nar armies of Ilrik the Black. Tetric would not have to continue with his destructive plans. She could show him the way back to the Light from Within, to life.

She curled her hands into fists, dropping the waterskin. He didn't deserve such kindness from her. His evil and deception had no bounds. He'd taken her own life forces to fuel his Power from Without, murdering Seer Prime Eshe Pashcot of Rün-Taran and her Defender Second Syne Develan. He had the blood of thousands on his hands. Those he had not killed outright, he took from them their capacity to direct their own lives with the Soul Harvest. Did such evil deserve redemption?

Mirana bent down and picked up the waterskin, studying it in her hands.

Was not the blood of more than one thousand Ken'nar lives on her own hands when she destroyed the bridges of Two Rivers Ford? Did she not drain a man's life from him so thoroughly with the Power from Without that she killed him? Had she not forsaken her mother and father for a tyrant?

If the Dark Trine Tetric Garis was beyond hope of salvation, was she?

No. She could not go home. Not yet. She had to continue to find the last keep passage hidden somewhere in the mountain-locked learning hall of Caladazh far to the north.

She rummaged in a saddlebag for something to eat but found nothing.

"Oh, that's not good."

Mirana took out the precious alabaster cylinder with Jasal's journal writings to search the bag further when it rattled in her hand.

"What?" She had been so overwhelmed by the revelations of Jasal's writings that she hadn't noticed there was something else in the container. She reached inside and felt a chain. She gasped. "It can't be." She pulled out the object.

An amulet.

The chain links, made of a lustrous metal purer than silver, gleamed in the fading daylight. Platinum? "No. Is this—?" The setting embraced half of a brilliant, colorless gem. A diamond.

"By the Light."

This was the amulet from her unceasing keep vision. It was beautiful, stunning in fact. And possibly the deadliest object on the continent. Would she somehow wreak destruction on Kinderra by connecting to white light through the amulet?

Lightning flickered, flaring in the full bellies of the clouds, raising the question of a growing storm. Thunder answered, loud. She flinched. Her mount sputtered at the sound.

"Hush, Ashtar."

The oval diamond had been split in half, the setting clearly made to encircle a much larger gem. How could such a thing happen? Why?

The diamond's facets glinted in the flashing storm. All other amulets she had ever touched cried out to her, demanded from her, forced themselves upon her. This one was different. Its call to her was tender. Gentle. Loving.

The amulet began to glow, warm and soothing in her hand. Not exactly a presence but a sense, a knowing, gently caressing her. The diamond.

It spoke to her. Only her.

She closed her eyes. The natural essence of the gem surrounded her, embraced her. Its essence was somehow both unique to the crystal yet mirrored hers. She opened her Aspects to the amulet. A sense of profound and utter peace surrounded her. The diamond's life sense was now no longer a mere reflection of her life but was melding with her, merging with her.

Becoming her.

"Wha-What is happening?"

She had chosen. She was chosen. Her Aspect connected, completed her soul, making her whole. At last.

She once told Teague—Was it only months ago? It seemed like lifetimes past—she was alone, alone in her Trine Aspects, alone in the dilemma of how to use them safely, alone in desiring and abhorring the choosing of an amulet. But this amulet—*this* amulet!—was hers. Jasal Pinal may have worn the diamond twelve hundred summers ago, but it now belonged to her. It told her so through a sense of conviction that defied explanation. She was no longer alone. The amulet was a part of her now, inseparable from her. And inseparable from the torturous knowledge she had gained by killing with the Power from Without. Never again would there be an amulet—or an Aspected—making choices for her.

"Ashtar, I might live or die by my decisions, but from now on, I will make my decisions to do the most good with all that I am. My Aspects. And *my* amulet."

Mirana's hands shook, her body both exhausted and exhilarated. And hungry.

Her stomach growled.

She laughed at the absurdity of the situation. "The most indescribable moment of my entire life, and what comes into my brain? The thought of Quartermaster Lasen's beef stew. Maybe my next decision should be to find food? Saving the continent can come after—"

Like a wave speeding toward the shore, a reflection of Jasal's presence broke over her. The world around her disappeared abruptly, drowning her in a remembrance.

She still held the amulet, but now it rested in another's hands. What was happening? Desperation and determination consumed her, the emotions not hers.

This was the amulet of Jasal Pinal. His amulet was the only one known to be made of diamond and platinum, the rarest of substances in Kinderra.

She saw herself laying the amulet on a stone table. The table inside the Quorum chamber within Jasal's Keep itself. Beyond the room, she heard screams, the clang of swords.

This was a memory, a memory seen through Jasal's own eyes.

In one hand that was not her own, she held a sharp chisel, pressing its beveled tip against the diamond. She gripped a hammer in the other.

No. Aspects Above, no. Jasal was destroying his amulet.

The hammer came crashing down on the chisel. Agony exploded in her chest as if someone had driven a sword through her heart. Her knees buckled, her hip hitting the stones that covered the chamber's floor. She pushed herself up, staggering to her feet. Again, she struck the amulet, crying out in anguish. Again. Again. Again!

She collapsed, the body that was not hers convulsing in pain. In her hand lay the bent setting of the amulet. It now held only half of the diamond. She tried to stand, but her legs would not allow it. She had to get up. She was running out of time. Once more, she hauled herself to her feet. The other half of the diamond lay on the stone table, torchlight shifting in its fractured facets. With Jasal's hands, she grabbed the diamond shard and the amulet and staggered out of the chamber.

The sweet coastal grass snapped back into reality. Mirana lay on the ground, rain falling on her face. She clutched Jasal's amulet in her hand.

He had shattered his amulet.

"But why?"

Each hammer stroke had felt as though he plunged a knife into his chest. Why in the name of the Aspects Above would he have done such a thing? Had he, too, seen destruction from his hands mediated by this very diamond? As she had, so very many times?

Slowly, she sat up and wiped the sweat and rain from her face. Was he trying to prevent himself from using his Aspects outside of himself? It wouldn't have mattered if he'd destroyed his amulet. He was a Trine. He could have used any amulet.

Rank terror, cold and hard as steel, sliced through her again.

"What have I done?"

An amulet was supposed to be a wondrous, miraculous relic. The crystal allowed the living presence of the Light of the Aspects Above within the Fal'kin to be made manifest outside of themselves, a testament to their commitment to protect Kinderra. Every Choosing Ceremony for millennia, primes recited those words from the sacred book of the Ora Fal'kinnen.

In her hands, however, an amulet would spell doom. She had seen it in her vision of white light at Jasal's Keep. She would wear an amulet, and Tetric would try to take it from her. To stop him, she would destroy him and everything else in an explosion of blinding light—including herself.

She gripped the chain to remove the amulet but paused.

She knew she would die at Jasal's Keep; she had never seen anything beyond the white light. But maybe that sense of glorious finality had been reserved only for her. Maybe she hadn't engulfed Kinderra in an otherworldly pyre of radiance. Maybe she would destroy only herself and the amulet, preventing Tetric from having it, and thus save Kinderra. But she would never know until she found the last of the Codex writings.

Mirana threw herself over her saddle.

"Ashtar, we must get to Caladazh. We're running out of time."

CHAPTER 2

"To see the skeins of the Future is a gift of the most
terrible kind. In my heart, I long for blindness. But one
cannot embrace both ignorance and knowledge."
—The Codex of Jasal the Great

Trine Tetric Garis parried the sword of the Rün-Tarani defender, deliberately leaving himself open. His move would instill overconfidence in his attacker and in the other two defenders who remained alive. His assailant moved in and gripped his amulet. With an unnatural swiftness, Tetric pivoted behind the defender just as his attacker released fire from his amulet. One of the defenders went down, agony and shock contorting his dying expression. The Trine immobilized his opponent, opened himself to the man's life within the Aspects, and pulled at it, feeling the power build gloriously within him. A heartbeat later, he released the power through his fractured hematite amulet and sent searing fire between the man's shoulder blades, turning his heart to char. He let the body fall and stared down at the one Rün-Tarani defender who remained.

The young woman froze in fear and defiance. "You killed our seer prime. You killed our defender second. You killed them in cold blood—you murderous traitor."

He leveled his long sword at her, but there could never truly be a stalemate. "All of you who cling to the misguided notion that communion with the Aspects can only be from within— you are the traitors. Traitors to the Aspects!" He swung his blade.

Then he felt it.

Life.

From her. Within her.

His preternatural reflexes could not stop his sword from burying itself in her abdomen. "No!"

The young defender didn't collapse so much as sink to the ground, as if all the strength from her limbs left her at once.

He dropped to his knees beside her. "You are with child. I can save you. Save you both. There is still time. You are a brave woman, a courageous warrior, and I need defenders like you. Please, follow me. Let me save your lives."

Blood pumped steadily out of the gash in her stomach. "I would rather my *biraena* and I remain in the Underworld for all of eternity than swear fealty to a traitorous bastard like you." With a blur of motion, the woman grabbed Tetric's blade and pulled it deeper into her body.

She made no cry, no scream of pain nor bitter victory; she just…died.

"No." He laid his hands on her ruined abdomen. "Aspects Above, no." He poured the Healing Aspect from his soul into the young mother's body, knowing it was already too late. There was nothing left to heal, no life remained to be saved.

The babe in her womb had been a mere sevendays old, a minuscule bit of flesh and primordial consciousness.

"Why wouldn't you listen? Don't you understand I'm trying to save you?"

If only Eshe and Syne would have listened to him! If only they had tried to understand and accept what he was trying to do, they would still be alive. This beautiful young woman and the little life within her would still be alive, as would the eleven other defenders who lay dead around him. He dropped his hands heavily to his thighs.

Was this not why the divine Aspects Above created him a Trine? Was he not trying to end the three thousand summers of bloodshed with every fiber of his being?

Tetric sat back on his heels, his shoulders bowed by the weight of his burdens and so much more.

"You killed her, Mirana. Not I. This woman would have seen you embrace the Light from Within and the Power from Without and would have understood. You do not know what you have done, child. You are not going to end this war. If you don't come back to me, Kinderra is doomed."

He loved Mirana. Although she had been born to another man, she was his daughter in the Aspects, another Trine granted to him by the godhead of the Aspects Above themselves.

Tetric cupped his amulet and reached for the Seeing Aspect. He must find her. He must bring her back. But instead of a present skein of time giving him some indication of Mirana's location, the future tore at his mind's eye.

In a time yet to occur, he would stand before her, his sword pointed at her chest while a storm raged around them. He would demand she back down from their senseless fight.

The vision continued to unfold before his mind's eye. Something around the girl's neck glinted in the lightning. An amulet.

For as long as he had known Mirana, she had been terrified of the very idea of choosing an amulet and had only used one when the consequences of not bonding with a crystal meant certain death. She was not afraid of death. He knew that for certain. Fighting the depraved warriors in the Vale i'Dúadar proved that, to say nothing of her surviving the battle at Two Rivers Ford. No, it was the power she could wield with an amulet that terrified her.

He sensed his desire for the girl's amulet. If only he had it, Kinderra would be his, and the senseless war would end.

The Aspects Above whispered to him it was Mirana's strange, if unique, connection to Jasal Pinal was her motivation for both drawing closer to her own Trine Aspects and running from them. Embracing yet shunning them. As she did him. And he, her.

End and beginning, in one, in both.

The words from the Book of Kinderra's Trine Prophecy chilled him in a way they never had before. He forced his connection deeper into the Seeing Aspect, his own amulet now hot in his hand as he held it. He saw himself lift an amulet's chain from Mirana's neck, desperate to have it and stop the girl from killing herself. The vision then exploded in a blinding, white light.

Tetric fell on his back, the vision's end stealing the air from his lungs with its suddenness. He gasped for breath as he fought to still the hammering of his heart.

Somehow, the keep was imbued with unimaginable power, a power that exploded in a brilliant magnificence. Once he controlled that power, the war would truly end. He didn't want to lay waste to Kinderra with that inexplicable light, far from it. In fact, he prayed he never had to use it. He hoped the mere threat of that power would be enough to quell any lingering resistance from the Fal'kin. Once he controlled Jasal's Keep, they would, at last, lay down their arms against his Ken'nar, and the fighting would cease.

He needed to know more about the amulet Mirana wore in the vision, one so important, she was willing to accept some unfathomable end its choosing would confer upon her. The amulet that hung around her neck would be a colorless gem, quartz or even diamond perhaps. The only diamond amulet he knew of was the amulet of Jasal Pinal. Could the amulet of the vision be the very relic of that long-ago Trine?

Despite Jasal Pinal's desertion of his Fal'kin and the innocents who depended upon him for protection during the siege of Deren, the keep did, in fact, save the citadel. The blinding white light in the vision. The Light and the Keep. Breath caught in Tetric's throat.

Amulet fire.

Could amulet fire, released from Jasal Pinal's diamond, be the light in the keep? As a Trine himself, he could control any amulet he chose, not just one as with those with a single Aspect, so why did this amulet and only this one matter?

Tetric laughed at his ignorance. He had been all wrong trying to stop Mirana from reaching Trak-Calan's learning hall in Caladazh without him, believing she would take whatever writings she found there and run from him again. Now he understood the opposite was true. Instead, she *must* arrive at Caladazh ahead of him. She would find the last lost entry from her ancestor's journal for him *and* bring him the amulet. She would give him both artifacts so he could finally unlock the secrets that had remained within Jasal's Keep for more than twelve hundred summers.

If she didn't—

… Hearken unto me, Ëi Seconde … Tetric called, pouring so much of himself into his mind-voice, his amulet burned his palm. He must tell his second to call off his search for Mirana. He waited. No mind-voice returned to him, only a living presence and a refrain of pain, both diluted by the great distance between the men. Had his servant been injured? He frowned. Pain was a better teacher than he would ever be. *… Sido … Answer me …*

He waited for long moments, but no call returned. Instead, a burning in his palm so hot it felt cold bit into his attempt to contact his lieutenant.

Tetric hissed in pain and shook his hand. An eschar, deep red and sickly white in the shape of his amulet, had burned itself into his palm. His efforts to heal the young defender woman and her babe, to find Mirana, and to call his seer second had critically injured his hand, maybe beyond repair.

He sank once more onto his heels.

Had Sido left him, too? Tetric clenched his wounded right hand into a fist, savoring the agony lancing up his arm.

The last time he had contacted the seer, the boy had pleaded with him to be claimed as his heir, even his legacy. Sido Rendel was the seed of unremarkable Fal'kin, weather seers from Kana-Akün. The young man, however, was hungry, ravenous for power, and had been consumed by the desire to rise above his parents' humble expectations, so the seer had sought Tetric out as a mere youth and had begged to be mentored by the Trine.

Tetric had never regretted the decision of accepting Sido as his *scholaire*, but suddenly dread seeped through him, heavy and ominous.

The memory of his second's vision of the aftermath following the future siege of Deren floated in Tetric's mind. Mirana had survived. Did this mean she would return to his side? Her and his second both? Deren would lie in ruins, but Mirana would stand smiling, victorious, before a broken, cheering people.

Despite the pain, he gripped his amulet, inviting a bond with the Seeing Aspect to provide further clarity to the memory. A figure stood next to Mirana, face indistinct, hazy with the impermanence of the future. She gave the person—a man or even a youth, perhaps?—a lingering kiss. The vague stature and physique of the man seemed familiar somehow.

A burst of anger exploded and stole the gasp of sudden recognition.

"Sido, you dare betray me?"

All the long summers spent shepherding Sido, making the seer stronger than the young man thought possible, making him stronger than Tetric himself thought possible. Sido had given him the freedom to move so many of his plans forward toward ending the generations of genocide. None other had been able to assist him in that capacity, but like so many other Aspected, his seer second's greed for power, for dominance, superseded that of Kinderra's need. Tetric refused to allow that to continue. Mirana did not belong to any man, least of all his second. She belonged to Kinderra alone.

Tetric bowed his head and remained on his knees a moment longer. He had no other choice.

Sido Rendel would never see Deren.

He sought the mind of his horse. He had sent his mount away when the dozen Rün-Tarani defenders out for vengeance attacked. Fal'kin were not so noble as to refrain from hamstringing the beast or slitting its throat outright to prevent him from escaping on his steed. Moments later, the midnight-black stallion neared with an easy gallop, snorting and pawing the earth when it reached him. Tetric stroked its neck, calming it. He paused before climbing into the saddle.

The dead woman and her babe. The bodies and ash of her comrades.

"We have work to do before we leave this place, *Ëi cara.*"

He gripped his amulet with both hands, feeding the Defending Aspect with his life's essence, white-hot pain searing his palm, up his arm, and across his chest. He welcomed it as amulet fire dug great furrows in the soft earth.

For was this not what the Trine of Kinderra did? Give of himself to all the peoples on the continent?

He panted in pain as he gently laid the woman in the grave and crossed her arms over her belly so she could forever hold her unborn child.

… Mirana, please come back to me …

The Ain Magne covered his eyes with his uninjured hand and wept.

CHAPTER 3

"Whilst we deemed the battle a victory, we still mourned, for the war waged on."
—The Book of Kinderra

"Regardless of what Teague, Morgan, and Binthe discover, we must station our forces here, here, and here."

Kaarl Pinal pointed to several locations on a map spread before him. He sat on the ground under a large tent with his wife Desde, and the leaders from Varn-Erdal and Sün-Kasal provinces. The tent served as a learning hall for Varn-Erdal's defender prime, Liaonne Edaran, and the map, drawn on a piece of leather, was just about the only thing Liaonne had left after the Ken'nar had burned her learning hall and the city of Edara to the ground.

As Steward of the Quorum of Light, Kaarl had little reason to be giving any advice at all, let alone devising a battle strategy for three provinces. He was supposed to have given up his role as a defender commander leading Fal'kin in battle. He was supposed to be an arbitrator, a politician. As the steward, he was supposed to merely advise on interprovincial policy and not become involved in war actions.

He had never cared for things he was *supposed* to be doing. He cared for his family, his Aspect, his amulet, and actions that might leave more people alive than dead.

"Your Fal'kin, Sahm, and most of your Unaspected, Desde, should be placed here." He indicated locations on the map along the Garnath River. "These are the most likely points where he will try to cross the river from Kana-Akün. Put the balance of our Unaspected here." He pointed to an area some miles north of Deren.

Desde frowned. "It's risky. That will leave Deren itself all but unprotected."

He knew he could only advise her—as Prime of Kin-Deren province, she alone had the final word on where her troops would be stationed—but she was a seer, not a defender. "Perhaps, but you need your armies to prevent the Dark Trine from crossing over the Garnath. Deren is a fortified citadel. Her walls and gates will hold against a large assault if he breaks your lines. If you can hold him off along the river, it might not even come to that. If it does, they will run into your forces and have Sahm's Fal'kin at their heels."

"How long can the walls and gates withstand a direct assault?" Rabb Plout asked.

Kaarl gave the Seer Second of Sün-Kasal an encouraging shrug. "Long enough."

"I agree with Desde. If the bulk of our forces remains here"—Rabb pointed to the river—"Deren remains vulnerable if the Ken'nar army manages to slip through our lines. Our forces will only be effective if he passes, say, within a day's ride."

"They might not even try to run your lines," Liaonne added. "What if he's already on the march, taking the windward side of the Dar-Anars? He could try to cross the Anarath and come at you from the southwest. The Anarath is wider, but it is likely shallow, too. That spit of rain we received after the Ken'nar attacked Edara is not nearly enough to make a dent in this damnable drought. The Dark Trine just might risk the long march."

Kaarl considered her suggestion. "It's possible, however, it would take too long. I know it seems like this accursed dry weather will never end, but it will. You are probably right about one thing—he will have to move soon. Before the autumn rains come. If he's moving an army of any size at all—and I fear he is—he would have already had to start his march. He will take the shorter road." He stabbed his finger on the blue line of the Garnath just above Silveren Lake.

Sahm Klai, Defender Prime of Sün-Kasal province, glowered at the map. "What if you're both right? While we were fighting five thousand of his Ken'nar bastards here at Edara, he could have already begun moving more of his troops across the Garnath toward Deren."

Kaarl heard his wife's jolt of alarm. It would be an utterly brilliant move. He wasn't sure what surprised him more, the possibility that the Dark Trine could be attacking Deren as they spoke—or that Sahm Klai thought of the tactic.

"He couldn't." Desde sounded to Kaarl like she was trying to convince herself. Aspects Above knew he was. "To have had five thousand troops here and another force marching on Deren at the same time? How would he even be able to command two battles of that magnitude at the same time?"

Kaarl and the others were silent. Only the Aspects Above knew what the Dark Trine was capable of. He could have dozens of battle seers, Ken'nar warlord defenders.

He forced himself to breathe slowly.

"Do we even know if the Ken'nar host is truly that large? They retreated from Edara with a scant two thousand," the burly Sün-Kasalan prime said.

Desde sat back on her heels. "He had five thousand at Two Rivers Ford, too. Until that battle, we didn't think he had more than two thousand in all. That's what we hope Teague and the others will be able to find out."

"To lay siege to Deren, the Dark Trine will need thousands of defenders as well as towers, battering rams, oil, trebuchets, and whatever else his diseased, Aspect-forsaken mind can dream up. To throw all of that at Deren, he must have an easy crossing. That means he must cross the Garnath River while it is still low."

"We cannot leave all our troops on the Garnath." Sahm thrust his finger down on the drawing of the river. "If he takes another route, all I have and most of what Desde has will be there, sitting worthless, with no one defending the south."

It was so bloody obvious. Two Rivers Ford had been destroyed, and the Dark Trine's land route was gone. Taking the route Liaonne had suggested around the Dar-Anars and coming up from the southwest would take far too long, not to mention risk discovery. "The Dark Trine must cross the Garnath, the quickest path to the south." Kaarl traced his finger from Falantir to Deren, a direct line south of the Kana-Akün capital.

The defender prime tugged at his beard and contemplated the map. "Two Rivers Ford, gone. How could stone bridges that have stood for thousands of summers just collapse?"

Desde squeezed Kaarl's hand. "They didn't just collapse."

"Desde." He did not release hers.

"Kaarl, there's nothing to be gained by hiding it anymore. Kinderra will know it soon enough. Many already do. Mirana destroyed the bridges. With the Aspects. Mirana is a Trine."

Kaarl tried to exhale, but his breath caught in his throat. Desde was right. Their lies could no longer save Mirana. The entire continent knew their child was a Trine. Now the only choice he had to keep their child safe was to kill the Dark Trine before he could kill her.

"But we have Tetric Garis. And the Dark Trine. Thr-Three Trines?" Sahm spoke slowly as if his words struggled to untangle themselves from disbelief. "There has never been such a thing. Your daughter? That small girl? She has only seen sixteen summers. The Trine Prophecy. What does this mean?"

Kaarl felt the others' minds shut, one by one. Rabb rubbed at a healing cut on his hand, studiously avoiding eye contact with Sahm. Kaarl had told the seer in confidence about Mirana's three Aspects. Obviously, the man had honored his word.

His heart constricted in his chest so tightly it hurt. "We don't know." Desde's hand remained in his.

"I was there at the ford. That wall of light that slammed into the rock. That was…" Liaonne swallowed. "That was your daughter?"

The big Sün-Kasalan shook his head, incredulous. "Why did you not tell us? Hiding an Aspect—hiding *Aspects*—like that is a capital crime. Bloody hell, it's more than a crime, it's sacrilege."

Kaarl released his wife's hand at last. "Sahm, if the Dark Trine knew of her, her life would be forfeit."

The defender glowered at him. "And how many others' children's lives were forfeit because of your lie? We could have had another Trine fighting for us." He clenched his massive hands into massive fists. "Where is she now, your daughter?"

He shook his head. "I don't know. I begged Garis to take her before the fighting broke out at Two Rivers Ford. I can only hope they are someplace far away."

His hands once held a sword and an amulet in defense of Kinderra. Now all they held were memories. He had led the il'Kin, the most accomplished fighting force the Fal'kin had, and yet he could do nothing—nothing!—to protect his child.

"She left us, left me. We lied. I never meant to hurt her. I meant to save her life. I don't know if I'll ever see her again."

"You were not alone in this, *Ëi ama*." Desde placed her hand on his back. "*Ai*, I wanted to tell her about her Trine gifts so many times, but I dared not risk it and put her life in jeopardy, no matter how much my heart ached hiding the truth from her. And hiding it from everyone else." She took a sharp breath. "In the end, she already knew of her powers. We knew there was always a chance she would discover them on her own, but we had hoped she would have come to us if she did." Her hand left him. "She never said a word."

"If the Trine Prophecy is to be believed, Garis's sole mission as the Light Trine is to destroy the Dark One," Sahm said. "Mirana could be in grave danger if Garis does indeed confront the Dark Trine."

"Sahm," Rabb cautioned.

"I know that," Kaarl snapped. "I am trying not to jump to conclusions. Please do not push me to make them."

Liaonne sat back on her heels. "You willingly gave your daughter to Tetric Garis?" She snorted a sharp laugh. "You must have been desperate."

He gave her a withering look.

"After the Dark Trine's army all but wiped my province off the face of Kinderra, I care more for the whereabouts of Garis's

Dar-Azûlan Fal'kin than where he is with your daughter. We need them."

The seer second nodded. He scowled a moment and ran a thumb around the edge of his brown topaz amulet. "Kaarl, you said some of his troops came with you to the ford. He told you he left the rest stationed up near Falantir." He let go of the crystal. "Do you know where his troops went after the ford?"

Kaarl sensed Desde's mind and briefly held her gaze. "We were focused on regrouping our forces."

Rabb nodded. "But still, Liaonne, Desde, did either of you see them follow Garis and Mirana? Or did they maybe meet up with those he left in Kana-Akün?" He gestured toward the forest province on the map.

Now it was Kaarl who shut his mind. The seer was probably just working his logic aloud, but the chain of the man's thoughts mirrored his own. "I never saw Garis's Fal'kin again after the fighting broke out."

Desde held up her hands. "Stop it. All of you. I know what you are thinking, Rabb, but this is Tetric Garis we're talking about. We've all fought alongside him. For summers." Kaarl reached for her hand again, but she pulled it from him. "He could have ordered his men to follow the Ken'nar that escaped north from the ford. He could have ordered them back to the Kana-Akün to rejoin the rest of his troops, or they could have all been slaughtered like so many others were. He could have done any number of things. How dare any of you insinuate that our Trine is a traitor!"

Kaarl studied his wife's beautiful, strained face. Her words defended the Trine, but she could not hide her thoughts, not from him. She suspected the same, but fear for their daughter drove the emotion behind her words.

Liaonne drew a slow circle with her finger around the star that marked Edara on the map. That faded bit of blue ink was all there was of a once-proud if rustic city. "I've always thought he was far too ambitious for a man who has supposedly dedicated his life to the whole of Kinderra. You talk about not wanting to jump to conclusions, but the healers' boy drew a pretty damning one alleging Garis ordered his parents and the herbsfolk to the Dar-Anar foothills to be slaughtered or captured."

"Teague was in shock. He had just seen his father commit suicide as a Ken'nar. He did not know what he was saying." Desde glared at the young prime, and to Kaarl's surprise, the habitually fierce woman cast her eyes downward.

Desde leaned forward and pounded her fist on the map. "You are talking about the man who is protecting my child."

Kaarl put a gentle arm around his wife and pulled her back. "Desde, I'm sure we are all tired and are simply overreacting." He called a warning to Rabb. He valued the man's insight, deeply, but they had enough to worry about. The fear growing in the pit of his stomach, however, wasn't because he believed the seer was wrong. It was because he believed the seer was right.

"Please, my prime, I did not mean to upset you," Rabb said to Desde. "I am trying to understand if Garis is trying to tip the scales in his favor to become Primus Magne, if he has become the Dark Trine, or if he has become just as bewildered as the rest of us as to how to stop the Ken'nar." He dipped his gaze. "I see now I spoke your own concerns. I will never know the particular fear for a child's welfare, but I can understand—"

Sahm Klai frowned. "And whose fault is that?"

Liaonne held up her hand, silencing the Sün-Kasalan. "Wait. Tetric Garis is trying to become Primus Magne? Take away our self-rule? When did he make this known?" Her yellow topaz brightened.

Kaarl closed his eyes, defeated frustration holding them shut a moment. Oh, he did not want to discuss all of this now. The Ken'nar host was nearly on their doorstep, for Aspects' sake. "He asked me as steward to support him when the council convenes during Quorumtide. He told me of his plans before we left for Two Rivers Ford. He said he'd be able to stop massacres—hell, the war—if we all united under him."

Desde grimaced. "That is assuming we'll still be hosting Quorumtide. After all of this"—she indicated the smoldering remains of Edara—"I'm not certain we should. Or can."

Liaonne shook her head. "Edara is exactly why we must convene the Quorum of Light. The primes of Kinderra need to know what's happened."

"But is it safe?" Rabb toyed with his amulet again. "All our Fal'kin leaders in one place? It may prove to be an irresistible target for the Dark Trine."

Kaarl rubbed his beard. There was also the issue of the practicality of calling off the meeting just sevendays away. "Could we cancel the convocation in time before the more distant provinces start heading for Deren?"

Sahm walked his fingers across the map, measuring distance. "Some of the Unaspected merchants may already be arriving to claim choice locations for the festival markets." He sat back and scowled. "I know Sün-Kasalans are. What are you going to do, Steward?"

A sickening coldness slithered through Kaarl's stomach, drawing his attention away from the desire to plant his fist in Sahm Klai's face. The big defender had just placed the safety of the Quorumtide celebration squarely on his shoulders. In truth, it was. He was Steward of the Quorum of Light for however long the convocation's members kept him at the post. Not to mention he and Desde would be the hosting province leaders. If all of the Underworld were unleashed upon Deren, innocent men and women—and children; families always made up much of the Quorumtide crowds—would be caught in the crossfire. Literally.

"If Garis tried to curry favor with me to support his bid for magnistate, chances are I'm not the only one," Kaarl replied at last. "He may have managed to convince some of the other provinces to support him. He'd have to have a vote by the Quorum to elevate him officially."

Rabb frowned. "Officially."

Desde shot him a concerned glance and sent a spike of emotion to Kaarl. "If he tried to become Primus Magne without a vote, he'd risk censure, even expulsion from the Quorum. But that means next to nothing for a Trine." She covered her face with her hands, attempting to hide her worried expression behind them under the guise of fatigue.

Kaarl knew better. He rested his hand on her shoulder but faced the group. "We must be ready with an alternative. I think we're all in agreement here that the Ken'nar have been emboldened to fight like never before. We need the provinces to come together to push the Dark Trine's forces back, maybe eliminate them altogether. But as independent peoples." Somehow. Desde squeezed his hand at the unspoken notion. "And that means we must meet to come up with a comprehensive strategy that preserves our freedom."

Liaonne shook her head. "I know he is a Trine and has turned the tide of battle when all seemed hopeless, but I don't care if the man can walk on thin air, he will get no support from Varn-Erdal to elevate him to Primus Magne. I will never bow to a sole leader, a sole *ruler*. Never. I cannot abandon my province for the council meeting to vote. Kaarl, you will take our votes to the Quorum of Light. You have all witnessed my words." She sat back, calming herself with difficulty.

Sahm Klai crossed his brawny arms. "Just because some of you think he has delusions of grandeur does not make him evil. I know the man as well as any of you. I, too, have fought alongside him."

Rabb nodded. "*Verdas*, but given what Teague Beltran said, there could be another reason why Garis is so bent on getting the Quorum to name him Primus Magne. A bloodless coup."

Sahm skewered his seer second with a ferocious look. "The boy was battle-shocked. How could Garis kill his own men? *Why* would he? It makes no sense."

"Unless he didn't kill them." Rabb's hand remained on his brown topaz amulet. It now glowed.

Kaarl exhaled explosively. "Rabb, please."

The Sün-Kasalan prime laughed without humor. "Do you all hear yourselves? This is absurd. Insinuating that Tetric Garis is the Dark Trine goes beyond the bounds of idiocy."

Rabb, Sahm Klai's seer second, squared his shoulders as if tensing for battle. "When young Teague spoke about his parents and Garis's order, my Aspect called to me. It was subtle and swift. I do not know what it means. Yet."

Kaarl held up his hands. "Please. All of you. No one is saying Tetric Garis is anything other than what we know him to be. We have more urgent issues than to sit here and gossip like scullery women. We need to decide where to put our forces to meet the Ken'nar. I'm telling you, the river is our only option."

"The only option?" Sahm shook his head. "I guard the largest province in Kinderra. I have another option. To draw my battle lines at home."

"Klai, our shallow victory here at Edara has done nothing more than give us some time and force the Dark Trine to change his cavalry to an infantry," Liaonne said.

Kaarl nodded. "She is right. He will strike again. We need to take advantage of what little time we've gained to prepare. You must place your forces along the Garnath."

The large man rose to his feet. "I told you before, I will not trade one overlord for another."

Kaarl came to his own feet. "I will forgive you that remark because of the trials we have been through of late."

His wife stood and held up her hand. "Enough. Sahm, Kaarl's advice is good, and I intend to act on it. I have sensed increased activity somewhere in the Kana-Akün, as have the other seers. I also agree with you, however. I have eight hundred Unaspected remaining, most of those Fal'kin who survived the ford. I will take three hundred back with me to Deren and leave the balance of my forces along the Garnath. I am asking you to do the same. For the sake of the rest of Kinderra. Liaonne can do nothing further, except perhaps send scouts into the territory."

The young Varn-Erdalan prime nodded. "Done."

"So, this is how it is?" Sahm Klai scowled down at the others. "This is exactly why I proposed a mandate against relations with Quorum members."

Kaarl stepped toward the big prime. "How dare you suggest that Desde is not her own woman just because she shares my name!"

The big defender did not move one inch. "That is not all she shares."

He had heard enough. He started for Sahm Klai, but Desde grabbed his arm. Liaonne and Rabb held the Sün-Kasalan back.

"Sahm, stop!" The seer second pulled on his prime's arm. "Stop. I, too, have seen what Desde has sensed. I have seen activity that could be consistent with a pre-war buildup and troop movements. I warned you before we even left Kasan."

Kaarl gritted his teeth and relaxed. His wife released him. He was far more furious with himself than he was with Sahm Klai. He had not picked a brawl since he was younger than Mirana, but it was all just so bloody obvious. The Dark Trine could not possibly move a large force by any other route. The Ken'nar bastard wanted a land route, and Mirana had ended any hope of that when she'd destroyed the ford. Crossing the river while it was low was the only choice left.

He took a step back from the large defender, exhaling his anger, and held up his hands in apology. "Sahm, forgive me. I implore you to leave your forces along the river, but you are prime of your province and only you can decide how best to protect your lands and Kinderra."

Instead of backing down with his own apology, the Sün-Kasalan took a step forward. "You came to me, begging me to go north to save Edara from the Dark Trine because if it fell, Deren would be next and then all the lands to the south. I heeded your words because I perceived a threat to my province. Edara *has* fallen. And it is only because of the might of Sün-Kasal that the wench still holds her province. The Dark Trine does not sit in her learning hall, but it has fallen just the same."

Liaonne shot to her feet and drew her sword. "*What* did you call me?"

"Liaonne, no!" Desde placed a hand on the defender's arm. "Sahm, what's the matter with you? For Aspects' sake."

"I lost men and women, too. Good men and women," Sahm seethed. "No, Kaarl. This time, the answer is no. Sün-Kasal will protect Sün-Kasal. As it should have done before."

"Sahm, please," his second said. "Be reasonable. I have seen—"

"I do not care what you have seen. He may or may not cross the river. He may or may not attack Deren. Your visions are just that, Rabb. Visions. I am a defender. I am prime. I deal in absolutes. My duty is to keep Sün-Kasal safe. And so I shall." He turned on his heel and stomped from the tent.

Rabb gave Liaonne a weary frown and shook his head. "I apologize for his remarks, my prime. Let me speak to him. Maybe I can get him to reconsider."

"Don't bother," she replied, her voice husky with vehemence.

Rabb curled both of his lips inward, perhaps to bite off a comment or a chuckle. He did neither and hurried out after the prime instead.

Liaonne exhaled harshly and clawed a hand through her white-blonde hair. "Klai is an idiot. Always was, always will be. But he did speak the truth about Edara, and me, as much as I hated hearing it." She straightened her shoulders. "Kaarl, your strategy is far from ideal, but I do not see any other defense than to make a stand along the river. I will send scouts and messengers to Tash-Hamar. I guarantee you, Fasen Aldi will not be happy to learn our Defender Prime Klai may leave a door open into his province if he doesn't help turn the Ken'nar back at the Garnath." She squeezed Desde's arm gently and then started to leave. She paused. "Desde?"

"*Ai?*"

Liaonne held her amulet, dropping her gaze to her yellow gem. "Speaking of Tash-Hamar. If Timir Sadhi is at Quorumtide…if he should come, tell him how deeply I regret not being there."

Desde smiled. "*Ai.* Of course."

"Tell him to be careful." Liaonne stepped out of the tent and left Kaarl and Desde alone.

He raised an eyebrow. "I thought her tastes were of a more feminine flavor."

His wife remained smiling and shrugged. "Liaonne is not a woman who limits her palate. But some tastes rise above others. *Ama ísi enigma.* Love is a riddle."

He sank back down to his knees, his eyes on the map. "Rabb will not be successful in changing Sahm's mind, will he?"

She kneeled beside him and leaned her head against his shoulder. "I don't know. The Seeing Aspect is too volatile right now. I see a myriad of possibilities." She rubbed her eyes and kept them closed as she pinched the bridge of her nose. "Oh, Kaarl, I don't know anything anymore."

He brushed his lips on her hair. ... *I wish your father were still alive, Ëi ama* ...

... *I do, too, if only to spare you this grief* ... She entwined her arm with his and pressed her lips to his shoulder.

... *You aren't just agreeing with me because you share my name and my bed, are you?* ...

She sat back. "Do you think so little of me that a pair of strong arms and eyes like moonlight on water would sway me to do something to jeopardize Kin-Deren?"

He pulled her closer. ... *But what if I am wrong?* ...

... *It doesn't matter if you are wrong or right* ... *It is not your decision to make* ... "It is mine. I am prime of Kin-Deren."

"Do you have a sense of when the Dark Trine may come?"

She shook her head. "And believe me, I have sought nothing else since the fighting ended here. I only get a vague impression of cold air and rain."

"Autumn?"

"Maybe. It's possible we wounded him badly and he will be forced to wait until early spring, but that seems remote. I will ask Liaonne's seers if they have seen something more precise. Even without a vision, however, it makes sense tactically for him to strike before Quorumtide. Certainly, before the snows come."

Kaarl frowned. "He'd attack that soon? Quorumtide is only a few sevendays away." He quickly squelched the memory of Sahm Klai's comment about the Ken'nar already sacking Deren.

"Have you ever tried to move a trebuchet through a foot of snow and ice?" She gave him a look, and he smiled at her logic. "Personally, with so many Fal'kin in Deren for Quorumtide, not to mention all the primes and their seconds, I couldn't think of a worse time to sack us. So maybe sometime after." She held her arms. "Or before."

He embraced her again. ... *Are you sure you are not a defender?* ...

She laughed. "I have to see what supplies we can leave with Liaonne, what we will need to leave with our troops on the Garnath, and what we require for the march back to Deren. That's what I *have* to do. What I *want* to do is wring Sahm's neck like a chicken." Now Kaarl laughed. "What's so funny?"

"You used to sound like that whenever you would scold Mirana."

"Maybe he's brought her back home." Her voice grew soft with emotion. "Maybe our *biraena* is home, waiting for us."

He forced a smile. "Maybe." He closed his mind to his wife.

CHAPTER 4

"Dïë ísi falé bé nöc, per nöc ísi falé tudsa bé dïë."
("The day is followed by the night, but the
night is also followed by the day.")
—Ora Fal'kinnen 145:83–84

Kaarl walked through the scattering of tents that was now
Edara. Someday, minstrels would sing of the Battle of Edara as
a victory, the Varn-Erdalans sacrificing their hall to keep its
precious treasure of fabled horses out of Ken'nar hands and the
Unaspected of Kin-Deren sacrificing their very lives in the
heroic contest. But for what? Liaonne—and Sahm Klai, for that
matter—had been painfully correct. Little had been
accomplished here, for either side. The Dark Trine's forces
might not be encamped in Varn-Erdal, but no Fal'kin were
guarding the northern half of Kinderra either.

He turned to the north for a moment. After both Two
Rivers Ford and Edara, the Ken'nar had retreated in the

direction of Falantir. The forest capital had fallen to the Ken'nar the past winter, that was all but certain. Never had the Dark Trine kept all his forces in one location, but scattered them across the continent, always having his men and women on the move and making them almost impossible to find in the vastness of Kinderra. The loss of one unit would never materially affect the whole of his army. While that might be a brilliant strategy from a certain point of view, it also meant the Dark Trine could only incite surgical strikes and skirmishes. Now, with consolidated forces, he could lay siege to any province he chose. That, however, left him vulnerable as well. Using all he had in one battle also came with the risk of losing all he had.

Kaarl smiled grimly as he continued through the camp. Perhaps the Dark Trine was growing overconfident. *Ai*, only twelve hundred Unaspected marched to Edara from Deren. The city, however, had a hundred times as many living within and near her walls. And the province as a whole held a thousand times more. Many might flee ahead of the Dark Army, even most, but not all. For every Aspected, there were a thousand such Unaspected. No, Deren would not fall prey to the Dark Trine quite so easily.

In the distance, Rabb Plout gesticulated emphatically on some point he was trying to make to Sahm Klai. The seer second's questions regarding Tetric Garis floated up in Kaarl's mind.

When Garis and his troops had arrived after the grynwen attack on the il'Kin outside of Falantir back in late Thirdmonth, the Trine had made some vague comment about following possible survivors, but he had said nothing about his forces coming to Falantir's aid. He certainly had not called to Kaarl to enlist the help of the il'Kin or even to warn him about what had befallen the forest city. He had made no mention of trying to prevent an attack on, protect, or liberate Falantir. Was it possible that Garis had not known? *Ai,* of course, anything was possible. Furthermore, if the Dark Trine had been but a few leagues away, the Ken'nar bastard could have heard Garis's warning call. That could have left the Dar-Azûlan no choice but to warn him in person. That, however, seemed like a thin excuse.

The man was extraordinarily skilled in the Seeing Aspect. How could he have *not* seen what had happened at Falantir? Mirana had, and later, so had Deren's seers. And what of Garis's Healing Aspect? Would not the deaths of hundreds have cried out to that most sacred of Aspects?

Kaarl gripped his amulet hard enough to feel its edge bite into his hand. How many times had he resolved to ride after Teague, Morgan, and Binthe, to see for himself what was hiding in the forests of Kana-Akün? Every fiber of his being had screamed at him to race to Falantir to find the Dark Trine and end this madness once and for all, but Teague had been correct. He had fought the Ken'nar for decades. They would know him. Binthe and Morgan, for all the time they had been with him, still didn't have the long summers he had spent tangling with their enemy. He could disguise his body but not his mind. Even cloaking himself under U'Nehíl would leave the Ken'nar suspicious.

Garis had told him Mirana would be safe while she was by his side. Wasn't his ultimate calling as a Trine, however, to kill the one who opposed him? Was that not what the Trine Prophecy foretold? Wasn't that why the Aspects Above created him?

A young girl with blue-black hair ran through the tents, laughing and shouting after some chickens.

Unless Mirana was the Trine that opposed him.

He stopped and stood motionless. Again, he fought to calm himself. He was being ridiculous. His fears were irrational, those of a father. *Ai,* concern for the safety of his child was the worry every parent faced. Maybe Desde was right. Maybe Mirana was home in Deren. And he'd make damn sure her home would remain standing.

He walked faster in Sahm Klai's direction.

"Sahm," Rabb Plout pleaded, "whether we fight him on the Garnath or at Kasan, we are still going to face him. Even your Aspect should be telling you that. At least if we take him on the river, we won't be risking Sün-Kasal. To do anything else is sheer stupidity."

The big man stepped closer to the seer. "I look the other way with your choice of companions. Others on the Quorum are not nearly so open-minded. If you insult me once more, I will see to it you will never use your amulet in service of Sün-Kasal again. Then where will you serve?"

"Sahm," Kaarl said as he approached the Sün-Kasalans. The big prime whirled around on him, frighteningly fast for a man of his size. He sent a back-off warning so forcefully to Kaarl's mind it hurt.

"Do what you must, my prime." Rabb closed his hands into fists as if he were holding his battle seer's long knives. "I am your second. I serve at your pleasure." The seer stalked off into the camp.

Kaarl crossed his arms. "That was uncalled for."

Sahm held up his hand. "Enough."

He remained silent but did not leave. The defender prime did not speak for a long time.

"You think I am an imbecile," he said at last.

"No. I think you are frightened. Like we all are. And none of us has any answers to assuage our fears. I do apologize for earlier. Truly. I should never have raised my hands to you."

"You wouldn't stand a chance, you know. You may match my height, but I outweigh you half again as many stone."

He smirked at the big prime's bravado. "We will be headed back to Deren soon. I don't want to leave things between us this way." He held out his hand.

Sahm studied Kaarl's hand a moment, then blew out the rest of his anger and gripped his forearm. "I should never have spoken about Desde that way. Or you. That was inexcusable."

Kaarl smiled. "I forgive you, but I am an easier one to convince of contrition."

The defender prime returned his smile briefly. He turned his face to the south. Kaarl could see nothing but the burnt stubble of dry grass. He was certain, however, that Sahm saw the rich fields of his home. "Do you remember the day Bystra died?"

Kaarl nodded. "Like it was yesterday."

"It has been eighteen summers. And a few heartbeats." The Sün-Kasalan shook his head. "Why does death pain us so? We Aspected, especially we defenders, know from the moment we are born we will probably not live out our natural lives. Why are we so surprised when one of our loved ones dies?"

A drizzle of dread trickled in Kaarl's stomach. He refused to let his thoughts travel any further than Sahm's words. "Your wife was a brilliant defender. And so were both your sons and your daughter. It was more than just the Power from Without that took them. I think we are beginning to learn we have not had a level battlefield for a very, very long time."

The defender swallowed loudly. "Bystra would be halfway to Falantir by now to attack the Dark Trine head-on with every last one of our Fal'kin and probably half of our Unaspected as well. Liaonne thinks she is Kinderra's she-wolf from the Underworld, but the girl hasn't even seen twenty-six summers. She is too young to have seen my wife in her glory. Bystra should have been prime of Sün-Kasal. Not I."

Kaarl put a hand on the man's shoulder. "You may be more cautious with your Fal'kin than the other primes, but I also know you march home with far fewer losses than any other. That is not the result of caution. That is the result of a good leader."

"Kaarl, do you understand what I'm up against? Truly? I feed Kinderra. Not just the Fal'kinnen, but the Unaspected, too. Everyone. Deren is the symbolic heart of all that is Kinderra, but in the end, it is just a symbol. I put bread in the mouths of babes. If I fall, no symbol in this world or the next will keep them alive."

"*Ëo comprende, Ëi cara,*" he replied. "*E ísi verda.*"

The big man grew quiet again. Kaarl squeezed his shoulder and turned to leave.

"What do you think of your chances against the Dark Trine? Honestly?" Sahm asked.

He studied the prime for a moment, unsure of how to answer. Did not the Ora Fal'kinnen say lies held no honor? The truth, once revealed, brought the suffering one meant to avoid.

"These are Unaspected, not Fal'kin," he replied at last. "Maybe some distant summer hence, Kin-Deren's populace might rise against the Dark Trine as he sits in Deren. Only the Aspects Above know, however, if there will be anyone left to lead them. We will do what we can, but honestly, Sahm, without you, I see no hope."

The prime heaved his massive shoulder as he blew out an exhale. He paused a moment then nodded slowly. "Sün-Kasal is a truer sister to Kin-Deren than any of the other provinces. It was cleaved from Kin-Deren not long after Jasal Pinal died. The siege by Ilrik the Black had so frightened Kinderra, the primes wanted another learning hall to protect our food."

"*Ai*, that's right." Kaarl smiled faintly. "I had forgotten my history lessons."

"Family fights together. And Fal'kin family, closer still."

Kaarl faced the other man. "As the adage goes." Dare he hope Sahm had changed his mind?

The defender turned and hooked his thumbs on his belt. "I told you and Desde I would not put my troops along the Garnath."

Why was hope always so frail, so damned fleeting? "You must do what you feel is right."

"Sün-Kasal will form a line in front of Deren itself. Desde's Unaspected can take out the Ken'nar war machines and maybe tackle the first wave of their vanguard. Then she will let those black-armored bastards through. To me." Sahm curled one side of his bearded mouth. "They will not even see your legendary gates."

Kaarl laughed, nearly weeping in relief. "That is a good move."

The big defender waved him off and laughed himself. "By the time I got back to Kasan, it would be time to head out again for Quorumtide. I might as well go now."

Kaarl raised an eyebrow. "And Rabb, too?"

The Sün-Kasalan prime frowned, one more of acquiescence than acrimony. "Am I pleased that he takes men to his bedchamber? No. I would much rather he find a good woman and beget a dozen more like him. He is one of the most gifted seers we have. I know I am blessed to have him as my second. You think I'm the reason we take so few losses? If we survive, it is because of him."

"Have you told him this?"

The defender sighed again. "Not nearly often enough."

"You are a good man, Sahm Klai. I am honored to fight alongside you, but I am even more honored to call you a friend." Maybe hope did remain after all.

CHAPTER 5

"Tears drown our hearts like the sea washes away the shore. The Ken'nar take thee, O thou children of Rün-Taran, to silent depths where even Mother Mer-Lima cannot."

—The Book of Kinderra

Teague Beltran charged over the high plains in the eastern reaches of Varn-Erdal province. Morgan Jord and Binthe Lima rode beside him, the three encased in the helmets and narrow plates of black Ken'nar armor. While the need for the disguise made sense and he welcomed it, the stiff armor made the already demanding ride grueling, even painful. How did the Ken'nar fight in these damned things?

He reached up to touch his father's heavy amulet where it beat against the metal breastplate as he rode. When they reached their destination, it would take more than a swift horse and plated armor to keep him alive. Falantir was the very den of the enemy. An enemy that turned his father into a soulless monster. An enemy that might still be holding his mother captive. Hatred filled him, and suddenly his sore muscles didn't seem so bad anymore.

The Dark Trine might be in Falantir, too. Teague might meet the Ken'nar leader face to face. He might throw aside his duty as an herbsman for good and find the strength to kill him.

Oh, who was he kidding? He was *so* going to die. The Dark Trine would turn him into a greasy pile of ash before Teague even had the chance to think about revenge, and probably step over his remains on the way to the latrine, too, for all the effort it would take. But if he died, he wouldn't be able to save his mother if she were alive or bring home what he could if she were not. He would never be able to tell Mirana how much he loved her. That simply would not do.

A volcano erupted in the pit of his belly.

No. That would simply *not* do.

He *would* find his mother first, and he *would* find some way to pledge himself again to Mirana. He had always loved Mirana and always would, no matter how she felt about him. For summers, she had confided in him that she had seen some horrific fate Kinderra would suffer at her hands. She had pushed him away because of this very nightmare. She must have believed breaking his heart would save his life.

"Miri," he whispered, "I don't care what we face, even death, as long as we face it together." He looked up at the sky. "I've always felt this way, but I was just too young, or stupid, or-or, I don't know, to have the right words until now."

If his arms could never hold her again, if his lips never touched her again—he let the thought sink through his chest, a bitter weight he could no longer avoid.

All he cared about was that she was alive and free. He had promised Mirana he'd never let her face the Dark Trine—any darkness, really—alone. By the bloody gates of the Underworld, he'd be damned if he would give up on that promise.

He gripped the hilt of his Ken'nar blade, savoring the way the finger plates of the armor disguise bit into his fingers.

He growled at his frustration, the expression loud enough to rise above the pounding of the horses' hooves. "Mirana, I swear to you, I will find you, and I will never leave you again."

Binthe glanced over her shoulder at him. "Did you say something?" Her question was nearly lost over the pounding of the horses' hooves.

Teague didn't respond. The seer had probably caught the gist of his words, and explaining would take too much out of him. He hugged Bankin's sides with his knees tighter and tried to concentrate on their ride, but again, the faces of the women he loved the most floated up in his mind. So much for keeping his thoughts in his saddle. He both desperately hoped they were in Kana-Akün and just as fervently wished they were anywhere else.

Irony. He huffed a laugh. He hated irony.

Lord Garis had seen the attack on Two Rivers Ford with his Aspects but had mentioned nothing about trying to prevent Kana-Akün's capital of Falantir from falling into Ken'nar hands. The Trine was one of the few who knew where Teague's healer parents would be stationed during the battle at Two Rivers Ford. He supposedly healed an il'Kin comrade of Binthe's, yet the woman had tried to kill the seer and him both as a harvested Ken'nar.

The Trine Prophecy only spoke of two Trines, the Light and the Dark. There was no mention of three. Regardless of what nightmares Mirana saw for her fate, Teague knew she was not and could never be the Dark Trine. That left her as the Light Trine and Trine Tetric Garis as…as something else.

Teague refused to let his thoughts go any further than that, but insidious little terrors boiled and broke like fever dreams in his mind.

For now, he could do nothing for Mirana. The Fal'kin depended on him, Morgan, and Binthe to find the Dark Trine's war machine hidden deep in the forests of the Kana-Akün province.

When Morgan finally slowed them to a halt, the sun blazed down from an unbroken expanse of blue.

"Why are we stopping?" Teague asked, his voice muffled by his Ken'nar helmet. "We have hours before dark."

The defender removed his helmet and wiped the sweat from his forehead. "The horses need a rest. As do we."

"I'm not tired. I would have thought you two, of all people, could ride longer."

Binthe set her helmet on her saddle pommel and combed her auburn hair loose of its braid with a gauntleted hand. "*Ai,* you are, too, tired. And so am I." She grimaced as she lowered herself from her saddle and stumbled on her healing leg.

He frowned and nodded. It would take her sevendays to fully recover from the leg wound she'd received saving his life when the Ken'nar attacked Edara. He was not a Fal'kin healer. He was barely a healer at all. He picked leaves, steeped draughts, sewed catgut and linen and silk through flesh, and prayed they'd work.

"We must use the cover of darkness to hide us as we get closer to Kana-Akün," the seer woman continued as they made camp in the tall grass. "We will rest for the remainder of the day and be in the woods tomorrow evening. The going will be slow once we enter the forest, but it will be safer than out here in the open."

He shook his head. "We can give the horses a bit of a rest, but then we need to continue. At least during the day, so we can see their swords coming at us."

The seer paused with a saddlebag. "This is not something to be rushed."

"Every moment we waste is another moment my mother faces in that hellhole," Teague said.

Morgan caught Binthe's eye and then turned away to tend to his horse.

"What? *Wha-at?*"

"I do not hold out much hope in finding your mother alive. I can sense nothing of her." She walked over to put a hand on his arm. "I've been trying."

He batted it away. "Maybe she's under U'Nehíl. Or unconscious. Did you think of that?" Or worse. He tore off his helmet and threw it from him.

"I know how much you want to find your mother, but we cannot rush into the Ken'nar stronghold, amulets blazing. We must be patient."

He held his hands out to his sides, exasperated. "Be patient? For what? For them to kill her?"

"That's enough."

He jumped, as Morgan had snuck up behind him. Dammit, he wished the defender would stop doing that. He stepped back and took a breath. "I'm sorry. I just—" He ran his fingers through his hair and winced when a break in his gauntlet caught on a lock. "Never mind. Neither of you understands." He yanked down his saddlebag.

Morgan stiffened. Binthe held up her hand, stopping any retort. "*Ai.* I would."

He didn't want the seer's soothing voice and demeanor, her kind words, her sisterly caring. He wanted his family and Mirana back, alive and whole.

"What I wouldn't give to have my family back, too," she whispered.

He let out a frustrated groan. "I'm sure Rün-Taran has seen its share of Ken'nar swords."

"They have. Ten summers ago, to be precise."

Morgan took the saddlebag from the seer. "Binthe. Don't."

The seer held the defender's gaze with her own for a moment and turned to Teague. "Both my mother and father died as a result of battling the Ken'nar to prevent them from entering into the Kin-Deren interior."

The revelation stunned him. He vaguely remembered some skirmish ten summers ago, but fights on provincial borders were almost an everyday occurrence. He knew her parents had died, but he never knew how. "They were killed then?"

"No. They were not." Her voice had taken on a brittle tone he had never heard from her before. "The Ken'nar swept down from the Dar-Calans and crossed the Bherath River. Jad-Anüna and Rün-Taran both answered Kin-Deren's call for aid. My father and I were away at sea. When they brought my mother home to Nuralima, she was more dead than alive, but not from any wounds sustained on the battlefield. She breathed yet she was gone. Her eyes. She just stared. She was an empty shell. We did not know what it was then, but seeing what happened to your father has answered many questions."

Morgan took her hand in his. She squeezed it and let go. "Unable to help my mother, my father's grief turned inward and drove him mad. One day, unable to endure it any longer, he killed my mother and then turned her sword on himself. I was there. And I arrived too late to stop him."

Teague's shoulders fell. "Oh, Lights! Binthe, I'm so sorry. I didn't realize—"

She stood toe-to-toe with him, a touch taller and infinitely more adept with long knives. "The army we will meet will not be some paltry hundreds or even thousands, but tens of thousands. The Dark Trine has harvested Fal'kin for a long, long time. So I would counsel caution before we ride into Falantir."

"Binthe, *siba*, I—"

Her sea-green eyes locked on his with the intensity of a searing amulet. "You are not the only one who would see the Dark Trine dead for killing loved ones, Teague Beltran."

CHAPTER 6

"I have seen Their Divine Plan."
—The Codex of Jasal the Great

The flat, brown ribbon of the Garnath River stretched ahead of Mirana. Leaden clouds butted their heads against one another as the hot breath of the wind blew the heat from the far western plains. Now and then, fat, cold drops of rain spattered on her skin.

She tried to rein in Ashtar, but the scent of water drove him forward. He stopped only when he stood in the middle of the river. She plunged into the water, as eager as the horse to slake her thirst.

Sevendays without rain had turned the wide, pounding river into a shallow creek. She drank the warm, muddy water anyway, grimacing at the grit sliding down her throat.

Mirana waded across to the far riverbank. Leagues of open country and another river lay between her and the mouth of the Darbinh Pass and Trak-Calan province. She stretched weary muscles as she turned east. Should she backtrack and cut through the jungle toward Salmasalar? She could take a boat to Yalahn. She would lose time getting to the port city, but once she set sail, it might save her sevendays.

And that would be exactly what Tetric would expect her to do. He could be waiting there for her. And he would never let her leave him a second time.

The quest to find the last missing page of Jasal's Codex had turned into a race. He would try to get the Trak-Calan keep excerpt before she did. She clawed her fingers through her hair, catching them on the knots tied by the wind of her ride. Overhead, a hawk cried. It dove like an arrow toward the water and winged upward at the last moment, a fish held in its talons. Her stomach rumbled.

She had finished what scraps of waybread remained in her saddlebags days ago. She bit her lip. How could she hunt without a bow or arrows? She could use her amulet, but she'd probably end up turning her dinner to ash. The reality of her situation sank in. She could push herself a little while longer, even calling on her Healing Aspect, but at some point, she had to get some nourishment. She could not waste the time hunting. Then again, she had to eat if she was ever going to make it through Trak-Calan province's mountain to Caladazh.

"Bloody hell."

Mirana picked up a piece of driftwood from the pebbly shore. The silty water obscured the river bottom, but if a hawk could find a fish, she should be able to sense one with the Aspects. She hunted well enough. How much harder could fishing be?

She whistled to Ashtar. He ignored her, munching eagerly on the brown, brittle scrub weeds that poked up through the stones of the riverbank. The poor beast was just as hungry as she was.

Mirana patted the horse's flank and rummaged through her saddlebag, pulling out a leather stay from her pectoral armor. She smiled and quickly tied her belt knife to the end of the driftwood to make a spear.

It turned out fishing *was* a lot harder.

Her prey eluded her every attempt to spear them, riled and wary from the bloodhawk. She stood back and paused in her useless splashing. She frowned. "Well, if you want a fish, think like a fish."

Mirana calmed her mind and slowed her heart's pounding from exertion and the anticipation of food. She closed her eyes. Almost immediately, warmth spread across her chest to her shoulders and arms. The primitive minds of fish and dozens of other creatures touched her consciousness. Startled, her eyes snapped open. Jasal's diamond amulet glowed, pulsing with an inner light as her Aspects meshed with it seamlessly.

Giddy laughter bubbled up from her empty belly. "This is almost too easy."

She spoke too soon.

Five more fruitless—or rather, *fishless*—attempts left her soaked and her stomach burning with hunger.

"Think, Mirana." She could now sense where the fish were, but they darted away with each stab of her spear. "Think!"

The fish swam away because they sensed a predator. How could she trick them into thinking she was—her stomach growled—well, *food?*

She grinned. Centering herself once again, she merged her Aspects with the amulet while opening herself to U'Nehíl. With the technique of mirroring her life's essence with that of the life she sensed around herself, she radiated the persona of a worm.

Several fish slowed their movements, swimming lazily once more through the murky water. One floated closer with the river current. Another swam even closer, determined not to lose its meal to its fellow schoolmate. It opened its wide mouth to gulp down a worm—

"Aha!"

Wriggling at the end of her makeshift spear were two fat river trout.

"You can keep your grass, Ashtar!" She brandished the trout by their tails at the copper-colored warhorse.

Mirana tromped from the stream and shook her wet hair out of her eyes. She had been so focused on fishing that she hadn't noticed the rain now pouring down from thick, dark clouds. No fire would last in this downpour. Then she smiled. No ordinary fire could be ignited in the rain, that was true. But she had an amulet now. She didn't need a blazing bonfire, just enough amulet fire to cook her fish.

Mirana knelt on the shore and removed the long knife from the stick. Slitting open one of the river trout, she groaned and turned away. "Ugh. And I thought rabbit innards were bad." She tossed the entrails into the water while Ashtar happily nosed the scrub. Could people eat grass like horses?

"Quartermaster Lasen's cod was very good. And I ate a snake. This can't be worse than that." She had an amulet but not the quartermaster's seasoned broth and spices. Or his cooking skills.

She centered herself and opened her Aspects to the diamond. The crystal bonded with her with alarming swiftness. The Defending Aspect shot forth from her and through the amulet toward one of the trout.

And completely incinerated it.

"Seriously?" Mirana squeezed her eyes shut, her head swimming from the exertion. Fine. She'd eat the other one raw.

She took a few breaths and popped a piece of the fish into her mouth.

Raw fish was indeed worse than snake. By far.

She gagged. Bitter as gall with a sickening sweetness like that of fetid eggs, it tasted beyond repulsive. She tried to swallow without tasting as the trout morsel slid down her throat like mucus. She retched again. Maybe she had fouled it in the way she disemboweled it? Nothing that horrible could be remotely edible. She forced two more bites down. It was the most hideous thing she had ever eaten, but it would keep her alive. She had wasted enough time on this nonsense.

"That's enough dinner for now, *Ëi cara.*" Mirana clicked her tongue, calling the horse to her.

Holding the remaining trout with one hand, she grabbed a stirrup with the other to pull herself up. She steadied herself against Ashtar until the dizziness passed.

"What to do with you?" she said to the trout. Maybe it would stop raining soon and she could build a proper fire. And eat proper food. And find a way to make Tetric see reason. And save Kinderra.

At that moment, her stomach demanded she save philosophical questions of salvation for another time. She forced down another bite of fish. It wasn't any better the second time.

Mirana gazed north; the distant mountains of Trak-Calan were lost in the mist. "Why do I feel like the closer we get to Caladazh, the further from the end of our quest we become?"

Ashtar sputtered and tossed his head.

"You choose *this* to agree with me on?" She patted her mount's thick neck and kissed him. "You worthless, wonderful beast." She wrapped the remaining trout in some plant leaves that grew near the water's edge and stowed it in a saddlebag.

Mirana swung up into the saddle and galloped north, surrounded by heavy rain, thick mud, clinging questions, and equally cloying answers.

CHAPTER 7

*"Periculus etim ísi inimica i'Oëa inimica, as gryphus e
aquila bath ten talus'e."*
("Dangerous still is the enemy of thine enemy,
as the griffin and the eagle both have talons.")
—Ora Fal'kinnen 45:12

Mirana tore across the muddy plains of far eastern Kana-Akün, heading northward toward Trak-Calan, Ashtar's hooves churning the rain-soaked grasslands into mud. The treacherous mire sucked and pulled at the steed's every hoof fall. He'd already slipped and fallen once, taking Mirana down with him. Riding blindly through the night, shrouded in rain and mist, she prayed she was still on course.

The gray dawn gave her precious little light and even less warmth. She was soaked to the skin, only the horse underneath her and the exertion of the hard ride keeping her warm.

The dim daylight faded again into a charcoal evening then true darkness. Fatigue now weighed her down. Her own needs did not matter right now. The only thing that mattered was getting to Caladazh and finding the keep passage. With her Healing Aspect, she could endure a certain amount of physical hardship over that of ordinary folk, even other Fal'kin without the Aspect. She could not, however, go on forever without food and rest.

Deep exhaustion settled into her bones, and she no longer felt hunger. The unending beat of her horse's hooves lulled her into a semi-wakefulness. Jasal's Keep flared in her mind. She shook herself back to consciousness. Ashtar was tired and his gallop faltered. She dared not risk winding him, but she had to make it to Trak-Calan and find the keep passage before Tetric did.

Mirana hid behind U'Nehíl, using her Aspects to camouflage her presence by mirroring the sense of life around her. Could Tetric find her the way she had once found her father? She had searched for the odd duplications of life forces that should not exist. Would he do the same to find her? What was to stop him? She pulled deeper within herself.

The horse's breathing now came in rasps. Red-tinged foam blew from his nostrils. She had long since stopped pleading for Ashtar to run, but he'd found some form of feral determination that rivaled her own.

The saturated ground turned into rivulets of silt. Lightning illuminated the clouds and the jaws of the Dar-Calan Mountains far ahead of her. The wind picked up, driving the unceasing rain into her face.

"If this rain keeps up, we'll be swimming, not riding." There were times she would have sworn the horse replied to her, but now, he was far too focused on his run to respond. The notion of what Ashtar would say to her—probably something like he'd be the one doing all the swimming—made her smile. She bent low in the saddle and kissed his mud-spattered neck.

In the distance, a thin gray line slashed through the muddy ground on the horizon. The Bherath River. If she'd had the strength, she would have cried out with joy.

Thyre's Crossing would lead her over the banks of the Bherath River. The mouth of the Darbinh Pass would be two days farther. She could make it one. Caladazh and the learning hall were a few days beyond that, high in the Dar-Calan Mountains. The Darbinh Pass was the only route to the learning hall.

And the only way out.

If Tetric managed to reach the pass before she did… She pushed the thought away and brought her concentration back to guiding Ashtar through the mud.

Ahead of her, the crude, wooden bridge spanning Thyre's Crossing swayed in the wind, its fraying rope stringers creaking. Aspects Above, she better not be hallucinating.

"Ashtar! We're almost there! Run!" Her voice cracked with exhaustion.

As if the horse, too, sensed they neared the last leg of their journey, he found a reserve of strength that made her want to weep with gratitude. The steed's hooves now drummed in a single beat as he ran at full stretch.

The worn path to the bridge beneath them suddenly disappeared, the muddy earth submerged underwater.

"No!" She pulled back hard on the reins but too late to stop her mount's charge.

Ashtar tripped over the hidden embankment and fell into the flooded thoroughfare. She pitched over his head and landed with a bone-jarring thud, tumbling several times to sprawl in the mud of the opposite bank.

She tried to roll over and sit up, but her body would no longer move. Ashtar lay on his side, his chest and forelegs on the embankment, the rest of his body below the muddy water.

"Ashtar, get up, boy. Get up." The chestnut neighed, more a wet cough than his usual baritone whuffle. "Get up, Ashtar." He floundered weakly in the mud.

Mirana pushed herself up and staggered over to her horse. She fell to her knees and tugged at his reins. He lifted his head and then dropped it again in the mud, making a wet slap. His sides heaved. Blood leaked from his nostrils.

"What have I done to you?" The beast could not get his legs under him. "All right, boy. All right. Rest. We will rest for a few moments."

She brushed off some of the mud from the animal's copper coat. After her father returned home from a fight, he would curry the horse for hours and make the warhorse's coat gleam like a ruddy mirror. Her father had said Ashtar meant more to him than his sword, maybe even his amulet. The chestnut destrier had saved his life as many times as Morgan Jord had. He owed the steed the attention—such paltry thanks for his valor.

She knew it was more than just showing gratitude. Those hours spent currying Ashtar had helped to clear her father's mind, giving him time alone to force the bitter memories of war to recede. He never wanted to bring such violence before Mirana and her mother. She'd known this. Overcome with joy at having her father home, she had crept out of bed once to meet him in the stable. She found him just standing still, his mind in a riot. She'd never bothered him in the stables again.

Father. *Paithe.* She had forsaken him for a traitor. Her father had believed there were two Light Trines. He was wrong.

"I am so sorry, *Paithe*. How could I have been such a fool?"

She forced herself to stand. "C'mon, boy. You've got to get out of the water." She pulled on his reins, willing the horse to get up.

Ashtar pawed at the mud, neighing, fighting frantically to stand. His hind legs strained while his fetlocks remained knuckled over in the mud. He neighed louder and pulled one front leg and then the other out of the mire. She called to her Healing Aspect as she pulled the horse with all her strength, and the pale amulet at her chest glowed as she wrapped him within the cocoon of her curing gift. He climbed out of the flooded path, sending her slipping backward to fall once again in the muck.

"Ashtar." Mirana held up her hand as she lay on her back. The horse nuzzled her palm.

Rain pounded down on her from a glowering sky as exhaustion and hunger ate away at her strength. The Healing Aspect trilled through her body like the last writhes of a dying fish. She must get up, too. Three breaths. She would give herself three breaths, then she would get up and continue.

One. Two. She breathed. Three.

Again, she pushed herself up. Her head swam and her legs buckled. Her body shut down. She could go no further until she ate, no Aspect need tell her that. She reached up and grabbed one of Ashtar's stirrups. Groaning with effort, she pulled herself to her knees, and finally, to her feet. She patted Ashtar's flank as he gulped water from a flooded gopher hole.

Mirana opened one of the saddlebags and dug out the leaf packet containing the river trout. The putrid stench of rotting fish assailed her nostrils.

"Oh, I really don't want to do this."

She had to eat.

Mirana found a morsel that appeared somewhat less spoiled and pulled it off the bones. She stared at it for a moment and took another breath. She shoved it in her mouth and swallowed. Immediately, her stomach clenched. She gripped Jasal's amulet before she could vomit and called to her Healing Aspect again, forcing the trout to stay in her. As soon as she released her hold on the Aspects, her stomach contracted again. She sank to her hands and knees and retched. The rest of the decomposing fish liquefied in the rain. She heaved again at the sight of it.

The Seeing Aspect coursed through her, stronger than the nausea.

His sword rakes across her abdomen. She sinks to her hands and knees, clutching at her wound, feeling her blood flowing hot over her hand.

She moaned, shaking her head to dispel the fragment of her keep vision. When the retching stopped, she cupped dirty water from the gopher hole with her hand and spat it out.

Mirana sank into the mud and gave a wearied sob. No tears came. Crying took too much effort.

Learning hall *brepaithe'e* had told stories of a winter famine that once gripped Kana-Akün summers ago. Many, many died, but some managed to stay alive by eating pine needles and clay. The hall's old ones also whispered others had stayed alive by eating something else. What exactly that something was, no one ever said.

She pushed herself up once more to sit and scooped up a handful of mud. She'd take a seer's bet it tasted better than rotten fish. Ashtar snorted.

"Easy for you to laugh." The horse snorted again. His ears shot forward, and he backed up. Out of the gopher hole slithered a snake.

She had not ridden the length of Kinderra to die from a snake bite. She pulled deep within herself, calling to her Defender's Aspect, and sent a finger of flame from Jasal's amulet. The snake wriggled then sizzled in the mud.

She lifted her face to the unforgiving sky. "Is it not within your will to send me a covey of quail?"

At least it was fresh. Mirana staggered over to the dead snake. A bulge distorted its body. Maybe its meal could become hers. She slit the reptile open, and a gopher, whole and undigested, fell out. She shouted, never so happy in her life to see dead *verminh*.

Mirana washed amulet fire over the rodent, this time holding back the Defending power trying to rush out of her. She put a piece in her mouth. Amulet fire burned parts and left others raw, but it was marginally edible. That made it a feast.

She tore into the meat with her teeth, and Ashtar wuffled. "You outweigh snakes by a thousand stone, you coward—"

The Defending Aspect prickled her awareness.

Mirana stopped chewing and listened.

Five men approach.

Were they friends or foes? She couldn't take the chance to find out. Tetric had been right about one thing—information about Jasal's Keep was something people would kill for. She had to get across Thyre's Crossing before she was discovered.

She let her gopher fall into the slurry and held her hand out to Ashtar. "Help me up." He trotted closer and she pulled herself to her feet with the reins. Had she been able to finish her gopher, maybe she could have taken on all five men, but not now. She was still too weak. Or was she?

The Power from Without.

Eshe Paschot's words came back to haunt Mirana. The Power from Without had left its scars within her, wounds that would never heal, the temptation to use it always there. The power had been limitless. She had been limitless.

No. Never again. Kinderra would be better off with her dying a noble death than if she continued down the path her former *patrua* had set her upon.

Mirana reached for Jasal's amulet. She was a Fal'kin. Her protection was the Light from Within.

She flopped over the saddle and dragged her leg around, the toe of her boot floundering for the stirrup.

"I don't know who they are, and I don't want to find out. Hah!"

She dug her heels into Ashtar's side. Once over the crossing and on the Darbinh Pass, she could hide among the rocks during the coming nightfall. She could try, anyway.

She glanced over her shoulder. Two dark forms loped out of the woods toward her. Grynwen.

"Oh, Lights."

Five dark-armored riders charged close behind the large carnivores. Ken'nar. The lead rider's form was lanky. Maybe the Ken'nar were just as starving as she was. Or maybe he was young. Whatever he was, he was high-ranking; she saw a flash of gold chain from his epaulets.

"Bloody hell. C'mon, Ashtar!"

Mirana's Defending Aspect called to her before her eyes saw the strike. Amulet fire exploded from one of the Ken'nar's crystals, the blue flame of a sapphire. She dove away from the deadly light and slipped from the saddle. Too weak to correct her position, she fell to the ground.

"Hold your fire!" the young Ken'nar commander shouted.

The Defender's Aspect welled up in her, reviving her from the fall, begging for release. She called to Jasal's amulet. She yearned for wholeness in a way she had never experienced before. She sought completion from the amulet, through the amulet. For the amulet.

The dark warriors closed in and attempted to surround her. She gripped the diamond and answered with her own fire, directing it toward the warrior with a sapphire. White flame exploded from the broken, flawless gem—and split into tendrils. Each finger of fire struck a rider squarely on his amulet, driving them from their mounts. The young commander screamed and hit the ground, holding his arm. The grynwen cowered and paced.

"What the—?" Mirana scrambled to her feet.

The lead Ken'nar curled into a muddy ball of pain. She hadn't struck him in the arm. She hadn't meant to strike him at all, only the warrior who fired on her. What was happening? The Ken'nar with the sapphire collapsed to the muck, but the others were already rousing, grabbing their amulets.

"I said hold!" The commander clambered back onto his horse and rode toward her. "If she is injured, I will cut out your black hearts myself." The grynwen took off again.

She dashed for Ashtar. One of the wolflike creatures leaped upon her back and drove her to the ground.

… *Attend!* … the Ken'nar called.

"Get off me!" Mirana struggled under the grynwen's weight. Wrapping the beast with a violent intent of the Aspects, she threw it from her, sending it yowling and skittering across the mud.

She flipped over, but fatigue and sludge prevented her from moving into a defensive crouch, and she landed on her backside.

… *ATTEND!* … The young commander's call to the carnivores pierced her mind again.

The grynwen that attacked her wobbled to its massive paws, shook itself, and slunk back to its master. Its pack mate paced and whined impatiently, its pupilless red eyes never leaving her.

The Ken'nar commander reached down low with one arm and dragged Mirana over his saddle.

She thrashed against him. "Let me go!"

His pale-green peridot amulet glowed in the gloomy twilight. She grappled for one of her long knives but could not reach it from her awkward angle.

"Stop. You are safe."

Like hell she was. She twisted out of his grip and fell back into the mud. Lying on her back, she glared up at him.

The man removed his helmet and dismounted. "Mirana. It's all right."

She gasped in recognition. "Seer—Seer Second Rendel?"

The driving rain plastered the waves of his sandy hair to his forehead in a matter of moments, rivulets of water trailing down a scar on his left cheek, his thin nose, and thinner lips. Yet his physique, the green in his eyes. In a dark alley, she could have easily confused him for Teague. His presence, though, was different. Vastly different.

Sido Rendel was Tetric Garis's seer second. He remained like a shadow in service to the Trine. His reputation painted him as impossibly—and ruthlessly—talented for one who had yet to see twenty-three summers. She had met him as a young girl only once during Quorumtide, and that had been little more than an introduction. She pushed away her fear.

"Stand down, all of you," he ordered. He turned back to her. "I had hoped to find you before you reached the pass. Your hold on U'Nehíl is most impressive." He held out his hand to help her up. She ignored it and wobbled to her feet.

"Seer Second, why are you not wearing the colors of Dar-Azûl but dressed as a Ken—?"

Understanding hit her like an armored fist. Sido Rendel was dressed as a Ken'nar because he *was* a Ken'nar. Shock, fury, and shame of her naivete pummeled her like an answering blow.

Tetric had sent his lieutenant to intercept her. If she tried to run, Rendel and his men would kill her. Bloody hell, again! How was she going to get out of this one? She could barely stand, let alone fight.

"It looks like you found me, Seer Second, but I'm afraid I must depart your cordial company," Mirana snapped as she rubbed a bruise forming on her shoulder. "I have urgent business elsewhere. *Ben dia.*"

Tetric must have told Rendel she was a Trine by now. Maybe if she acted tough, they'd…what? Leave her alone? Just let her go? Well, they hadn't killed her yet.

"I know." The seer nodded. "And I'm coming with you."

What? Rendel seemed like he wanted to escape just as much as she did. What was happening? "And I have three Aspects that say you're not." She turned to the remaining three defenders as they approached. "I'm leaving—"

The fourth defender, the one with the sapphire, remained on the ground and moaned.

Mirana frowned. "—as soon as I take care of him."

She'd begun to tromp through the mud toward the fallen man when Sido grabbed her arm. "Do not approach him."

She yanked her arm back. "I only meant to stop his attack. I will not let him die. Even if he is a Ken'nar."

The seer held up his hand, staying his men. "Leave him alone. It is better this way."

"I will not let a man die if I can help it." She hurried to the fallen defender and knelt beside him. "Rest easy. I'm going to help you." She called to Jasal's amulet and let her Healer's

Aspect emanate through the diamond, setting it aglow. She lifted off the man's helmet.

Sido sucked in a breath. "Mirana, I'm warning you. Stay away from—"

She stared at the downed man with uncomprehending eyes. "Dav! It's me, Mirana Pinal, Kaarl and Desde's *biraena*." The man's eyes gave no flicker of recognition. She turned toward Sido. "Why is he under the banner of the Ken'narren? Defender Commander Koehl is my mother's provincial commander. He would never leave the Fal'kin."

Mirana moved his sapphire amulet aside, revealing a gaping wound in his chest. "No. Oh, Dav. I'll fix this, I'll heal you. I promise." She hadn't hit him that hard. How did this happen? "Help me get his armor off."

"It is better to let him die," the seer second said.

She snapped her head around again, pinning the seer with an icy glare. "How dare you? This man is a hero."

He cautiously walked toward her. "He is no longer who you think he is."

She ignored the seer and placed one hand over the man's wound, holding Jasal's amulet with the other. She reached into Dav Koehl's mind with the Healing Aspect—and found nothing. No, that wasn't quite right. He was alive, barely, but he held no emotions. None. She sucked in her breath and turned to Sido. "What have you done to him?"

With lightning-fast reflexes, the dying Ken'nar grabbed her throat with an iron fist. "The Fal'kin must be stopped at all costs." Blood leaked from his mouth as he rasped the words in a monotone. He bore no hate; killing was simply his reason for being.

An enormous pull from his Power from Without drained life from her, and she collapsed against the Ken'nar. He cried out in agony and maniacal glee, his amulet blazing painfully bright. Sido yanked her away and threw them to the ground as the wounded Ken'nar's sapphire flared. The man who had once been Dav Koehl turned himself into a human pyre.

Mirana sat back in the seer second's arms, riveted by the pile of ash that had been one of her family's closest friends. Dav Koehl, as much as Tetric Garis, had taught her how to use a blade.

Sido helped her out of the mud as the rain turned the ash into watery silt. A life, a brilliant, courageous life diluted into puddles as if it had never existed at all.

One of the defenders picked up the abandoned sapphire. "What should we do with this? It's useless now."

"We'll sell it. We're running low on food," the seer replied.

Instead of acknowledging the order, the man laughed. "I'd rather buy something else."

She could not see the defender's eyes behind his helmet, but she felt the weight of his leer all the same. She clenched her teeth as her hand flew to her amulet. "The only thing you've bought yourself is a hole through the head."

Sido pulled her hand away from the diamond and turned to the defender. "Check the riverbank. Make sure it is still passable."

The dark-armored warrior nodded. "*Ai*, Lord Second." He gave a low chuckle and tossed the sapphire lightly against his palm before slipping it into his belt pouch. He and the others rode toward the bridge.

Sido leaned in close. "I must speak with you."

Mirana pulled her wrist from Sido's grip. "What happened to Dav?"

He motioned her away from the ash slurry. "Tetric Garis is what happened. That is the result of his Soul Harvest. He is just one of tens of thousands."

She worked her jaw for a coherent question. None came. "Tens of—? Tens of *thousands?*"

Sido nodded grimly. "Tetric doesn't kill the Fal'kin he wounds and captures. He strips them of their amulets and uniforms, anything they could cling to as a Fal'kin, to break their will and destroy their hope in the Aspects Above. Then he harvests them, obliterating their wills, leaving them living shells. Killing machines. That's how he's been growing the Ken'narren. For summers upon summers."

Was there no end to the horror her mentor had hidden from her? "Why are you telling me all of this? You're a Ken'nar. By all rights, you should be trying to kill me."

"Because I need your help." He smirked. "And you sure as hell need mine."

Just how stupid did he think she was? She returned his sneer. "Like the help you gave Dav Koehl? *U'gratas.*" She turned and stepped toward her horse.

He moved in front of her to block her way. "Wait. Please. We have the same goal."

"Really?" She arched a brow and placed her fists on her hips. "Do you honestly expect me to believe you, Sido Rendel, Tetric Garis's second, commander of his armies, heir to his—"

The sudden glow of his amulet matched the flash of anger in his eyes. "I am heir to nothing!" He shifted his gaze to the men inspecting the bridge. "Not anymore."

She blinked, surprised. Was it possible the Dark Trine's own second held no truck with Garis's desperate, despotic aspirations for peace? Or was this just a ploy to gain her confidence before he delivered her to Garis?

Oh, why was everything always so hopelessly complicated?

Better to find out the truth now while she faced the seer alone. "So you've been part of the Dark Trine's plans all along. Even while wearing the heraldics of Dar-Azûl province?"

He said nothing but flattened his lips in an accusing expression eerily similar to their mentor's. She glanced at the other men. Her heart felt like it had just turned to ash in her chest. "You mean, all the Dar-Azûlans—?" Turning back to the seer, her fists clenched into tight balls. "All this time? All the Dar-Azûlans—?!"

Something snapped inside her. All the pain, exhaustion, and starvation receded as fury like raw amulet fire exploded within her.

"You rackin' sons of bitches!" She slammed her fist into his jaw. Sido rocked back on his heels into the mud.

He held up a hand. "Wait—!"

"We sheltered you when you came home with *Paithe* after Falantir!" Mirana spun around and landed a boot on his hip, sending the seer several feet away to flop on his stomach.

"Mirana, let me explain," he groaned, attempting to roll over.

"We tended your wounds! We fed you! I even *peeled potatoes* for you bastards!" She reached down, amulet alight, and hauled the Ken'nar seer to his feet as she pulled her arm back for another blow.

"Mirana! Stop!" Sido caught her fist before it could bury itself in his face. "I need your help to stop Garis."

She panted in rage and exertion. "I will help you taste my amulet." How could the second-in-command of all the Ken'nar armies possibly think they had the same goal?

"Neither of us wants Tetric to gain control of Jasal's Keep," he replied.

She hesitated and released him. "You know about Jasal's Keep?"

"*Ai.*" He wiped his split lip and spat blood. "That's why you've left him, isn't it?"

At some point, Sido had indeed been a part of Tetric's inner circle because he apparently knew everything his master did about her quest. "What about them?" She indicated the men by the river with a jut of her chin. He shook his head. "And Tetric? Does he know you've finally grown a pair of—"

"No. If he did, I'd already be dead." Sido squinted through the mist to the mountains in the distance.

"He will find out. And when he does, he will kill you." And at the moment, she wasn't sure if she'd stop him.

"*Ai.* That is if I matter enough to him for him to bother expending the energy to execute me."

Something trembled within the young man's Aspect. Sadness? Genuine sadness? Not the loss of power, status, women, or whatever else the seer second held as important?

Movement caught both their eyes. The men were returning.

The seer leaned close. "But I have no intention of dying before I see everything Garis has worked for slip through his fingers."

She could not care less about his thirst for revenge at the moment. "How did you learn about the keep?"

"I'm a seer. A very good one." He shook his head, dismissing her questions. "We don't have time for this."

"You honestly think I'm going to let you accompany me?" She laughed. "You are my enemy."

"I am *not* your enemy," Sido whispered. "Or at least, not anymore. Tetric Garis made us both who we are. We both believed he would show us how to be something more than what our destiny called us to be. Instead, he lied to us both. I want to see him destroyed as much as you do."

That was just it. She did want to see the Dark Trine destroyed but not Tetric Garis. Sido was right, however, about one thing. No one in Kinderra understood Tetric as she did. Except for Sido Rendel. She had no reason to trust him and every reason to hate him, and yet, he spoke with conviction when he said he wanted to stop the Trine from gaining control of the keep.

"You don't trust me." He straightened. "Well, then let's think more practically. Do you know your way through the Darbinh Pass?"

She scowled. "Don't you just follow the—"

"And if the pass is blocked by a landslide? Or you run out of food and don't know where the lemmings hide? Or how to start a fire when the air is so thin you can hardly breathe? Shall I continue, Lady Trine?"

Mirana clawed some mud from her hair. Slowly. She needed time, a moment, to think. Could she trust Sido Rendel? Now that was a laughable thought. She glanced up at the mountain pass in the murky distance. She'd nearly broken her neck on Deven's Stair through the Dúadar Pass. If Tetric hadn't been there to save her from falling— Later. Was she really going to do this?

She was really going to do this.

She leaned close enough to feel his breath against her cheeks. "Do *not* make me regret this, Seer Second, or you'll have *two* Trines wanting your blood."

He barked a laugh. "It's always nice to be wanted."

Ruthless and snarky. It was going to be a long trek. "What will we tell your men?"

"Maybe it is time for Lord Garis's Trine Second to start giving orders." He jutted his chin at the approaching defenders.

Mirana opened her mouth, stunned. "I—what? What should I—?"

"The crossing is flooded but passable, my second," one of the Ken'nar said.

"Good." She fought for composure. "We have business with the Lord Trine—"

Sido touched her arm with his fingertips … *Ain Magne* …

"—with the Ain Magne elsewhere." She gave a curt nod. "You will return to the installation in Falantir—"

The seer's grip tightened. *…How did you know— …*

…Obsca! … "—and await us there."

The defender sat back in his saddle. "And what makes you think I'll take orders from a little *cunaré* like you?"

"What. Did you. Call me?" She made a slight movement with her head as her amulet flared. The man flew from his horse to land flat on his back in the mud. She drew her sword and held it to his throat under his helmet. "You will take orders from me because I said so." The tip of her blade indented his skin. "And the next time you even think about using a derogatory word like that toward me, your amulet will not be the only thing I remove."

"We've wasted enough time." Sido stayed her arm and helped the man up. "Bhrecht, all of you, give me your waterskins and the food from your packs."

Bhrecht snorted in disgust. "Lord Seer, you can't be serious?"

"Now, Defender, or I foresee a very short disagreement between us." His left hand gripped the hilt of his sword. Bhrecht handed over his waterskin and supplies with brusque movements.

The young seer second put the food in his saddlebags. Mirana, however, took whole squares of waybread and stuffed them in her mouth. He raised an eyebrow.

She chewed and swallowed quickly. "I couldn't waste the time to hunt." He frowned and gave her a piece of dried beef. She scowled as her fingertips brushed his hand.

Pain. Deep. Throbbing.

She crammed the beef into her mouth. "Whash wrong wi' your ahrm?"

He ignored her question as she took three more pieces of jerky from him.

"Easy. The more you shove down—"

She stopped chewing. "Oh no." She dropped to her hands and knees and vomited.

"—the more will come back up." Sido sighed. He took a step back and wrinkled his nose. "Bloody hell, girl. What have you been eating? I wouldn't even feed that to my grynwen." He handed her one of the waterskins.

She took a sip and spat it out. "So the seer is now a healer?" She took a long pull, but it didn't stay down any longer than the food did.

"And the water, too. Stop. Stop!" He crouched down beside her and took the waterskin from her hands. "Small sips." He held the skin as she complied and took it back from her before she could drink more. "I am no stranger to starvation. You're in no condition to ride, much less handle anything else we may encounter."

"I'll be fine." She lurched to her feet, snatched the skin back, and took another small mouthful of water.

He frowned. "I hope you have a warmer travel cloak than that. It is always winter in the Darbinh Pass."

She lifted her chin. "I will use my Healing Aspect to fend off the cold."

His thin lips leveled into a hard line. "Of course you will." Sido snapped his fingers at Defender Bhrecht and pointed to Mirana. The man yanked off his cloak and threw it at her. The seer caught it and draped it over her shoulders. "It's not fur-lined, but it will have to do."

Mirana nodded. "*Gratas Oë*, Defender." The man didn't reply. Well, she had just drawn a sword on him.

Sido held his amulet and pale green light seeped through his fingers. "It will take two days to reach the entrance to the pass. It's several more days on the pass itself before we reach Caladazh, but it will likely take much longer. This rain will steal our speed."

She climbed onto Ashtar's saddle. "I am willing to prove you wrong."

"Many are willing. Few succeed." Sido swung up onto his mount's back and turned to Defender Bhrecht. "Head back to Falantir. We should return with the Ain Magne within a few sevendays." She bit the inside of her cheek. It was an out-and-out lie.

The seer held up his hand. "Attend." The grynwen stood at rigid attention. He pointed to the dim line of the forest behind him. "Go." The predators began to trot away then paused and turned back around, their vermilion eyes shifting between the seer and her. He sighed and called something—an emotion, for lack of a better word—of well-being. The grynwen broke into a run after the retreating Ken'nar.

Mirana tapped Ashtar's sides, easing him into a swift trot. "Are we really going to have to eat lemmings?"

CHAPTER 8

"Thou hast favored me above all others. Wherefore hast
Thou blessed me? I beseech Thee to make Thy servant
worthy of Thy Gifts."
—The Codex of Jasal the Great

The Ain Magne Tetric Garis stood at the entrance of the Trak-Calan learning hall, running his hand down the rib of the moon arch, wiping off the fresh snow. It had once been painted with red lacquer, but that was a very, very long time ago. The bitter wind and ice had long since scoured the lacquer away. Now the remnants of the pigment stained the wood brown like dried blood. He supposed it had been just as worn when he last stood here. Somehow, he remembered it being more vibrant. Everything about Caladazh had been more vibrant then. The joy. And the pain. It had also been a very, very long time since he stood here last.

No defensive gates separated visitors or intruders from the hall's entrance. To outsiders, it would seem there were no protective elements at all. He smiled. No, Caladazh's protection sat elsewhere.

He passed under the arch and into the courtyard, slowly but deliberately.

Somewhere behind the clouds, the sun had set, the twilight taking on a bluish cast. The familiar square of the learning hall still rose three stories—it had seemed so much taller when he was younger. Its four arms stretched long to embrace a courtyard. The well, sunk deep into the marrow of the rock, sat in the center and gave mountain spring water, pristine, cold, and sweet. The memory of its taste lingered on his tongue. Granite blocks dry-fitted together upheld clay-tiled roofs, their curved eaves curled upward pagoda-like, cupped hands pleading into the chill air. Peaked towers jutted up at each of the corners.

He had often wondered why the hall's founders had built such a large edifice. The complex never held more than two hundred Fal'kin within its walls. Perhaps they had never anticipated the day when Aspected would stop at nothing to kill each other.

The courtyard appeared to be deserted, but like so much else in Caladazh, it was an illusion. The long porticos were not entirely straight but ran at slight angles. One standing at the moon gate would never see the defenders and battle seers waiting at the edges.

He tied his horse off at the well. "It has been a long time."

A man approached from out of the shadows to lean against one of the portico's support columns, his arms folded across his chest. Creases at the corners of the man's eyes and his mouth were more noticeable now than the last time he had seen him. As were his own. The man was thin, lithe. Lethal. A dark beard and mustache framed his mouth and chin, and his long, straight hair was pulled back, as much silver as black, doing nothing to obscure the sharp blades of his cheekbones nor his hard, dark brown eyes. Other than the orange garnet amulet about his neck, he appeared harmless. Yet another of Caladazh's illusions.

"You look older," the man said.

"I am. As you are." Tetric blinked against the tiny, dry snowflakes drifting down from a darkening sky.

"I would welcome you home, but you are not welcome, and this is no longer your home."

"I gathered as much." He cocked his head at the defenders lurking in the upper stories.

The man unfolded his arms and walked over. "Merely a precaution. Nothing more."

"Indeed." He gripped the man's forearm in greeting.

The Fal'kin paused before returning the gesture. "Why are you here?"

Tetric smiled faintly again as he scanned the hall's upper stories. He could not see the defenders and battle seers, but they were there. "I am looking for a girl. I had hoped to catch up with her in Salmasalar when I took a ship to Yalahn Harbor. I didn't see her in the Calan foothills either. Is she here?"

The Fal'kin released his arms. "It is said that Kinderra's Trine can find a single mind among thousands. Surely, your blessed gifts would tell you if the one you seek is here or not."

Tetric said nothing and straightened his stance.

"A long time ago, your heart was broken as well as your faith. I am surprised you have any heart left after that to even be captured by another."

He flattened his mouth and fought the urge to stretch against the growing tension in his neck. "Mirana Pinal is my *scholaira* and exceedingly skilled in U'Nehíl. Is she here?"

The Fal'kin guided him by the elbow to stand under the portico. "Prime Desde and Kaarl Pinal's daughter? What are you doing with their—?"

"Koben. She is very important to me. And her life may be in danger. I must find her."

Koben Ryotan, Prime of Trak-Calan, shook his head. "No. We have received no visitors in quite some time. However, my Seeing Aspect showed many have perished in the westlands. I'm not sure who is left to travel."

Tetric did not know whether to be relieved or concerned. For a heart-stopping moment, he wondered if she had decided to forsake the keep and head back to Deren.

No. The keep's answers were far too important. She knew her fate was tied to the keep.

"She will come here, but when she sees me, she may flee again. If she does, she will die."

Koben scowled. "Why?"

"I would not have come if I had another choice. Please, Koben, I need your help."

The seer's dark eyes sought his own for a moment. He nodded. "Come."

The prime's chambers were spare, just as he had remembered them. The same small window overlooking the courtyard and the mountains beyond. The long-necked oil lamp that chased away Tetric's nightmares as a toddler. A bed lay in one corner, the bed in which he had lain with a fever and could not be left alone. Behind the desk was the same black-lacquered cabinet traced with gold from which he had received his first long knives. Two things were missing from the room, however. A tiny fir tree on the desk and the old man who had tended it.

Koben sat down in a high-backed chair behind the desk, but Tetric remained standing. "That is a different chair."

"I am a different prime," the seer replied. "So tell me. Why would Pinal's daughter run from you?"

A single knock on the door interrupted his reply. A young defender entered. "Do you require anything, Seer Prime Ryotan?"

The young woman had addressed Koben but had not taken her eyes off Tetric. She hooked a thumb on her belt near the hilt of her sword. He smiled at the girl's inept attempt at a threat. Did she think he'd slit the man's throat in his own chambers?

"*Gratas*, Hinsah. Send in some food if you would. I am sure the Lord Trine is weary from his journey. The heavy rains in the highlands made for even heavier snows in the pass."

The defender woman bowed and left.

He raised an eyebrow, and Koben raised his hand in a dismissive gesture.

"Please forgive my new commander's second. She is young. Nineteen summers."

"Is she any good?"

"Very." Koben smiled but with cunning, not joy. "But enough of trivialities. I do not know Kaarl Pinal well, but I know him well enough. He hates you. Why would he release his daughter into your keeping?"

Oh, if only the prime understood the full measure of his words. "Mirana is a Trine."

"What?" For the first time since they met, Koben's expression changed. Shock and wonder furrowed his brows. "There had been rumors summers ago that she might defend as well as see, but this is…" He shook his head slowly. "Why is she under your banner and not Desde's?"

"She came to me more of her own accord than Kaarl's, or Desde's, for that matter. They had lied to everyone, including

Mirana herself, about her Trine Aspects. She needed—needs—my help."

"It is not a good thing to come between a parent and his child." Koben settled deeper into his chair and regarded him with hooded eyes. "But I suppose there is no one better to train a Trine than another Trine."

He nodded and bolstered the walls around his mind from the man's attempts at intrusion. He took a seat at last. "*Ai*, that is definitely part of it."

The seer curled a corner of his lip into a sneer as his eyes remained narrowed. "Would the other part be that young Mirana destroyed the ford itself?" He gave a noiseless chuckle at Tetric's startled expression. Koben. He had forgotten just how precise the man's gift was. "Are you all that surprised that I should know? Regardless of my Seeing Aspect, we are not as isolated as you think. I also hear many things. Such as that both the prime of Rün-Taran and her second are dead. Murdered, it is said. Is that why you seek the girl? Is she the murderer?"

The door opened once again, this time of its own accord, and Hinsah appeared with a food-laden tray. Once she had left, Tetric slammed the door behind her and locked it without so much as moving a finger, ensuring no more interruptions. If he'd wanted to kill Koben Ryotan, the man would already be dead.

The seer smiled again, and again without humor. He gestured to a cup on the tray. It floated over to his waiting hand. "Is she the Light Trine or the Dark Trine?" He took a sip. "Or do you not know and that is why you keep such close scrutiny on her?"

Tetric ignored the food. "I put little stock in prophecies."

"Too bad Shalas believed in them." Koben took another sip from his cup, a longer one, and peered at him over its rim.

He clenched his jaw, forcing his anger down. He'd wondered how long it would take for Koben to mention Shalas's name. "I had hoped you would have left the past in the past." He wanted to say something more but gave up. What was the point? "I loved him. And you. He was the only father I had ever known, you, my only brother. How many summers will it take before you believe that?"

"There could never be enough," Koben replied, his voice cold.

"I had only seen seventeen summers. I had no idea the Healing Aspect could be manifested in that way."

The prime set his cup down on the desk, a hard, falling gesture of his hand. "You were no child. It wasn't your Healing Aspect alone. It was the way you used it. And used me."

Tetric wanted to be furious, for this anger had smoldered within his heart for nearly forty summers, but he couldn't bring it to a full blaze on the man who had once been his foster brother. He had no fuel left to stoke this fire. "You always seem to remember what happened to Shalas, yet you never seem to remember what happened to me."

The seer pinned him with his gaze a moment longer. He sighed and nodded and studied his hands in his lap. "After you left, all I had was fury and guilt."

"I had a little more. I had fear as well, *Ëi sibe.* And loneliness. You both abandoned me because of what I believed."

"Is that why young Mirana has left you? Does she not understand, not accept the majesty you claim comes from the Power from Without?"

He examined a cut on his knuckle he'd received from slipping on ice in the pass. "*Ai.* She does not understand. Yet."

He rubbed it with his thumb, and it disappeared. "She is not alone."

Koben noted the incident with a flicker of a smile, not a smile of pride or awe, but wariness. "And neither are you. Some thousands of Ken'nar wholeheartedly agree with your perspective."

"Self-righteousness does not become you, *sibe*." Perhaps coming to Caladazh had been the wrong decision after all. "Any Fal'kin who has ever dealt blood and has not at least been tempted to use the Power from Without has lied about either his valor or his piety."

His brother laughed tersely. "There is an ocean of difference between temptation and action."

Tetric rose from his chair to stand by the small window in the prime's chambers. The sky remained dark charcoal for the moment, but it would soon clear and reveal countless stars shining like amulets in the heavens. His Seeing Aspect told him so.

"I did not come here to reopen old wounds."

"They never closed."

He hung his head and took a breath. Temptation and action. He didn't need to slit a throat to kill. "Did Shalas ever mention an artifact of Jasal Pinal here in the hall?"

He caught Koben's clear sense of confusion. "No. Why would a relic of the disgraced Kin-Deren Trine be here in Trak-Calan?"

His fervent hope had been that somehow his foster brother would know where the keep journal entry lay or even give it to him outright. Now he would have to compel Mirana to search for it when she came. She might not be so easily convinced. He took a measured breath, willing himself to calm.

"Jasal's Keep in Deren is some sort of weapon. One of the secrets to its construction, written in Jasal Pinal's hand, is hidden here. The girl can hear some sort of manifestation of her ancestor from within the Aspects. I cannot. Without the girl, I will never learn how to tap into the keep's power and use it. Without that watchtower and whatever weapon is within it, the war will continue, and eventually, Kinderra will be destroyed. I am going to ask the primes to name me Primus Magne. With the entirety of the Fal'kinnen and the keep under me, the aggression will cease. Immediately. Once and for all. Together, Mirana and I will stop this war. Our past is already lost. I will not let our future be destroyed as well."

His foster brother became silent, and Tetric granted him the time. He found it ironic that the two men in Kinderra whom he actually trusted were Koben Ryotan and Kaarl Pinal, two men who wanted nothing more than to see him dead.

"And if we primes don't support you?" the seer asked, his voice hushed.

Tetric spun around and slammed a fist on the desk. "Have you heard nothing I've said? I'm trying to *save* Kinderra."

Koben did not move. "What makes you think the Dark Trine and his Ken'nar will simply lay down arms because you control some mythical weapon?"

He stared at his foster brother, formulating and rejecting many answers as he did so. "I am trying to build a new future," he replied, fatigue from so many things dragging at his voice.

"For yourself."

"*Ai.*" The familiar ache spread across his shoulders. "For myself. For you. For all of us. As Primus Magne, I can do this. I *will* do this. It is what I have been called to be."

Koben's horror and anger leaked past his own mind's barriers to Tetric, the seer's sunset-colored amulet suddenly brightening. His brother had been his last hope. Without his belief and support, he had no choice but to take the magnistate by force. His Defending Aspect told him so.

He slowly shook his head and turned back to the window. He swallowed back the burning, almost painful sensation in his eyes, one he had almost forgotten. "Mirana is like a daughter to me, Koben, a child I had not yet even begun to hope for with Cerise. There is no one on the face of Kinderra who understands the burden of being a Trine except her. If she runs from me again, she will die. Help me to help her, *sibe*."

Koben rose and stood behind him. He laid a hand on Tetric's shoulder. ... *The prophecy speaks of two Trines, the Dark and Light ... That young girl is not the Dark Trine, sibe...*

... I do not believe in prophecies ...

The seer pulled back his hand as if stung. "Tetric, if you try to kill Mirana Pinal, it is you who will die."

... And you with me, brother ...

His Healing Aspect told him so.

CHAPTER 9

*"I know not where the Aspects Above are leading me,
but with my Beloved beside me, the road is smooth."*
—The Codex of Jasal the Great

Mirana pulled the Ken'nar cloak tighter around her as she and Sido led their horses up the steep Darbinh Pass. Her leather armor helped but not much. Her companion had shed his metal armor for practicality on the arduous hike, but she envied him for the quilted tunic he wore underneath.

The blinding sun shone from a sky so saturated with blue, it could have been dusk. During the night, the storm clouds finally wrung themselves out and scuttled away in a keening wind. Gusts blew bits of ice in her face, prickling her skin like needles.

Her Healing Aspect flared along with her amulet. *Pain.* Sido's crystal glinted as he drew in a hiss from between his teeth.

"Your arm is still bothering you. Maybe I should take a look."

He shook his head. "Not mine. I thought I saw—ah. There you are." The seer reached in between two rocks. "Easy."

Mirana scowled. "What—?"

Sido withdrew a squirming lemming from the crevice and pulled a thorn from its front paw. "Now, scat." When he set the creature down, it remained where it was. "*Phsszt!*" The rodent shot away and disappeared among the crags.

Mirana stared at him, mouth agape.

"I wasn't hungry." A corner of his mouth twitched.

A joke. Sido Rendel just made a joke. And saved a tiny being's life. She laughed, but she wasn't sure if it was at his jibe or in wonder of his action.

Mirana tried to draw in a deep breath, but the elevation made breathing difficult. With each step, her lungs burned as though she had run a mile. Her father once said the Dar-Calan Mountains were the highest in Kinderra, and winter always kept at least a finger on them. *Paithe.*

"Those grynwen," Mirana said. "They're your pets?"

The seer second snorted in disgust. "Hardly. But they make damn better friends than half of the people I know."

Given the people Sido knew, he was probably right.

She hurried to his side. "How can you possibly train grynwen? They can't be tamed."

Sido kept his gaze on the pass. "They can be if the dam is dead, and the pups are young enough."

"You killed their mother?" She rushed ahead to block him.

The seer rolled his eyes. "No, someone else did. I just—" He looked everywhere but at her. "They assigned me the job of raising the pups. My defender commander at the time thought it would be funny if I were eaten alive by newborn grynwen pups. I bottle-fed them for weeks." He laughed and watched his crystallized breath rise in the frigid air. "Imagine Commander Lyer Khorr's surprise when he tried to mess with one and it all but took off three of his fingers." Now he riveted her with his hazel gaze. "I absolutely didn't mean to call the command so forcefully. Of course not. That would be a terrible act of insubordination." He stepped around her and continued trekking up the pass.

Grynwen. Ordered to attack.

Mirana squeezed her eyes closed. The question on her lips begged for an answer, even as she didn't want to hear it. Aspects Above help her, but she couldn't quite muster bitter hatred of her new companion. She should. She had every reason to. Liking him, however, was becoming oddly easier. He was honest, brutally so, like everything else about him. After so much deception from everyone in her life, she craved honesty in whatever form it came.

"You were the one who sent the grynwen to ambush my father, weren't you?"

"I wondered just how long it would take you to ask." He continued to trudge ahead of her, his boots crunching and squeaking in the fresh, powdery snow.

She stopped. "You weren't simply trying to get him and the il'Kin to leave the area. You wanted him dead. Why?"

He barked a sharp laugh. "Why do you think?" After a few steps, he paused. His shoulders fell as he tossed his head back to stare up at the bright sky again. "The il'Kin came too close to Falantir. We could not risk any information reaching Deren."

"Why grynwen? Were you afraid of my father's amulet?"

At last, Sido turned around, his gaze drilling into her, green and dark like a stormy sea. "Your father and Jord would have heard our horses coming. That sea slag—Binthe Lima, is it?—

would have seen something, no doubt. With grynwen, your il'Kin would have detected nothing more than a pack of predators."

Part of her brain understood the logic—and she hated that she agreed with it. Long, nighttime conversations with Tetric had hammered such viciously efficient strategies into her head. Another part of her, however, couldn't believe she now allied herself with the man who had tried to kill her father.

Maybe the ambush hadn't been his choice.

"Did he order you to do it?"

He looked away from her to focus on the granite walls of the pass. "It's war, Mirana."

"I know, but—"

"But *what?*" The disbelief in his voice echoed around the columns of rock.

She bit her lip. "It doesn't have to be. Not anymore, at least."

He laughed, the sarcasm as cold and brittle as the air around them. "'It doesn't have to be.' The one thing I hate worse than an idealist is a hypocritical one."

"Hypocritical?" She stepped closer and balled her fists on her hips. "You tried to kill *my father*, for Aspects' sake! What? Did you try and murder my mother, too, while you were at the ford?"

"I suppose your mother's Fal'kin were there to invite me to tea, and I was just mistaken that they wanted to turn me into a pile of ash." He leaned toward her, a snarl pulling at the scar on his cheek. "A woman whose company I *very* much enjoyed now lies as a wet splatter at the bottom of a canyon because *you* destroyed the bridges of Two Rivers Ford!"

The familiar, nauseating drizzle of guilt trickled through her stomach. She had wanted to faint when Tetric had first told her how many she had killed at the ford. One thousand sixty-one. Including fourteen of her own Fal'kin who couldn't escape the destruction in time. It was so much easier to think of the lives lost as one large person rather than a collection of individuals. Individuals who had been fighting for their own world vision. Sido's words shattered that last wall of protective-yet-damning denial. "I-I'm sor—"

"Don't you dare even think that word!" He glared at her a moment longer, then turned and resumed his trek up the steep pass.

She tried to follow him, but her legs would not move. She had killed someone he loved. Or at least cared for on some level. If she could be surprised anymore, she would have been at the idea of the caustic seer second being coupled with anyone. No, she couldn't hate Sido Rendel for actions of which she was also culpable.

"Tetric was most displeased with me," the Ken'nar muttered. "With the grynwen. He would have killed some if your father hadn't first."

Her father had killed some of Sido's closest companions. And he grieved that loss, hated that loss. She could sense it. They were bodyguards, friends. Like Ashtar.

Her gaze fell from Sido to the snow covering the toes of her boots. "He was displeased with me, too. With the ford. And he did kill one at the ford. A grynwen, I mean."

He slowed his pace. "That wasn't him. That was me. Tetric had ordered me, in no uncertain terms, to make sure you were not harmed. You are…important. To many."

Mirana snapped up her head. "You killed one of your pets to save *my* life?"

The seer whirled on her. "For the last time, they're not pets! Now can we please just keep walking?"

"Of course." Mirana lowered her eyes back to the snow, but Sido was already annoyed with her. What was one more perplexing, pointed, and painful question? "How did you know about the keep?"

He stopped. "Bloody hell. I should have listened to you and awaited my execution in Falantir. It would have been easier." He gave an explosive sigh. "I wasn't supposed to. I may only have one Aspect, but my Sight is three times as powerful as any other seer. *Ai*, I have had my own vision of Jasal's Keep."

A flurry of deep emotion tumbled through Sido's mind, only to be quickly hidden behind U'Nehíl. He had said he wanted to see Tetric lose everything he'd worked for. Did he see her destroying their mentor's vision of conquest? Maybe he bore complex and confusing feelings about her, too, because of it? Did he see her as a ruthless killing machine in the guise of a lost and strangely vulnerable young woman? Maybe he, too, wanted to hate her, but no longer could and was trying to find a way to like her.

Those hard, hurting slate-green eyes made her heart flutter, a sensation both frightening and exhilarating. "How much do you know?"

"Jasal's Keep is some sort of weapon."

"*Ai*." Mirana nodded, concentrating on her footfalls over chunks of ice and rock to close the distance between them. "But we don't know what kind or how it works. No one does. Jasal Pinal, or one of those in his inner circle, split the secrets to its construction from his Codex into four entries, one given to each of the learning halls in existence in his time. Tetric and I found three. The last is in the learning hall in Caladazh." She teetered off-balance when her boot found a chunk of ice hidden in the snow. "If he finds it before I do—*oof!*" She slipped into Sido's back, knocking him into the rock wall. He bit back a cry of pain through clenched teeth and clutched his right arm.

Cold. Weariness. Pain. Agony.

Mirana scowled. "Sido?"

He doubled over and panted. "Obviously, we have to find it before he does."

"Are you all right?" *Laceration. Deep. Muscles torn. Tendons, ligaments, severed. Something else. Insidious. Invading.*

He squeezed his eyes shut against the pain. "I'm fine."

"Lights! Let me see your arm." She rushed over to him, reaching for the hand protecting his arm. "Did I hurt you at Two Rivers—?"

"No!" He spun away from her. "Guess what? People fight in a war. Injuries happen."

She frowned. "Let me see it."

He backed away from her before she could touch him. "Just…just give me a moment."

She balled her hands into fists and set them on her hips. "If Tetric reaches Caladazh before us, we'll have to fight our way in *and* out of the province. I would prefer you had the use of both your arms. Or are you planning on holding your sword with your teeth? Now, shut up, hold still, and let me see." He guarded his wounded shoulder and guarded his mind a moment longer before giving her a curt nod.

Mirana helped ease him down into the snow. She held Jasal's amulet with one hand and laid the other on Sido's chest. He trembled beneath her fingertips. She hadn't meant to frighten him but simply needed to get him used to her touch and her mind. Could a man like Sido Rendel ever be frightened?

Immediately, heat from his body radiated to her hand. Illness, not fear, caused the shiver. "You're burning with fever." She unlaced the opening of his padded tunic and shirt. She peeled the sleeves from his shoulder to reveal a dirty poultice. She gritted her teeth. "I will control your pain, but this might sting a little."

Sido retreated against the rock face. "Never mind. Forget it. I'll be fine."

"I said hold still!" She poked him in the chest to push him back, then took a breath and closed her eyes. … *Just relax* …

"I don't think that's possible with you around."

Mirana cracked open an eye and smiled. Centering herself again, she directed the Healing Aspect to calm the nerves of the seer's shoulder.

Pain! Pain! Shearing. Screaming. Pulsing. Burning.

Sido wasn't merely uncomfortable, he was in agony.

She peeled away the spent poultice, flooding the man's arm with soothing sensations when the bandage stuck. "Oh, Sido." She failed to hide her look of disgust when the wound was revealed. "Why didn't you tell me this wound had festered? This is serious. You should have had this tended to days ago. You could lose your arm."

His mouth sank into a frown. "Your bedside manner leaves something to be desired."

A deep laceration cut across his upper arm just below the shoulder. Dark purple bruising encircled the wound, and angry red streaks jagged away from the gash. The crude stitches of a suture tried to hold the wound closed but his sudden movement had torn them through the flesh. Crusty clots of dried blood and sickly yellow-green pus clung to the thread.

He trembled again. His fever was rising. Mirana removed her cloak and covered him to keep him warm in the frigid air. When she took out her belt knife, he grabbed her wrist with his good hand in a reaction bordering on a Trine's ability for its swiftness.

"I thought you were going to help me keep my arm?"

Ben Kin, did he think she was going to cut off his arm? With a belt knife? "I'm just going to remove these stitches."

His fingers remained encircled around her wrist. "Do you know what you're doing?" He motioned for the knife. "Give it to me. I've cut arrows out of my own body."

She rolled her eyes. "Stop being such a baby. I do, in fact, know what I'm doing. I spent a lot of time in the Healing Hostel in Deren and learned quite a bit. Now hold still."

The seer leaned back from her once more. It reminded her very much of the youth Maark Bedane's reaction when he had come to the infirmary.

"I'm not going to let you feel something like this. You shouldn't feel anything."

He hissed a curse. "Pain is the greatest of mentors. One learns quickly to never again allow what caused the injury."

Oh, how many times had she heard that while flailing with her sword against her *patrua* on Bartus Alhambre's ship?

"Haven't you been healed before? At least by Tetric? You're his second. Surely he would not have let something like this go unattended."

"Most of the time, he wasn't with the main host but...elsewhere."

Mirana bit her lip. Elsewhere. Pretending he was the Trine Kinderra thought him to be.

Sido turned away and tightened his jaw, steeling himself for the treatment. "Not even Belessa Tir has ever healed me. My mother said the prime's sainted Healing Aspect was only meant for Unaspected and those who faced battles, not hall seers like us. Now the old woman no longer heals."

Mirana called to his mind a questioning intent.

"I was born to Kana-Akün."

That wasn't the answer she wanted, but she didn't pursue it further.

"Well, I won't hurt you." At least, she hoped she wouldn't. She had certainly suppressed pain before, but this wound was also infected. How was she supposed to heal that, even with an amulet? She had no salves, no tinctures, nothing.

When the Ken'nar continued to protect his arm, she called *… Sido … Open your mind to me … I will not hurt you …* Tentatively, like a dog that had been beaten too many times and was unsure if its new master would harm it, he allowed her mind to reach his.

Pain screamed a shrill stanza through her. The wound was serious, far deeper than a simple cut. And here he had been climbing a mountain alongside her, never saying a word.

She cut the black thread with the tip of her belt knife. As gently as she possibly could, she pulled the filament from the wound. "Whoever your herbsman is, you should let him go. A blind man could have made better sutures."

"Herbsfolk have the annoying tendency to kill themselves rather than treat a Ken'nar." He grunted with pain. She paused. "Have you ever tried sewing up your own arm? It's not exactly easy. And it hurts."

She had imagined Tetric Garis's Ken'nar worshipping him as some sort of demigod. Did the man not even care for the welfare of his own men and women?

Mirana's Healing Aspect rose within her again, deeper, stronger, drawn from her by the need of Sido's wound. Warmth like liquid sunshine flowed across her chest from the diamond resting at her breastbone. She surrounded him with that soothing warmth, sending him into a light sleep. The grating noise of the torn flesh filled her mind, the raw life notes of the wound vibrating against each other. Now, with a connection to an amulet, she could more than merely perceive injuries, she could heal them by calming the discord, the cacophony, willing what was rent back to completeness. Slowly, ravaged muscle knit itself closed, bit of flesh by bit of flesh, note by note. The dissonance turned to unison as the frayed ends of the cords of sinew reached toward each other and meshed whole once more. The fibrous bands of scar tissue pulled together what flesh could not.

She could not mend an infection like a wound, however. Something more dangerous, more sinister lurked here. She washed more of the Healing Aspect through Sido. Strange images played before her mind's eye. Small creatures, infinitesimally small, invaded his wound, gnawing at his flesh though they had no mouths, secreting poison though they had no stingers. Other round, floating grayish forms engulfed these creatures, but the gnawing, poisonous, tiny beasts far outnumbered them.

His heart beat against her Aspects. With each pulse, fresh blood rushed to the wound, washing away some of the creatures.

Mirana hesitated. Could that be the answer? His blood would cleanse the wound from the inside out, but if he lost too much, he would die as surely as if it had festered.

Could she do this? What if she wasn't strong enough? He would lose his arm. He would lose his life.

No. She was strong enough. He needed her to be.

She held Jasal's amulet tighter and called gently to the seer's heart with her Aspect. Blood flowed to the laceration. Pus and blood began to seep from the wound over her hands as her Healing Aspect sang to his body, joining with it.

Sido's essence shifted within him. Another melody played over the music of her healing, a different song entirely. Fresh warmth spread from him to her, having nothing to do with his abating fever. Emotions now wept into her mind. Confusion. Disbelief. Astonishment. Longing. Desire.

Gratitude.

His gratitude was more than a simple notion of thanks. It was deep and abiding. A heart-rending, encompassing gratefulness like nothing she had ever experienced.

Tears welled in her eyes, freezing at the corners.

All she'd ever wanted was to use her Trine gifts to heal Kinderra. And Sido, in all his ruthlessness, exposed his vulnerability and let her.

She rolled back the shields defending her emotions and allowed her own gratitude to leave her mind for his. His heart beat faster on its own accord now. As did hers.

At last, she had helped someone, healed someone with her Aspects. Truly. With an amulet of her own. With the Light from Within. As a Trine. Sido had shown a part of himself he had probably never shown anyone, and he had given that trusting part of himself to her. Her. A person he should hate. Instead, he had set aside that hate to trust her. And with that, he had swept away the last of her self-doubt.

Mirana fought the urge to embrace him. More of his blood flowed over her hands as clean flesh formed, driving out the diseased, dead tissue.

Slowly, she lifted the pain-soothing veil from Sido's mind and body. Her heart, though, continued to race with the man's nearness and her own overwhelming storm of emotion.

The seer blinked. "Wh-What happened?" He looked at his arm with uncomprehending eyes. Where a grisly wound had rent his shoulder, now healthy skin covered it, marred only by a thin, red scar.

Mirana shook from the bone-chilling cold, from the strain of healing, from the intensity of the connection they had shared. "You, uh," she swallowed, "you will have a scar."

"I don't understand. I—" His words stopped as if they had failed him entirely. She knew hers had. … *Gratas … Gratas Oë* …

She stared into his slate eyes at the naked honesty residing there. "A man who frees trapped lemmings and nurses grynwen pups cannot be a monster." She smiled. "Not completely, anyway."

He dropped his gaze. "Or maybe he's a monster who loves lemmings and grynwen."

She lowered her head to meet his eyes so he could see her smile had not wavered. "Well, that's a place to start."

The blood and putrescence of the wound covered her hands. Sido scooped up a handful of clean snow and took her hands in his, gently washing her scarred palms.

Warmth spread through her. That same strange, warm life song that had drifted within the Aspects from Sido now came from her.

… You thanked me … But I should be the one to thank you … Her hands remained in his.

His expression softened, his eyes focusing on her lips. *… Why? …*

Her gaze lowered to Sido's mouth. His lips. Thin, perhaps. But they spoke honesty. *… Because you've given me a place from which to begin to tame my own monsters …*

This time, Mirana did envelop the seer in her arms. And he did not move away.

CHAPTER 10

"Ama ísi enigma. Ama ísi u'ben e ben. Ama ísi fuádain e tudempre. Ama ísi frágil brea tuda. Ama ísi forte brea tuda. Ama ísi enigma."
("Love is a riddle. It is cruel and kind. It is fleeting and eternal. It is the most fragile of things. It is the strongest of things. Love is a riddle.")

—Ora Fal'kinnen 301:1–6

Mirana had glimpsed something within Sido Rendel she had never expected to see, something she had never thought she'd receive from another man besides Teague. That fact, however, wasn't the one from which she wanted to flee. Denial was a cunning enemy she'd never give quarter to again. The same passionate, even needful emotions had flooded her as well, as sudden and urgent as a battle cry.

She continued to plod up the rocky pass through the snow and ice, Sido marching slowly by her side. Her mind wound itself into a relentless coil of questions.

She had betrayed Teague's love, telling him his lack of Aspects would make their lives together impossible. It wasn't true, of course. Teague's Unaspectedness didn't matter to her, it had never mattered to her. By pushing him away, however, didn't she make her prejudice true? She didn't believe he could escape her damning destiny precisely because he did not have the Aspects, just as he didn't believe she could perpetrate it.

Sido Rendel, Seer Second of the Ken'nar, however, was the only one who could understand the pain of betrayal such as that. He understood it all too well. He had revered Tetric Garis, as she had. And the Dark Trine had cut the seer from him like a diseased limb because he thought Sido was something less than worthy. Just like she had, in a sense, with Teague.

Could she ever start again with someone else? Was this an opportunity? A chance to show she had learned well from her failures and would not make those mistakes again?

She exhaled in confusion. An opportunity and maybe a little bit of hope? She nodded. Teague deserved his freedom from her.

"When did you know you were a Trine?" Sido asked.

Mirana huffed a laugh. "It was less of a 'when' and more of a 'how.'"

He stopped and turned, a brow arched in a question.

"When I was very young, I didn't know my Aspects were different from anyone else's." She toyed with the diamond at her chest. "When…when a friend and I were twelve, he fell from a tree and broke his arm. The urge to heal him was, well, compelling to say the least." She squinted up the pass. "There was no longer any question that I was a Trine." That might have also been the moment her heart understood she cared more for Teague than just as a playmate. She shook her head, dispelling the memory.

Sido resumed his trek up the icy path. "Would that friend have been the Healers Beltrans' son?"

She followed the seer. "We were friends. Good friends."

He stopped again and turned. "And what are you now?"

Good question. Actually, no. There was no longer any question here, either. "He has his life." She nodded again. "And I have mine." The pain of severing Teague from her life still hurt enough to keep her from smiling, but the warmth of a burgeoning new future poured through her.

Sido made a noncommittal grunt as the snow crunched under his boots. "Still, it seems to me you Fal'kin are a rather dense lot. Wouldn't they, or at least your parents, have thought something was unusual about you when their amulets flared every time you entered a room?"

She rubbed her eyes. There had to be a nook in the rocks someplace where they could finally stop for the night.

"They did know."

"Who?"

"My mother and father. My grandfather. And probably Teague's parents as well. They probably knew the moment I was born, if not before."

He stopped again. "And the amulets?"

It all seemed so obvious now. Obvious and pathetically ridiculous.

"My parents drummed into my head that amulets were sacred, not just pretty baubles or weapons, but something holy that shouldn't be touched until I was much older."

He remained facing her, wanting more of an explanation.

"They would drape their amulets over a shoulder when they hugged me or held me. But once in a while, contact with an amulet couldn't be avoided. It would all happen in fractions of a moment, so neither I nor anyone else could tell if I had caused their amulet to glow or if it was their own unconscious thoughts. With my parents' amulets, though, their crystals would glow, and I felt…" She shrugged. "I guess I thought it was my parents' doing. I thought that was what love felt like."

He regarded her a moment longer before continuing up the pass.

Why had the Aspects Above chosen her to be a Trine when she was so foolish as to have not known her own powers for most of her life? Why had the godhead given her their gifts when she was too naïve to not know what Tetric Garis for whom he truly was? How could she possibly save Kinderra when she drained the life from an innocent man, too drunk on the Power from Without to not notice she had murdered him before it was too late?

Mirana stifled a cry. Nothing more could be done about those sins. No, they were written indelibly on her heart. But she had also healed a man who, against everything, had put his life—maybe a part of his soul—in her hands. Literally. Her heart held that, too.

Sido paused again and sent a questioning intent from within the Aspects.

"What made you want to become a Ken'nar?" The seer's face drained of expression.

Mirana bit her lip. Too soon.

Sido frowned then acquiesced to the question with a nod. "I suppose it's only fair to answer your question."

"Sido, you don't—"

He held up a hand, silencing her. "I hate the limitations of the so-called 'Light from Within.' It's as simple as that."

"Simple?" She laughed without humor. "There's nothing simple about choosing whether to give of one's self or to steal life from someone for your own motives."

He stepped closer, towering over her. "Is that what you think the Ken'nar do? Suck the life from people to warp it for our own dastardly deeds?"

Mirana straightened. "That's exactly what the Power from Without does, what the Ken'nar do!"

He lowered his face inches from hers. "A defender I respected had her flesh burned from her bones. Slowly. Bit by bit. By a Fal'kin with his amulet. Using his oh-so-altruistic Light from Within." Now he stood back. "I escaped. But not unscathed." He pointed to the scar by his mouth. His mind pressed against hers. "We have killed your people, just as you have killed mine!"

She couldn't disagree with him on that point. "I hate this damn war. I hate it so much. All the killing, the depravity. It's got to stop! People deserve peace, freedom." The answers had to be within her ancestor's keep. There was no other option.

Sido laughed, a harsh, cutting sound. "What makes you think the Ken'nar want subjugation and tyranny any more than the Fal'kin do? You Fal'kin believe in such lofty notions as freedom. To the Ken'nar, freedom is our life. The freedom to use our Aspects how we will. I was little more than an infant when I unknowingly used the Power from Without. I loved the horses in Falantir's stables." He laid a hand on his horse as if acting out the memory. "As I stroked one, I had slipped into some sort of communion with the horse's life force. Now that I think about it, it was not so different from using an amulet. And I saw it. A vision. A killing winter storm. I had no idea what I had done. I didn't even know there was such a thing as the Power from Without. I just knew I saw something important. I immediately told my mother and father about the coming storm. My father asked how I came by such a vision as neither they nor any of the other seers had the prescience of a blizzard. I told them I had been petting the horse and the vision just came to me." He turned and stalked closer to Mirana. "And you know how they thanked me? My father hit me, trying to terrify me out of ever using the Power again. They ignored my warning of the blizzard. But it came. And thousands died. *Ai*, I'm evil for stealing that horse's life force and using it for my own motives."

He stomped up the path.

"Sido! Please. Wait." She hurried to catch up with him.

The seer closed his eyes as his shoulders sank. "What?"

"You were too young to have known what you did, and you ended up becoming a victim as much as the horse. Maybe even more so as no harm came to the horse. Instead of beating you, your parents should have warned the prime and then gently explained to you about the path to Without." She laid a hand on his healing arm. "That's why the Power from Without is so treacherous. One *can* do good with it, but the choice to use others for a power source instead of oneself becomes all too easy." His gaze rested on her hand. "What you did that day was good, Sido. And how you were punished was wrong. Very. They should have thanked you and taught you about the Power from Without."

"No one's ever—" He took her hand in his. Turning it over, he brushed his lips against the scars on her palms.

Mirana gently raised his chin, his mouth so close to hers. So achingly close. His fingers, nicked and cut, cradled her head, tipping her face up to his, pulling her closer—

The Defending Aspect screamed a warning through her.

Mirana gasped. "What the—?"

He leaned back in surprise. "*You* were about to kiss *me*. Do not blame—"

She shook her head. "Not you. Something's wrong."

A series of sharp cracks reverberated through the mountain crags. The horses neighed and whinnied, pawing at the ice.

She froze. "What's that sound?"

"Nothing good." Sido swallowed and held his amulet. It glowed for a moment, then he let it fall back against his chest as he gave an explosive exhale.

"What—?"

The rest of her question was lost as the cracks gave way to thunderous explosions.

Sido grabbed Ashtar's reins. "Get against the rock!" He shoved her against the granite wall of the pass, dragging the horse to shield her with its body, then doing the same with his mount. The roaring went on and on.

When it finally stopped, Mirana stood on tiptoes to peer over Ashtar's back.

A small mound of fluffy snow obscured the pass as it jagged sideways around a rock buttress. When Mirana stepped around the granite outcropping, her stomach jagged sideways, too.

She groaned.

An avalanche of snow, ice, and stone had completely obliterated the Darbinh Pass ahead of them.

"How are we going to get around this?" She gestured to the enormous hill of snow and let her hand fall, slapping her thigh.

"I'm thinking." Sido eyed the mountain walls on either side of them.

"You said you've been through the pass before. Do you know another way?"

Sido pursed his lips a moment. "Well, *ai*, I did mention avalanches, but I never said I'd been to—"

Mirana's jaw dropped. "You *lied* to me?"

"No, of course not." Sido barked an unconvincing laugh. "I was completely truthful about lemmings. And I was right about the avalanches."

Lights! He had perfected the art of omission lies like their mentor. Lights, again. She conveniently omitted telling the seer about her role in the keep.

"So you've never been through the Darbinh Pass?"

"The Ken'nar had never bothered with Trak-Calan. The province is too remote from the rest of the continent to provide any tactical advantages."

"Sido!"

"No, I haven't. But Tetric has. I've seen the way. In his mind. He dreams of this place."

The path ahead of them seemed insurmountable. "I was not aware he ever truly slept," she replied.

"He used to." The seer faced the mountain of snow. "If we can't go around it, we'll have to go over it." He unsheathed his sword and stalked over to the looming white mound.

"You're going to cut your way through?" Mirana asked.

"I never know if you're serious with your questions or are just trying to annoy me." He plunged the blade into the snow level with his waist, using it for leverage as he began to scramble over the obstacle.

"Whoa! Wait." She rushed over. "That snow is unstable. You could fall through or trigger another slide, this time carrying you right off the mountain."

He looked down at her. "Well, what other choice do we have?"

"Let me think." Mirana eyed the wall of snow, one hand on her amulet. "If we can't go around it or over it, we'll go through it."

He hopped down from the snow hill. "That's a terrible plan. It would take us sevendays to tunnel through."

"Who said anything about a tunnel?" She grinned.

He did a double-take from the white mass to her. "What do you mean? You're not going to—"

She nodded. "If I brought down an entire ford, I can clear this snow pack." Maybe. Hopefully. "Take the horses. Stand back."

"Mirana—"

"If I don't do something, we'll die of exposure and starvation."

The seer flattened his thin lips and led the horses back a few paces.

Mirana cupped the half-diamond amulet with her hands and opened herself to the Aspects. Molding and shaping the powers within her, she called to the Defending Aspect, the other two Aspects adding to its strength.

Once again, she would destroy the wall that separated those for whom she cared from freedom. Once again, she would become the Aspects, the Light from Within.

She would become fire!

Mirana held her Defending Aspect close, letting it grow and condense. Heat built inside her, and the Healing Aspect whispered to her of pain. Burning.

Burning!

She released an explosion of pure-white amulet fire at the wall of ice. She cried in triumph as her Defending Aspect manifested, incendiary light melting snow and ice. She continued the onslaught, washing the avalanche detritus with a wide beam of unceasing fire.

Something slammed her in the chest, wrenching her from her communion with the Aspect. She screamed at the abrupt separation as a deluge of water poured over her. Floundering in the flood, she desperately searched for purchase to keep her from drowning and being swept away.

A strong hand grabbed her by the collar of her borrowed mantle and dragged her up out of the river she had created.

"Sido!"

They crouched on a boulder just above the pass. The horses likewise stood on rocks above the flood.

He grinned down at her as he held her in his arms. "For future reference, ice melts into water. A lot of ice equals a lot of water."

"Yeah. I'll remember that next time." She laughed.

His slate-green eyes sought silver ones. "You are a miracle, Mirana Pinal."

An intense shiver ripped through her. "What I am is *cold*."

"That's because you're completely soaked." The seer took off his cloak and wrapped it around her. "I've got to find you some shelter before you freeze to death."

Her skin might have been frigid, but the fire Sido had ignited, no mountain cold could extinguish.

CHAPTER 11

"The Light from our greatest Jewel shines elsewhere."
—The Codex of Jasal the Great

Sido and Mirana made camp for the night in a small cave within the granite boulders to shield them and the horses from the ever-present wind. The seer attempted to start a fire with a flint, some lumps of charcoal from their packs, and dried lichens he had gathered, but could not produce a spark in the thin air. He tried a few more times and gave up, cursing.

Mirana cupped Jasal's amulet. "Let me try," she said through chattering teeth, accidentally biting her tongue.

Sido shook his head. "You've done enough already."

She smiled. "I think I've proven I sort of have an affinity for fire."

She called to her Defender's Aspect as gently as she could and ignited the tinder with her amulet. It worked but not well. They huddled with their horses around the sickly flame.

Sido wrapped the bedrolls and extra clothes around them and held her close for warmth. "Tell me about the keep. What sort of weapon is it?"

She weighed her words before answering. "I don't know for sure. All I see is a blinding white light."

His gaze drifted to the diamond peeking out from her Ken'nar cloak. "I have seen that vision as well. Jasal's Keep exploding in pure white light, brighter than the sun."

He had mentioned that before, but she had been preoccupied at the time with starvation and wondering if he and his Ken'nar were going to turn her into a pile of ash. How was it possible that he had seen the keep vision, too? It was her vision, hers alone, condemned upon her by the Aspects Above. It wasn't meant to be shared with anyone.

Then again, Sido was a very talented seer. Why *wouldn't* another with the Seeing Aspect have seen something so…so dramatic? No. Terrifying? Explosive? Damning. She could insert any description she wanted to of the keep vision, and none would ever do justice to what it meant to her.

Sido's acknowledgment of seeing her vision felt oddly comforting, however. She now knew unequivocally it wasn't just a nightmare or her imagination. It was real. And someone else knew it. Aspects Above knew Teague had never believed her.

Tetric, of course, claimed to have seen it as well. But he couldn't have seen all of it, or he would have recognized himself within the vision. Or maybe that was another of his lies.

His lies—always wrapped in truth, layered beneath his noble, true desire to free Kinderra from war, preserved his innocence. And she'd believed him, believed *in* him, because so very many of his ideals were *good*.

Ai, that was the whole damning thing about Tetric. He didn't want minions groveling at his feet. He didn't want to slaughter those who opposed him. He hated killing, detested it. He believed elevating the Power from Without as the one true philosophy to attain communion with the Aspects would bring peace to all people—Fal'kin, Ken'nar, and Unaspected.

Except he was wrong.

She refused to give in to denial or delusions. She knew exactly what would happen if she couldn't make him understand just how wrong he was.

Mirana pushed the thought away. The day had been traumatic enough.

The seer threw another bit of lichen on the anemic flame and moved to sit closer to her. "If we nurture the right future skeins together, we will be victorious."

"What do you mean?"

He scowled. "You must have seen it, too?"

Wait. What? What was he talking about? "You've seen something else? Something beyond the white light?"

He nodded. "Tetric is not in my vision. But you are. And so am I."

She had so many questions. No, not questions but elation. A myriad of emotions came to her mind faster than her tongue could speak them. "You've seen something *after* the light? After the explosion?"

"*Ai*." His brows drew together in concerned confusion. "You mean…you have not?"

Mirana shook her head slowly. "No. Nothing," she whispered, hope and dread vying for the same place in her heart.

She'd had this same vision, or parts of it anyway, her entire life, but there was never an "after," no victory, no happy continuance. It all ended in failure, bleached away by the white light. Like the finality of Jasal Pinal's emotions locked within his Codex, she had her own sudden and final conclusion. Could there be something more? With Sido?

She leaned closer, taking his hands in her own. "Tell me what you've seen. Am I in your vision?"

He smiled, the firelight reflecting in his green eyes. "*Ai.*" He brought her hands to his chest, his amulet. "Strong. Brave. The whole of Kinderra kneeling at your feet. *Ai*, Mirana, you will survive this. And I will be by your side."

"I've never seen anything of this. Just the light." And the finality of it all. She looked at their entwined hands. "Who else survives?"

"You're asking about the herbsboy, aren't you?" He dropped her hands.

"No!" She screwed up her face in confusion. "*Ai.* Maybe. Sido, I didn't mean to upset you. *Ai*, Teague Beltran. But I also want to know if so many others will outlive the coming cataclysm."

One that she might bring with her very hands.

"You are a seer, a Trine. Surely you could see his fate if you wished." He gave the fire several stabs with his sword.

"I just told you. I've never seen this part of the keep vision. Not once." When he continued to jab at the flames, she reached for his hand. "Sido. Please."

He gave a curt nod and set his blade aside but did not reply further. She toyed with a bit of lichen and said nothing.

The fire ate away at the lichen as it curled black in a death throe. The altitude stole the strength of the flame. It was not strong enough to keep them warm. It would be a cold night.

Mirana reached for Sido's mind. She wanted his warm melody again. The one she heard while healing him. The one as warm as the melody singing through her now.

"We met each other once. At Quorumtide," she said at last.

"I remember. You wore a beautiful, pale-blue dress. Like your eyes."

"That's right."

He turned to her. "You were a child at the time."

"Hardly a child. I was fourteen. And I am certainly not a child any longer." She dug through one of her saddlebags and took out the alabaster cylinder with the keep passages. "Sido, your revelation that maybe, somehow, I might survive, that *we* might survive the future, has given me more hope than I've had—"

Since Tetric Garis stopped her from killing herself.

"Here." She handed the pale document tube to the seer. "The keep is constructed of amulets. It's lined with them. Thousands."

Sido's eyes widened in disbelief. "By all the Power that surrounds." He opened the cylinder and leafed through the writings, scanning what words had not been washed away from the parchment. "So the light we both see, it's—"

"—some sort of massive amulet fire, *ai*," Mirana finished. "It must be."

"After my vision, I knew it was a weapon, but I never imagined it was something like this." His amulet glowed an icy, pale green as his eyes searched the flames. His lips curled with a sort of feral hunger. "A weapon of such magnificence. Whoever controls it will be invincible."

And just like that, he extinguished her hope like the frail fire before them.

Mirana crossed her arms and leaned away from him, the granite cold and hard against her back. "How naïve you must think I am."

He turned quickly to face her. "What?"

"You didn't come with me to offer any help whatsoever."

He scowled. "What do you mean?"

"You came to learn about the keep, how to control it." She pointed to the cylinder. "And you made a grave mistake by doing so."

He raised an eyebrow, the action drawing on his scar. "Have I, now?"

"Think, Sido. The keep is of no use to you. And never will be." She took out her amulet from her shirt and held it up. "Only a Trine can use another amulet besides the one he or she has chosen. The keep is nothing more than a pile of pretty stones to you."

"*Ai*, that is true. But not to Tetric. Your success means his failure. That's what I want. If you didn't trust me, why did you agree to have me come with you? Why did you tell me all that just now?" His mind brushed hers, searching for a connection.

She looked away from his penetrating gaze. "I need you as much as you need me. It's going to take the both of us to prevent Tetric from gaining the keep. And, more than likely—" The words were harder to speak than she expected. "More than likely, I will have to kill him to do that." She shook her head and laughed sadly. "Even more likely, he'll kill me." She closed her eyes and leaned back against the cold stone wall of the cave. Solid. Strong. But cold. "He's wrong, Sido, about the way he wants to bring peace to Kinderra. But he's right about so many other things."

He laughed darkly. "Do you honestly think you can change Tetric's heart?"

"I don't know, but I have to try."

"Maybe not all of us are meant to be saved." He placed the leaflets back in the cylinder and laid the container in her lap. "He no longer cares about me. He never truly did. I was only a means to an end." He nodded. "And, oh, it ended, all right." He hefted his sword and struck at the weak flame again, punctuating his words.

Mirana put a hand on his arm. "You are his second. He placed you above all others."

He grabbed her wrist. ... *Except you* ... He threw her hand from him as he threw her words back at her. "I gave him everything he ever asked of me. Without question. Everything. I have lied for him, sacked my own province for him, killed for him, bled for him. I willingly suffered his torture, time and time again." The horses stirred at the harshness of his voice. "And why? So I could see the glory of his Ken'nar on a throne." He curled his long fingers into fists, clenching and releasing them, again and again. "All he wants are harvested slaves. None of us mean anything to him. Only power." And you," he said as he stabbed a finger toward her, "you want to take my one chance at revenge from me, the one thing I have left—*the one thing!*—so you can save him from himself?"

His face held fury. His emotions, however, held sadness, a heart-crushing despondency as acute as anything she had sensed from Jasal Pinal. "I never realized what he put you through."

"'What he put me through.'" The bitterness in his voice cut her words to shreds. "I sought him out when I was only fifteen summers old. I was a terrified boy searching for a way to rise beyond the shallow role of a seer divining weather for the Kana-Akün prime. And do you know how he demanded my fealty?"

She shook her head. "Sido, please. Don't—"

"He had me murder my parents." This time, he grabbed her hand and shackled it in his grip. ... *And I did* ... *Because I believed in him* ... *And now he has betrayed me* ... "I will help you take the keep from him and I will gladly help you kill him. But save his Aspect-forsaken soul?" He shook his head. "That's a journey you walk alone."

Was there no end to the nightmare her life had become? "Tetric saved my life when I didn't want to live. He's done things. Terrible things. And so have you. But so have I. I may do still more terrible things. And yet he believes in me. He believes I can make a difference and help Kinderra."

Or had Tetric saved her from herself only so she could become the very tyrant she feared? A life-stealing mortal amulet he would wield with cruel efficiency?

"I know he truly does want the war to end. Maybe that is a place from which we can start again."

The seer laughed in disgust. "The end of war under Tetric Garis does not mean peace. You must know that by now."

Ai, she did. "But if we can get him to understand that freedom doesn't mean the ability to do what you want with another's life, maybe there's a chance. Maybe."

She picked up the cylinder from her lap. "The keep," she continued. "I don't think even a Trine can choose thousands of amulets at once, much less control them." Not with the Light from Within. "When all I see is failure and destruction at my own hands, Tetric sees something else. That is the only hope I have to cling to."

"Tetric Garis offers no hope." Sido jumped to his feet and threw his arms out wide. "Do you know how many times he has tried to kill your father? He even wanted you dead until he understood your power. He has given you nothing but lies disguised as truth." He jabbed a finger at his chest. "Have I not just told you that you will outlive this conflict? You and me, together. Why, in the name of the Aspects Above, do you want to save him, Mirana?! Why do you even care?!"

She shot up to stand, dropping the cylinder. "Because I have to believe there is a way back! There must be a way one can come back from evil!" She turned away from him. "There has to be." … *Or I am already lost* … "Sido, everyone, even Tetric, deserves the chance, the choice to turn his or her life around for the better. If not, if all of us are beyond redemption for our sins, then why live at all?" The Trine Prophecy said only hope would remain. Hope was one name for it. The other was denial.

Mirana wiped at her face. She was so tired. Tired of fighting. Tired of trying. Of searching for questions and only finding answers even more convoluted. Of moral knots and slick faults. Tears wet her fingers as she held them over her eyes.

"I need to give Tetric Garis that choice. To know that such a thing is possible. For myself."

He stood close to her. … *You are not evil* … *What I saw in your eyes in my keep vision* …

She looked over her shoulder but remained with her back to him.

… *What I felt from you as you healed me* … *When I pulled you from the flood* … *I've never felt from another living soul* …

The warm life music grew once more in him. And in her. "I wanted to help you."

"And you did. But you did something more. Much more. You've made me think about other possibilities," he said slowly, as if he wasn't certain how to convey his emotion. "Or start to, anyway. Mirana Pinal, you've completely disarmed me." She could feel the heat from his body as he moved closer still, his chest touching her shoulders, his lips brushing her ear. "And I hate it." With a gentle but persistent hand on her shoulder, he turned her to face him.

She searched Sido's face, so like Teague's but thinner, the angles of his nose and jaw sharper, harsher. He wasn't so much sculpted by the Aspects Above as he was cut by them. So much like Teague but harder. Hardened. Hurting.

"Give me your hand." He took her hand in his and placed it over the pale green peridot of his amulet. She inhaled sharply at the sudden intimate connection. … *Open your mind to me* …

As she did, a vision formed before her mind's eye, a future skein, loose in its weaving, insubstantial in a time yet to come, if at all.

Deren lies in ruins. Great blocks of stone crumble, gaping wounds left in the great walls. Hundreds, thousands of people stand before her, Aspected and Unaspected. Together as one, they kneel. A man, a young man with sandy hair, takes her hands in his. She turns to him, but she cannot see his face clearly, as if her eyes are misted with tears, the threads of time yet to be fully woven. But she feels the unmistakable power of love. For him. From him. Undying love. The young man kisses her, deeply, then kisses her ruined palms.

She blinked as the vision ended abruptly.

"I am glad the herbsman left you," Sido breathed.

The seer's amulet felt warm against her palm. She began to tremble but not with cold. "He didn't. I left him. I knew if he stayed with me, the Dark Trine would kill him. I thought I could save his life if I broke his heart. And I did. But I broke mine as well."

"Your heart doesn't need to remain broken." He covered her hand over his amulet with his own. His face was close to hers, his breath misting the chill air.

She didn't want to speak the words, to give them the power to become real, but they fought for their freedom. She had to release them, or they would continue to spread like a virulent disease and consume her. "I can't do this alone anymore. I can't. My whole life, I've been alone. Teague tried, but he never truly understood what I was up against. I thought Tetric could help me become who I need to be, but I was wrong. Then I thought if I shut everyone out of my heart, the choices I made wouldn't hurt so much. That was wrong, too."

His mind pressed against hers, desiring a deeper connection, and she let him in.

"This amulet"—she laid her fingers on the half diamond—"is the closest thing I've ever had to a true partner. But in the end, it's nothing more than metal and crystal."

With his fingertips, he traced the outline of her cheek, and she turned her face into his caress. He drew his fingers slowly down her neck to touch a silvery link of the amulet she wore. And paused when he touched the scorched mica face of the peda blossom pendant.

"And this?" He pulled it from her shirt.

"It was a promise neither of us could keep," she breathed.

"Then why does it remain close to your heart?"

She shook her head. "I don't know."

"You are not alone. I know exactly what you are battling, Mirana." Sido slowly lifted the peda blossom over her head and let it fall to the stony floor.

Was the weight on her shoulders lessened? Or made heavier?

"Whatever Trine powers Jasal Pinal used with the keep, you must find a way to use them as well, and right now you have no answers. You want to turn Tetric Garis back from his sins, but you know you cannot." He trailed his fingers down the chain, link by link, resting them on the diamond that lay between her breasts. Her heart pounded, loud in her ears. "If he remains lost to you, you believe your soul will be just as lost. You know you will have to kill him, the man you worshipped, who then broke your trust and your faith. I know that agony as well. We are bound to each other. By him." The Healing Aspect spoke to her of his quickening heartbeat. The sense of it drew breath from her, faster, needful. "I know this because I am Aspected. As you are. That is something the herbsman can never be. He will never understand what the Aspects Above placed within you and me. But I do." His lips brushed her forehead, the bridge of her nose.

She lifted her face to his. ... *I don't want to be alone anymore ...*

... You have me ...

He covered her mouth with his, his mind driving through hers, not in an attack, but in need. A need she returned. He pulled her closer, holding her tightly against his body. His lips parted hers, opening her mouth to his. Passion washed through her, stealing her breath and lighting her Healing Aspect with its intensity. His want rose, an urgent, insistent song. A harmony echoed, her own body's aching descant singing through her. Sensations, physical and Aspected, began to merge. She took in what his body was experiencing and released to him what her own awakening body was just beginning to understand.

The last time she kissed Teague, they, too, had been surrounded by cold, and yet Teague's embrace always held warmth borne of love. Sido's heat radiated around her now, through her, fueled by hunger. Teague had all but called her keep vision a fantasy. She knew it was not. And so did Sido. Sido had spoken her deepest fears, not to terrify her, but to empathize with her. He was a man, six summers her senior. Teague shared the same Reckoning of her birth—no longer a boy, but the summers of adulthood lay ahead of him, as they did her. Teague shared her secrets, her dreams, her hopes. Sido shared her Aspect, her truth, Tetric's betrayal. Sido shared her raw desire.

Mirana drank in his kisses, sparring with his mouth. She tore open his shirt, tasting his naked skin, trailing her tongue over his amulet. Male hardness between his hips pressed against her, drawing soft, needful sighs from her.

His hand traveled up her back. His long fingers untwined the plait in her hair, freeing it. He gripped a handful of it, pressing her even closer into his embrace. He kissed her mouth, her throat, her neck, inhaling the scent of her hair, of her.

Sido had killed her Fal'kin. She had killed his Ken'nar. Sido used the Power from Without. She, too, had killed a man with the Power from Without. Sido wanted to stop Tetric's domination of Kinderra. Sido wanted this war to end. Just like she did.

Sido had seen the keep vision, believed it, and knew it was real. As real as his embrace now, as real as the need his body demanded from hers. The crescendo of desire, hers indivisible from his own, built within her, a motif that set all her senses on fire.

His hand slid farther inside her shirt to cup her breast. Desire, raw and lightning-bright, shot down her spine, penetrating throughout her body in a liquid warmth. She gasped into his kiss, the pleasure, painful and delicious in its intensity, filling her. An aching need coiled tightly deep within her. He pressed his hips more tightly against hers, holding her against the wall of the cave, and pulled her mind deeper into his. A rhapsody swelled and burned within her as she moved against his body, desperate to relieve the ache in her own.

Sido's lips were cold against her. Sido was so like Teague, hair the color of burnt honey, his body comfortably tall, deceptively strong, but his eyes were a deep, slate green, not hazel as she had first thought. They held no softness, no illusions.

She needed the hard and assured strength of Sido's life-song to resolve the aching, burning dissonance deep, deep inside her. Now.

Sido understood her. He wanted her. But Teague had loved her. Teague would have run away with her had she asked.

Teague was willing to die for her.

Sido was so like Teague. Yet he was not.

Mirana pushed him back from her and gasped. "You—" She swallowed a gulp of air. "You need your rest."

He continued to hold her fast, his own breath coming in quick bursts. "You don't sleep?"

She brought her hands up, laying her palms against his chest to push him away, but his body's seductive music threatened to pull her back into his embrace. "We have a long journey tomorrow. I will keep watch tonight."

Sido did not move away. He also did not prevent her from stepping around him. "I would rather watch you tonight."

"I...I need..." What did she need? Oh, so many things. And all of them seemed as wrong as they were right. "Get some rest."

Mirana snatched the fallen blossom pendant from the ground and hurried out of the cave. She breathed in the frigid night air to clear her head and cool her blood, clutching Teague's peda blossom pendant close to her heart.

CHAPTER 12

"Ama ísi enigma. Ama ísi u'ben e ben. Ama ísi fuádain e tudempre. Ama ísi frágil brea tuda. Ama ísi forte brea tuda. Ama ísi enigma."
("Love is a riddle. It is cruel and kind. It is fleeting and eternal. It is the most fragile of things. It is the strongest of things. Love is a riddle.")

—Ora Fal'kinnen 301:1–6

Mirana stared at Sido's back as he plodded ahead of her. What could she possibly say to him now? They had resumed their trek in the high Darbinh Pass before daybreak and hadn't spoken a word or called a thought to each other since dawn.

She couldn't go forward with Sido, yet she couldn't go back to the beginning with Teague. Nothing made sense anymore.

Once again, she had no one to blame for her tangled heart but herself. With Teague, she had chosen her fear over what she held dear. And for what? Her keep vision had not changed. Pushing Teague from her had done nothing to save his life. He still perished in that crushing premonition.

She still loved Teague. But another equally undeniable truth was she held deep feelings for Sido. Not love, or not the kind of love that led to a union and a family anyway. But deep admiration. Sido had unlocked in her the hope, no, the fact that she could inspire someone to take a different path. Or consider it.

She watched the seer march up the pass.

Or at least consider considering it.

Tetric had tried to have her abandon all her beliefs instead of helping strengthen her resolve in them. As much as she wanted a change in her former mentor's heart, to give up the Power from Without and so much more—and she held fast to giving him a final chance to do so—she doubted it was possible.

With Sido, though, it was different. He listened to her, her ideas, even her hopes to find a way forward from her sins, and reflected on them himself. He didn't like it. But he was thinking about it.

Mirana dug her heels into the snow and marched up the sloping trail. The Darbinh Pass wound its way around columns of granite and ice. Now and then, shorter pinnacles allowed a glimpse of the mountain range. Waves of stone undulated into the distance, some peaks cresting above the clouds.

The pass finally flattened and widened, opening to a broad glacier. The vista stole her labored breath. She drank in the sprawling ranges around them, providing a momentary respite from the relentless answers and the even more dogged questions.

She squinted across the white plain, shielding her eyes with her hand across her brow from the blinding sunlight reflected from the snow. Sections of ice bore striations, so many claw marks from an enormous mountain tiger. Holes and depressions pocked other areas like Quartermaster Lasen's lacy, mellow cheese. The edges of a yawning glacier field pushed against snowcapped, blue-gray towers of rock. High up in their eaves sat the learning hall of Trak-Calan. Clouds obscured its foundations, giving the hall the appearance of floating above the rock rather than being built from it.

Sido stumbled on a rock hidden by the snow. She caught him, but he said nothing.

He was tired. *Ai*, his body told her Healing Aspect that. But he was tired of so many things. Of pain, physical and otherwise. Of struggle. Of loss. His life had been ruined by his own choices as much as it had been by Tetric. He was as lost as she was.

"Did you love her?" she asked at last. "The woman I—the woman at Two Rivers Ford?"

"We had…an understanding." Sido's steps slowed but did not stop.

She stood still. "I'm so sorry."

"Do not ever speak that word to me."

"I am, though."

His eyes remained on the jagged horizon. "You love him. Why, I don't know."

She made a sad smile. "Maybe because I champion lost causes."

"Now that I do believe."

She hurried to catch up to him and stood in front of him, blocking his way. "Please try to understand. I've known him my whole life. We shared everything. He was the only one I told about my Trine Aspects. I will always love him whether he comes back into my life or not. I realized that too late." She lowered her gaze to his peridot amulet. "For all of us."

He moved closer to her. "And yet, you were in *my* arms last night."

"That's not fair." But he was right. For a few moments, being in his arms was exactly where she had wanted to be.

The seer exhaled and relaxed his stance. "After you healed—" He paused and shook his head. "Mirana, when I first had my keep vision, I thought I could use you and control the keep through you."

"Oh, really?" She arched a brow and folded her arms. "And how exactly would that have worked?"

He held up a hand to silence her. "Please. I'm trying to explain myself. Or-or apologize. Or. Something. None of which I do very often." Mirana bade him continue with a nod. "That was all before I realized…before I met—" He took a frustrated breath.

She closed her eyes. "Sido—"

"You've been nothing but kind to me."

"I slugged you in the jaw." She pointed to a fading bruise. "I really should take care of that."

"There is no reason on the face of Kinderra why you should want anything else from me but my death. And yet you are absolutely relentless in trying to, well, *care*."

He was right. She did care. "Why are you telling me this?" she asked slowly.

"I am not a good man, Mirana."

"Because you have fought and killed Fal'kin? Because you use the Power from Without? Because you made horrific choices that led to horrific actions?" She shook her head sadly. "Do I wish it were otherwise? *Ai*. But I have my own sins."

Sido lifted his head toward the towering granite walls surrounding them. "Even Tetric, for all his corruption, has an ethic he follows. I hold no such illusions. I do what I need to do for my benefit and no one else's. I feed my Aspects with the lives of others from Without, and I make no apologies. I have killed many, and I hold no regrets."

He took a few steps on the frozen trail, leading his mount. "I have killed il'Kin with my sword and have let others be harvested. I have tried to kill your father and mother."

She fought to keep her expression calm. "Y-You would have never succeeded. My father is one of the greatest defenders Kinderra has ever seen."

"Defenders see five moves ahead. Seers, fifty," he replied, reciting the adage.

She made no move to follow him. "Defenders don't need to see fifty moves ahead or even five. They only need to see one move ahead. Enough time to shoot amulet fire. That is something no seer can do."

Sido faced her now, his expression strained. "You cannot be that trusting. I just told you I've tried to kill your parents."

Mirana wanted very much to give the seer a matching bruise on the other side of his face. But that would solve nothing. Well, it would solve the need of venting her anger. "If they were here now, would you still try to kill them?"

"I wouldn't just stand here and let your father put a hole through my chest." He shook his head slowly. "But I—no." He made a frustrated chopping motion with his hands. "But that's not the point."

"Then what is the point?"

"I—" He blew out another exasperated breath. His mind's desperation reached out to her, a frantic but frail need to believe in something he knew might not be possible. In another man, she would have called it hope.

"What do you want from me?" She stepped closer and held her hands out at her sides. "Do you want me to hate you? Do you want me to keep you as my enemy? How will my hate help us? How will hate solve anything? Am I appalled at what you've done? *Ai.* And I *hate* those parts of you. But this war has turned us all into monsters." Her shoulders fell, defeated by the same fragile need to believe in something she knew might not be possible. "What matters now, the only thing that matters now, is to find a way to do more good than the evil we've already caused."

He curled his scarred lip into a jagged sneer. It almost hid the tears that glinted in the corners of his slate-green eyes. "What evil could you have possibly done?"

Hope. Denial. Both were beliefs chosen over something else. The only difference separating the two was how much one was willing to lie to oneself.

Exhaustion ate away at her, a real, penetrating, debilitating loss, leaving her limbs and her spirit empty. How much longer could she keep trying to find a path where there didn't seem to be one?

"I killed an innocent man, an Unaspected," she replied, her voice struggling to rise above the wind moaning through the granite.

Sido barked a wordless comment, too pained to be a laugh yet filled with sarcasm. "All of us killers have. It's the hazards of the job."

Mirana wanted to hit him again. Or cry. Or both. "I almost took the life forces of his mates as well, mates whose only crime was trying to save my own misbegotten life. The Power from Without I used to do it was intoxicating. Limitless. I didn't want to stop. Only that man's death, the silence of his life from within the Aspects, prevented me from killing the others." She held her arms, shivering as much from the memory as the cold. "That power tempts me still, though I abhor it."

"How different is that from when the battle takes Fal'kin defenders?" Sido shook his head in disbelief. "They become so consumed by fighting and the need to use the Defending Aspect, they kill with impunity. They use the oh-so-blessed Light from Within and you call them heroes."

"We do *not* call them heroes. We don't—" She scrubbed her eyes with her knuckles in frustration. "I killed more than a thousand Ken'nar when I destroyed the ford. I also killed fourteen Fal'kin—my own provincemen—who simply couldn't escape in time. And I killed both with the oh-so-blessed Light from Within." She let her arms fall heavily to her sides. "The point I'm trying to make is that it makes absolutely no difference who I killed or how. Fal'kin. Ken'nar. Unaspected. I cannot blame all these deaths on my ignorance or even my Aspects. Using another's life to murder instead of one's own power might seem like a small difference, but it makes an already heinous act infinitely more damning. It's like killing twice. At least to me. And there's nothing I can do now about those sins. We have all done things that scar our souls, Sido."

She passed by him and started up the trail.

"I torched Edara." His voice was flat. She stopped walking. "Not just the learning hall. The entire city. Tetric commanded me to take Varn-Erdal's horses to mount his troops because you destroyed the ford bridges. There were no horses. There was nothing. We searched for sevendays. He commanded me to capture Fal'kin and take them back to be harvested. There were not enough Fal'kin for me to even bother risking my troops. He commanded me to kill Liaonne Edaran, but she escaped. We were defeated at every turn. So I burnt Edara to the ground."

She closed her mind. She didn't want to hear this. She didn't want to feel this from him.

"I sacked Falantir in Kana-Akün. My home. On my order, I let no one escape," he continued, his voice soft and chilling. "I held Belessa Tir while Tetric harvested her. She gave me a sweet biscuit once when I was six summers old. I predicted lightning from a storm would start a forest fire. I held her as Tetric ravaged her mind, and the old healer woman fought mightily."

Mirana turned slowly. "Sido, please—"

"I told you I was no stranger to starvation. We Ken'nar don't have the luxury of an Unaspected tithe to feed us. I told you I was only two summers old when the winter famine gripped Falantir, but I remember it well. Do you know how we survived?" His mind now pressed against hers. He stepped closer, his lips nearly touching hers. "We ate the dead, Mirana. *We ate. The dead.*"

She tried to move farther away from him, anything to escape his grief, but her legs were frozen. He now held her gaze, her expression reflected in the pain and fury of his own. A wave of emotion washed from him through her. Guilt. Hatred. Desperation. They overwhelmed him. And her. Her Healing Aspect flared, lighting the half diamond at her chest.

"I-I don't know what to say." Cold tears stung her eyes. "I want to help you, but I don't know how."

"You rackin' little silver-eyed—" He sighed again. "You healed me. For no other reason than I was wounded. In my keep vision, you look at me with such kindness. No one has ever done that." His lips tightened, betraying his struggle to control his emotions. "I know what you said about your herbsman, but my vision has never wavered. I told you who I am, what I am. You could have killed me when we first met. You could have let me succumb to my wounds on the pass. But you didn't." His hand held hers, his palm warm.

Her chest constricted as she fought back grief and guilt. Sido Rendel loved her. He hadn't meant to fall in love with her.

Ai, she'd had a momentary question in her own heart when she thought Teague was lost to her, but she could no longer believe the lie. She had distanced herself from the seer since that moment, however, it was pointless. The damage was already done.

Now she would have to break Sido's heart, too, just when he was finding it again.

She squeezed his hand and released it. "Your vision has given me courage, but it's not one that I've seen. I don't know what that means."

He grabbed her arms roughly. "It means you love me." He loosened his grip but did not release her.

She held his arms, not to ready for a fight, but to form a pathway to his mind from hers. She wanted—needed—him to sense the sincerity of her caring because her next words would hurt. The faintest echo of his healing arm whispered to her Healing Aspect. "I'm not sure it's you in that vision."

"Who else could it be?" Desperation glinted in his green eyes, so like Teague's yet not.

"The vision you showed me, the hazy figure of a young man, the brownish hair, the height of him." She swallowed back against the burning in her eyes. Now was not the time for tears. There never really was such a time. "You were seeing someone else with me." Her throat tightened even more. "If it had been you, you would have never seen him. You'd be standing in his place. You're a seer; you know this."

He released her and stood motionless as the sunlight glinted in the wet corners of his eyes. "No. No, you're wrong. I know what I felt from you in that vision. And when you healed me. When I held you in the cave. I know what I saw. I know what I felt. I see the truth and accept it. It is the one Fal'kin belief I still hold."

She blinked back the ice-tears forming on her lashes. "Sido, you are one of Kinderra's most powerful seers. You know that isn't you in the vision. That doesn't mean I don't care about you. I do. Deeply. But as a friend. And that's something I truly need in my life right now."

He remained still.

By the Light, she was exhausted. Exhausted in her body. Exhausted in her mind, in her heart. Exhausted in her soul. "Please, let's just get to Caladazh and get that over with."

Sido rushed in front of her. "He walked away from you and yet you still love him. You pledge your heart to a boy who does not even know what love is."

Like water slipping through the spaces between her fingers, Sido was slipping from her, heartbeat by heartbeat.

"He didn't walk away from me," she said. "I walked away from him. But you are right about one thing. You and I do share something no other two individuals in Kinderra do. We were created by Tetric Garis. We know what he is capable of. I *do* need you in my life. Someone who understands, someone I can rely on. I need you to help me stop him. Please."

He gripped her arms. "You have my Aspect. But Teague Beltran has your heart."

"You also have my trust. My respect. My admiration. My friendship. Aren't they enough?"

He pinned her against the rock wall. "I want all of you."

"Sido." Jasal's amulet brightened in the morning light. He let her go. "I don't love you, Sido. I care for you too much to not tell you that. I love Teague. I made a mistake, a horrible mistake, and I will always beg your forgiveness for doing what I did. And his, too, frankly. But I love Teague. I always have and I always will." The Defending Aspect whispered to her. Surely Sido wouldn't try to hurt her now? No. The quiet sense of warning came from somewhere or something else. This heart's impasse needed resolving before she could divine what else the universe was about to throw at her. "You said you were not a good man, and maybe you weren't. But you can be. If you choose it. Please, Sido. You've come so far."

He leaned close, his lips nearly touching hers. She tasted the salt of his tears as they trailed freely down his chin onto her lips. "You belong to me, Mirana. Not him. Me. I want you. For my own. Forever. Not as a possession or object of desire, but as a companion. In every sense of the word."

"I don't belong to anyone, Sido. I choose to be with Teague. If he'll take me back. If he lives. If we live." Jasal's amulet gleamed brighter against her chest.

"And if he doesn't take you back?"

"Sido—"

The Defending Aspect prickled in her chest. *Danger.*

"I know what I saw for Deren's future," the seer continued. "It is our future. I know what I felt from you—"

"*Obsca.*" She held up a hand, listening.

"Bloody hell, girl! Do you know how many women have thrown themselves at me?"

Her focus on the warning within the Aspects prevented her from crafting a snappy retort. She'd let him have it later. A snap cracked across the plain. "Do you hear that?" Now a creaking groan sounded through the air, like that of tree limbs breaking in a storm. "What is it?" She searched the snow plain, trying to find the threat.

He shielded his eyes from the sun and peered into the white around them. "The glacier." He scowled and held his amulet, light spilling between his fingers. "It's…it's moving."

She looked from the glacier to the seer and back to the river of ice. "Moving?"

"Only a seer would notice, but *ai*, it's moving. That's what's making the sound."

She reached for her amulet and the Seeing Aspect and closed her eyes. "*Ai*. By the Light, it *is* moving." She bit her lip. "And cracking."

He swallowed. "And cracking."

As if in answer to his words, a low noise rumbled across the plain. It grew louder, followed by a popping sound. Fissures began to appear in the snowfield behind them.

"We can't stay here." She tensed to start running but he grabbed her arm.

"Do. Not. Move." He looked out across the blinding expanse of white, his brow furrowed in concentration. "You'll force more cracks and fall through." His gaze remained fixed on the white expanse.

"We have to find a way across." But how? Mirana stretched out with her Aspects. Life lay beneath the snow, faint but unmistakable. "Something's living here." She scowled. "Plants?"

He nodded slowly. "*Ai*. Algae. Like pond scum on snow. We'd get blooms of it high on the slopes of the Dar-Tinal Mountains in the north of Kana-Akün. The wind blows dust and silt down from the mountains. Muck grows in it."

She raised an eyebrow.

"I know more about the wind than a person should." When she didn't change her expression, he frowned. "Did I not say my parents were weather seers? Never mind. Come."

"Wait a moment." She turned back to the glacier. "It's strongest in those pits, but less so in the holes. Do you feel it?" The ground rumbled again.

He nodded. "In the shallow pits, algae bloom closer to the surface, closer to the sun." He tightened his grip on his amulet. "Some are deeper than others. Life feels farther, fainter in those. Some are very deep."

She bit her lip. "Making the ice unstable." She scanned the edges of the glacier. A solid surface had to exist somewhere. Rock surrounded them, for Aspects' sake.

The seer motioned her behind him.

A subtle but nauseating tug pulled at her vitality. "No. Stop." She gripped his arm. "Don't use the Power from Without. Please. We can do this. Use your Light from Within to sense the plants or algae or whatever, but you don't need to use their lives. By letting us know where they are the strongest, they will tell us where the ice holes are shallower and therefore where the glacier is thicker. We only need to sense them, not use them. Please."

"You can't be serious?" His condemning glare accused her of abject stupidity.

"I can't do this alone. You must reach out with your Aspect, too. You haven't lost your ability. You've just chosen to not use your Light from Within."

The glacier creaked and snapped again, the noise closer. "Do you really want to have this discussion now? Find the damn path!" He pointed the way forward.

"If you are so much as a finger's width outside of my footsteps, you could fall through the ice. Sido, please. This time, don't pull in life. Reach out with your own and see what is hidden. The Aspect within you is your birthright."

He glanced behind him, small fissures widening at their heels now. "The Light Within is not strong enough."

"*Ai*, it is, because *you* are strong enough. I need you to try." … *Please* … She squeezed his arm and released him. "Reach out and follow me. Step only where I step."

Mirana cast out her Aspects and began to cross the cracking glacial field. She walked where the glimmers of life were strongest, where the ice was thicker, Ashtar following her like a shadow. Sido stood motionless, holding his horse's reins, waiting for her to put some distance between them. Treading as lightly as a cat, she stepped on the crusty snow. It snapped like twigs under her feet but did not break. After she had gone several yards, she bade the seer to follow her. He walked across the glacier, placing each foot only where her boots had imprinted on the icy snow.

They'd already picked their way across to the middle of the icefield when she heard a loud crack near Ashtar. She stood still. "Oh, no. Oh, you big brute."

"Who are you calling a brute?" the seer asked.

"Not you. My—uh oh."

Neither she nor Sido had considered that Ashtar was at least a hand higher and considerably heavier than the seer's sleek thoroughbred.

A hairline crack expanded from between several ice pockmarks near her horse's hooves, but instead of engulfing her, it snaked away behind her. Huge chunks of hard-packed snow fell to oblivion as a crevasse of blue ice yawned open before them.

"Sido! Run!" She took off, heading for the rock ledge on the far side of the glacier.

The seer moved slowly at first, then quicker. He released the reins of his horse and broke into a run. He followed her footsteps, trying to outrun the zigzagging fissure. The noise became deafening. Great slabs of snow and ice fell away into the abyss behind him. Sido's horse screamed in fear and dashed away in panic toward the safety of the granite ledge where the pass resumed through the mountains. Like a gaping maw intent on swallowing the seer whole, the fissure stretched and widened as it approached him.

Her Seeing Aspect flared, and Mirana slid to a halt. He would not make it. "Sido!" A deafening boom echoed around the glacier plain. A fissure opened and the seer disappeared. "No!"

She ran back, ice breaking and falling away under her feet. Reaching the chasm, she dropped to her knees. "Sido!" He clung to a sharp outcropping of rock buried beneath the snow. Below him, the crevasse yawned away, its bottom lost in the deep turquoise gloom. "Hang on!"

"Obviously, I'm already doing that!" He snarled with exertion as he attempted to climb from his precarious position.

She ignored his comment, lay down on her stomach, and reached down to him. "Grab my hand."

He struggled to extend one arm toward her, but he could barely touch her fingertips. Pieces of snow and ice fell and disappeared in the aquamarine darkness. "I…I can't!"

She stretched as far as she could, the frozen crust crumbling underneath her, and cursed in desperation. Her height—or lack thereof—was once the source of good-natured teasing between her and Teague. It now had dire consequences. Could she call Sido to her? What if she dropped him?

Ashtar neighed behind her.

"Hold on. I think I have an idea."

"Again, not helpful." He groaned again and tried to pull himself up to the outcropping. "Do something. Hurry."

Carefully, she backed away from the edge. Stepping in her own footprints, she led her horse to the chasm, praying the rock shelf under the ice on which she stood would not disintegrate beneath her. She untied his reins and looped them into a knot, making a long rope. Why hadn't she asked the sailors to show her some knotting skills? With cold-numbed fingers, she tied one end to the pommel of her saddle and the other around her ankle.

"I need your help, Ashtar." She held the warhorse's great head in her hands and pictured herself grabbing Sido down in the chasm and the steed backing away, pulling them to safety. The horse blinked and tossed his head.

"I hope that means you understand because if you don't, you'll have to pick apples yourself to eat from now on." Her knot-tying skills had to be better than the captain's were.

She leaned over the edge of the chasm until she felt the leather around her ankle grow taut. "Grab my hand. Reach. Now!"

Sido swung one arm up, their fingers touching, but he could not get a firm grip. "I'm trying!"

She inched forward and hung over the edge by her waist, trusting all her weight to the reins. She stretched again, and this time, the seer grasped her wrist.

"Ashtar, pull!" She called as clear an intent as she could to the horse's mind. The freezing temperatures numbed her hands, and she knew she could not hold Sido for long. She wrapped him with her Defending Aspect, the ice melting under her amulet. Again, she called a picture to Ashtar's mind of him pulling her out of the crevasse. A moment later, the leather strap tightened painfully around her ankle as the destrier backed up.

The seer swung free from his handhold, clutching her wrist with both hands. She now held him with both hands but slid forward under the full weight of his body. "Pull, Ashtar, pull!"

The leather reins constricted around her ankle, cutting off her circulation. Sharp ice scraped and cut the skin of her arms and chest as the seer clung to her. The Defending and the Seeing Aspects rose as one within her.

The reins. Breaking.

She cried with effort and pulled back with all her might and her Aspects. Sido shot out of the chasm just as the leather straps snapped.

He landed beside her, both panting. He said nothing, but stared at her, his eyes wide, incredulous. The soft, warm refrain of his deeper emotions sang out to her.

Tetric had once told her he'd rather have her trust than her understanding. Sido's trust was worthless to her if he didn't understand her—and himself. That tenuous thread gave her hope. She would give such hope back to him. Maybe it would be enough for the both of them.

The question still lingered in his eyes, but this time, they held more gratitude than doubt.

She smiled. "I told you, I'll not let a man die if he can be saved." The snow around them began to creak once more. "Move!"

They scrambled to their feet and dashed over to Ashtar. Mirana mounted the copper-coated warhorse with one swift movement; Sido vaulted onto his back behind her. She dug her heels into her horse's sides, willing him to ride faster than he ever had before. The warhorse sped away, charging across the icy, shifting ground, his hooves pounding up clouds of snow as he ran.

She grabbed fistfuls of Ashtar's mane, guiding him across the path that lay hidden beneath the snow. In a last desperate effort for safety, the destrier leaped over the widening fissure. He landed hard on the granite shelf at the far end of the pass, sparks flaring from his iron-shod hooves. The seer's horse pranced anxiously on the landing.

She cried with relief. "No defender has ever been so brave as you, *Ëi cara*." Ashtar's sides heaved from the strain in the thin air. Breathless herself, she dismounted and untied the reins from her ankle. She kissed the warhorse's neck.

The seer slowly dismounted and took the reins of his thoroughbred.

She gulped another breath and smiled. "You did it."

"I hate being a slave to the Light from Within." He remained facing his mount.

Once again, the sense of his presence disappeared. Mirana frowned. Ken'nar were exceedingly good at hiding themselves under U'Nehíl. Grasping at life to harness the Power from Without, it was just a step further to reflect it. "How is using your own power being a slave? It's the most self-empowering thing one can do."

Sido sighed in exasperation. "Can we save your unending philosophical posits for another time? I nearly died."

"But you didn't." She smiled again.

"That had more to do with you than me."

She wanted to argue but let it rest.

"Besides, Tetric might have felt my power draw if I'd used the Power from Without."

"We don't know if he's reached Caladazh yet," she replied. "We could be days, sevendays ahead of him."

"He's here. I doubt he even had to use a single Aspect to find his way." He peered up to the learning hall nestled in the distant peaks. "Caladazh was Tetric's home."

"His home?"

She whipped her head around to the granite columns lining the pass. Tetric's name was synonymous with the remote, barren province of Dar-Azûl. Her heart sank as fast as her stomach rose. He might know exactly where the missing journal entry from the Codex was located. He would certainly have a better idea of where to look than she did. "I thought Tetric was from Dar-Azûl."

He laughed grimly. "No one is from Dar-Azûl."

Mirana nodded soberly. "I suppose not." She reached over to stroke the nose of his thoroughbred. "You are a brave man."

Sido laid a hand on his steed. "You want me to cast aside my keep vision as if it never happened. You want me to pretend last night never happened. You want me to embrace a connection to the Aspects I swore I'd never touch again. You want me to become some paragon of Fal'kin virtue, starting anew as if all that I've done in the past never existed." His voice was muted in pain, almost childlike. He shook his head. Sadness? Frustration? Both. "You want all this from me, but I'm not sure I can give it to you. I'm not sure anyone can come back from this kind of evil. Not me. Not Tetric."

Something more called to her, something buried deep within his internal storm. She had broken through the ice imprisoning his conscience's heart. And that left him completely undone.

"You must believe there is, too, or why would you be telling me all of this?" she replied quietly.

He shrugged, a slight gesture that could have been one of defeat. "I wanted you to know exactly what it is that you are trying to save. And decide whether it is worth the effort."

He resumed his trek, closing himself off again behind the indelible wall surrounding his mind.

"It is always worth the effort, Sido."

He did not respond but kept trudging up the pass.

Anyone—everyone—was worth the effort. But was she strong enough to show him the way?

CHAPTER 13

"We girt ourselves with the weapons of stealth and courage and defeated the enemy in a way no sword could."

—The Book of Kinderra

Teague pulled back on Bankin's reins as Morgan raised his fist in the air. Binthe paused before motioning them through the thick growth into a moonlit clearing. Falantir—and Aspects Above knew how many Ken'nar—lay less than a mile ahead of them. If he could have made the palfrey ride on tiptoes, he would have.

Hundreds of tree stumps and smaller felled saplings surrounded them. They grew in an odd pattern, not random but in concentric circles—or rather, they had grown that way before they had been chopped down.

He slipped down from his saddle. "They must be using the trees to build their siege towers."

Binthe nodded. "They are going to attack Deren. And soon." The Ken'nar helmet muffled the seer woman's voice.

He frowned. The Ken'nar forces could have licked their wounds a little longer after Edara.

Morgan trotted his horse closer to the seer. "What else do you see?"

She clasped her amulet. A small image shimmered in the air before them.

Teague gasped. "By the Light!" They had found the main host of the Ken'nar army.

The Fal'kin defender shook his head in disbelief. "There must be ten, twelve thousand. Deren will not be able to repel this."

Teague continued to stare at the scene before him. Such numbers didn't even seem real, let alone possible. "Are you sure you're looking at a current time skein and not something from another time?"

"*Ai.*" Binthe's armored shoulders sagged. "Unfortunately."

"What if we get Fal'kin from other provinces? If we could get word to Tash-Hamar, even Jad-Anüna—"

The seer closed her hand and the floating nightmare disappeared. "There is no time. I sense urgency among the Ken'nar."

His mother was somewhere in the garrison, surrounded by tens of thousands of Ken'nar, every one of them trying to suck the life from her. "We've got to do something. We can't just let them march through Deren."

Morgan put out a calming hand. "I have no intention of letting that happen. The Garnath River will be impassable soon with the autumn rains if it is not already." As if lending weight to his reasoning, a low rumble of thunder rolled out from the overcast sky.

The seer held her amulet again. "Something does not make sense."

"What?" Teague peered into the dark forest around them.

"The encampment. It is enormous. It goes on for a league in all directions."

Morgan gripped his amulet. "They have been here a long time."

"*Ai*, but that's not what concerns me. There should be more." She caressed the face of her emerald with her gloved thumb.

Teague opened his mouth, aghast. "*More?*"

The defender waved a hand at him to keep still. "What do you mean?"

"The encampment is built to contain an army twice this size. At least."

Morgan shifted in his saddle. "Can you call to the past? Find what happened to the rest?"

Teague could not see his friend's expression hidden behind the Ken'nar helmet, but he could hear it in his voice. He was scared. Teague had never seen the man frightened. Ever.

Binthe shook her head slowly. "I don't understand. I saw no troop movements south. I saw no troops at all." She faced Morgan. He held her arm.

"*Wha-at?*" Teague asked. "Would you *please* stop doing that?"

"I have no visions to explain where the other Ken'nar are." Emotion hushed the seer's words.

Morgan squeezed her hand. "It's all right, *Ama*. Maybe the Seeing Aspect isn't ready to give you answers yet. Or-or there are no answers to be had."

Teague's heart lurched with a few sloppy beats. Binthe was stumped. That couldn't be good. "Maybe there aren't any more

Ken'nar. Maybe they just wanted some elbowroom in their camp." You never knew. "If the Dark Trine—"

"They call him the 'Ain Magne,' the 'Great One,'" Binthe interjected. "To the Ken'nar, the Dark Trine is not evil but a savior. Nearly a deity."

"Fine." He didn't care if the grynwen whore's son was dark, light, or spotted purple—the Ken'nar leader certainly was no savior, and Teague sure as hell hoped the bastard was no deity. His hand closed over the hilt of his Ken'nar broadsword. "If he already has an army marching on Deren as we speak, what are all these troops for?"

Morgan nodded. "A very good question." The defender turned to Binthe. "We have to find out what else the Dark Trine has planned."

The seer woman exhaled, the sound tinny from within her helmet. "It will be dangerous with so many."

Teague shook his head. "Maybe not." Even from this distance, he could see the faint glow of campfires. "With ten thousand other Ken'nar roaming around, they may not notice three more."

"No, Teague," the defender said. "You cannot go. You do not have the Aspects. The sentry guards will sense it."

"Did you think I just came along for the ride? Of course I'm going, Morgan. My mother is in there."

"You don't know that."

"*Sibe*, Morgan is right," Binthe replied. "You will destroy our cover. You will be killed, and us, too. Stay here. We will be back by dawn. If not, you must ride south and get a warning to Deren any way you can."

"I can't just hide in a bush." He chewed on the inside of his cheek. "You're right. I would ruin our cover if they're expecting me to be a Ken'nar." He began stripping off his armor as fast as he could.

"What are you doing?" Morgan's voice dropped to a harsh whisper as he looked everywhere at once for dark-armored fighters. "Are you *trying* to get yourself killed?"

Teague stuffed his borrowed armor in some thick scrub. "I'm a spy. You know they use Unaspected to do their dirty work. You two are perimeter sentries escorting me in. I have news only for the Dark Trine, the—the—"

"Ain Magne," Binthe said.

"The Ain Magne himself." He reached into one of the saddlebags on Bankin's side and slipped a shirt and a travel cloak over his head. He lifted off his father's amulet. He hesitated, then looped it over his belt.

The seer put her gauntleted fists on her hips. "You're not serious?"

"If he were here, we'd probably be dead already. If they think I have something that important, maybe they'll let us through the encampment unescorted."

Binthe turned in her saddle toward Morgan with a sigh. "I don't have any better ideas. Do you?"

The Fal'kin lifted his helmeted face to the sky, the first few drops of rain making a soft plinking sound on his armor. "No."

Teague climbed back onto his horse and started down a path made by the felled trees.

"So what is your news that only the Ain Magne can hear?" Morgan asked.

Oh! "Uh. Well, I—"

Three Ken'nar emerged from the woods just ahead of them. Panic seized him. Two Ken'nar crossed lances, denying them further entry into the encampment. Another held up his hand, his other palm drifting to his broadsword. A defender, most likely.

"Halt. Name and rank."

"Pieter Jord. I'm a scout. I must make my report. Let me through." His own ready words surprised him.

"This one says he has information." Morgan reached across from his saddle and gave Teague a rough shove. He didn't have to be that realistic, did he?

The Ken'nar defender guard cocked his head slightly. "He is Unaspected filth. And you two let him into the camp?" He drew his sword.

"He said it's important. Meant for the Ain Magne only," Binthe replied. It was all he could do not to turn around and gawk at her. She had completely changed the character of her voice, sounding like a feral wildcat. A bead of sweat rolled down the back of his neck.

"Of course I'm Unaspected, imbecile," Teague snapped. The annoyance in his voice almost sounded genuine. "The Fal'kin scum won't think to look for me as I spy on them, will they? Now let me through. I must speak with the Great One." He tried to urge Bankin forward, but the lancers remained where they were.

"If you're one of our Sightless *vermihn* spies, then why do you wear the mark of a Fal'kin?" The Ken'nar defender lifted the amulet on Teague's belt with the point of his sword.

He screwed up as evil as a smile as he could. "A trophy. She won't be needing it anymore. But I will remember her fondly. Very fondly. Now let me pass."

"The Lord Trine has yet to return to Falantir. Or weren't you aware of that, spy?" the guard said. He couldn't see the man's face behind the skeletal helmet, but he could definitely hear the sneer in his voice.

The Dark Trine wasn't there. That was good news. On the other hand, the Ken'nar sentries were not believing his ruse. "I have been out doing my job. I won't be able to say the same for you when he arrives and finds you impeding the information he desired."

The guard turned to one of the lancers. He probably called something. Teague ground his teeth together. If there was one gift he wished he had, it was to hear mind-words.

"You may pass." The guard motioned him through as the sentries uncrossed their lances.

"*Gratas.*" Teague made an overly grand bow from his saddle. He rode a few paces and stopped. "Guard, where is the healer woman?"

"We have little time for this nonsense, boy. Come." Morgan waved him forward.

"Which one?"

Which one? Again, he beat down his panic. Did he mean Belessa Tir or his mother? Oh, Aspects Above, could he mean Mirana? "The Tash-Hamari. I heard she is beautiful." He tried to keep his voice even. He was pretty sure he failed.

The sentries laughed lasciviously. "She is," the Ken'nar defender replied. The others joined in low snickers. "But you lie with her, you'll never wake up again. Only when she was unconscious could we tame her. She doesn't fight so much anymore, eh, *Ëi cara'e?*" The three Ken'nar laughed again.

Teague's hand went for his sword, but Morgan reached over and clamped his arm with an iron grip. "We have tarried long enough, maggot. Deliver your news so we can be done with the sight of you."

He glared at his disguised friend, but to do anything further would break their cover. He forced himself to guide Bankin farther into the Ken'nar camp. A few paces in, he reached for his broadsword again. They'd touched his mother. They'd violated her. Fury shot through him, hotter than an amulet. He yanked at the gray's reins, jerking her head back around.

"I am asking you to leave it," Morgan hissed in a low whisper, his helmeted face nearly touching his own as the man's hand restrained Bankin's reins. "For now."

"But they—"

"I know." The Fal'kin laid a hand on his shoulder, gentle but unyielding. "Clarienne suffered the same fate. And I want them all dead more than you can possibly know. But Kinderra is counting on us." He squeezed his shoulder and straightened in his saddle. "We will have our justice."

"We need to move," Binthe whispered.

Teague nodded and forced himself to concentrate on the path ahead.

The image of the army Binthe had projected through her amulet did nothing to prepare him. Dozens of siege towers and other war machines stood like foreboding sentinels in the rain, replacing the tall timbers from which they were built. Dozens of Ken'nar fit other bridge-like structures with bladders made from animal skins. Fire pits burned and hissed in the damp, fed by charcoal made from the very trees that surrounded them. Smiths pounded metal into swords, arrowheads, and large grappling hooks. Campfires blazed farther off into the woods, creating trembling shadows in the gloom.

He had been to Falantir a few times with his mother and father. It had been a second home to his parents as children while they learned their Healing Aspect from the Healer Prime Belessa Tir. The aged healer had even come down to Deren to help his mother deliver him. He remembered her as a strong-willed but gracious woman, somewhere between sixty and a thousand summers old. How many lives had she saved? To think her blessed gift had been so hideously perverted only to die imprisoned within the Soul Harvest.

The learning hall of Kana-Akün still stood, barely, gutted and burned. For more than eight hundred summers, the sprawling wood-beamed structure shouldered the ages, a place of peace, knowledge, and healing. The Ken'nar had at last worn down what even time could not. On stanchions flanking the once-welcoming doors, tatters of the province's standard, a golden hart on a green field, wafted in the night air.

And everywhere were Ken'nar. Thousands upon thousands. They moved around the hall like a pestilence, a black infestation of creatures that could only remotely be called mortal.

Teague reined in Bankin, too numb to be frightened. Morgan and Binthe sat motionless on their mounts next to him.

The Dark Trine's plan to cross the river was now obvious. He would use animal bladders to float sections of bridges, towers, and trebuchets across the river, the pieces secured to each other with iron hooks. Those hooks would then lash the towers to Deren's walls, rendering the impenetrable structure meaningless. The bladders would be filled with naphtha and set aflame in the trebuchet. All the engineering functioned for multiple purposes with nothing wasted, built for maximum use, maximum death. It was so simple and oh so effective.

A loud thunderclap broke his thoughts. He had seen enough. "You two go on ahead. I'm going to find my mother."

Binthe trotted her horse a few paces closer. "It's not safe for you alone."

"You said we won't have much time, and we won't if we stay together." He stole a glance behind him. So far, none of the Ken'nar had seemed to notice them. "You finish the reconnaissance, and I will find my mother. Meet me in the forest south of the learning hall at dawn. You'll find my mind. And hers, too."

Morgan sighed. "Teague."

The words of the Ken'nar sentries boiled like scalding acid in his stomach, but they also gave him hope. Did his mother no longer fight them off because she was stalling for time, awake and aware, playing her own ruse? Or—he swallowed against a throat two sizes too small—had she already been harvested?

He growled in frustration. "I know, Morgan, but I have to do this. I must find out for certain."

The defender squeezed his arm and nodded.

Binthe reached over to push back his rain-soaked hair. "*Kin ísi Oëa, Ëi sibe.*"

He watched his friends slip farther into the woods and disappear. His mother could be alive. Or not. A chill trickle of rain slid down the back of his neck and under the collar of his shirt, setting off an identical sensation in his belly. If his mother had been tortured, abused, and turned into a mindless slave, death might be a kinder fate. The trickle turned into a full-on sluice of guilt. Was he really thinking this? In some sort of giddy mortification, he accepted he'd rather have his mother dead than have her face a life of agony trying to recover from such unimaginable torment.

Whether his mother was a captive or a harvested slave, she would be an asset to the Ken'nar. It only made sense they'd keep her someplace well guarded.

Teague gulped down another helping of fear and slid from the saddle, walking Bankin closer to the carcass of the learning hall. The horse sputtered as he tied her off to the remainder of a lance shaft near the entrance stairs.

"If you're calling me an idiot, Bankin, *Ëi cara*, I actually agree with you this time."

He let out his breath and climbed the stairs. The heavy oaken doors swung open without warning, causing him to stumble back to avoid being smacked in the face.

A Ken'nar stood before him, arms folded. His baldric was of dark leather, and like everything else in Kana-Akün, had once been of fine quality. Combat, scarcity, and hardship had weathered it like the man who wore it. Beyond him, the once-grand gathering hall stood like a prince turned into a beggar. The carved oak figures on the chamber's support columns had been hacked and burned. Scorch marks were everywhere. The long tables were scattered with the remains of what he hoped were meals. Against the soot-stained walls and in corners were piles of clothing.

Fal'kin uniforms. Hundreds of them.

He swallowed.

Several dozen warriors sat in small groups, eating, studying maps, scribbling on parchment. They wore no helmets, and most were not in full armor. That answered one myth: the Ken'nar were indeed human. Had he not been equal parts fury and fear, he might have thought the men and women looked like, well, ordinary men and women.

"Begone, maggot. Commanders only," the warrior intoned. He had four silver chains on his shoulder marking him as a high-ranking commander. Great.

Teague blinked. "*Ai*, sir. I, well, I'm looking for—"

"Khorr! Ask him if he'd like to join us in some target practice," a woman shouted from one of the groups eating dinner. She rubbed the belly of a grynwen—*a grynwen!*— with her booted foot. "He can be the target, and we'll practice." Loud guffaws resounded around what was once the hall's main gathering space.

"Don't be so inhospitable, *siba*," another woman replied, her voice both seductive and menacing. "He's adorable. Maybe he dances well."

Before Teague could answer, a stiletto whizzed by his ear, taking a few hairs with it before embedding itself in a wooden entrance post. He jumped and absolutely did not scream.

"See! I was right!" The sultry woman laughed.

"Enough!" Farther within the hall, another Ken'nar raised a hand, silencing the others. Five silver chains over his shoulder jingled with the movement. He was the senior warlord, perhaps the leader of the whole installation—not the Ain Magne nor his second but close enough. Three other grynwen lifted their muzzles at the man's sharp order.

Teague swallowed. Oh, he was so dead.

"Forgive me, sir," Teague replied to Khorr, the commander who had stopped him at the door. "I'm looking for the healer." Thankfully, that was the honest-to-Aspects-Above truth, so it wouldn't be perceived as a lie.

Khorr didn't budge an inch. "You don't look wounded to me."

"Ah, no, sir." He licked dry lips with a dry tongue. "I was sent to care for her."

"Sent by whom?"

If he pretended to be brave any longer, it might turn into the real thing. "I don't know his name." He lowered his head and squinted against a sudden, uncomfortable buzzing behind his forehead.

Khorr waited long moments before replying. "You are unfamiliar to me."

Oh rackin' no. The man was in his head. In. His head. He lifted his gaze. Now or never. "*Ai*, sir. I'm from Edara. I know something about herbs. I was told to treat the healer woman."

The buzzing made his eyeballs feel as though they were rattling in their sockets, then the sensation stopped as quickly as it appeared. The commander nodded. "That way." He jerked his head toward the hall's enormous hearth.

Teague entered the great room as his heart leaped in his chest—only to finish the beat seemingly in his stomach.

At the end of the sprawling room, a fire blazed on the andirons, and a woman sat motionless on a stool next to the flames.

It was not his mother.

"Prime Tir?" Teague whispered in horrified awe. He crossed the room in stunned silence.

Healer Prime Belessa Tir had always looked remarkably young to Teague despite having seen almost one hundred summers; the Aspects Above may have favored her for her noble work. The woman who now sat before him was almost unrecognizable.

Belessa Tir had turned into a withered caricature of herself. Her thick, snowy mane of hair had become brittle and wispy. Brilliant green eyes stared out, vacant. Her cheeks were sunken, her face cadaverous. Blood vessels had broken beneath her skin, creating bruises and red wounds as if her body could not cope with the strain. The healer's verdant robes hung in tatters on her skeletal frame. Golden threads, ripped and torn from the once-elegant brocade, unraveled like spider webs over emaciated arms.

"*Matrua* Belessa!" he breathed. Without a word or even a spark of recognition, she returned her gaze to the fire in the hearth. "What has happened to you?"

It was a stupid question; he already knew what happened to her. Healer Prime Belessa Tir, healer of healers, prime of a province for twice as long as most Fal'kin lived, had succumbed to the Soul Harvest.

Whatever was left of his fear was consumed by an incendiary volcano of rage. He fell to his knees before the woman and took a bony hand in his. "They will pay for this. I swear it." He didn't care if he had been heard.

Her eyes slowly tracked to his. "Another little one to add to my lord's army." Her voice sounded like pottery breaking. Then she smiled—a grimace in a skull thinly veiled with flesh. "Have no fear, Ungifted child. You will be remade anew for a higher purpose, for even the Unaspected have a place in the Ain Magne's new world of peace."

Teague tried to pull his hand from hers, but her grip became like a vice. "Lights, Belessa! Let go!"

"Hush, now, child." The fingers of one skeletal hand touched his temples.

"Belessa, stop!" He batted her hand away. She fell off the stool, dragging Teague down with her, his other wrist enclosed in her claw-like grip.

The deep-green tourmaline of her amulet flared with verdant light. She snarled and sent a bony knee into Teague's stomach as he tried to rise. "You *will* serve the Trine."

"Stop, Belessa!" He grappled with the old woman. Shouts behind him were followed by the sound of heavy boots nearing.

"Unaspected scum, what do you think you're doing?" Khorr called out from across the room.

Belessa wrapped the sides of Teague's head with her hands as she hissed some unintelligible curse.

He grabbed her wrists. "No! Don't do this!" Sudden pain blazed like a spike being driven through his brain. Swinging his leg for momentum, he rolled over with the old healer now on her back. Belessa screamed as her body became rigid. A trail of blood leaked from her nose.

"Belessa? *Matrua?*" He looked down at her face contorted with pain, her wrists still in his grasp. She gurgled and went still. The old Healer's breath rattled in her chest. Her body had been pushed too hard for too long, forced to harvest souls for the Dark Trine. Teague placed his fingers gently on her purple-mottled wrist. A pulse, as fragile as the woman herself, brushed his fingertips and faded.

"No. Belessa. Please, don't die. Not yet. I need you. I need to know if my mother is here. Niah Beltran. My *maithe.* You know her. You were as dear to each other as her own *maithe.* Belessa, please. Help me. Bel—" The healer's body appeared to collapse in on itself as she slumped to the side. Teague caught her and gently lowered her to broken slate tiles before the fireplace. At least they were warm.

"*Ëi Matrua.*" He laid a hand across the old woman's eyes and closed them. "Go home to the Aspects, Belessa Tir. *Oë ad pace.*"

He wanted to cry. Every tear he shed would be an oath of vengeance against the Ken'nar and everything they stood for. But no tears came. Maybe someday. But not now.

"What the bloody hell is going on?" Khorr's baritone voice boomed behind him.

Teague crossed Belessa's arms over her chest and rose to his feet. It was all he could do not to launch himself at the man and rip that deep voice from his throat with his bare hands.

The Ken'nar commander toyed with a small blade in one hand. "You kill her, boy?"

"I wish I had. Long before now," Teague growled. "She died."

"Died?" Khorr stepped closer, standing toe-to-toe with Teague. "We needed her. You were supposed to tend to her. You filthy little maggot, you killed her."

Teague shook his head and held up his hands. "No! She died. You pushed her too hard."

"I'll gut you like the worthless Unsighted worm filth you are," the Ken'nar snarled.

"I did not kill her." There were at least thirty Ken'nar between him and the doors to the hall. So much for an escape route. "She died trying to harvest me."

"Then it looks like it's up to me to take out the rubbish." Khorr swiped at Teague's stomach with the dagger.

Teague sucked in his stomach and spun in the opposite direction of the strike. Coming around, he hammered a fist on the Ken'nar's wrist, forcing the defender to drop the blade, but in a blink, the Ken'nar recovered and planted the tip of a broadsword at his chest.

"Khorr! Stop this! Now!" The senior warlord rushed over and twisted Teague's wrist, forcing the knife from his grip. Had he not fallen with the move, the Ken'nar would have broken half the bones in his arm. The senior officer turned to his subordinate. "Do you not have better things to do than fight with this—" He looked down at Teague with a mixture of disgust and pity and weariness. "This."

"Staine, who made you Ken Lord?" Khorr's sword remained unsheathed.

"Is the bridge construction complete?" Staine replied.

It was an order, not a question. Teague swore he could see the Defending Aspect itself crackle around Staine.

"I am not some errand boy." Khorr pounded his chest as he glared at the commanding officer. "I lead men and women here, too, Staine."

"You will be neither unless you carry out my orders."

No, it hadn't been a hallucination. Angry streaks of light did indeed spark and snap from the blue gem in Staine's amulet.

Khorr held his ground before sliding his blade into its scabbard. "When the Ain Magne returns, Staine. When the Ain Magne returns." He nodded and made a low chuckle as he left, slamming his shoulder into the other man's for good measure as he passed.

Teague exhaled. "*Gratas*—"

"If I see you again, I will kill you myself." Staine jutted his chin toward the hall doors.

Teague made his way from the great room almost without running. The man probably read the gratitude in his mind anyway.

As he swung up into Bankin's saddle, he saw Staine kneel by the body of Belessa Tir and lower his head. The doors closed themselves on protesting hinges. Teague clicked his tongue and nudged his horse deeper into the Ken'nar camp.

CHAPTER 14

"Aspecta'e Alta ten marcaó Oëa cora as Biraen il'Kin."
("The Aspects Above have branded your heart
as a Child of the Light.")
—Ora Fal'kinnen 15:15

Teague rode aimlessly for a long time and still had not reached the limits of the encampment. Knots of Ken'nar rushed through the camp back the way he had come. Other dark warriors moved the heavy siege weapons. Others stood in small groups, calling and speaking in low tones. Others simply sat. They only acted when some Ken'nar gave them an order.

The harvested. They all still wore the heraldics of their provinces. He gripped his father's amulet at his belt.

He studied the Ken'nar that passed by him, watching for one that might have his mother's gait or bearing. If she was wearing a helmet, as many of the Ken'nar were, he might never find her. They, too, wore the colors from the Fal'kin provinces.

Why? He shook his head. He'd figure that out later. He was running out of time. He would have to ask.

Teague sat erect in his saddle and screwed up an air of irritated confidence as he approached several Ken'nar testing newly made swords. "You, there. Where is the Tash-Hamari healer woman?"

One Ken'nar, who had what looked like a braid of human hair looped on an epaulet guard, brandished a blade as wide as Teague's hand. He stopped its point so close to Teague's throat that it scraped as he swallowed. "Well, *Ëi cara'e*, it appears as though we have ourselves a target after all."

Okay, this was getting old.

Another Ken'nar sheathed his own sword with a decisive snap. "Ungifted maggot. Why the Ain Magne and his Second have allowed Unaspected *verminh* into our ranks, I will never understand."

Teague's stomach contracted into a hard knot. He forced his mind not to give a name to this "dark second." Too late. Mirana's beautiful face and starlight eyes pushed their way through his consciousness.

The point of the Ken'nar's sword at his throat brought his attention back. He batted the blade away. "I don't have time for your games. Where is the healer?" He tried to sound just as menacing as the braided Ken'nar, but to his ears, he failed quite miserably.

The defender chuckled evilly. "She is working her gifts on the prisoners." He pointed to an area farther in the trees. "Unless the second has found a new duty for her."

"She must be keeping him plenty busy. I haven't seen him in sevendays," a third warrior replied, a wicked scar by his eye drawing the corner of the bottom lid at an angle as he snickered. The others joined him, lust thick in their voices.

Teague fought the impulse for a little target practice of his own. Instead, he focused on his relief—his mother was alive. And this second was apparently a man. Not Mirana.

"I have seen the work of healers such as her," he replied, "so I would caution you, *Ëi cara'e*. She might decide to work her gifts on you."

He did not wait for the guard's retort and rode in the direction the braided Ken'nar indicated, their laughter ringing in his ears. Something whizzed past his ear. An ax, its blade wider than his palm was long, split a scrawny sapling in half next to his head. He required all his resolve to keep riding and not stop, not turn around.

Moments later, he came to another clearing. A small group of people with their hands bound behind them knelt in a row. None wore amulets. They had been severely beaten. One appeared unconscious, maybe dead.

He dismounted and approached with caution.

"Stop! I beg of you! Please! No!" a man cried out, his words shrill.

Another voice spoke from the other side of the trees out of his line of sight. It was a woman. He started to breathe faster. Her voice was melodious but completely devoid of warmth.

"Do not struggle. It will only be a moment. Then you will understand our Ain Magne's glory for you."

A man wearing the red horse uniform of Varn-Erdal stood lashed with chains to a tall pole. He screamed again and writhed against his bindings. Teague gritted his teeth against the soul-wrenching shriek. It continued for an agonizingly long time. At last, the Varn-Erdalan slumped in the chains, his face now expressionless. The woman turned.

Teague could not move. His body, his heart, his soul could not comprehend what he saw.

The creature who had been his mother stared at him, her beautiful, deep brown eyes blank. Bruises purpled the soft caramel skin of her cheeks, over one eye, and on her throat. Dried blood caked a split in her lower lip. Several amulets hung from the rope she wore for a belt that held the shreds of a bloodstained tunic about her. Lacerations cut her bare legs and feet.

He snapped out of his horror and ran over to her, grabbing her arms. "Mother, it's me. Teague. Mother, you must wake up. Mother!"

She looked at his hand holding her arm, then lifted her eyes to his face. His heart leaped in hope. "*Ai*, Mother. It's me. It's Teague. I've got to get you out of here." He pulled her arm, expecting her to follow, but she did not move.

"You have no Aspects." Her words came in that sweet, sickening almost-whisper she had used on the newly harvested Fal'kin. Her brows drew closer together on her otherwise placid face as if she did not understand what she sensed.

She did not recognize him. She was gone. Like his father. Like *Matrua* Belessa.

His chest tightened. "Mother, please come with me. I can make you better. I can make everything all right. You and Father taught me everything. I'll make you better somehow. I promise."

"The Ain Magne needs those without gifts to draw enemy fire." She smiled, a mockery of the compassionate expression that had once soothed away his nightmares, and placed her palm on his forehead.

He felt the ground slip beneath him. He tried to roll away, to pull himself from her, but he no longer controlled his body. A strange ache settled behind his eyes and radiated down to his chest. His mother's pale-rose quartz amulet began to glow like the light of a spring dawn. It flared, and the pain grew exponentially, like a lance piercing his brain and his heart.

"Mother, please! I'm your son!" The pain grew. He heard someone shout his name, but he could not respond. Excruciating agony ripped through him as if his mind, his soul were being torn from him. He could not breathe, he could not think. He opened his mouth in an earsplitting cry of anguished torture.

Suddenly, the pain stopped. He gasped for air. He forced his eyes open and found himself staring into his mother's face. She, too, lay on the ground, unmoving.

She was gone. Like his father. Like *Matrua* Belessa.

He raised himself on one elbow. She had fallen on her stomach. A gaping wound in her back smoldered. He looked over his shoulder. Morgan's amulet remained in his gauntleted hand. Binthe held a fighting stance by his side, her long knives drawn.

Truly. Gone.

White-hot rage flared up inside him. He screamed and launched himself at the defender.

Morgan wrapped his arms around him, preventing a strike from his fist. "She was trying to harvest you."

"You killed my mother, you bastard!" He fought with every ounce of strength he possessed.

"Teague, she was already dead. Your mother was dead, Teague. Teague, listen to me. Listen to me." Morgan held him tighter, immobilizing him with armor-clad arms. "That creature was no longer your mother."

"No." Tears burned in the corners of his eyes. "No. Not my mother. Not my mother and father both. No."

"Morgan." Binthe indicated with a tilt of her helmeted head toward several Ken'nar coming to investigate the disturbance.

He nodded. "We have seen enough. We are leaving this Aspect-forsaken place."

Teague, shaking with despair and unrequited rage, stood his ground. "I will not leave her."

The seer inhaled sharply and grabbed the amulet from his belt.

He spun to grab her wrist. "What the—?"

In a swift move, Morgan hitched one of Teague's arms up behind his back and dug his fingers into the sides of his neck.

"What happened here?" a Ken'nar inquired. Three chains over his shoulder identified him as a unit captain. His broadsword, one with a well-worn serrated blade, identified him as a defender. The jagged scar across his right cheek identified him as mean. None of those things were good. Spots danced in front of his eyes as Morgan tightened his grip on his throat. He stopped struggling.

"We caught this maggot trying to pilfer amulets from the newly harvested." Binthe held up his father's amethyst.

"What happened to her?" The Ken'nar commander stalked over to Teague. He drew his belt knife and stuck its point in the hollow of his throat. "Did you do this?"

He tried to move his arm a fraction closer to his own sword, but Morgan pulled tighter on his arm, nearly pulling it from its socket.

"He got close enough to the Fal'kin *verminh* on the pole for him to loose amulet fire. This coward"—she pointed at Teague—"shrank away, and the healer was hit by accident."

"By accident?" The Ken'nar dug the knifepoint into his skin, drawing blood.

He winced in pain. "Plea—Please, sir. He wasn't going to need it anymore."

With a flick of his wrist, the Ken'nar sheathed his knife. "You Unaspected are not worth the air you breathe. You know the Ain Magne needs the harvested to keep their amulets. How else will he control his armies?" He turned to Niah and flipped her over onto her back with the toe of his boot. "Pity. She was beautiful."

Teague struggled against Morgan, intending to rip the Ken'nar apart with his bare hands, but the defender held him fast.

"We will take him to the hall to await the Ain Magne and the second," Morgan said.

"You may have a long wait. Neither are in Falantir. Lord Garis and Second Rendel will meet us in Deren. We leave before dawn. Kill him." The Ken'nar then slammed his steel-plated fist into Teague's face.

He collapsed in Morgan's arms. The entire right side of his face felt like it had caved in. When the Ken'nar disappeared into the encampment, the defender gently lowered him down.

"Are you all right?"

"No." Lancing pain screamed up his face to his temple. He turned and spat out the blood from his mouth. His eye had already swollen shut. He worked his jaw, surprised it was still connected to his face. "I taught you that hold, you know." He rubbed his neck.

"*Ai.*" Morgan nodded. "And it's a good one."

Teague's mind then stopped as understanding hit him like the Ken'nar commander's fist. It was true. Tetric Garis was the Dark Trine. A second fist of thought pummeled him harder than the first. "Mirana's with Garis."

The Fal'kin did not reply.

He crawled over to his mother's lifeless body, sprawled on the ground. Tetric Garis had done this, turning her from something held sacred by the Aspects Above into a sacrilege. What if he had harvested Mirana like he had his parents and Belessa Tir? Teague's mind shut down. For a moment, all he could do was sit in pain.

Large groups of Ken'nar streamed toward the learning hall. Morgan laid a hand on his shoulder. "We need to leave. Now."

Teague shook himself from his shock. He cut the rope belt around his mother's waist and removed the amulets. His hands shook as he arranged her clothes and her arms. Mother. No, no, she was gone. This corpse was just some flesh that looked like her. It wasn't her. She was gone. He covered her with his cloak. He reached for her amulet and hesitated.

"You're with Father now." He lifted her amulet from her, closed her eyes, and kissed her forehead.

Binthe helped him to his feet. "Come."

"Wait. We need to free them." He pointed to the Fal'kin prisoners. "Then we leave." He did not wait for their response.

Teague ran over to the captives. A man lay in the pine needle-covered mud with his eyes closed, his hands bound behind him to his ankles. The Ken'nar bastards didn't want this one to escape. He didn't move, unconscious or harvested. The man was young, a handful of summers older than himself. Blood leaked from a gash on his forehead and from his nose down over his split lips. Older bruises faded to green and yellow discolored his temple and jaw. Scars from amulet burns covered his forearms. A fresh one traveled down from his collarbone to disappear under the rags of his shirt.

Teague cut the rope binding the young man's wrists. With a lightning-fast move, the Fal'kin grabbed Teague's wrist, forcing him to drop his belt knife. A defender then. Definitely.

"You'll need more than that to kill me, *verminh*. Haven't you learned that by now?"

Teague glanced over his shoulder to make sure no one was watching. "We're not going to hurt you. We're here to free you."

The young Fal'kin's brows knitted in confusion. "What?"

"The Ken'nar are marching south. Head west to Edara. You won't find much left, but you will be safe there." He cut the ropes around the Aspected man's ankles.

The young defender rubbed his wrists. "Then it's true? They burnt Edara to the ground?"

Teague said nothing. He held out the captives' amulets he had taken from his mother.

The Fal'kin reached for a battered gold amulet holding a deep magenta rhodolite crystal. It glowed at his touch. He slipped it over his head and gasped. Clutching the amulet close to his chest, he closed his eyes.

"For more than a summer, I have been severed from my amulet. I thought I'd die from that alone. Then I wished I had. I escaped three times, but they found me each time. Without my amulet, I was useless as a defender. Without my amulet, I—" His shoulders shook as he wept.

Again, Teague searched the rain-soaked forest for guards waiting to fry them both where they sat. They didn't have much time. "What is your name?"

"I am Drei Carada."

He blinked in shock and sat back on his heels. "Son of Trein Carada and Marienne Tans? From Edara. Varn-Erdal."

The young Fal'kin nodded and scowled, equally surprised by Teague's recognition. "*Ai.*"

Teague's face broke into a smile. He hissed in pain with the expression but remained grinning. Illenne had never given up hope that Drei might still be alive. She never gave up her love, despite the passionate, fraught moment she and Teague shared. He wasn't sure what he wanted to believe about the Aspects

Above anymore—the Ken'nar encampment surrounding him pretty much proved they didn't exist—but if there was ever a sign for him to still hold Mirana in his heart, finding Illenne's betrothed alive was it.

"You must hurry. Illenne Talz waits for you."

Drei Carada stared back in hopeful astonishment. "Ille? She-She's alive?"

He nodded and smiled. "*Ai*. And she loves you. She has never stopped loving you."

"I am sorry, but we are running out of time," Binthe said as she and Morgan freed the rest of the captive Fal'kin. "We must hurry."

"Don't keep her waiting any longer. Go now." Teague helped the young defender to his feet.

"Who are you?" Drei asked as he steadied another weeping Fal'kin whom Binthe had just freed.

"I am Teague Beltran." He straightened his shoulders. "Son of Tennen and Niah Beltran, the healers of Kinderra."

Drei gripped his forearm. "*Gratas Oë*, Teague il'Beltran, son of healers." He ran off to disappear into the dark woods unnoticed, the other freed captives close behind him.

Teague swung up onto Bankin's saddle and jabbed his heels into his horse's sides. He charged into the dank forest, Morgan and Binthe beside him. He would never again fear the Underworld. He had already been there.

CHAPTER 15

"Caladazh, Sister of Deren, sits upon the roof of Kinderra. From her lofty perch, she provides clearer vantage. To the land. To the Aspects. To the truth."
—The Book of Kinderra

Mirana thought of and discarded dozens of words to start some sort of innocuous conversation with Sido as he trudged in the snow beside her, his Aspect lost in his solitude. If he wanted to be alone with his thoughts that badly, she would give him his privacy. It was just as well. The altitude made breathing difficult even with her Defender's and Healer's Aspects augmenting her stamina. She could not even imagine how the seer must be struggling.

The learning hall had better not be much farther. She was not about to spend another long, cold night in a dark cave. Teague's pendant warmed her palm as she held it.

The sun disappeared behind the mountains, painting them blue, the air turning sharply colder. She turned her concentration from the path under her boots to cast her Aspects around them. Minds, lives, returned to her.

She picked up her pace. The sooner she found the last of Jasal Pinal's keep writings, the sooner she could return to Deren and do—something. She slipped a little on a small patch of ice. The Ken'nar steadied her but continued walking, saying nothing.

The pass led to a narrowing between the cliffs. Sido took Ashtar's reins from her, allowing her to go through first. As she passed through, a semi-circular archway came into view, disfigured by flaking paint, framing the entrance to the learning hall. The arms of the moon arch embedded themselves into the rock, but oddly, it embraced no gate. Her grandfather once told her that Trak-Calan's learning hall was the first to be constructed after the Sundering. Only the learning hall in Deren was older. A learning hall without a gate—with the glacier field, Caladazh didn't need one.

She reached out again to sense the hall's residents, but now, only hazy, mirrored life essences of mountain creatures returned to her. The Fal'kin of an entire hall had cloaked themselves under U'Nehíl. *Ben Kin*, why? She posed no threat. She wanted to claim a torn piece of parchment—one that rightfully belonged to her now that she thought about it—and be on her way.

Sido came up behind her as she approached the entrance. She stopped in her tracks.

The moon arch opened to a courtyard. In the courtyard stood Koben Ryotan, Seer Prime of Trak-Calan.

Next to the prime stood Tetric Garis.

"I knew you would never truly leave me."

Mirana stood under the arch, unmoving. Tetric's mind now unveiled itself and sought hers. Relief. Dread. Hope. She clenched her jaw, shards of betrayal and hate filling her mind. Splinters of hope scraped, too, at her heart.

"I didn't leave you," she replied. "You left me. With your lies."

Tetric eyed his former second but didn't speak to him.

Several Fal'kin appeared out of the lengthening shadows to block the entrance behind her and the seer. Others surrounded them in the courtyard and still others held bows, poised high on the parapets.

Mirana heard Koben Ryotan give a call. The defenders held their positions. "Please, come," the seer prime said. "There are no enemies here." His placid gaze slid from her to Sido and back. His mind, however, opened just enough to let his apprehension leak out. He couldn't possibly be wary of her, and yet he stood close by Tetric's side.

"Then why make me your prisoner?" She gestured with her head over her shoulder, indicating the Fal'kin that surrounded her and Sido.

"I wanted to make sure you would not run from me again before we had a chance to talk," Tetric answered.

She held her ground. "And say what? More lies?"

"I never lied to you. I have always told you the truth. Unlike the viper coiled behind you."

The seer's own unease flared for a moment before disappearing behind his mental walls.

"If it wasn't for me, *Ëi Ain Magne*," Sido hissed, "your precious Trine girl would be buried in an avalanche. You should be on your knees thanking me." He smiled. "She did."

Mirana bit her tongue to keep her fury at Sido's remark. She didn't fault the seer for his bitter hatred of their former mentor, but now was *not* the time to goad Tetric into a fight. She wanted to get whatever clue Caladazh had of Jasal's Keep and get back out again as quickly as possible and in one piece. Fighting the Trine was not something she wanted to do now, and hopefully, not ever.

Tetric's eyes grew hard as obsidian. "Apparently, my Aspects must be failing me because I thought I saw it was she who saved your worthless life."

Now was not the time for a violent confrontation. "I didn't know about the weaknesses in the ice until he told me. Only then did I know to search with my Aspects."

He curled one corner of his mouth. "How very noble of him. Mirana, Sido mistakenly believes that if he is your lover, he will be able to control the keep through you."

She matched her former mentor's expression. "I am aware of that."

The seer's fury cut through her anger. She reached back to stay his hand before he could make a move.

"You will suffer nothing coming between you and the girl and the keep," Sido snarled. "A sad attempt at some sort of adoption through convenience is a rather poor substitute for a true dynasty built by blood. One Mirana and I will build. Together." He gently lifted her ebony plait and brought it to his lips. Pretense or not, she was not about to be pawed at like a pleasure woman. She took her braid back from him and squeezed his hand. Hard. Defender hard.

Tetric's hematite amulet glowed a pale, dusky silver in the evening light. "I see it now." He laughed quietly. "You've been caught in your own trap, boy. You sought to capture her heart. Only now it is you who is held captive. Even your pathetic Light from Within will not bring her to your bed."

She caught a flash of intent from within the Aspects and gasped. "Sido, don't—!"

The Ken'nar launched himself at their former *patrua*. The Dark Trine made a small gesture with his hand and sent the young seer flying across the courtyard. He slammed against one of the portico columns and dropped to the ground.

"Sido!" Mirana ran over to him. She then turned to face Tetric, curling her hands into fists. "Stop. Both of you."

The Dark Trine gripped Koben's arm and pulled him closer, lifting his eyes for a moment to the upper stories of the learning hall.

"I saved the girl's life, and this is how you thank me?" Sido spat blood oozing down into his mouth from a wound on his temple. "Did not your Mistress Sight tell you I would? She spoke to me. But then you know the Seeing Aspect often has chosen to speak to me over you. Is that not why you made me your second?"

She stiffened as the Trine's Aspects flared. ... *Stop this!* ... *NOW!* ... Tetric blinked and took a step back. Sido hissed in pain at her call.

Koben Ryotan pulled his arm free of Tetric's grip. "This adolescent brawling is most unbecoming of you, *sibe*." Her *patrua* made no attempt to immobilize the seer prime again but remained close by his side.

Mirana scowled. "Brother?"

The prime nodded. "In every way that once mattered." He stepped forward and helped Mirana bring Sido to his feet. Tetric hovered like a shadow. The prime sent a notion of caution to her mind. If one of the defenders shot an arrow at Tetric, it could strike Koben. By the same token, Koben couldn't attack Tetric. Outmatched by the Trine's reflexes, he'd be dead by Tetric's hand before he could draw his knife.

She and Sido were not the only prisoners here; Tetric Garis was using the seer prime as a human shield against the Fal'kin leader's own defenders. They didn't dare risk retaliation.

"Do not think for one moment, Seer," the Trak-Calander prime said, "that Trine Garis could not stop your heart with a single thought if it pleased him to do so. So I would counsel caution."

She tried to reach closer to the seer prime's mind. His emotions did not match his words.

"You will soon no longer counsel anything, my prime," Sido retorted. His words were snide, but the sense from his mind was one of grim concern.

"Enough." Tetric held up his hand. "Koben is right, we will settle our differences later. Mirana, I know you have come for Jasal Pinal's journal entry, but I came here for you. Please put away your doubts. I am still the same man who stayed your hand in Deren's library. Let us finish what we've begun." He held his hand out to her.

His hand had indeed stopped her from slitting her own throat in that library. She could never give him such devotion again. The only way she would consider returning to his side was if he admitted everything he believed was wrong and vowed never again to use the Power from Without. Saving him was so very impossible, but she had to try. Every life was worth saving. Even his.

She made no move to take his hand. "I want to. But not with a Dark Trine."

Her former *patrua*'s hand fell to his side. "How can you believe this of me? You know me. *Biraena*, don't do this."

"Prime Ryotan, your brother is the Dark Trine," Mirana said. "He has been for a long, long time."

The seer prime's dark eyes flashed. "He is many things. Some, I pray, are not lost. Some are gone for good."

Sido snorted with disgust. "Seer's double-talk. You think me a traitor for using the Power from Without, Ryoten? I wonder how long you sat in a stone chair during Quorumtides suspecting your 'brother' of being the Dark Trine, never saying a word of it to your fellow Fal'kin primes?"

The prime's shoulders fell like a man giving in to defeat— or fate. Both were possible. He looked down at the snow-dusted paving. "One can look and still not see. That is a particularly distressing fault for a seer."

"The truly sad thing is Mirana has come for him as much as the keep writings. Some ridiculous attempt at reclaiming his soul." Sido's lips twisted into a sneer. "My purpose here isn't nearly so honorable."

Tetric set his dark eyes on Sido. "Enough of this." He turned to Mirana. "The keep has waited long enough for us. Come, *Ëi biraena*. Let us learn its secrets."

Mirana made no move to follow him. "I am not your daughter. I never was. All you ever wanted was a pawn you could control with the Power from Without."

Tetric shook his head. "You chose to use it of your own volition."

She gritted her teeth. "*Ai*, and I will never find forgiveness for what I've done. It is wrong. And I will never use it again. Tetric, it is *wrong*. You know it is."

Maybe this was the crossroads of her life. If she turned away from the quest to unlock the secret to the terrifying power of Jasal's Keep, if she chose not to seek its revelation, maybe her vision, her destiny of using the keep to destroy Kinderra, would finally be lifted from her. And from Tetric.

The cold stung her eyes, making them water. *Ai*. It was the cold. And Tetric. "If you leave with me now for Deren, we will not need to find Jasal's journal passage. Nor his keep. All it will take to end the war is your choice to do so."

"You know there is so much more that is needed for true peace. More than you or I can give alone. We need the keep."

"You're wrong, Tetric. We can create peace together. Come back with us. We can talk to my mother and the primes. We will find a way to have the Ken'nar lay down their swords. We will find a way to heal the harvested. We will undo what has been done." Her words tumbled out in their haste to make themselves heard. "If you come back with me now, we will not need the light in the keep." She grabbed his hand and tried to lead him from the learning hall.

He held his ground. "I once told you ending the war with the keep is just the beginning. For that peace to remain, we must control Jasal's Keep." He took both of her hands in his. "Mirana, Jasal Pinal is here. I know you can feel him. Hear what he has to tell you, see what he would show you. If you do not, Kinderrans will continue to die. By the thousands. And those deaths will be on your hands." He turned her palms up, reminding her of their scars, before he let them go.

If she refused to search for the remainder of the Codex, Koben Ryotan would be the first to fall in a new onslaught of violence such as Kinderra had yet to see. He would make war. Upon her. If she walked away now, Tetric might somehow find the last stanza on his own and divine the answers to the keep. If she left the quest, his armies would still put Deren to the sword.

He would destroy Kinderra. And all those she loved.

She looked up at Sido. His jaw was set. Koben's defenders had not moved, nor could they for fear of risking their prime's life. She was trapped. She couldn't go back to her old life of ignorance and denial. Her destiny—and Kinderra's destiny—was now balanced on the edge of a knife called hope. The only way open to her lay ahead. With Jasal Pinal.

Mirana nodded at last.

Tetric guided Mirana and Sido into the hall, his hand on his foster brother's shoulder. A heaviness pervaded the corridors. Tapestries hung limply on the walls, their images faded. Thousands of voices whispered just beyond her senses. Memories, echoes of the past, weighed down on her.

The immense age of the learning hall pressed down upon her. It settled onto her shoulders and seeped into her bones. Every life that had walked within Caladazh's corridors left its mark on the hall. Flitting like wisps of mist in the furthest reaches of her mind, the tailings of presences long lost to memory struggled to make themselves heard.

"Tetric told me you seek the writings of Jasal Pinal," Koben said. "I know of nothing like that here."

"The mandalas sigil," the Trine intoned. When she and the prime paused, he continued, "Where else would something so precious be kept?"

Mirana turned to the prime. "What is this mandalas sigil?"

Koben eyed Tetric, his expression unreadable, as was his mind. "In here."

The older seer opened the doors to a windowless gathering room. The chamber was much smaller than the gathering hall of Deren. The one hundred or so Fal'kin who called Caladazh home could fit in the chamber but not many more than that; the hall at home could house thousands. Long wooden tables sat surrounded by thick-legged chairs. Other than a few tapestries and lights, there were no other decorations. None were needed.

Suspended high on the wall at the far end of the room was an enormous jewel-encrusted disc. Wider across than three tall men stood, the crystals sparkled in the flickering rushlight. Mirana stopped at a low set of stairs that ascended to a dais.

"It's beautiful."

Koben cast his gaze ahead of her. "*Ai*. It is thousands of summers old. Each one of those amulets was once held by a prime. The more beautiful it grows, the more disheartening, because one who has led us has gone home to the Aspects Above. Some not so willingly," he added.

"Koben." A warning edged Tetric's voice.

Another presence touched her mind above the miasma of others, but this one was distinct, familiar. Intimate.

Jasal.

He, or rather some essence of him, was near. But with so many amulets in the sigil, she couldn't find exactly where.

The seer prime took her arm gently and escorted her up the steps. ... *For summers, I refused to let my heart see the truth about my brother ... I must pay for my self-delusion, but you need not ... Do as he says or he will try to kill you ... I will do what I can ...* She fought to keep her face expressionless at the prime's call.

His call was private—but never private enough to hide from a Trine.

Tetric grabbed the Trak-Calander prime's arm and roughly pulled him away from her. "Do not drive her from me. I will not lose her again." He waved a hand, and the doors behind them slammed shut. The locking bar fell into its supports with a bang.

"Tetric Garis murdered Shalas Yutan for loving him like a son. He murdered Shalas and used my Aspect to do it." The older seer remained in his brother's grip.

"What?" Mirana stared in shock at the men.

A despondent weariness flowed from her *patrua*'s mind to hers. "Shalas Yutan tried to kill me. I was trying to stop him, not murder him."

Koben stood toe-to-toe with the Trine. "He died because of you. Because of the Soul Harvest."

She knew Tetric was capable of unthinkable things, but all had been couched in some malignantly skewed sense of logic. This, however, held no reason, skewed or otherwise. "Tetric, is this true?"

He did not take his face away from Koben's. "I meant to stop Shalas. I had no idea the Healing Aspect could do such a thing. How many times must I tell you that, *sibe?*"

"How could you kill the man who loved you as a son?" She wasn't sure if she truly wanted an answer.

Sido's amulet glowed. He swallowed audibly. "One is capable of anything if pressed hard enough." He reached for her arm with a sense of urgency she could divine even without his touch but pushed his hand away. Tetric would not tolerate again either man trying to communicate with her mind to mind. Furthermore, she needed no warning of danger. It had surrounded them the moment they passed through the moon arch.

The Trine shoved the seer prime aside and moved toward her. "Mirana, please. You know me. Do not listen to these traitors. Look to the sigil, *biraena*, look to Jasal for the truth."

The reflection of Jasal's presence called to her, muted by so many other memories emanating from the amulets. When she located her ancestor's writings, what would she find within them? Did Jasal's darkness include patricide? By the Aspects, she did not want to know that. She did not want to see that.

"Mirana, in a moment, Trak-Calan's learning hall will arrive in a futile attempt to rescue him. A pitched battle in enclosed quarters is very bloody," Tetric said, his voice as brittle as the ice outside. He flung out a hand and released a jet of black-tinged silver flame from his amulet, melting the locking bar.

She and Sido flinched and ducked at the sudden, violent strike. Already, distant shouts reached her ears.

"That will only slow them down. I do suggest you find Jasal's writings quickly."

She looked to the sigil and back to the Trine. "There are so many—"

… Now! …

She winced at the force of his call. How many Fal'kin could he kill before he went down? If he could be killed at all. She might not be around long enough to find out. Sido and Koben certainly wouldn't be.

Mirana clenched the half-diamond amulet in her hand and looked up to the sigil. The Codex portion she found in Tash-Hamar had been hidden behind the mosaic of Antiri, Jasal's wife, hidden behind something that mattered to Jasal. But what was here that would be significant to her ancestor? He had never stepped foot in Trak-Calan as far as she knew.

"Hurry," Sido growled.

"I'm trying."

"Try harder."

She chewed on her lip again. Maybe Jasal never came here, but did he have an ally, a friend from the province that came to Deren, maybe during that long-ago siege?

"Prime Koben, which amulet was the one chosen by the prime during Jasal's time?"

"That one." The seer prime pointed to a muddy brown smoky quartz.

It was as good a hunch as any, only she didn't have the luxury of time to guess again. If she didn't find the keep entry immediately, the whole blasted Underworld would be released in this room.

She held the half diamond close to her heart. The dusky quartz illuminated and sent a tendril of sienna light to the amulet next to it. She gasped. It wasn't Jasal, but something—someone else. A golden topaz set in an amulet shaped like a tiger's head now pulsed with light in time with its darker mate.

"Shalas Yutan." Koben smiled coldly. "Does his voice cry out to you the loudest? Perhaps it should."

Shalas Yutan's sulfurous gem pulled at her along with the brown quartz. Another crystal adjacent to the two now flared, adding its blue light to the gold and brown. Then another. And another. One by one, the other amulets began to scintillate. The mandalas sigil transformed into a whirling kaleidoscope of color.

Dozens, hundreds of other memories forced themselves into Mirana's mind. She could not control the visions that raced through her. Images, faces, places rushed by as if to show her the entirety of hundreds of lives in an instant. They flooded her, drowned her, overwhelmed her.

Jasal's amulet flared from her chest, splitting into fingers of light, each one touching an amulet embedded in the mandalas sigil.

Mirana screamed.

CHAPTER 16

"I knowest that which maketh my heart tremble."
—The Codex of Jasal the Great

The torrent of memories abruptly, painfully ended, and Mirana opened her eyes. She stood in the prime's chambers in Deren, the one from which her mother now led Kin-Deren and her *Brepaithe* Toban before her. She held the back of a chair.

It was the same chamber, and yet it was not. Everything appeared newer, the tapestries shone more vibrantly, the windows not as etched. The items on her mother's desk were different.

A tall, handsome man with fair hair and piercing silver eyes regarded her, a grim expression weighing his young face. Around his neck, he wore a simple amulet of platinum, its crystal a clear, flawless diamond.

Jasal Pinal.

She had never seen his face, but she knew intuitively it must be him. He was not alone. Others were in the room, primes, wearing the colors of their provinces.

Jasal shook his head. "I do not want the honor."

"Jasal, *Ëi cara*, you are Trine. If you do not take up the mantle of Primus Magne, the Ken bastard Ilrik will overrun Kinderra." Mirana heard herself speak with a voice that was not her own but a man's. Panic seized her. What was happening?

She was inside the memory of the Trak-Calander prime in Jasal's time, not merely watching it. Living it.

Jasal turned around, his indecision palpable through the Aspects. "My own province is burden enough to carry. Now you want me to be responsible for the whole of Kinderra?"

A strikingly beautiful, dark-haired woman drew near to the Trine. The blue-green amulet hanging at her chest glowed faintly. Mirana knew that amulet. That amulet had saved her life against a sea monster. The woman threaded her arm through Jasal's, her honey-colored eyes holding love and concern. Antiri. It was Antiri Amil Pinal, Jasal's wife.

"*Ëi ama, Oë Trinus.* You are already responsible for Kinderra. You have been so since before you were born."

He hung his head and said nothing for long moments. At last, he faced the group, determination now replacing doubt in his penetrating eyes. "Let it be done."

The scene faded again before Mirana's mind's eye, and Jasal faded while Antiri remained. This time, grief muted the seer woman's beauty, and her amber eyes were red-rimmed. She was dressed in black robes, a dark, translucent veil covering her head.

Antiri sat astride a horse. Two others flanked the seer on steeds, as did Mirana. Lush grass waved in the breeze around them. The hands with which Mirana held her horse's reins were different from the previous vision. A woman's hands. The weathered, scraped hands of a defender.

A newborn infant slept in a swaddle tied next to Antiri's chest, a peaceful sight so incongruous in such somber company.

Antiri stroked the babe's head, a shock of pale hair shining from the wrapping. "I was not certain any of you would come. They have already begun to paint him a coward, even a traitor. I did not know if you would believe them."

"Jasal was our Trine. *E Ëomus cara.*" Mirana now spoke with a woman's voice. She must be the new Trak-Calan prime, installed immediately after her predecessor was killed in the Siege of Deren.

"Do they not understand he gave everything to save Kinderra? He would never abandon us," Antiri said, her voice strained with heartbroken indignation. "Ilrik knew he had lost— his troops were decimated. He chose to immolate himself with Jasal's body. Jasal had no way to return. I tried to stop Ilrik myself, but Jasal called to me and told me to flee. For Jasan's sake." She held the babe close and drew yet another ragged sob.

The seer kissed her son and composed herself. She took out three pieces of parchment from the folds of her cloak and handed one to each of the primes. "Each of you shall bear a portion of his legacy. Guard it well. Guard it with your lives. Guard it beyond your graves. If such information should ever fall into Ken'nar hands, it would be our undoing."

Mirana examined the parchment piece her ancestress had given to her:

> *It is enough to fail for one's own sake, but to fail for the*
> *sake of others is unredeemable. I must be strong. Never*
> *have the Aspects led Their servant astray. That is why*
> *I, and I alone, shall bear the burden. For not only am*

I the Lock, I am the Key. This is the one purpose for which I have come into the world. At last, my destiny is upon me. And I will choose it!

The keep passage of Trak-Calan.

Mirana's heart beat wildly. Was it truly her heart or that of the prime whose memory she was witnessing?

Jasal's grief was deepest here in this excerpt, a soul-deadening dread. *Ai*, to be stripped of the Aspects' greatest treasure did mean the amulets, as the ancient Trine wrote in the Rün-Taran excerpt, but now it took on a deeper meaning. The treasure of life. Was he to bear the burden of so great a sin, he could not speak it? Lock and Key. Within and Without. Life and Death.

"What if such information is needed again, my lady?" Mirana spoke in the Trak-Calan woman's voice, soft yet harsh.

"One will come who will know how to find it. The Thrice-Blessed of the Prophecy. Jasal saw this," Antiri replied. "I have kept some of his miracle in his Codex."

"But our Jasal was the Thrice-Blessed," not-Mirana said.

"No, he was not." The seer woman shook her head. "But, *ai*, he was blessed. To us." She looked down at the babe in her arms and began to weep again. "Until the answer to the Trine Prophecy comes to us, use all the Aspects within you to keep his writings safe." She held her son close.

Not-Mirana gripped the hilt of a sword at her waist. "We cannot allow the lies about Jasal to continue."

Antiri tried and failed to suppress a sob. "We must. The lies will safeguard what Jasal did."

"What of his amulet?" A man spoke, the prime from Tash-Hamar she recognized from the previous scene. "If the Thrice-

Blessed rises, so will the Thrice-Cursed. A Ken'nar Trine could also use Jasal's amulet. And his keep."

"No. Not with Jasal's design." She tried to smile. "Jasal's amulet is secure. That is all you need to know, *Ëi cara*. It is safer for you that way. Safer for all of you."

Mirana watched the Tash-Hamari prime trot his horse closer to Antiri and place his battle-scarred hand on her arm. "It is time to come home to Rhadaz, Tiri. You and Jasan will be safe there."

"My heart beats for nothing more than to return to the province of my birth. It is Jasan's heritage as well. But I cannot. The law demanded I sunder my ties to Tash-Hamar when I joined in union with Jasal. I would be put to death if I returned as recompense for abandoning my province and taking my Aspect with me. Jasan would die."

The Tash-Hamari straightened in his saddle. "Am I not prime? I can change the law."

"No, Amahl. Laws do not change minds or hearts." Antiri smiled in gratitude. "*Gratas Oë cin Ëa cora tuda.*"

The third prime, a man wearing the capricorn heraldic of Rün-Taran, cantered his horse a few steps closer. "Then you shall come with me to Nuralima. I will guard you and your babe as if you were my own. Rün-Taran has far more than heat to protect Jasan."

Mirana could attest to that. Her ankle throbbed at the thought of the capricorn.

"*Gratas.*" The seer nodded. "My gratitude for all of you is greater than the grains of sand in Tash-Hamar. We shall go to Rün-Taran." She turned in her saddle to face the Tash-Hamari prime. "However, there is a favor I would ask of you, Amahl."

"Anything."

"In my saddlebag."

The defender prime reached in and took out a book.

"For the rest of Jasan's life, Kinderra will speak the name of his father as a curse. Give this to Jasan when he is old enough to understand what his father has done. When he is willing to hear the truth. I will not—" She took a shattering exhale and laid her fingertips on her amulet. "I have seen I will not be able to give it to him myself."

The plain leather-bound cover. The simple brass lock. The Codex of Jasal Pinal.

A cry of anguish escaped Antiri's lips. "How could Ilrik have done this? He once loved Jasal as a brother. How could he kill him?"

The scene swirled again.

Mirana sat behind a plain wooden desk, one she did not recognize. Light from the setting sun bled into the room from a small window through the teeth of the mountains beyond. An uncommonly tall, darkly handsome youth stood before her, no longer a boy yet not a man. She sensed his anger simmering just below the surface.

"But you must let me go, Father," the boy implored. "You have trained me with an amulet for summers now. Let me ride out to the battle. Our forces have been decimated by the Ken'nar. Let me go. Let me do what I was born to do."

"You cannot yet, *Ëi biraen*. You must not." Mirana spoke in the heavily accented, musical voice of a man more comfortable with the lyrical language of the Old Tongue. He sounded tired, fatigued from speaking of far too many losses, too many arguments.

She was living a memory from Shalas Yutan himself.

The young man held out his hands, exasperated. "Why?"

"Your powers grow too strong, too quickly, Tetric. I should have taken that amulet from you when you were still a little one before you truly knew what you had done."

Tetric Garis.

Young Tetric clenched his teeth, his jaw muscles tightening. "I knew exactly what I was doing. That is why I did it."

"*Ai*, and you gave yourself a connection to the Aspects for which you are clearly not ready."

"You are allowing Koben to go, and he is a summer younger than I."

"Koben is not you. You are not Koben."

Tetric leaned on the old man's desk, his face close to the prime. "I am three times as ready as Koben to fight."

"You are three times as powerful as Koben, but you are not ready to fight." Shalas-Mirana covered one of the boy's hands with his own. "Especially when you choose to touch the Aspects from Without." A trace of fear crossed Tetric's face only to be chased away by anger.

"Koben. I will kill him." Tetric's voice had become a venomous whisper.

"Koben did not tell me this. You are not so powerful yet as to keep everything hidden from me." The prime smiled sadly. "You use the Power from Without at the expense of the Light from Within because you think it makes you even stronger. It does not. All it makes you is a thief."

Tetric leaned back and crossed his arms, flattening his mouth into that now-familiar line. "What do you think it is I steal?"

"Life." The seer prime replied as weariness filled the marrow of his bones. He was old. It was sheer willpower that kept him alive now. He would not leave for the Aspects Above until this boy was a Fal'kin, in mind, heart, and soul. "The Aspects Above have blessed you a Trine. How much more power do you need, *Ëi biraen?*"

"There is never enough power. Not when it comes to saving Kinderra." Tetric slammed down his fists on the desktop in front of Mirana-Shalas. "I must go."

"Tetric." Mirana-Shalas gripped the edge of the desk and called a warning to the boy, letting the full magnitude of his Seer's Aspect wash over him. He was not above reminding Tetric that the boy was not the only one who held great power, even if it was only one Aspect.

Tetric blinked back the harsh intent. "Koben has twisted your heart against me."

"I have raised you and Koben as brothers. I have raised you as Fal'kin. You must not touch the Power from Without. That is the way of the Ken'nar. The way of evil."

Young Tetric leaned over the desk once more. "Why? Because it is dangerous?" He then smiled, a slow, cruel turning of his thin lips. "Or because you fear what you do not understand? I understand the power, both from Within and Without."

Mirana-Shalas reached for Tetric's hand once more. "I love you. You are as much my son as if you were of my own blood. But it is you who does not understand. Think, Tetric. You look at the Power from Without as freedom from the limits of mortality. But it is a prison. You will forget you are a Trine in your heart, and you will live only to bleed the lives of those around you. Then you will be right. Then there will never be enough power."

Tetric snatched his hand away as if burned. "You speak of prisons? Why would the Aspects Above have imprisoned us in such frail cells"—he struck his chest—"when they entrusted

Kinderra to us? They have called us to use it. They are calling me to use it.”

“Where have you learned this?” The first tendrils of fear slithered their way through the seer’s mind into Mirana’s.

The youth smiled grimly again. “I learned it from your very lips, Father. ‘*Oëme u’pleasé, quod etan u’gente defende Crearae tuda.*’ They were not pleased for there was no one to protect all of Creation.”

Horror clenched Shalas Yutan’s—and Mirana’s—heart. “The Ora Fal’kinnen does not condone—”

“‘*Mane il’Aspecta’e reacé a gente cin digita’e i’fulmena. A Oëmea cora’e touchá cin Kin, daá Ken il’Aspecta’e.*’ The Hand of the Aspects reached out to the people with fingers as of lightning. To those whose hearts were touched with Light, were bestowed the Power of the Aspects. I have been given all of Creation. It is my birthright as a Trine.”

“No, Tetric.” Tears burned in Mirana-Shalas’s tired eyes.

“I am sorry, *Paithe*. I have been given the power, and I intend to use it.” Tetric turned on his heel and strode purposely toward the chamber doors.

“And I will not let you damn Kinderra nor yourself.”

Mirana felt the old prime’s heart break as his Seer’s Aspect welled up inside. Shalas Yutan’s form shimmered. Feline savagery engulfed her. Out of an enormous tiger’s maw came a bloodthirsty roar. The beast leaped over the desk and crouched in front of the door, ready to pounce on the youth if he tried to pass.

Tetric stumbled back, eyes wide with fear, knocking over a chair. Then he laughed. “Tricking my eyes as if I were a child you could frighten into behaving? I thought better of you, old man.”

He shoved the tiger aside and reached for the latch. The tiger lunged and pinned Tetric to the floor with two great paws on his chest. The young Trine gave a strangled cry of fury against the weight holding him down. A blur of motion from the youth's hand produced an ebony stiletto. Tetric sank the blade into the tiger's haunch. The animal roared again then disintegrated, the knife protruding from Shalas Yutan's shoulder.

"Please, my son. Listen to me," the old man gasped in pain, blood running from between his fingers as he removed the stiletto. "My ruse was enough to make even you hesitate. One created only by my Light from Within. If such a power does not require drawing life from another and can still bring enough fear to a Trine to cause him to stop in his tracks, is it not the more powerful gift? The more selfless gift?"

Tetric, breathing hard between clenched teeth, glared at his foster father. "Selfless, *ai*. But not more powerful. The Light from Within can never beat the Power from Without. Ever! It is limitless!"

Tears filled Shalas's eyes. "*Ai*, it is limitless. That is why it is so dangerous. If you continue this madness, all the lives you feed upon will not be enough for you. You will destroy all you wanted to save. All you were born to save."

"You dare try to stop me from answering my destiny? Me? The answer to the Prophecy?"

"Do you not understand, *Ëi biraena*? I am trying to stop you, not from fulfilling your destiny as a Trine, but to stop you from damning yourself."

Tetric sneered in disgust. "You are no longer worthy to call yourself my father, Shalas Yutan. I am the child of the very Aspects Above themselves."

The door to the prime's chambers slammed open. "Father! I felt—! Tetric—?" A young Koben Ryotan ran in. His panicked gaze fell on their bleeding foster father. With a cry, the younger seer reached for his belt knife. The blade flashed and sliced through Tetric's forearm.

Tetric's face contorted in fury. Koben was fast, but he was no match for the young Trine. Before his foster brother could attack again, Tetric wrested the knife away with his Defending Aspect. It clattered on the stone tiles next to Shalas Yutan. The elder seer batted it away.

"Stop. Both of you." Mirana-Shalas staggered heavily to his feet on old legs and dragged Tetric back from Koben. The Seeing Aspect raged through Shalas's body, through Mirana's body. "Tetric, if you take up the Power from Without, you will not gain the strength of the Aspects you so desire. You will instead sacrifice your soul. It will cost you. Everything."

Tetric made an inhuman snarl. With one long-fingered hand, he grabbed a fistful of Koben's shirt, and gripped Mirana-Shalas's robes with the other. "I *will* follow my destiny!"

Searing pain ripped through her mind. She heard Koben scream, and a cry of agony came from Shalas's mouth. The old seer clutched at his robes with a gnarled hand. Pain seared through his chest and her own. Tetric's Healing Aspect was constricting Shalas's heart. Breath sounded loud and ragged in her ears. She could no longer see the scene.

"What have you done?" Koben's voice sounded more distant still. Someone's arms wrapped around her body.

"F–Father?" Tetric sputtered his words in panic. "*Paithe?*"

"You used—you used the Power from Without to attack our father."

"He wanted to prevent me from becoming the Trine of Kinderra, Koben."

"You used me, Tetric! You stole the Aspects from me to kill our father!"

"I-I just wanted to stop him. Stop you both."

She heard more words, but they no longer made sense, overtaken by an agony that shattered the soul.

The vision dimmed as young Koben Ryotan's words rang in her mind. Her pain, instead of fading with the vision, grew in intensity, the sense of overwhelming failure adding to it. She needed to wake up, she needed to stop this. She didn't want to see these memories anymore.

She gasped in pain on her hands and knees. Her sword lay just beyond her fingertips. It might as well have been miles away. Her vision.

No. No more. She had to wake up. Koben's Fal'kin would arrive at any moment, and eventually, they'd gain entrance into the gathering chamber. And then—

Mirana's heart hammered, the pain across her abdomen flaring with each beat. It was not real. Not yet. She was a seer, a Trine, she could stop it at any time. She could wake up. Now.

The scene remained.

The gravel of the stone paving under her hands dug into her palms. Cold rain pelted the back of her neck like shards of ice. Blood gushed thick and hot over her hand and down her side.

"You used me." Her voice cracked with emotion and exhaustion. "You never loved me. You only loved the keep. You only love power."

A tall, dark figure stood before her. "No, Mirana. Never. I never wanted to hurt you. You must give me the amulet. It is time now. This foolish fight is over." His deep baritone was tender, his intent cruel.

The Dark Trine. Tetric Garis.

She didn't want to hear this. She didn't want to see this. Still, the Seeing Aspect held her.

The rain continued to beat down on her. Her blood dripped into a grout line in the paving, diluting in the water. It swirled in the rain like rusty smoke.

Just beyond the Dark Trine, a door opened to the spiraling staircase within the keep. It was important. Escape? *Ai*, but in her pain-filled haze, it was not quite the escape she believed.

"It is over, *biraena*. Give it to me."

Panic filled her. If she made a sudden move, could she knock him away and make for the door? No. He was too fast. Could she strike out at his knees, crippling him? No. He had armor. Could she back up? No. His Ken'nar, minds clear with cognizant loyalty, waited behind her. There were no options. She had failed.

"Mirana! Don't give it to him!"

Teague.

The Dark Trine flung out his arm, sending Teague flying into the stone of the pinnacle. Her beloved fell, making a wet, final slapping sound as he hit the stone. He did not move, a pool of dark blood expanding beneath him. Others—they seemed familiar, but their faces were indistinct with a time yet to come— tried to run over to help Teague but were held back by Ken'nar swords. ... *He has but moments left ... I can still save him ... Give it to me or your herbsboy dies ...*

This was the moment that had made her separate herself from Teague, believing he would be safe if he was no longer with her. Her heart hammered against her chest.

She would have to choose now. Sacrifice Teague for the Kinderra. Kinderra for Teague. She could not make a choice like this. Not this. There had to be some other way.

She must wake up. She would not see this. Not Teague's death. Not this. She. Would. NOT!

The Mirana-Yet-To-Be sat back on her heels and bowed her head, weeping. Tetric's long-fingered hand rested on her head as if to grant her some sort of benediction but banal, profane.

"He would have never understood what we are doing. He would have only caused you far more pain had he lived. In time, you will move beyond this loss. It is over now, *Ëi Biraena Trinus*. Kinderra is ours. As you knew it would be. As it was meant to be."

She had waited too long. Teague was gone. Everything was gone.

His cold fingers gently brushed the hair away from her neck, and her skin crawled in revulsion at his paternal touch. He grasped the chain of the amulet she wore and lifted it over her head. She gasped at the sudden absence of its protective weight, crying out in agony at its separation from her. Life had been severed from her. She was left blind, abandoned. Alone.

The destruction of Deren surrounded her. Buildings burned despite the driving rain. Cries of the dying, so numerous before, now grew fainter as they succumbed to their ends.

It would not stop here. It would go on and on and on until Kinderra was consumed. There was no hope. The Thrice-Cursed had won. Kinderra was lost. Teague was gone. Without Teague, there was no reason to fight her death anymore.

She had failed.

Fire lanced in her back. Pain, a universe of it, enveloped her. Pain was her new reality, her eternity. And she deserved it for sins of which she would never be absolved. She screamed without a voice, begging for death from a godhead trinity who no longer recognized her.

A nothingness surrounded her. Absolute.

It was an agony in and of itself. She no longer knew if her body still existed, and she wasn't certain she cared anymore. She wanted an end. To all of it.

The world exploded in white light.

To fail for the sake of others.

She had died in failure. Had Jasal Pinal been afraid that he, too, would die before he finished the keep? He'd bargained all he had to save Deren. Everything.

He had died by his own hand. But he hadn't committed suicide. He'd given his life to choose the amulets in the keep. *All* of his life. *All* his Light from Within.

Only in Their unmatched Wisdom could such a design be conceived. Woe to the enemies of the Light! They will be their own undoing!

The keep truly was a thing of divine inspiration. With Jasal's Trine Aspects and his very life fueling the amulets within the keep, the light released was the most powerful weapon to have ever existed.

I, and I alone, shall bear the burden. For not only am I the Lock, I am the Key.

The keep. Magnificent. Terrible. Life-saving, life-destroying. In one, in both.

But to hearken unto Their Will requires a decision I am loath to make. My choice is before me.

Jasal had emptied all that he was from his body and soul to choose the keep's amulets, leaving only a shell behind. He left more than just his mortal body behind; he had to leave Antiri and his beloved newborn son. Then Ilrik did the unthinkable. He destroyed Jasal's body along with his own. With no dwelling place to which his Aspects could return, Jasal died. Truly.

All her life, Mirana knew that if she took up her destiny, it would mean the destruction of everything and everyone she held dear. She was right. And so very wrong. All that she loved would indeed be destroyed. For her. But not for Kinderra. To save Kinderra and her people, she would have to walk in Jasal's footsteps and leave everything behind. She would have to leave her mother and father behind. She would have to leave Teague behind. To her, all would be destroyed because she would no longer bear witness to it.

I must be strong.

Tetric had told her time and time again that she was not strong enough unless she used the Power from Without. She had believed him. Once. She had used the Power from Without. Once. It left a wound within her soul that would never heal, but it also left knowledge. The Light from Within was a sacrifice of oneself on behalf of others. Selfless. The Power from Without was a sacrifice of others for one's own gain. Selfish.

Rememore Kin en Forte.

The scripture in the Kin-Deren passage was not wrong, it was not a misspelling, it was not a mistranslation. *Rememore Kin en Forte.* Remember the Light *in* the keep. Jasal Pinal himself was the Light in the keep.

This is the one purpose for which I have come into the world.

To save Kinderra and all that she loved, she would have to reenact Jasal Pinal's miracle at the keep. Everything would indeed be destroyed to her as she must pour out all that she was. She would no longer be aware—or alive—to perceive the land and the people she held dear.

At last, my destiny is upon me. And I will choose it!

But was she strong enough?

Mirana's cheek pressed against something smooth and cool and substantial. The echo of her scream still rang in the gathering hall. She opened her eyes. She was lying in Sido's arms.

The mandalas sigil of Trak-Calan was at rest, its dozens of amulet crystals dull points of color once more.

Now, however, there was an empty socket. The amulet of Shalas Yutan lay on the floor nearby. In her hand, she clutched a piece of parchment.

Sido helped her to her feet as Tetric rushed over, ignoring the shouts and fists banging on the doors outside the gathering chamber. "What does the Codex entry say? Tell me." The Trine gently opened her scarred hand and took the scrap of parchment.

"The keep will destroy us both." She let her hand fall to her side. "Let it go, Tetric."

"It is the only thing that will save us." He scanned the parchment. "What is this? What does the gibberish mean, Mirana? Lock and Key? And the other entries? 'Stripped of their greatest treasure'?"

Sido grimaced at the locked door. "It won't take them long to break through." As if in answer to his words, the metal hinges creaked and the scent of burning wood drifted through the chamber.

She wouldn't be a lock or a key to anything if she and the seers couldn't escape the gathering hall. But how? Sido and Koben couldn't create amulet fire. Maybe the men could take on Tetric by themselves while she concentrated on opening the door, but for how long?

Dammit! Right now, their chances were better against the accidental crossfire of a hundred angry defenders out for Tetric's blood than remaining the Dark Trine's prisoners. She needed just a few moments to gather power to blast the door open. Sido and Koben had to give her those moments or they were all dead.

"It doesn't matter. To awaken the keep will take more than we can give." She made her way down from the dais, edging closer to the doors, Sido by her side. "Lay down your sword, Tetric. Recant the Power from Without. Walk away from the keep. End the war."

Sido inhaled sharply. "Mirana." He cocked his head over his shoulder to indicate the doors. The hinges were glowing orange; the defenders outside were melting the iron right off the entrance.

The Dark Trine remained unmovable. "I will ask you one last time. Why is Jasal's amulet the only one that will ignite the keep?" The hematite crystal glowed, pulsing like a heartbeat.

"Tetric—"

Sido's amulet lit briefly then went out. He pulled Mirana close. He reached down her shirt with his free hand and pulled out the half-diamond amulet. Mirana struggled against him. "Sido!"

"The keep is made of amulets, *Ëi Trinus,*" the young seer said, holding up the amulet still about Mirana's neck. "You saw how it reacted to the mandalas, light, fire from one amulet connected to another—"

Mirana struggled in his grip. "For Aspects' sake, what are you doing?"

"This one connects them all," he continued. "Imagine, Tetric. Fire from hundreds, thousands of amulets. Power beyond all telling."

A hinge, now molten metal, dropped with a heavy, hissing thud.

Tetric stepped close and placed a hand on her cheek. "I always knew you were special, but you are too young to bear such a burden. Give me the amulet, Mirana. I, too, can wield it. Don't you see I am trying to spare your life?" The Trine's voice was so loving, so kind. So devastating.

She turned from his paternal touch and pulled her arm from Sido. "Perhaps my life is not meant to be spared." She picked up the Codex parchment from the floor and tucked it inside her shirt next to Jasal's amulet. She backed away from him toward the groaning, smoking doors. "My life is meant for the good of Kinderra. As yours should have been."

… Mirana, Ëi Trinus biraena, please … he called, his mind pressing painfully against her attempt to keep him from entering any further. *… If you leave me, I will be forced to kill you … I will ask you one last time … Give me the amulet …*

No tears came to her eyes with his words. That surprised her. She had expected to feel devastated when they parted for good. This pain far outstripped her ability to feel it. The loss was too deep, the grief too consuming. Only the loss of Teague's love had been worse.

Maybe she had been a fool for hoping it would be otherwise, but she held no regrets for trying to turn him from his destiny of destruction. She had tried everything she could. She would never let a man die if he could be saved. However, such salvation for Tetric—nor anyone—could not come from her. That choice had to come from one's own earnest desire to turn back from the darkness in one's soul.

"No." She lifted her chin and filled the half diamond with the Aspects, setting it alight. "If I give my life, that is my choice. If you kill me, that is yours and yours alone."

Mirana threw her arms wide and loosed an enormous gout of white light at the gathering chamber doors. They flew off the remnants of their hinges, and dozens of Trak-Calan defenders poured into the room.

… So be it … the Dark Trine's voice intoned in her mind. *… You have made yourself my enemy, Ëi biraena …*

CHAPTER 17

"Our Enemy gnashes at our heels like mongrel dogs."
—The Codex of Jasal the Great

"Down!" Sido launched himself at Mirana, tackling her to the floor.

A jet of silvery black lightning shot overhead, narrowly missing them both.

Mirana's plan to blast the doors open and have the Trak-Calanders tangle with Tetric was working.

The problem was the plan *was* working.

Deadly lightning of all colors zigzagged around the room, a visual counterpoint to the *clang* of swords.

Dazed by Tetric's strike and the energy she had leveraged, she shook her head to clear it. Through the smoke and seething mass of bodies surrounding the Trine and the prime, Koben wrestled with Tetric behind a wall of silvery fire.

A protective flame wall? Was that even possible? By the Light, there was still so much she had to learn. Would nothing take down that man?

"C'mon!" Sido hauled her to her feet.

"Let go of me, traitor!" She fought to free herself. "Koben!"

Koben called to a chair and hurled it at Tetric through the wall of amulet fire. "Mirana! Run!"

The Trine repulsed the chair and sent it flying at the prime. The older seer fell, sprawling in agony amid the flames. "You have stood in my way for the last time, *Ëi sibe*." Tetric drew his long sword and slashed at the seer prime.

"Koben!" Mirana yanked her wrist from Sido's grip. She concentrated the Defending Aspect within her but could not get a clear shot at the Trine with so many Fal'kin in the way.

The awful finality of life silenced rang through her mind. "No!"

"*Come! On!*" Sido dragged her with him through the door. She and the seer took off running down the hallway.

Moments later, a deafening explosion drove her to her knees. She was shaking her head to clear it when the young seer lifted her by her sword scabbard strapped across her back and pulled her down a side passage.

She struggled. "Let me go—"

Sido clamped a hand over her mouth. … *U'Nehíl … Now* … He grasped his amulet and closed his eyes. She fought a gasp as she watched the seer and herself run down the hall, into the courtyard, and out the gate. The Dark Trine tore after them.

The seer's ruse Sido created was good. Very good. And if she hadn't been so furious with him, she would have told him so.

"Damn you." She wrenched herself from her companion. "Your ashes can follow Tetric Garis to the Underworld and rot—"

Sido leaned into her face. "He was going to kill you if you did not tell him about the keep. I saved your life. Actually, twice in as many breaths." He pointed to the hallway where their conjured doubles had been. "Damn stupid of me if I was a traitor."

She frowned and nodded. "Well, I—" Dozens of Fal'kin charged down the corridor after the Trine, interrupting her reply. However, there were fewer than there had been in the gathering hall. "You're a very good liar."

"And a hell of a lot more." He winked at her.

She hardened her mouth. "Really? Now?"

He ignored her and peered down the hallway. "Tetric will be busy with Koben's defenders, but a seer's ruse lasts only so long."

She leaned back from him, impressed. "That was you? I mean, that was us? From you? But it was from the Light from With—" She shook her head. "You know what I mean."

Sido rolled his eyes and motioned to her. "Come."

They dashed under the porticos, keeping to the shadows, to reach their horses. The tall Trine fought with the defenders surrounding him.

As Mirana lifted her leg to a stirrup, she stumbled and fell, groaning as vitality bled from her like a sudden, mortal wound.

No! No more! She would not be used like an accursed Ken'nar's tool!

She surged back to her feet and wrapped the courtyard well's bucket with a ferocious intent from her Defending Aspect. Hurling it at the Dark Trine, she smiled in grim satisfaction as it struck him in the back of the head. He dropped to his knees before the circle of Trak-Calan defenders.

She snarled as she drew her sword and launched herself toward the fray.

Sido pulled her back and shoved her toward her horse. "Save the vendetta for later. Go! Now!" He vaulted into his horse's saddle.

She swung up onto Ashtar's back and dug her heels into the warhorse's sides. "Ride!"

Stone, ice, and wood crashed down in front of her. The chestnut destrier leaped over the debris and charged down the Darbinh Pass, the young seer and his mount on Ashtar's tail.

They drove their steeds through the moonlit pass. A sharp outcropping, obscured by shadow, scraped her thigh as she rode past. She gritted her teeth in pain. The full moon would light their way across the glacier—and put them in plain view as it did so. She clenched her teeth harder.

Tetric's Aspects called to her, reaching for her, pulling at her. His mind attempted to breach her protections, his presence surrounding her. She cried out and dug deeper within herself, the diamond she gripped now hot against her palm, and pushed against the Trine's mind assailing her.

The trail narrowed, forcing Mirana and Sido to ride single file. The seer took the lead, his horse bred for speed.

Her Healing Aspect rose sharply. Ashtar was failing. Exhausted from the journey already behind him and the altitude they now endured, he ran on sheer willpower. "Please, Ashtar. Just a little more, boy."

The frigid temperatures quickly sapped Ashtar's muscles, making his footing unsure. She missed a patch of snow-covered ice lost in shadow and one of the horse's hooves struck the slick spot. He slipped, throwing her, and she slammed into the granite wall of the pass. Stunned, she fell to the snow. Her head ached fiercely, and something warm trickled down her forehead. Groaning with pain and effort, she pushed herself upright. Out of the night came a fork of silvered black fire, striking Ashtar's flank. She scrambled to the warhorse. "Ashtar, get up. Get up!"

Sido reined his mount around. "Leave him."

She pulled on Ashtar's reins. "No. I will never leave him."

The drumming of hooves drew close then slowed. She snapped her head up. A black rider on a black stallion, held in shadow, stood over her. "Mirana, stop this foolishness. Now. Come back to me. You are my child."

"I was never your child," she snarled, tightening her grip on the fallen chestnut's reins.

"Mirana! Let the damn horse go!" Sido cried.

"Would you be the one to take her from me, *Ëi Seconde*? I trusted you above all others."

The seer made a noise in the back of his throat that was as much an anguished sob as it was a sarcastic laugh. "You never trusted me. I was a tool. A convenience. And nothing else."

Mirana pulled deep within herself, willing out her Healing Aspect through the broken diamond, flooding Ashtar with her power.

Tetric reached down with his hand. "The horse's life is forfeit. Do not make yours so as well."

She tugged again on the warhorse's reins as the animal tried to rise.

The Defending Aspect. Warning.

She screamed and rolled away just as the Dark Trine's long sword swept down, slicing across the horse's neck. Ashtar shuddered then lay still.

Emptiness.

A rhapsody of a life ended in mid-refrain.

"ASHTAR!!"

He was more than an animal, more than a horse. He had saved her life when nothing else could. Now he was dead.

… It is over… Come…

Slowly, inexorably, the love for her horse—no, her protector, her friend—was replaced by the only emotion just as strong.

Mirana held her amulet, infusing it with her fury, and locked her gaze on Tetric. "You are damned right. It *is* over."

The Defending Aspect exploded from the diamond. A jet of pure white flame arched unerringly for the tall Trine's hematite crystal, the force of the blow sending him flying from his saddle into the rock wall.

"You will not have the keep nor Kinderra." Mirana loosed another volley of amulet fire, sending ice and rock crashing down. A tendril of light peeled off from the blaze and curled back on itself, striking Sido's amulet. The seer cried and fell from his horse. "Sido!"

Tetric threw his arms wide and hurled the avalanche away before it could crush him.

The staccato sound of hoofbeats reverberated around the pass. Amulet fire—blue, red, yellow—curved around the rock walls. The Trine spun to avoid three different beams of deadly light.

"Damn you, girl!" Sido heaved himself up from the icy path. "Do you not understand by now I'm trying to help you?"

Her anger had made her forget the broken amulet's fatal flaw. "I didn't attack you, I swear it." She steadied him. "You go. I need to save Ashtar."

"Your horse is dead. We are not, and I intend to keep it that way." He swung back up onto his mount and dragged her over his saddle in front of him. He stabbed at his horse's flanks with his heels and drove hard toward the open expanse of the glacierfield.

Moonlight shone on the snow, lighting the path they had made during their crossing but leaving them exposed. The seer slowed his horse so as not to ride off the path and into the crevasse a handsbreadth away.

Mirana stole a glance behind them. Out of the shadows of the pass's mouth emerged a stallion as black as the midnight sky. A creaking sigh rolled across the icefield.

Behind her, the seer groaned softly as he fell forward against her back. "Sido?" The edges of a fissure next to them pulled together and closed the seam. The seer's arms about her fell slack.

By the Light! Tetric was draining Sido's life from him to feed his Aspects and melt the glacier cracks and pits back together. With the path they had made now hidden, they would fall to their deaths.

"You! Will! Not! Have him!" She turned in the saddle and grabbed her amulet with one hand, holding the thoroughbred's reins with the other. Light, white and hot, shot from her amulet toward the Dark Trine pounding across the glacier behind them. She fought the amulet fire's urge to fracture and concentrated her will on the dark figure closing the distance between them.

Sido cried out as his breath and vitality returned. She caught an intent of thanks as he urged his mount onward.

"He's right behind—" The Seeing Aspect welled up in her, urgent, stealing her breath. The path disappeared from her mortal eyes.

Three dozen Trak-Calanders. Riding. And falling.

"No! It's not us! It's the Fal'kin he's going to kill!" she shouted over the hoofbeats of Sido's steed. "We have to warn them about the glacier path."

As they re-entered the narrow channel of the Darbinh Pass, she pulled the sleek thoroughbred's reins, dragging its head around.

"What in the hell are you doing?" Sido yelled.

The Dark Trine rode across the glacierfield like a wraith from the Underworld. Before his Aspects, the crevasse healed with a thin skin of icy snow like a closing wound. He slowed his gallop and turned around to face the oncoming Fal'kin.

… Retreat! … Pull back! … Pull back! … Mirana called to the defenders.

The Trak-Calanders charged across the bright moonlit expanse toward the solitary, still figure of the Dark Trine. One, two, four, five riders fell through the seemingly whole ice. Some pulled back hard on the reins of their mounts, but their comrades came from behind them at full charge and could not stop. They disappeared into the deadly crevasse, a tidal wave of men and women and horses, breaking through the thin crust of snow and ice.

Mirana gasped as lifenotes erased themselves into a sickening quiet. "No!"

Sido cursed. He pitched a large stone at a snowy overhang across the pass from them. Snow and granite gave way, crashing down to block the pass behind them.

Tetric would be slowed but not stopped. Nothing would stop him now except death itself.

Mirana's Trine Aspects told her so.

CHAPTER 18

"Thou art my Beloved. Thou art my fourth Aspect. The Aspect of Love."
—The Codex of Jasal the Great

Mirana and Sido raced through the forests of Kana-Akün on the seer's thoroughbred, leaving the frigid Dar-Calan Mountains behind them. Tetric Garis's presence had disappeared from the Aspects. He no longer called her to come back to his side, to be his daughter. He no longer reached out for her, willing her to hold fast to her courage. He was just…gone. She was dead to him now. He would now try to make that expression real. That didn't worry her. It terrified her.

She guarded herself under the cloak of U'Nehíl with all her Aspects. They had to get to Deren. She had to warn her parents. She had to choose the keep. She had to stop Tetric from committing more of his chilling brand of benevolent evil. Somehow.

Day and night blended into one long expanse of time as she fled from the Dark Trine with the Ken'nar seer. Exhaustion and fear gnawed at her. She could not sense Sido's emotions—he had hidden his presence as tightly as she had—but he held fear in his eyes as his gaze darted around the forest. Tension knotted his muscles against her body as they rode.

She supported the seer as best she could, strengthening him with her Healing Aspect when even his formidable endurance began to leave him. Using her Aspects to keep them both going and to remain hidden herself, however, cost her. More than once, the seer's arms around her alone saved her from slipping off the saddle.

At last, Sido reined his horse to a trot for a few paces and pulled it still.

Mirana looked around the forest for some danger. "Why are we stopping? He can't be far behind us."

He dismounted and steadied himself against a tree, grimacing. "My horse is tiring. He's nearly winded. We already lost one horse, and we cannot afford to lose another."

Mirana nodded as she slid from the saddle. She winced against sore muscles from the hard ride. "He is a brave one." She patted him and wiped the foamy sweat from his neck. Did the Ken'nar love their horses as much as the Fal'kin did? "What is his name?"

The seer took a quick sip from a waterskin. "He has no name. He answers to a call."

She grabbed the skin from Sido. "For Aspects' Sake, give the damn beast a name. He deserves that much." Ashtar. She exhaled and shook her head.

He took back the skin and squeezed it, watering his horse. "I am sorry about Ashtar. He was very brave."

She nodded in acceptance. She would mourn the death of that beautiful beast—and everything and everyone else—someday. But not now.

"And I'm sorry about that amulet strike. I wasn't even aiming for you." She rubbed her eyes and kept them shut. She missed home. And safety. And food. Her mother and father. Teague. "You figured it out before I did back at the Caladazh learning hall. The amulet longs for its other half. It reaches out for any other crystal to make itself whole once more."

"Well, don't do that again." He rubbed his chest. "It hurt." He handed her back the waterskin, but a corner of his scarred mouth tugged upward.

Mirana returned his smile. "I am sorry. I truly don't want to hurt you." She toyed with the skin. "Your seer's ploy back in Caladazh. That came from Within. As did crossing the glacier and a dozen other little actions you didn't think I'd notice."

He crouched down to study the ground in the tree-filtered sunlight. "The ground is still damp from the rain. The pine needles will cover our tracks. We won't be as lucky by the time we reach the open plains."

She held the skin and waited for him to think of a real reply.

Now he exhaled. "You asked me to try. So I did."

She smiled. "*Gratas.*"

He rose slowly and pretended to study something on a tree. "For saving your life?"

"*Ai.*" She smiled wider. "And for saving yours."

His hand went to his amulet as he peered through the forest. "You are an annoying pain in a grynwen's ass."

She laughed, grateful for some of the tension easing between them. "And I think you know exactly what that's like—"

The Defending Aspect whispered a warning to her. *Lives. Approaching.*

"Ken'nar." Sido stiffened. The sound of hoofbeats dulled by the pine needles on the forest floor thudded through the forest.

She reached out with her Aspects. "Ken'nar? But Falantir is days north of us."

"Garis has twenty thousand hidden in these woods."

"Twenty—? When you first told me that, I thought you were just exaggerating to frighten me. You're serious?"

"He has been building his armies for a long, long time." He reached for the horse's reins and motioned to her, their conversation abandoned in the urgency to stay alive. "Garis has likely warned some of the commanders about us. Come. We have stayed here too long."

She and Sido charged southward. Out from the dense forest, a rider dressed in a simple linen shirt and breeches cut across their path on a sparely built gray filly. The palfrey reared to avoid colliding with the seer's mount, throwing her rider to the ground. Two black-armored Ken'nar quickly surrounded them. She ignored the armorless rider and kept her focus on the Ken'nar and their blades.

One of the Ken'nar drew closer. "Mirana?"

The Ken'nar sounded like Morgan Jord. That was impossible. Unless he had been harvested. She gripped her amulet. "Let us pass, or I'll turn you all into ash before you can even think of attacking us." Behind her, Sido's sword sang as it left his scabbard.

"Miri?"

Mirana looked down at the fallen rider.

She could not speak, she could not even breathe. He was alive. He was real. Disbelief, longing, guilt, sorrow, hope, love, and a thousand more emotions collided within her to merge as a single, nameless ache.

Teague.

She slipped from the saddle as he climbed to his feet. Teague stood before her. He had changed. *Ai*, he was taller, his hair had grown longer, his jaw more chiseled, his shoulders broader, more muscled. But those were superficial changes. He had changed within too. From pain, from loss, from sacrifice. From her words. Pain had written its indelible epitaph on his soul. It had torn away what had been left of his innocence. Pain had tempered him like steel. She had left him a sixteen-summers-old boy. What stood before her now was a sixteen-summers-old man.

Pain had wrought its cruel forging on her as well. Death—witnessing death at others' hands, death at her own hands, death of her own innocence and trust—and the painful understanding it brought had torn her asunder and forced her to fashion herself into something new. Something perfectly imperfect. Broken yet unbreakable. Half a diamond but diamond-hard nonetheless.

"*Ëi ama*," Teague whispered. Tears shimmered in his eyes. He was not the same. But he was alive. He was real. He was now.

Mirana rushed over to him, and he gathered her into his arms, kissing her fiercely. She drank in his love, letting it fill her. His breath became her air. His heartbeat, her life. His essence, her life song. She would never let go of him again. He was her love. He *was* love.

He was her fourth Aspect, the Aspect of Love.

"I am so sorry," she cried, laughing and kissing him all at once. "I was so afraid you'd be killed because of me. I thought pushing you out of my heart would save your life."

"I know, I know. And I don't care." He held her face in his hands. "I was a fool. I should have realized all that sooner. I should have never left you. Whatever danger you must face, we will face it together. I want to. It's my decision to, whatever the cost. I will never leave you again. I swear it." He pulled her to him again and covered her mouth with his.

A sharp pang of emotion cut through Mirana's mind. She parted from Teague to catch Sido's gaze. "I—" She bit her lip, and the seer lowered his head. There was nothing more to be said about her love for Teague.

She turned back to Teague and reached up to caress the bruises on his face, her hand soothing away his injuries, Jasal's amulet illuminating them both with her Healer's Aspect.

The other two warriors dismounted and removed their helmets.

"Binthe! Morgan!" She ran to them and cried in the tangled embrace of their arms.

"Miri. Thank the Aspects you're safe, *Ëi íuven siba*," Binthe said.

"My parents. Are they—?"

The seer smiled amid her tears. "They're fine. They should be in Deren by now."

Morgan released her to hold his amulet. "Where is Ashtar? Why do you ride with this cur? If he has hurt you—"

"Morgan, he is with me. Ashtar is—" She took a breath. Later. "Tetric Garis is the Dark Trine."

He pulled her behind him. "And this grynwen's spawn is Tetric Garis's second."

Sido's sword remained in his hand, but his eyes shifted between Mirana and Teague. "At ease, Defender. She is in no danger from me."

"Morgan, stop. Sido is with me. He and I were both deceived by Tetric Garis. We all were."

Teague took her hand. "We know. Now."

"We must get to Deren and tell my parents Garis is the Dark Trine before he attacks."

"And bring this pig's *excra* into our very Quorum chambers?" The defender pointed to the Ken'nar with his sword.

She walked over to the seer and pulled him to the group. "Sido may be the best defense Deren has. He knows Tetric's forces, resources, tactics."

Teague eyed Sido warily. "It may already be too late."

"What do you mean?" she asked, scowling.

Binthe frowned. "He may already be on the march. We just came from Falantir. I think your warlord commanders"—she indicated Sido with her chin—"gave the order to move out."

Mirana bit her lower lip and snapped her head around to the south, toward Deren. "No. We need more time to get home." She held Binthe's arm, the diamond amulet shining brilliantly. "All the primes and their seconds."

Binthe's face blanched.

"The Dark Trine will have all the heads of the provinces trapped." Teague frowned.

Morgan squeezed his eyes shut. "At Quorum."

"Holding them hostage." Mirana put her hands to her mouth and squeezed her eyes shut.

Father. Mother.

Sido stepped from the group. He, too, now faced south toward Deren. "They will have no choice but to name Garis Primus Magne. They will be forced to elevate him, or he will kill them. If they resist, he will slay them, and every province will be left leaderless."

The Trine Prophecy. Mirana raked her fingers through her hair. O Aspects Above. "'The chosen shall be like a ship without a keel.'" She took a shuddering breath as the insidious genius of her *patrua*'s plan continued to unfold in her mind. "If I try to call to my mother or father from here, Tetric will hear me. He'll kill them." And most likely her, too. She gripped her amulet.

"Do not lose hope so soon," Morgan said. "Your mother and father are not so easily fooled, nor so easily bested in combat."

"They cannot fight this." She waved her hand behind them, indicating the army that still lay hidden somewhere in the forest.

She should not have left Caladazh. She should have remained until Tetric was dead. Or she was. Mirana covered her eyes with her hand. "What have I done?"

Teague enveloped her in his arms. "*Ama*, you are as much a victim as any of us, perhaps his greatest. Garis only allowed you to see what he wanted you to see. But he hasn't won yet."

"We can make for Deren ahead of the main legion of his army if we hurry," Sido said.

Mirana nodded wearily. "I suppose five do move faster than twenty thousand."

"*Twenty thousand?*" Teague and the Fal'kin cried in shock simultaneously.

The Ken'nar seer pursed his lips. "Give or take."

Mirana rubbed at her face. Teague was wrong. She was not a victim. A victim was powerless. She could give in to her sins, her indecision and hopelessness, her weakness. Or not. She had three Aspects. And the determination to do good with whatever time she had left. She was no one's victim, not even to herself. Not any longer.

"We'll beat them back with Jasal's Keep," she said.

Morgan scowled. "The keep?"

"Jasal's Keep is made up of amulets. Thousands of them. It is a weapon of the Aspects Above themselves."

Sido finally sheathed his sword. "The most powerful weapon ever built."

Binthe narrowed her eyes at the other seer. "But a Trine can choose any amulet. What is to prevent Tetric Garis from choosing the amulets within the keep?"

"This." Mirana lifted the half-diamond amulet from beneath her shirt. Teague and the Fal'kin looked at each other then back to her. "This is the Lock and the Key. It would be impossible for either a Fal'kin Trine or a Ken'nar Trine to choose every amulet in the keep. Jasal's amulet is the only way. It seeks completeness." She looked up into Teague's eyes and touched his peda blossom pendant as well. "Wholeness." He gathered her in his arms once more and kissed her. She held his face. "Get me to Deren."

"I'll get you there before the wind arrives."

"Nice." She laughed. "You've been practicing."

He swung up onto Bankin's saddle and then reached down to help her up. His arm encircled her waist as she settled in front of him.

"You four go on ahead," Sido said. He held the thoroughbred's reins. "Maybe I can do something with them." He pointed a thumb behind him to indicate the remaining Ken'nar horde.

Mirana bit her lip and turned in the saddle. "You'll be killed. You just said Tetric has warned his leadership of your—our treason."

"I said he *probably* did." He made no move to mount up.

"Come. Please. We need you. Deren needs you."

"Do you?" His gaze shifted to Teague. "Now?"

"More than ever," Mirana replied with a smile.

"I'm going to regret this, aren't I?" The seer swung up into the saddle and tapped at his horse's sides with his heels.

"Hopefully," Teague answered. "I'm sure you deserve it."

Mirana flattened her smile. This was going to be a long, long ride.

CHAPTER 19

"They will be their own undoing!"
—The Codex of Jasal the Great

Tetric Garis traveled up the road to Deren's gates, letting his black stallion pick its own pace. Leaden skies thickened and lowered above a chill wind foretelling the change of seasons. It was too cold for this early in Tenthmonth.

Music carried outside of the gates from the festival pavilions interwoven with the murmur of crowds. Children laughed and ran through the revelers.

A gust of wind blew, fanning Tetric's black cloak out behind him. Deren's great gates, built by Jasal Pinal himself, stood wide open, beckoning all to enter. It was as much a gesture to the peace for the season as it was a practicality. Thousands from across the continent streamed into the citadel. Thousands. He smiled as he rode through.

So many people filled the streets, he could hardly ride his horse through the crowds. The Unaspected dressed in their finest. The Fal'kin's uniforms shone in rainbow colors, the heraldics of their provinces emblazoned proudly on their tunics. Most laughed and sang, enjoying the festival, setting aside the horrors, fears, and trauma of war for a time. Some talked and argued; politics had always been a part of the Quorumtide pageantry. Others danced and flipped coins to street minstrels and mummers. Many, however, walked silently, slowly toward the learning hall.

He smiled. Quorumtide.

From side streets and alley shadows, a handful of men and women emerged wearing the black and argent griffin of Dar-Azûl province. They nodded to him, and he returned the respect. Ah, these. *Ai*, these were some of his finest. Aspects Above knew he needed no bodyguards, but it wouldn't do for the Trine of Kinderra to arrive for Quorumtide without honor guards. It was thoroughly ridiculous, but the people of Kinderra expected such shows of fealty to a man such as he.

He hadn't celebrated Quorumtide in Deren often as a child—Caladazh in Trak-Calan was much too far to come with each change in the Reckoning—but he did remember those times he had. Oh, the spectacle. The minstrels playing in the city squares. The puppeteers making him and Koben laugh even though they did not understand most of the ribald humor. Vendors in the market stalls selling wares from Kinderra's farthest provinces, delicacies and trinkets beyond even his ferociously active imagination.

And the banquets. He and Koben were allowed to attend the feasts, an honor accorded as sons of Shalas Yutan, the Seer Prime of Trak-Calan. His mouth watered at the memory. Roast meats done to a turn. Poultry steeped in milk then reclothed in plumage made from glazed fruit and slivers of almonds. Venison made succulent by some Unaspected magic the kitchens of Trak-Calan surely did not practice on its goat meat. Even salted fish from the oceans was made tender and flaky again.

He and Koben had been strongly admonished by Shalas before the banquets to be on their best behavior, that attending the feasts and the dance pavanes afterward was a privilege, especially for such young boys. And when their behavior was more like that of the young boys they were? A disappointed expression in Shalas's eyes was more crushing than any scolding.

Tetric smiled at the memories, both pleasant and poignant.

A squeal of joy from a little girl momentarily broke through his thoughts. The child, a multitude of tiny, black braids bouncing as she jumped, clapped her hands before receiving a rag doll from her mother and father. Tetric's smile grew. He pulled the stiletto from his belt.

There was not a child who had ever lived that did not become breathless with the expectation of a Quorumtide gift, and he had been no exception. On the eve of the convocation of the Quorum of Light, Shalas had presented him with his first knife. He was eight summers old. The blade was exquisite, a thin stiletto longer than his palm as a child, forged hard from Tash-Hamari steel, the handle made of exotic ebony wood from Jad-Anüna and inlaid with pearl from far-off Rün-Taran. Shalas had told him it represented all the blessings of Kinderra in one instrument, just as he, a Trine, was all the blessings of the Aspects Above. But with something so precious, Shalas had cautioned, came great responsibility. As a Trine, he, too, had a great responsibility for his Aspects. Neither was to be used without purpose.

Tetric shoved the ebony-and-pearl stiletto back into his belt.

The Quorumtide he'd attended when he was fifteen summers, however, still made his heart race with excitement and bitterness in equal measure. That was when he had seen her for the first time. Hair the color of flame. Eyes greener than any emerald. Her skin so fair and flawless it seemed to be crafted of the same marble of the statues in Deren's library he hid behind as he spied on her. She was so utterly different, so thoroughly intoxicating, from the people of Trak-Calan with whom he lived. She was the daughter of one of Healer Prime Belessa Tir's high-ranking Kana-Akün defenders. Because of her status, she, too, was allowed into the feasts and pavanes within the learning hall.

Cerise.

The Quorumtide dances, seemingly so ridiculous when he was a small boy, suddenly became the most important part of the celebration. He had sworn to his fifteen-summer-old self he would not leave Deren until he danced with her. He had searched for her, only to learn she had left the festivities early with others from Kana-Akün. Seers had had visions of Ken'nar attacking the northern borders of their province. He had been furious. It would be summers before he saw her again.

He had been broken when he arrived in Falantir in Kana-Akün. He desperately needed help and understanding of the powers that raged within him. Belessa Tir had been the only person left in Kinderra to whom he could possibly turn. That was until he met Cerise again. With Belessa he found knowledge. But with Cerise, he found understanding and acceptance—and so much more. He had shared everything with her, as she did him. His mind, his body, his soul. His love. And his belief in the sanctity of the Power from Without.

For summers, she had watched the Ken'nar cut down her Fal'kin comrades. Her five brothers and father had all been slaughtered on the battlefield. Grief over their deaths had turned her seer mother into an empty shell. His beloved had told him the Power from Without was an abomination to her, but it was the only way she felt vindicated from so much loss the Light from Within had failed to protect. She had planted trees in ever-expanding rings in the thickets outside of the Falantir learning hall, one for each life she took with the Power from Without, giving life back in recompense.

When Belessa Tir finally had discovered Cerise's secret, she stripped her of her amulet and expelled her from the province. Rather than be separated from her duty, from her people, cut off from her Aspect, Cerise had taken her own life. He found his beloved just as she fell on her sword. Not his Healing Aspect, not even all three of his Aspects, could bring her back.

Tetric smiled again.

He had worshipped Belessa—she had helped him unlock the deepest powers of his Healing Aspect—but the healer prime had not told him about Cerise's sentence until it was too late. In the end, he saw to it that Belessa gave him lives back, harvesting the minds of Fal'kin until it killed her. *Ai*, she was dead now; he no longer sensed her presence among the living when he searched for it. He still wasn't sure the woman had paid enough of a price.

All of that was so long ago, Cerise might have belonged to a different man. Cerise—Shalas, Eshe and Lindar, Koben, and *ai*, Belessa—were gone, lost to him, sacrificed, like so very many things.

Anger welled up in him now. What father would bring his daughter back home closer to war instead of leaving her safe, hundreds of leagues away from harm, as Cerise's father had? What father would lie to his daughter about the miracle of her Aspects, driving her to attempt to take her own life?

Tetric held his amulet, the one Mirana once had held and saved lives with. The one she had fractured.

He had saved Mirana's life, and instead of using her life to accept her role as a Trine with greater understanding, she chose to betray him. Betray her love as a child given to him by the Aspects Above.

Mirana Pinal chose to cut herself off from the fullness of the Aspects. From him. She chose to cling instead to the lie that was the Light from Within, that its limitations somehow made it more sacred.

He had made his own choices as well. Kinderra came first, as it must. As it always had. That fact, however, did not make his choices easier. No, it made them all the more painful.

Was there still time? Was there still hope?

Quorumtide celebrated the miracle of Kinderra's harvest as much as it did the confederation of provinces. Out of the earth, left for dead by winter, arose a bounty that fed all. Would Mirana finally understand that his harvest of Aspected was the most important one ever pulled from Kinderra's soil?

He had spent so much of himself—physically, mentally, spiritually—to remake those who would have been lost needlessly. They had pledged their lives in service to Kinderra, understanding and accepting the ultimate sacrifice that was an indelible part of being an Aspected. Through him, they remained in union with the Aspects Above and Kinderra, and would continue to do so when it came time for him to take up his destiny as Trine of Kinderra.

He did not want death, not even for his enemies. Death sickened him with its soul-silencing emptiness. No, he wanted life. To preserve it, he would sacrifice anything but Kinderra itself.

An old Unaspected woman reached up to him, calling his name as he and his honor guard rode through Deren. He briefly held her hand. Soon others, dozens, hundreds rushed over, Unaspected and Fal'kin, calling out to him, wanting some favor from him.

He had come to Deren not to be adored by the crowds, but to ensure its freedom. Their laud was necessary to rebuild the land.

His eye caught a group of men dressed in the heraldic of Kana-Akün. One nodded. He did not return the gesture, but he noted it just the same.

He would ensure the freedom of Kinderra by force if necessary. That, however, depended on the Quorum of Light.

Tetric lifted his head as he let his horse pick its way through the masses packing Deren's streets. The ponderous edifice of the learning hall loomed ahead. The massive, rambling structure had frightened him as a small child. But as enormous as the learning hall was, it was nothing but stone and wood. It was built by mortals, for mortals. When buildings no longer served the purpose for which they were created, they would be reconstructed to adapt. Or torn down completely. The learning hall was fallible. Everything was. Everything except for the Aspects Above.

Kaarl Pinal, however, stood as the keystone. *Ai*, Desde Kellis was prime and could see things many other seers could not, but she did not hold the hearts of the provinces the way her husband did. Many detested Pinal for his tainted heritage, but not a man nor woman on the continent could deny his courage and integrity. They all owed something to him, the safety of their province, their Fal'kin. They may hate his legacy, but they trusted the man.

Kaarl Pinal and the Quorum of Light would stand with Tetric, make him Prime Magne. Or they would not.

He did not bother calling to his Seeing Aspect to glimpse the future as it would have no bearing on his actions. He would do whatever was necessary.

Mirana must understand that a sacrifice of this magnitude might be necessary to bring peace to Kinderra. When both the Fal'kin and the Ken'nar were united under his amulet, the war would end. Immediately. Was that not worth this sacrifice?

Tetric raised his eyes toward the featureless gray sky. Jasal's Keep soared above Deren, its pinnacle as faint as a wraith behind the cold, damp fog. Sheltered halfway between its base and its pinnacle sat the chamber of the Quorum of Light itself. They would be there already, waiting for him.

Some would never believe in him, never accept him, no matter what words he chose or how much of his own blood he spilled. They were the true enemies of peace. Not the Ken'nar. Not the Fal'kin. Those who did not believe why and how he would end the war that had scarred Kinderra for three thousand summers—they were the dark ones. Not he.

She had called him evil. She accused him of betrayal. It was *she*, however, who betrayed *him*.

His amulet glowed with the rise in his Defending Aspect. The throng around him gave a hushed murmur. The amulets of the Fal'kin called out to him, each one touching his heart, his Aspects. This time, he savored the sensation instead of walling himself off from it. Would it be like this but even more glorious? Would it be like this when he chose the keep?

She would give him the amulet. They had both seen it. Jasal's amulet was the key. To have a cleaved amulet would create such an insatiable need to be whole, it would draw everything from him.

This was why the Power from Without was necessary. It was more than necessary. It was the only power that could be used. To use only the Light from Within would kill her. There simply could not be enough power within a mortal to choose all those amulets. The very power that she turned her back on was the very power that would save Kinderra.

If she would not use her Aspects in service to Kinderra, she was no better than an Unaspected. No. She was worse, far worse. She was anathema. She was a cancer within the Aspects, one that only he could excise. She was the embodiment of the most grievous sin one could commit. A single philosophy on the Aspects had no place in Kinderra. All paths must be accepted. His new Kinderra would hold no room for her lack of belief.

He could not feel her presence anymore—she was far too skilled in cloaking herself under U'Nehíl—but he knew she would come. Soon. His Seeing Aspect told him so. He had reached Deren ahead of her. The autumn rains had begun, and he had means of crossing the swollen Garnath River that she did not. The strong current had slowed her down. He wished the river had stopped her altogether. He had prayed it had. But she was determined to reach Deren. He knew of her indomitable determination. He had forged it within her, diamond hard.

A man rushed over, carrying a young boy in his arms. The child's hand was badly deformed. The man begged him for his Healing grace. If he did not do something, the boy would grow to be a cripple. Unable to ply a trade, he would not be able to feed himself. The child would die a beggar in the streets.

Tetric slowed his horse. He took the child's hand in his own, placing his other hand on his amulet. The boy's arm was encased in a silvery black light. Long moments later, he released the child. The boy and his father looked at the limb in wonder as he flexed it. The hand was made whole. The man sank to his knees, clutching his child to him, weeping.

Tetric smiled.

Mirana held Jasal Pinal's amulet, the key to his keep. Jasal's Keep was the key to peace. If she would not give him the key, if she stood in the way of peace, he would make whatever sacrifice was necessary. Even if that sacrifice was Mirana herself.

CHAPTER 20

"I am but Their humble carpenter; They are the Architect."
—The Codex of Jasal the Great

Kaarl tossed down a stack of parchment sheets on his wife's desk, sending up a small cloud of dust. He wiped his face with both hands and let his forearms fall heavily upon the desk. The chain mail he wore under his formal tunic made the action louder than he intended and left small, half-circle impressions in the wood.

"If I ever doubted my service as a defender, these parliamentary procedure covenants have proven to me my amulet is held in the right Aspect. How did your father ever wade through this morass every day?"

Desde stood in front of the window in her study. "I don't know. It numbs my mind, too, but he loved it."

He rose from her chair to stand behind her, wrapping his arms around her. She looked stunning, radiant in a gown made of cream silk shot through with gold threads nearly the color of her hair. Delicate embroidered red eagles decorated the neckline, giving it the appearance of a ruby necklace. Her bodice was tied tight, hiding her breasts yet hinting at them. The tiny eagles rose and fell slightly as she breathed. He yearned to return to their chambers where he could set those eagles free instead of heading the Quorum meeting.

… Have you heard anything from her? …

She shook her head.

People filled the streets of Deren as they celebrated by the market tents and performance stages. The learning hall itself was a beehive of activity as the primes, their seconds, and their entourages arrived for the Quorum meeting. In the courtyard below, people laughed, filled with the spirit of the season. Acquaintances from different provinces shouted to each other, renewing friendships. He longed to be down there with Desde and Mirana, content to be together with his family once again. Safe.

Rain had begun to fall, pattering gently on the leaded window. Desde traced a tearlike rivulet with a finger as it ran down the outside of the glass.

He moved from behind his wife to stand next to her. "It's cold. Too cold for so early in Tenthmonth."

"*Ai.* But at least we are finally getting some rain. It will be good for the soil."

"I'm sure you're right." After the parching summer heat and the Unaspected who had gone off to war with them, there had been few to work the fields. The winter would be a lean one. What good would nourishing rain do now?

The Quorum of Light had always been a time for celebration, but they did not have much to celebrate this time. It had been sevendays since Teague, Morgan, and Binthe went into the Kana-Akün province, and he had heard nothing from them. He could only hope his friends were on their return. He steadfastly refused to ask Desde to see what had befallen them. If she knew something, she would have told him by now.

When he was the il'Kin commander, Kaarl had looked forward to Quorumtide. Skirmishes with the Ken'nar were incessant, but the coming winter snows kept major hostilities at bay for months. The sevenday-long celebration was a time of rest for his battle-weary troops.

"Do you think we did the right thing still holding Quorumtide?" Desde asked softly as if she didn't want to voice her doubt.

"I think the point is rather moot." Kaarl indicated with a nod the Fal'kin and Unaspected laughing and milling about in the courtyard below.

… I want a real answer …

"*Ama*." He held her once more. "Do I have concerns for everyone's safety? Ai. But the importance of meeting with the primes to discuss a collaborative strategy against the Dark Trine's army cannot be overstated." He pressed his lips into her hair.

Quorumtide had been a time he cherished spending with his family when he could live as a man once more, not as a murderer uniformed in self-righteousness. Family.

Mirana.

He missed her so much, it was a visceral ache. Damn Tetric Garis. No, damn himself.

He should have gone after Mirana when she left them at Two Rivers Ford. Instead, he entrusted her to a man he hated.

Now he knew he had put her in the hands of the Dark Trine himself, the very monster from which he had sought to save her. He had no proof that Tetric Garis was the Dark Trine except for the conviction of his Aspect, but he knew.

He was no longer the il'Kin commander anymore. The il'Kin were gone. He was the Steward of the Quorum of Light, both the most powerful and least powerful man in Kinderra. Tetric Garis would try to convince the primes and seconds that the only way to save the land would be unification under him as Primus Magne. Kaarl would try just as hard to convince them not to support the Trine.

Damn himself.

The scene below grew blurry.

Kaarl rubbed his eyes. It was not long past noon, but he felt as though he had already battled the whole day away.

… Toban, why in all the Aspects did you name me your successor? …

"Because you are the best man for the role." Desde slipped her arm around his waist, straightening the Kin-Deren red eagle on the saffron-gold field of his uniform with her other hand.

He gave her a tender kiss on the forehead. "I wish I could believe you."

"You must be strong today. The shadow I've sensed has grown. I fear this meeting will be a difficult one. Even," she paused, "a dangerous one."

"I, too, have sensed things will not go well."

She blinked, considering his words for a moment. "The skeins of time have woven themselves much more tightly for you to also have seen."

"I only sense a foreboding danger." He smiled tightly. "But nothing about her."

She sank into her chair. "I just wish she were here." She swallowed loudly and shook her head.

… You would know if something happened to her … I would know … Those were the words he told his wife to keep her from breaking down.

… What if we are right about Tetric? …

… She is more important to him as an ally … He would not dare harm her … Those were the words he told himself.

"What if she is no longer his ally? The prophecy, Kaarl. He will not let her live."

He pounded his fist on the windowsill, the panes rattling in their lead caming. "Then I will kill him. I will call him the traitor he is, and I will kill him."

"No." Desde rushed over to him. "If you openly accuse Tetric Garis of being the Dark Trine, you will be the hated one. That will only serve to strengthen his hold on the other primes. We must play his game."

"Play his game? Desde, how can you even suggest such a thing? I will make this easier for all of us." He drew his sword. "I will block his vote."

"No, Kaarl. You must not. If he is the Dark Trine and you confront him, he will kill her. You are Steward of the Quorum of Light. You hold the votes of those provinces that are not present. Liaonne has remained in Varn-Erdal. You will be her proxy vote."

He felt a spark of hope warm him. "And Kana-Akün."

She smiled.

"And the votes of their seconds, too?"

She shook her head. "Unfortunately, no, *Ëi ama*. There was many a time when my father asked for that ruling, but that would give too much power to the position. You get one *absentia* vote per absent province, my steward."

He frowned again. "I read as much." He gestured to the stack of moldering papers. "There was no harm in asking. But I do break a tie."

"*Ai*. If it should come to that. And you, of course, have Kin-Deren's vote."

"Well, I have at least three assured votes against the bastard."

"Maybe four?" Desde's smile turned into a worried frown. "If Mirana does arrive, I will name her as my Prime's Second. If she will consider it. If she will speak to us at all." She toyed with her amulet, but it remained dark. He understood. What seer parent would call to her Aspect and risk a vision of her child's death?

He held her again. "It's a start."

A soft knock on the door interrupted them. Kaarl made a small gesture with his hand and the door drifted open. "*Ai?*"

A young Fal'kin *scholaire* boy bobbed a bow. "My Steward, Lady Prime, the primes are assembling in the Quorum Chamber."

"And Lord Trine Garis?"

"*Ai*, sir."

"Is my daughter with him?"

The boy shook his head. "I have not seen her."

What was Tetric doing with her? Or had she run from him? Or were they denying the obvious because it was too impossible to comprehend?

"*Gratas*, lad."

The boy nodded once more and left.

"Come. It is time we see exactly what our Trine has planned for us."

Kaarl started to leave then paused, looking back out the window at a Fal'kin below. The man stood in the courtyard and spoke to no one. His face wore no expression. He wore the heraldic of Kin-Deren and bore a sword, but he did not recognize the defender.

"Desde?"

"*Ai?*"

"Bring a knife."

CHAPTER 21

"We do as we are called. We are the Chosen. We are Fal'kin."
—The Book of Kinderra

Mirana crouched low in the dead corn stalks a few miles north of Deren. Teague, Morgan, Binthe, and Sido knelt next to her. A cold, wind-driven drizzle had begun to fall. So many times, Tenthmonth remained warm and sunny, wringing the last of summer from the weather. Why couldn't she ever catch a break? She rubbed her hands together to warm them and ignored the discomfort. The rain might dampen the sound when they made their final dash to Deren.

"Sido, get the horses down," she hissed in a harsh whisper, motioning with her hand. The seer made a low noise and his thoroughbred immediately complied, folding its legs under. He pulled on the reins of the other horses, driving them down into the brittle husks.

She peered at the dark line of Ken'nar off to the west. It stretched on and on but held its position. She gritted her teeth, dread rising with her Defending Aspect. "Where are our troops? Why aren't they here?"

Morgan likewise watched the Ken'nar. "Your parents, Varn-Erdal, and Sün-Kasal were deciding where to position our armies before we left for Falantir." He cursed under his breath. "With his damnable rafts, the Dark Trine had an easier time making it across the Garnath River than we did."

Sido scowled. "This is all he's brought?"

"Like that isn't enough?" Teague replied, jabbing a thumb in the direction of the dark line.

"Defender, you were in the camps at Falantir more than I of late," Sido said to Morgan, ignoring Teague's comment. "Wouldn't you say they seem to be missing a good third of their complement?"

The defender's hand remained on his amulet. "Your Aspect's grasp of the obvious is most impressive, Seer." Sido smiled with contempt at Morgan's remark but said nothing. Mirana frowned at the men. "*Ai*, Rendel," Morgan replied. "I agree."

Binthe sucked in her breath, clutching her amulet. "I see another army. Four, maybe five thousand."

Mirana quickly grabbed her own amulet and snapped her eyes shut. "Sün-Kasal. A league north of Deren's gates." She smiled at the group. "The Ken'nar have no idea they're marching into a trap."

"Maybe not." Teague swallowed. "The Ken'nar are just standing there."

Sido's scowl deepened. "It's not the lack of advancement that bothers me but the lack of troops."

Teague screwed up his face in disgust. "What? Did the others stay at home to babysit the captured Fal'kin?"

Sido shook his head, his focus remaining on the dark army in the distance. "They should have all been harvested by now. We had two healers."

"You rackin' sonofabitch!" Teague snarled. "How dare you mention my mother." He pulled his arm back, ready to strike the seer.

Mirana winced at his flare of anger. "Teague! No!" She grabbed his arm.

The seer stepped closer to Teague, his hand nearing the knife in his belt. "Do you really want me to show you just how tired I am of you, herbsboy?"

"Stop it. Enough," Mirana hissed at the young men. The Seeing Aspect tickled at the back of her mind. Something Sido had said about the harvested Fal'kin. "Sido, what was Tetric planning to do with those he had harvested?" Her hand reached for her amulet.

He shrugged. "Stuffing them in the alloyed armor." The seer now gripped his amulet.

Teague laughed in objection. "Why make Ken'nar armor? Just use all the captured Fal'kin armor."

"What do you mean?" Mirana and Sido asked together.

All four Aspected now faced Teague. "All the, um, armor. Uniforms. The, ah—" He waved a hand in front of his chest. "The heraldics. Piled in the corners of the Falantir gathering hall. Hundreds. Thousands maybe." He glared at Sido. "You must have seen them. You lived there, for Aspects' sake."

Mirana turned to the seer. "You told me the captured Fal'kin were stripped of their uniforms to demoralize them. Why were they not burned? Or-or used as blankets or bandages or something?"

"The uniforms," Sido whispered in shock and held his pale-green amulet, light spilling from between his fingers. His gaze met Mirana's, the color draining from his face. "He kept them to reuse them."

Mirana brought her hands to her mouth and turned southward. "Oh, Aspects Above, no! 'They will be no defense against an enemy from within.'"

"Mirana?" Binthe laid a hand on her shoulder. "*Siba?*"

"It's an excerpt from Jasal Pinal's Codex, his journal. Deren's walls wouldn't be enough to protect the citadel from Ilrik the Black's forces. Because his Ken'nar were already inside the city."

"Wearing the captured Fal'kin uniforms," Sido and Teague replied together, with each frowning a moment later. Mirana suspected neither of the men wanted to acknowledge they were of a like mind.

"Rendel, I should have killed you when I had the chance," Morgan snapped. With a blur of movement, he drew his sword and moved on Sido, the seer answering with his own blade.

"I did not know this part of Garis's plan." Sido stepped back and sheathed his sword but kept his eyes on the defender. "He stopped trusting me a long time ago." He lifted his hands in acquiescence, facing Morgan. "Go ahead, Defender. Kill me. You'd be doing me a favor. And you'd get to know for the rest of your misbegotten life you murdered an innocent man." He pursed his lips. "Well, innocent of this particular crime."

Mirana turned to Binthe, who shook her head in hopelessness.

"To the problem at hand," Binthe said, clipping each word as with one of her long knives, and eyeing the three men. "If Sido is right, some of the Dark Trine's forces may already be in the city, maybe within the learning hall itself."

Mirana shifted position, peering through the corn stalks at the way ahead. "If we ride hard, we will be in Deren within the hour."

Sido gave a sharp laugh. "How do you intend to avoid alerting them to your presence?" He jutted his chin in the direction of the waiting Ken'nar host.

She now smiled, a genuine one. "A seer's ruse. It will be a little more difficult this time with the horses, but we have three seers."

He raised an eyebrow. "And just how is this ruse supposed to work?"

"I will cover Teague and Bankin. Binthe has Morgan and their horses. You have yourself and your horse. The ruse is simply reflecting through our amulets whatever you see around you. And a healthy shroud of U'Nehíl can't hurt."

Sido's brow remained arched. "Do both? At the same time?"

Mirana's smile faded. "Well—"

"We have no other choice," Binthe answered but shifted her uncertain gaze to Morgan.

Teague shook his head and turned toward Mirana. "And assuming we're not piles of greasy ash in the next few minutes, what should we do once we're inside the gates?"

She bit her lip. She had not gotten that far in her plan. "We, well, we'll get lost in the crowd. I must get to Jasal's Keep before Tetric does. We're wasting time. We've got to move now before it's too late. C'mon."

Sido commanded the horses to rise with a motion of his hand. "That's your plan, Mirana?" She shot him a hard look as she swung her leg over Bankin's saddle. The seer rolled his eyes. "Aspects Above save us. We're doomed."

CHAPTER 22

"Only in Their unmatched Wisdom could such a design be conceived."
—The Codex of Jasal the Great

Kaarl pushed past the other primes as they conversed in the circular Quorum chambers within Jasal's Keep to stand before Tetric Garis, brushing the pole of a provincial standard and setting it wobbling in his haste. "Where is she?"

The tall Trine shook his head slowly. "I do not know."

He clenched his teeth. "What do you mean you do not know? Where is Mirana?"

Tetric's expression turned flat, almost dead. His eyes were as black as coal, his pupils not even discernible from the color around them. "She has hidden under U'Nehîl."

The man was inhuman, and Kaarl intended to show all Kinderra that.

"You are a Trine. You can pierce the veil of U'Nehíl if you wish." He locked his gaze on Tetric's eyes. "I will ask you one last time. Where. Is. My daughter?"

"She has turned against me, Kaarl. She has turned against us both."

He sensed the Dar-Azûlan now spoke something nearer to the truth, but when he pushed closer into the Trine's mind, he found not only anger but despair. His own anger disappeared, to be replaced by something far more consuming.

He grabbed the straps on the Trine's pectoral armor. ... *What has happened? ... Where is she? ... Tell me now!* ...

Immediately, Tetric clamped down with his psychic protections, painfully blocking Kaarl's attempt to further read his thoughts. Kaarl's Defending Aspect rose tenfold.

The taller man made no move to pull out of his grip as profound sadness eminated from his mind. "We have lost her. She has chosen the way of war. It is up to me, and only me, to end this now. As it always has been."

Terror swelled within Kaarl's chest like a billowing storm cloud. The prophecy. *Light will be dark.* Mirana had been so terrified of her Trine powers she had hidden them. *Dark will be light.* The Dark Trine had stood in their midst for summers under the guise of a hero. *One will come forth, thrice-cursed, to destroy.* Tetric Garis had systematically brought down one province after another. *One will come forth, thrice-blessed, to rebuild.* Mirana would be his opposition.

But wait. If she had chosen the way of war, that meant his daughter had turned her back on the Trine, recanting whatever diseased beliefs he had foisted upon her. Pride and hope replaced some of his dread. *End and beginning in one, in both.* She would seek to kill Tetric Garis.

It replaced some of his fear. But not all.

Tetric Garis would seek to kill her.

He pulled the Trine close, their faces nearly touching. … *What have you done with her, Garis? …*

… *What has she done to me? …* Tetric tore Kaarl's hands from his armor, his words cutting like knives into his mind.

Every instinct, mortal and Aspected, begged him to cut down this monster that stood in front of him. Every moment he kept Tetric in the chambers, however, was another moment Mirana had to gather her strength to oppose the Trine. He had to keep the traitor here. When she came to confront him, she would not fight alone. If Kaarl had to give his last breath to atone for his deceit and help his daughter triumph, there was no sacrifice he was more eager to give.

"Kaarl? What is it?" Desde laid a hand on his arm. "Tetric, where is Mirana?"

"She has taken a different road to Deren, *Ama*," Kaarl replied. "She is coming." He gripped her hand. It was all the warning he could give her. "Take your seat. I will begin momentarily." With their daughter hidden under U'Nehíl, he had no way of finding her, no way of getting word to her. He had no choice but to wait.

His wife lightly touched his forearm, making a pretense of straightening the fabric of his shirt as he lowered himself into the steward's stone chair. … *You are lying to me …*

… *We must keep him here … For Mirana's sake …*

Her expression did not change as the color drained from her face. … *Representatives from most of the provinces are not here …*

He nodded. … *One must wonder why …* He needed at least one member from each province, nine in all, to be in attendance for any policy decision to be ratified.

But not to hold the meeting.

"I know there are troubles in Kana-Akün and Varn-Erdal, but no Rün-Taran?" Fasen Aldi, the Defender Prime of Tash-Hamar, noted. "Or Trak-Calan? Or Jad-Anüna?"

The prime's nephew, Defender Second Timir Sadhi, took the seat next to him. "Did they send messengers?"

"No," Kaarl replied. "Perhaps they were delayed in their journey. We will give them some more time. I will address Kana-Akün and Varn-Erdal in a moment. We have much to discuss anyway."

Tetric's vicious little gutter snake seer, Sido Rendel, was also missing. Apparently, the Trine was confident enough that he did not need the extra vote from his province of Dar-Azûl. That worried him. What games was Tetric going to play? Five present votes, if all went well. Five absentia votes. Ten votes. The fate of Kinderra hung on just ten votes.

Kaarl cleared his throat and sent a quick, silent intent to the Aspects Above. "Toban Kellis departed for the Aspects Above in Twelfthmonth of the last Reckoning. He left instruction that, at least for this Quorum, I would preside as the steward. The issues before us are far too distressing for pleasantries. For those who might not know, perhaps you would like to tell us what has befallen Kana-Akün, Lord Trine?"

Belessa Tir, Healer Prime of Kana-Akün, was old but immensely powerful. If there had been a way for her to make it to Deren, she would have. That was proof enough for Kaarl that she was dead. Now he'd make Tetric prove her death—along with so much else—to the rest of the primes and their seconds.

The tall Trine remained standing as the others settled into their seats. "Falantir fell to the Ken'nar last winter and has remained under their control since." His gaze shot over to Kaarl. "As witnessed by the il'Kin back in Thirdmonth." Kaarl returned the glare until Tetric averted his eyes. "Healer Prime

Belessa Tir was aged. It is doubtful she would have survived the conflict. Her seer second, Thieer Pannen, would have been useless to the Ken'nar. If he did not die in the fighting, he would have been executed outright. Their deaths, particularly Belessa's, are a tragedy. May the Aspects Above bless them with their presence."

Several Fal'kin gasped in shock. Kaarl tightened his jaw. Buried in those words, the man insinuated that Kaarl somehow had suppressed this information. The heat of his garnet amulet reflected against his chest. "It is indeed a tragedy. Kinderra now has no healers."

Fasen raised his hand to speak. "It is more than a tragedy given that Varn-Erdal was sacked. Half of the continent lies crippled."

Kaarl looked at the defender prime, confused.

Tetric, at last, took his seat, languidly crossing one long leg over the other. "I have taken the liberty of already informing everyone of the Two Rivers Ford campaign and the razing of Edara before you arrived."

Kaarl raised a brow. "And how did you know about Edara? I don't recall seeing anything of Dar-Azûl there."

The Trine lifted a corner of his mouth. "I can call to the Seeing Aspect. Among others."

Desde frowned. "*Gratas Oë*, Lord Trine, for your assistance." She turned slightly in her seat to face the rest of the Quorum members. "We sent the Ken'nar into retreat at Edara, but the damage was done. Liaonne Edaran has stayed with her people to help them recover and rebuild."

Sahm Klai, Defender Prime of Sün-Kasal, glowered at the group. "What of Trak-Calan or Rün-Taran? I expected the journey to be too difficult for Eshe this time, but Syne is a tough old dog. I would have thought he'd be here at least. Nambre

Dinir, however, probably didn't want to leave the warm sun of Jad-Anüna for this foul weather."

Fasen snorted a curt laugh. "I left my warm sun. This meeting is far too important."

"I think we are all aware that Two Rivers Ford was destroyed," Timir said, "but this news of Varn-Erdal is beyond disconcerting. The north lies virtually unprotected. I, too, wish Seer Primes Koben Ryotan and Eshe Paschot were here. Their vision would aid us greatly."

Rabb Plout, Sahm's seer second, sat rigid in his chair, not taking his eyes from Tetric. His ruddy topaz amulet brightened briefly then faded. "Where *is* Koben Ryotan, Lord Trine?"

"Am I expected to know the whereabouts of every Fal'kin in Kinderra? The autumn rains have come. Delays are to be expected."

Kaarl curled his hands into fists on the arms of the stone chair. No, Tetric was not expected to know the whereabouts of every Fal'kin. Just the ones he killed. He quashed any chance of Kaarl using those conflicts to convince the others to vote against the Trine's magnistate. Had Tetric already stacked the deck against him? Kaarl expected he'd have to work harder on Sahm Klai, but he hadn't been concerned about Fasen and Timir. He should have been.

"I am less concerned about the whereabouts of the other primes than I am someone else." Tetric's dark eyes rested on him. "As our interim steward said, the issues before us are distressing, one of which is his daughter. By now, many of you know that Mirana Pinal has been revealed as a Trine."

Kaarl's limbs tensed, and his hand ached for his sword. ... *Kaarl ... No ...* His wife's call speared into his mind as her hand gripped his forearm, begging him not to act just yet.

The Trine continued before he could answer. "And while this is a blessing beyond anything for which we could have hoped, apparently the girl had known for some time of her three Aspects and yet still refused to take up an amulet. She ran from Kin-Deren's Choosing Ceremony. She committed a capital crime in a most public way. We could not adjudicate her offense at the time as the attack on Two Rivers Ford was imminent, so I felt it was best to bring the matter here. Now."

Desde jumped to her feet. "My daughter was terrified of a vision that had plagued her for summers. She did not want her amulet or her Aspects to be manipulated by the Dark Trine."

Kaarl glared intently at Tetric. ... *That's why she left you, didn't she? ... She found out who you really are ...*

The Dar-Azûlan shook his head slowly, regret in his eyes as his gaze traveled around the room. "The Dark Trine. You refer to the thrice-cursed of the ancient Trine Prophecy. The one who would destroy Kinderra. Is that not truly what she feared in this vision of hers? The prophecy speaks of only two Trines. I sit before you, as I have for thirty summers. And none of you has any evidence of just who sits at the head of the Ken'nar, regardless of the narrow-minded euphemism you use. So what does that make our young Mirana? Was she terrified that she would turn into the Dark Trine of the Prophecy herself? Is that why she preferred committing a capital crime in full public view rather than doing her duty as an Aspected and choosing an amulet?"

Kaarl rushed out of his chair toward Tetric, blood coursing through his veins like liquid amulet fire. "How dare you?" The Trine remained unmoving in his chair.

Desde rose and grabbed his arm. "Kaarl! No! Please!"

He felt her anger melt into alarm along with his own. "Tetric, you promised me this Quorum would judge her fairly," he said. "For that, she needs to give her testimony. We cannot decide what, if any, punishment she should receive until she can speak for herself."

"Prime Kellis Pinal," Tetric began, ignoring Kaarl, "you gave her to me as my *scholaira,* so her fate rests in my hands now. Not yours. I do not even have to bring it before the Quorum." He slowly turned his head to face Kaarl. "I only do so out of respect to you."

"Tetric, please," Desde whispered. "Not my daughter. You promised me you'd keep her safe."

"And I did while she remained under my protection. But she has left me." He looked once again at Kaarl. "Which is why she is not here to speak on her own behalf. I cannot guarantee anything now."

Kaarl's hand drifted to his amulet.

… Do it, Pinal … Tetric's mind seared through his. *… Yours will be the first Fal'kin execution seen in Kinderra since before the Sundering … And your daughter will be no safer …*

Fasen now rose to his feet. "What in the blazes is going on here? The girl is truly a Trine? Kaarl, where is your daughter?"

His chest burned with the effort of holding back his Defending Aspect and not releasing every ounce of it into Tetric Garis's body. He clenched his fists so tightly, cuts from his nails bled his palms. "Ask the Trine."

"Tetric? Where is the girl?" the Tash-Hamari defender prime asked again.

"I do not know. She has run from me and is hidden under U'Nehîl. My Seeing Aspect has given me some sense that she approaches Deren."

Hope and fury warred within Kaarl as his wife grabbed his hand. "Why did she run from you?"

Tetric half-lidded his dark eyes. "You don't want to know." His voice dropped low in mock sympathy. "The answer would be far too painful for you."

Desde stifled a cry as she sank back into her chair. "Tell me what has happened to my daughter." Her hand trembled in his own.

The Trine surveyed the group for a moment before answering. "She used the Power from Without." He dropped his gaze to his lap. "And killed a man. An Unaspected."

Horrified gasps echoed around the room. Kaarl would have added his own if he were able to breathe. Desde's body slumped against his. He turned quickly to catch her before she could slip from her chair to the floor. No hellfire of the Underworld would burn hotter than that of his amulet when he finally released his vengeance upon the man.

… You bastard … She was terrified of becoming the Dark Trine … And that's exactly what you tried to turn her into … Just like you …

Tetric sat back in his chair, his eyes remaining locked on Kaarl's. "I am all but certain the man's death was purely accidental. And I am willing to completely exonerate her because I alone understand the terrible cost of wielding such power without a compassionate hand for guidance. Trines, however, serve all Kinderra, not just one province. So, even if I am her legal *patrua* of Dar-Azûl province, perhaps the Quorum's decision is indeed more appropriate.

"I do have to wonder, however," he continued, "just how a young Trine could have lived in our midst for summers and those closest to her did not even suspect the powers she held? If they had such knowledge, and knowingly withheld such a saving grace from Kinderra—that would be a crime of particularly heinous deviance. This Quorum would have no choice but to find such individuals guilty and sentence them to be relieved of their amulets and expelled. Immediately. Or, given the precarious state of affairs, perhaps a more final punishment should be meted out. But…" He settled deeper into his chair. "Did you not say we have other priorities, my steward? Perhaps we can table your daughter's fate. For the moment."

Kaarl stepped backward to his place at the table, stumbling and nearly falling into his seat, as understanding threatened to crush him. Their daughter might not be within the Quorum chambers, but she was still Tetric Garis's hostage. As were he and Desde.

Mirana could never have killed a man in cold blood with the Power from Without. She was either tricked or coerced or perhaps it truly was an accident, if not an outright lie. He knew his daughter. She was the Light Trine. He knew this with every fiber of his being.

If he did not support Tetric's bid for Primus Magne, the Trine would expose their hiding of Mirana's Aspects to the Quorum members. He and Desde—and their votes—would be immediately ousted from the Quorum. The Fal'kin would elevate Tetric to Primus Magne and unwittingly hand over Kinderra to the Dark Trine. He and his wife would not just be expelled, they would be executed. Tetric could then do to Mirana whatever he chose.

Kaarl frantically sought a way out of Tetric's trap. Whether he chose to support him or accuse him openly of being the Dark Trine, Kinderra would be lost. His beloved wife and his only child would be dead.

He gripped his amulet, and it warmed his palm, the Defending Aspect giving him strength, but it was useless at the moment. He would have to make words his weapons now. His own life meant nothing to him, but he would be damned if he would die before he saw his family safe and Kinderra rid of this monster.

"All of us know Mirana, and we all know it is inconceivable that she could commit such an act without some extenuating circumstance that goes far beyond the extraordinary—if such an act even truly happened," he said. "Her case will be tabled until we can hear the facts from her own lips." He pierced the Trine with a fierce gaze. The Dar-Azûlan held his tongue, but his dark eyes glittered with satisfaction.

"*Ai*, the situation has grown perilous, *Ëi cara'e*," Kaarl continued. "We believe the main host of the Dark Trine's army had been encamped in Kana-Akün and is on its way to march on Deren. We must stop him before he can move any farther south. It will take all of us working together to do so. Varn-Erdal and Kin-Deren herself do not have two hundred Fal'kin between them. You can no longer rely on them alone to protect the south."

Fasen shook his head and gave a sharp laugh. "Then your Fal'kin must sprout like mushrooms because I saw plenty of red eagles flying out in the streets."

Kaarl scowled. He caught the spark of confusion from Desde's mind. She was just as mystified as he was.

Before he could question the Tash-Hamari prime, Tetric raised his hand. "If I may speak?"

He nodded. And he was most interested to hear just what the Dark Trine had to say.

"The steward is right. We can no longer do this individually."

One by one, the primes and seconds nodded. Kaarl's heart sank. So Tetric had succeeded in culling their favor before Kaarl could even make his own case of strengthening the provinces with Unaspected. Furthermore, the Trine had just made it sound like he had given Kaarl his support. The amulet fire in his blood returned.

"The incidents of these last months have weighed heavily upon Kin-Deren," the tall Trine continued. "You were forced to augment your ranks with Unaspected." He shook his head. "The arming of the Unaspected. If this is not a clear example as to the extreme duress our land faces, I, for one, can think of no other."

The Tash-Hamari prime rocked forward in his chair. "Unaspected?"

Desde did not bother to raise her hand. "*Ai*, Fasen. I asked the Unaspected to stand with us at Edara. We had no choice. It *was* an example of extreme duress. One that was ultimately successful, however. We destroyed three thousand Ken'nar out of the five thousand we met in Varn-Erdal."

"A 'success,' Seer Prime?" Tetric replied. "The learning hall was burned to the ground."

She raised her chin in defiance. "*Ai*, but it can be rebuilt. The people, the horses, still live. Liaonne Edaran lives. Varn-Erdal lives. My primes, the Dark Trine holds an army larger than any in Kinderra. Only the Unaspected themselves are more numerous. Our handfuls of thousands, even if every province fought together, may not be enough to stop him. The Unaspected share a legacy with the Aspected. We were created from them. The time has come at last that they must stand alongside us. Together, we will protect Kinderra from the evil of the Dark Trine."

Kaarl wanted to cheer at her brave words. The fire of a battle seer had always burned within her heart. Her brown eyes took on the strength of agate as she looked into each face around the table.

Tetric's smug expression melted into one of pity, softer and just as maddening. "Our days have grown dark indeed if we should turn to those we are sworn to protect to now protect us. You may have won a victory in doing so at Edara, but I wonder if you truly understand just what you've done? You have pulled the first thread that will unravel the very fabric of our society, Desde."

Fasen pointed at the Trine. "Tetric, you are out of line."

"Am I?" he replied, his voice as hard as steel. He turned back to Desde. "Show me one passage in the Ora Fal'kinnen that supports you. Where in the Book of Kinderra does it state the Aspected were so beleaguered that they could not even carry out their reason for being? Even your husband's ancestor, the once-lauded Jasal Pinal, defeated Ilrik the Black without unnecessarily endangering the lives of the Unaspected. Use your Aspect, woman. Tell me what you see."

She leaned on the table, her hands curled into fists. "I see freedom. Freedom from the oppression of the Dark Trine. Keeping this land free—*that* is our reason for being."

Kaarl held his wife's arm, determination sweeping away the last of his fear. "Perhaps if you and your Trine gifts had been present at Edara, Lord Garis, there might have been another way. Just where were you?"

Tetric glared at him for a moment, then relaxed deeper in his chair. "Looking after your daughter, Steward Pinal. As you begged me to do." Kaarl's own hands now clenched in fury. "You care for but one child. I, my steward, am here to keep everyone's children safe."

Sahm gave a disapproving snort. "That's blunt, even for you, Garis. Unless she has truly gone over to the Ken'nar with this ridiculous Power from Without nonsense you've alleged, we need Mirana and her Trine Aspects now more than ever. I would think you, of all of us, would welcome the help. Where is the girl?"

"I told you before, I do not know. Mirana Pinal will arrive in Deren in her own time," he snapped at the big defender prime. "Give me your armies and this war will end. Make me Primus Magne and I will guarantee the first true peace Kinderra has known in more than three millennia. I offer you the simplest path to peace, the surest road to end this conflict." He sat back. "Or choose the path the Pinals offer. Not only will the war continue, but Unaspected will be slaughtered, and Kinderra as we know it will eventually be destroyed. That, *Ëi cara'e*, is what you must decide today."

Kaarl willed his body to relax. Tetric thought he could stack the vote against him. Maybe he had, but Kaarl could stall the vote itself. "We can't decide this now. We do not have enough members present in this body to do anything more than gossip."

"*Ai*, we do," the Trine replied. "In the Reckoning of 2865, Kinderra was decimated by the Red Plague, and many primes and seconds had succumbed to the disease. Healer Prime Tilenatete Nasta of Jad-Anüna served as Primus Magne and codified that if there should ever be a time where a Quorum could not possibly be called, then a simple majority vote—with no absentia votes—suffices in all rulings."

Damn him. The bastard had found the very same loophole Kaarl was going to use to vote against him. How would he stall the vote now? Kaarl held his anger in check. "I suppose you have proof of the extenuating circumstances that are delaying the other primes and their seconds and preventing a full Quorum from being called?"

The Dar-Azûlan chewed the inside of his cheek for a moment. His amulet glowed faintly, its light uneven across the crystal's fracture. "Sün-Kasal was correct in saying the trip to

Deren would have been too arduous for Eshe Paschot. And *ai*, her Defender Second Syne Develan had seen more summers himself than any here. It is with deep sorrow that my Healing Aspect showed me both their passings."

Kaarl felt faint. Tetric had pulled off a coup, but instead of wiping out Kinderra's leaders en masse, he had killed them one by one. He rubbed the beard on his chin under the guise of digesting the news. That hand really wanted to crush the vertebrae in the Trine's neck.

"Where is Koben, Tetric?" Rabb asked again. The seer sat, rigid, his reddish-brown topaz amulet in his hand.

The Trine folded his hands, appearing to study them. "The weather has been unpredictable in the Dar-Calans of late. Certainly, our esteemed seers here could also predict something as simple as a snowstorm followed by rain. The glacier that fronts the entrance to the learning hall collapsed. The way out of the mountains will be impassable for months." He looked up from his hands. "Koben and I were raised together, as you know. I, for one, would have appreciated his full support. What's more…" He took a deep breath. "I can no longer detect his presence."

Kaarl swallowed. He killed Koben? And Eshe? Syne? Dear Light Above! Had he killed everyone who objected to his magnistate?

And what of Nambre Dinir and his Jad-Anünans? It was not often he fought alongside the Fal'kin from the far-flung jungle province, but they were a sight to behold, elegant and terrifying. "Nambre Dinir of Jad-Anüna has seen seventy summers himself. Are you telling me his summers caught up with him, too? The il'Kin supported Jad-Anüna and Defender Second Aber Haberi just three summers ago, and he appeared plenty hale. The man is built like a brick wall."

Tetric unwove his hands and rested them on the arms of his chair, thronelike. "I do not know where the representatives of Jad-Anüna are. I am concerned, however, with all the primes and seconds gathering in one place for this very meeting. It does make Kinderra vulnerable to attack on many fronts. I would hate to think the Jad-Anünan delegates ran into Ken'nar who found the situation irresistible."

Rabb glanced at Kaarl and Desde. "We all share your concerns, Lord Trine. However, in the aftermath of Edara and Falantir, Sün-Kasal and Kin-Deren—and Varn-Erdal, for that matter—decided that holding this Quorum was more than worth the risk." He turned to Timir. "Liaonne decided to stay with her people under the catastrophic circumstances, but she gave her vote to the steward."

Kaarl noted the flurry of emotions called from the young defender to the seer second. "Defender Prime Edaran was most emphatic that she would vote against any Primus Magne. I have three others who witnessed her decision and could attest to her wishes."

"Liaonne Edaran is a spirited and talented young woman," Tetric said. "Unfortunately, as I said a moment ago, her proxy vote is nullified as we have invoked the hardship clause for a simple majority of votes by those present."

Desde gripped her own chair arms, her knuckles white. "You have all the answers, don't you, Lord Trine?"

"*Ai.* I do. That is why I am here." He now sat forward, his long index finger stabbing the tabletop in front of him. "*I* am the answer Kinderra has sought for three thousand summers."

A sharp spark of warning leaped from his wife's mind to Kaarl's own. She grabbed his hand. ... *Dismiss the seconds ... Do it ... Now ...* Desde called.

Rabb now stiffened in his chair.

Why? He needed every vote to counter Tetric. "So grave a decision should only be made by the primes. I motion the seconds leave the chambers."

Tetric set his jaw. "They have equal representation here, Kaarl. They stay."

"You are not Primus Magne yet, Tetric. Those present will decide," Desde said.

"Unless there are more dissenters than Dar-Azûl?" Kaarl eyed the two primes. Neither said a word. "Then the motion stands. The seconds are dismissed."

Rabb Plout rose from his chair, concern written on his face. "*Ai*, this is indeed a grave decision. One that should be decided by as many present votes as possible. I wish to stay."

Timir nodded. "I agree with Rabb."

Desde sat, her back steel-straight, her eyes riveted on the Trine. Kaarl's Defending Aspect ratcheted up even more. "You both should leave. Now." Her words were not a suggestion.

Rabb shook his head. "I will abstain from the vote if I must, my lady, but I must stay."

Kaarl tried to call to the seer and the defender, but they were all but hidden under U'Nehíl. "Is this your desire as well, Sün-Kasal?"

"Rabb is his own man. He may stay if he wishes," Sahm replied.

"Timir?"

"I will not leave."

Desde stood. "Rabb, Timir, this vote is not for you. Leave." Kaarl put a hand on her back and found her body tensed, battle-ready. She gave a forced smile. "Go. Find Mirana. Help her prepare an adequate defense before she comes to the Quorum chambers. Please."

Kaarl smiled, a genuine one—she asked them to fight alongside their daughter.

"I understand, Desde. I understand everything. But Sahm will need me here," Rabb said, his voice soft, his amulet brightening.

"I know." Her smile disappeared. "But Mirana will need you more." She turned to Timir. "The both of you."

The seer blinked as his amulet briefly glowed a muddy amber and went dark. He nodded slowly. He gripped Sahm Klai's shoulder. "May the Light of the Aspects Above be with us, *Ëi cara'e*." He and the Tash-Hamari defender second filed from the room. Desde, at last, sat back down.

Kaarl folded his arms low across his stomach. One hand touched the hilt of a ceremonial dagger he wore at his waist. His father had given it to him many Quorumtides ago, and he had worn it for every Quorumtide since. He had never even thought about drawing it until this moment.

Tetric slowly unwound his legs and stood. For a long moment, he leaned on the table, hanging his head like a doomed man. Kaarl tensed, wary. "Honored primes, you have had time to consider my offer to be your Primus Magne. Now you must decide whether to choose peace under my hand. Or death."

Desde inhaled beside Kaarl. His Defending Aspect honed its own form of Sight. The death the Trine spoke of was not some distant consequence of continued strife but something much more imminent.

His hand still on her back, his wife moved ever so slightly forward in her chair as if she were ready to spring into action. "There may no longer be war under your hand, but there will be no peace, either, Tetric Garis."

Sahm rested his fists on the stone table, clutching invisible blades. "How can you say that? You were at Edara. You were at

Two Rivers Ford. With Kana-Akün gone, and the rest of the provinces in disarray, we have never been more vulnerable. The question is no longer whether we need a Primus Magne to help us defend Kinderra. It is whether we can continue to defend Kinderra without one."

Kaarl held up his hand. "Sahm, hold. You have no idea what this man is capable of."

The Trine curled one corner of his mouth. "And just what would that be, Pinal?"

Fasen rose to his feet. "Kaarl, you of all people should be supporting Tetric. How many of your il'Kin walk Kinderra now?"

"Fasen—" Desde interjected.

"I agree with Fasen," the big Sün-Kasalan replied. He turned to face Desde. "I was at Edara, too. Nothing is left standing. And Two Rivers Ford? My seer showed me from his very amulet his vision of what happened there. The Fal'kin of two provinces were emptied in that one conflict alone." He shifted his hard brown gaze to Kaarl. "Or at least that's what you told me, Pinal, when you begged me to come to Edara. Why do I see so many Kin-Deren defenders in Deren's streets? Are you uniforming the Unaspected now, too? Is that the only answer you have for us? I do not wish to cede control of my Fal'kin to a Primus Magne any more than you or Fasen or any prime, but I have witnessed what the Dark Trine is capable of, as have you. Only Trine Tetric Garis can stop this horror."

Fasen held out his hands in a pleading gesture. "We're not giving him our provinces, Desde. He will only be acting as our battle seer when the Dark Trine comes. The same position you once held."

"It is a position I still hold," she snapped. "And you are a fool if you think Tetric will be content with simply calling troop movements to your defenders. Ask yourself just how he knew the fates of all the other primes. Ask yourself why such a fate did not befall you."

Tetric sighed and shook his head. "*Ëi siba*, I see the poison from your husband's mind has infected yours as well. You once called me your friend. I even once told you not to lose faith, for your empty womb would be filled with a blessing. Was I wrong?" He leaned toward her. "I saved her *life* when she tried to kill herself after *you* all but forced her to choose an amulet for which she was not ready."

The blood drained from Desde's face. She worked her mouth to try to speak but no words came for a moment. "Wh-What?"

"You bastard!" Kaarl shot to his feet, holding Desde's arm. "You swore to me!" His wife turned to look at him. Every word he had ever uttered in confidence to Tetric, every promise, every action was another arrow the Trine would use to bring him down. He was such a fool. Such an Aspect-forsaken damn fool.

"Ka–Kaarl, is this true?" Her voice quivered, soft, like that of a lost lamb. He turned to her, his mind searching for words he could not find. "How could you keep this from me? Our daughter? How could you not tell me?" Tears welled up in the rims of her eyes and spilled down over her lashes.

"*Ama*, I—" He stabbed Tetric with his gaze. ... *I will kill you, you Dark bastard ...*

... No ... You won't ... The Dar-Azûlan held his dusky amulet, his thumb caressing the crystal's rift. "Mirana has left me. The Aspects Above alone will decide whether she remains a blessing or a curse to Kinderra. If it turns out she is a curse, I will be forced to act. Using all the armies of Kinderra to stop her."

Desde said nothing but gripped the stone table as she swayed in her seat.

Kaarl sank back down into the cold, stone chair and clenched his teeth. If he did so any harder, he was certain he'd crack them all. ... *We still have time yet ... Give him the rope to hang himself* ... he called to his wife.

Fasen held up his hand. "Wait a moment. Mirana was in my own chambers with you, Tetric, only months ago. I highly doubt she is the Dark Trine, even if she did use the Power from Without. But more to the point, I am not about to let you control my forces directly. You said we would still maintain the leadership of our provincial armies. Is that not true?"

The Trine's amulet remained in his hand, but he no longer toyed with it. He now held it as a defender. Kaarl's muscles tightened with wary readiness. "If I am Primus Magne, you will not need a battle seer. There will be no need to fight at all."

"How?" the Tash-Hamari asked. "Do you expect the Ken'nar will simply drop their swords and amulets at the mere sight of you?"

Sahm shrugged his massive shoulders. "It has happened before. The Ken'nar fear him."

Fasen shook his head. "I would never have agreed to support you if you had said you would directly command our Fal'kin. You always were ambitious, Garis, but now you have gone too far. *Ai*, I will take the information you call, but I will give my own orders!"

Tetric shot to his feet and slammed his palms on the table, the noise echoing around the room. "Do you not understand I am trying to save your lives?"

Kaarl rose from the chair to meet him. "How? Will you save us with your oh-so-sacred Healing Aspect? Or will you use it to wield the Soul Harvest on us if we don't comply?"

The Trine's eyes widened. The apostolic fervor that had always resided in the man's gaze now leached away before Kaarl to be replaced by a barbarous determination bordering on madness. Whether or not the other primes caught the expression, the Dark Trine had revealed himself.

"The Soul Harvest," Kaarl continued. "Is that why so many of my fellow provincemen are in the streets when days ago there were none. Is that why young Atan Robaar, a boy I once trained, tried to take me down? Is that why Tennen Beltran tried to kill his son?"

Tetric remained silent.

Kaarl's eyes remained locked on the Trine's, his hand on the ceremonial dagger at his waist. "Lady Prime, gentlemen. It is time to vote."

The Dar-Azûlan raised his hand. "Hold. I am not a petty man, so I will look past such insults. But votes deciding the fate of Kinderra are too precious to be mouthed by criminals."

Sahm exhaled loudly. "Tetric, enough of this. It is more than painfully apparent you hate the Pinals and they hate you, but I know for a fact they are no criminals. I have fought alongside them. I know their honor."

"You know for a fact, do you, Klai? Kaarl and Desde knew of Mirana's Trine Aspects since the girl's birth." His eyes flicked to Desde. "Perhaps even before. And they hid their daughter from us. For sixteen summers. We have traitors in our midst."

Sahm turned to Kaarl. "Is that true?"

Kaarl's Defending Aspect pulsed through him. Desde rose and stood beside him. Now his words would have to do what even his Aspect could not. "*Ai*. And we would do it again." His wife took his hand. "We did it to save our daughter's life. We do have a traitor in our midst, but it is not I nor Desde, and certainly not Mirana." He pointed to the tall Dar-Azûlan. "That man has deceived us all. For thirty long summers. Tetric Garis is the Dark Trine."

The Quorum chambers fell silent. Only hope remained now. A hope he called Mirana.

Tetric's shoulders fell. "All my life, I have given everything that I am to Kinderra." The Trine's words sounded distant yet edged with pain and sorrow to Kaarl's ears. "I have given the lives of my men and women. I have given my own blood. All to bring peace to Kinderra. What have the Pinals given us? A despicable coward who left the Unaspected, his Fal'kin, his wife, and his newborn babe to die at the sword. Lies and deceit spewed from their own lips. And an insolent child who has turned into a murderous, thrice-cursed traitor."

Tetric laid his large hands flat on the stone table and now stared intently at Kaarl. He fought to keep the man's mind at a distance from his own. "Mirana's Trine Aspects made her more my child, Kaarl, than she could ever be to you."

Whatever sadness or despair had colored the Trine's baritone before now vanished, leaving a venomous, hushed rasping behind. Kaarl released Desde's hand. He would need both to fight.

"Had you given your daughter to me when she was born," the Trine continued, "her Aspects would have always been in service to protect our people. Not just our Aspected, but together we would have been able to protect untold thousands of Unaspected souls that have since been lost in this bloody conflict. Only I could have made her the Trine she should have become. Together, we could have ushered in a new age, an age more glorious than Kinderra has ever known."

Tetric's eyes, black as midnight, continued to bore into Kaarl. "Instead, you corrupted her against me. You turned your daughter into the Dark Trine. She will destroy Kinderra. Not I."

His gaze traveled around the room, slashing across Fasen Aldi and Sahm Klai to finally stab once more at Kaarl. "If you believe that all the sacrifices I've made on Kinderra's behalf, on the behalf of your very lives and the lives of those you've loved, are evil, then you no more deserve to live than Kaarl and Desde Pinal."

Sahm looked down at his hands in his lap. "I gave my three children's lives to Kinderra." He snapped his head up. "Three."

Desde held out her arms, pleading. "Sahm—"

The large defender rose and crossed the room to stand in front of Kaarl. "Do you not think for one moment I would have liked to have held them back? To hide *their* Aspects? Do you think my pain, my fear for their safety was any less than your own?"

"Sahm, can't you see Tetric for what he is?" Kaarl cried. "Had we not hidden Mirana from him, he would have murdered her before she could walk! She is the reason why he doesn't sit in your hall. She destroyed Two Rivers Ford to stop his army from advancing. She is coming here now to help us defeat the very Ken'nar your troops will engage at any moment. Tetric Garis is the Dark Trine."

The big man pressed close. "You lie. Just as you lied about your daughter." His voice twisted into a snarl. "Give me your amulet, Pinal."

Fasen rose to stand next to Desde. "Klai, step down." His hand moved to the hilt of his sword.

Kaarl's eyes flicked from Sahm to Tetric. The tall Trine stood motionless, his dark eyes shining like his hematite amulet. "Sahm, if you take my amulet, neither of us will leave this room alive."

The Sün-Kasalan gripped the chain of Kaarl's garnet amulet. "But you'll have a much more difficult time killing me without it."

Desde held the defender prime's arm. "Sahm, *please!* Do you not see what is about to happen? You are about to hand over Kinderra to the Dark Trine."

"Step back, Klai," Fasen warned again. "We will deal with the Pinals later. Right now, we need to stop this madness before we lose everything to a dictator. Tash-Hamar will never bow to a Primus Magne. I vote no."

Desde's topaz amulet scintillated like a miniature sun. "Kin-Deren stands with Tash-Hamar. I vote no."

"Sün-Kasal?" Tetric intoned.

"Sahm, please," she pleaded again.

The big defender released Kaarl and stared defiantly at the others. "We've all fought alongside Tetric Garis. He couldn't possibly stand here and offer us a path to peace while he kills our own Fal'kin. We need him. We need a Primus Magne. Sün-Kasal votes *ai*. It is our only hope."

The Trine's hand drifted to the hilt of his long sword, his mouth contorting into a sardonic smile. "Dar-Azûl votes *ai*."

Kaarl's blood-red amulet warmed his skin through the fabric of his tunic, his Defending Aspect raging through him. If Tetric wanted Kinderra, he would have to take it by force. "You called for the simple majority ruling, which precludes absentia votes. I still stand as steward, and my power to break a tie still remains. The steward votes no." Now he smiled. "You are defeated, Lord Trine."

Tetric Garis's amulet surged in brightness as his call slashed through Kaarl's mind. ... *I saved your daughter's life, and all I asked for in return was your trust ... I begged you not to become my enemy ...*

Kaarl stabbed back with his own piercing call. ... *You have been Kinderra's enemy since before Mirana was born ...*

The Trine's mouth curled into an unfamiliar smile. "No, *Ëi cara*. It is you who has been defeated.

The doors to the Quorum chambers burst open, their hinges warping. A sea of Ken'nar stood outside.

Kaarl reached for Desde's hand. And drew his blade with the other.

CHAPTER 23

"It is enough to fail for one's own sake, but to fail for the sake of others is unredeemable."
—The Codex of Jasal the Great

Mirana released her hold on the seer's ruse, fighting to recover her breath after the frantic ride over the last miles to the citadel. Teague raced through Deren's great gates after her, Morgan, Binthe, and Sido close behind.

"I think we fooled them." She tucked her chin to gulp a breath. "We have to hurry to the keep."

"I think we were not the only ones to use a ruse to slip past an army." Sido pointed to something behind her.

She whirled around. "Oh, no." Galloping hard through the path they had made in the trampled cornstalks were fifteen black-armored warriors. "No."

"Only fifteen?" Morgan gave a sharp laugh. "There are ten times as many Fal'kin in this square alone. This makes no sense."

Teague pointed to the east. A dozen riders, wearing a blue-fielded golden lion on their uniforms, neared the citadel's gates. "Look! Jad-Anüna comes."

Unaspected straggled through the gates, laughing, oblivious to the approaching danger. She jumped off Bankin and ran back. "Hurry! Get inside! Get inside!" She motioned for the revelers to run.

Dozens of Unaspected travelers turned to see Ken'nar charging toward them and ran screaming for the safety of the citadel.

"Mirana! Get back!" Morgan yelled.

… *Jad-Anüna…* She called to any mind she could find. … *Ken'nar … Approaching from the north … They must not come closer …*

As if hitting a wall, the Jad-Anünan delegation veered their horses to the north and surged toward the Ken'nar.

Morgan's amethyst amulet glowed. "Come. We are running out of time."

Her Defending Aspect assailed her consciousness. *Warning.*

A blinding explosion of wrongness forced her to her knees. The discord of injury slammed into her, driving her out of communion with her Defending Aspect.

Teague jumped off his saddle and held her. "What is it? What happened?"

From farther within the city came a sound like the far-off cry of a grynwen. It grew louder, a keening wail in the air.

"No." Mirana lifted her eyes. Jasal's Keep stood in the distance, a dark monolith shrouded in mist.

He gave her a gentle shake. "What happened?"

Binthe held her amulet, eyes searching the crowd. "What do you see, Mirana?"

"We are too late." She staggered to her feet. Tetric Garis was within the keep. Father. Mother. She had no reason to keep silent anymore. She had every reason to let them know she had come.

… MOTHER! … FATHER! … I AM HERE! …

Sido, Morgan, and Binthe turned to her, grimacing at the strength of her call.

She spun around and stood before the enormous gates and spread her arms wide. Screaming, she released a burst of white amulet fire from the diamond on her chest. The jet of silver-white flame fractioned itself into hundreds of fingers, each one striking any oncoming Ken'nar who had passed through the Jad-Anünan line.

Around her, by the hundreds, other Fal'kin and Unaspected turned, stunned at the display of power.

"Fal'kin! Unaspected! The Dark Army comes," she cried. "Kinderra needs us to protect her. Deren must not fall. We! Must! Not! Fall! *Rememore Kin en Forte!*"

The people, Aspected and Unaspected alike, took up the battle cry and streamed out of the citadel to meet the advancing army. Hundreds more, however, turned on the crowd, drew their weapons, and cut down everything in their path. Stunned, commonfolk, defenders, and seers fell before the swords of the harvested Ken'nar clothed as friends.

… Please, Mirana … Forgive us …

… Father? … No mind came back to her. *… Paithe? …* "Father!"

She gripped Jasal's amulet. The Dark Trine would not have the keep. Nor Kinderra.

Mirana jumped into Bankin's saddle as Teague swung up behind her. She dug her heels into the horse's sides and charged her way through false Fal'kin toward the learning hall.

*   *   *

"Fools! All of you!" Tetric Garis launched his words like arrows. "Do you not understand I would have handed you the peace you all so desired?" He shook his head slowly and pinned Kaarl with a look of pure venom. "Or is it because you do not want peace? If there were no Ken'nar to fight, what use would Kinderra have of the Fal'kin? Kaarl Pinal, I had hoped that you, of anyone, would have understood. Your daughter did. For a time."

He tightened the grip on his sword, his red garnet scintillating. "What have you done with my daughter?"

The Dark Trine stabbed a long finger at his own chest. "It is what she has done to *me*."

Ken'nar fighters poured into the chamber, their Kin-Deren heraldics mocking them.

Before Kaarl could react, a mind pushed its way into his. *… MOTHER! … FATHER! … I AM HERE! …*

"Mirana?" Desde's voice came softly, filled with both joy and panic.

"Desde! Get down!" He gripped his amulet and loosed red fire at the Trine. Tetric ducked, Kaarl's attack narrowly missing him.

"I offered you peace, but you chose war instead. So be it." He pushed past Sahm Klai and swung his blade at Kaarl.

He spun away, but the tip of the tall man's sword grazed his temple. He drew his own blade and parried the Trine's blow just before it could cleave him in half, holding the long sword at bay with his own. "We trusted you. How could you do this?"

Tetric answered with his sword, swinging it with frightening speed at Kaarl's throat. In his effort to block the strike, Kaarl stumbled and fell against the stone table. Using the table as purchase, he shoved himself toward the Dar-Azûlan and pressed his blade back. He stood only a handsbreadth apart from the Trine, his gaze locked with the other man's. "I fought alongside you. How? How could you murder your own people?"

"Many were harvested, their minds opened to receive my will. Those who died gave their lives so that others could live in a unified Kinderra. Kaarl, I asked you, I *begged you* to be a part of that unified Kinderra. I need a man such as you. I did not want this. Even now, you can help me stop it. For Mirana's sake, I'll ask you again. Please join me."

He could not comprehend what kind of obscene logic would move even the Dark Trine to take the lives of his followers, turning them into the living dead or the dead in truth. "I would sooner join the damned."

With a lightning-fast move, Tetric slid his sword from Kaarl's blade and swung again. "Deren is surrounded by twenty thousand Ken'nar, Kaarl, and Mirana is somewhere out there. Cease this pointless fighting now. Have Desde pull back her troops. Or Mirana will die."

Kaarl shut his mind against the horror that he had sent his daughter willingly into the Dark Trine's hands. He countered his assailant's move, cutting down hard with his blade. "I will not let you near my daughter again." With a twisting motion, he forced Tetric's wrist at an awkward angle, sending his long sword flying away.

The Dark Trine reached out and pulled Desde in front of him, curling his sword arm around her neck. Kaarl froze. "I wanted peace. I begged you for peace. But you chose war. And so you shall have your war." With his free hand, he gripped Desde's amulet. His wife screamed in pain as he loosed amulet fire from her topaz.

He had not anticipated such a move. The amulet fire struck full in the chest, his own amulet lighting to deflect a blow that should have killed him. He dropped to the floor, stunned by burning pain. Desde whirled around and slashed at Tetric with a small knife she had tucked in her bodice. It caught him across the collarbone. He smashed his fist into her face, sending her flying.

Kaarl shook his head to clear it. "Desde!"

Arcane light flashed around the room, and the scent of burned flesh filled the air. Fasen Aldi leaped up and ran across the great stone table to defend Desde before a Ken'nar could cut her down. The Tash-Hamari struck a Ken'nar and cleaved off the arm of another attacker. A powerful blast of amulet fire knocked the defender prime from his feet. Before Desde could drag him to safety, blasts from five amulets from outside the chamber found their marks. The defender prime died in flames before he had a chance to scream.

"Fasen!" Desde called the fallen Tash-Hamari's sword to her hand and swung at three Ken'nar. All three sighted her with their amulets.

Sahm dragged her behind him. "Desde, I'm a fool."

She shook her head. "Sahm—"

Kaarl staggered to his feet. "Sahm! Down!"

The big defender loosed amulet fire from his smoky brown quartz at a Ken'nar defender. A pillar of multi-colored flame rose between them as the energies opposed each other.

Kaarl gripped his garnet, searching for an angle of attack. The Sün-Kasalan prime was powerful but not powerful enough. The Ken'nar amulet fire from three Ken'nar amulets overcame the Sün-Kasalan's deflection and wrapped him in a bright column of flame. Sahm's roar of agony cut off abruptly as his body turned to ash.

Kaarl shrank back from the brilliant light of the strike. "Sahm!"

Desde gripped her topaz amulet and she loosed an image of sulfurous fire. "Kaarl!" It poured over the three Ken'nar. The warriors froze, expecting to die.

He saw his advantage and sent his true amulet fire at the attackers. "Sün-Kasal shall not die unavenged!" The dark warriors' dying screams were cut short when they disintegrated.

Dozens more Ken'nar poured into the room. These were not mindless minions but black-armored fighters who willingly added their own obsession for victory to their fury. He again willed his Aspect through his garnet amulet at Tetric, and the force of the blast sent the Dark Trine into his own Ken'nar. Sensing Desde's peril, he grabbed his sword and hacked his way toward his wife through a sea of dark armor and false red eagles.

Dread and understanding seeped through him. The Quorum chamber had only one entrance and tens of thousands of Ken'nar were just outside. All the primes would be killed. Just as the Trine Prophecy had foretold, Kinderra would be like a ship without a keel with no primes to lead the provinces.

He sent a Ken'nar slamming into the stone wall with a brutal intent of his Aspect. The dark warrior slid to the floor and lay still. He parried another Ken'nar's sword with one hand, and slashed at still another with his ceremonial knife, catching his assailant in the throat. Both Ken'nar dropped without a scream. He dropped a third with his amulet, scarlet fire enveloping her without him even gripping his crystal.

… Kaarl … We must help Mirana … Desde called, her mind's voice panicked. *… We must get to her …* She tried to fight her way out of the chamber door but was repulsed back by arrows and swords and amulet fire.

Kaarl saw the arrows before his Defending Aspect could make his body react, a strange, suspended moment in the precious immediacy of his Aspect's own type of Sight. A bowstring pulled by a gauntleted hand. He didn't have time to scream Desde's name.

He moved and put his body between the bow and his wife.

At first, he merely heard the three arrows as they penetrated his back, three thuds, and the faint jingle of his chain mail as the projectiles sliced through his body. Then he felt them. The fletching burned as it sawed through his muscles and a lung. The barbed arrowheads scraped at his ribs on their way through his chest.

Desde held his arms, her expression confused. A small trickle of blood leaked from the corner of her mouth.

He looked down. Two black arrowheads stood out from him like birds of prey trying to peck themselves free from his chest. A third stain also bloomed but held no projectiles. Yet another bloody blemish expanded across his wife's beautiful gown. The third arrow had traveled completely through his body to embed itself in her heart, its fletching standing out in stark, black contrast to the pale fabric of her dress.

"Tell her I love—" Her knees buckled. She grabbed the arrows from his chest as she fell, pulling them from his body.

… Desde? … No … Desde! …

He wanted to scream those words, but his body was far past screaming. He landed hard on his stomach near her, losing his blade.

… Mirana has set herself against me … Against Kinderra … For that, she must die … the Dark Trine's presence intoned in his fading mind.

His Defender's awareness told him Tetric moved in close. He gripped his amulet underneath him where the Trine could not see. He had just one moment and only one. He flipped over to strike Kinderra's traitor down with amulet fire, but a sudden agony stole his failing breath. Tetric's sword plunged through his abdomen.

The heaving bodies locked in battle slowed. He tasted rusty salt in his mouth. Excruciating pain flared once again then disappeared. He collapsed against his wife.

The stone pavers were cold against his back. Everything felt cold. Except for Desde. She still felt warm. … *Please, Mirana … Forgive us …*

CHAPTER 24

"I must be strong."
—The Codex of Jasal the Great

Mirana swung her sword again. The Ken'nar pulled back his mount from Bankin but did not fall. His hand reached for his amulet, but he turned to ash as lavender light engulfed him.

Morgan released his amulet. "Are you all right?"

She was as far from "all right" as she could be. The city was in complete chaos. The deaths of so many assailed her Healing Aspect, and her Sight was feeding her fragmented, frantic images, sending her Defending Aspect burning through her. Her parents' lives were threatened.

And she could have stopped all this evil. All of it.

She ignored him and dug her heels into the sides of the horse she shared with Teague. "Hurry!"

The mists had given way to rain, and finally, a frigid downpour. Lightning stabbed at the sky as brutal punches of thunder struck overhead. Fal'kin and Unaspected fought the swarms of Ken'nar, and all perished in the streets. Fires, unabated by the rain, turned what had once been homes and shops into charred ruins. Grynwen howled in famished glee at the unexpected feast. Somewhere, above the din of battle, a child's cry was suddenly silenced.

Sido grunted on his horse next to Mirana as he shook off a glancing blow from a Ken'nar broadsword. He swung his blade at his assailant's throat as Teague's broadsword embedded itself between the Ken'nar's chest plates. "Not bad, herbsboy."

"She said you saved her life, so, you know," Teague shouted above the din. Binthe slashed with her long knives, blinking back her fractured visions.

Mirana stifled a scream, trying not to slide off Teague's horse as they tore through the streets toward the learning hall. Her Defending Aspect shrieked within her, begging to be released in response to the fighting around her.

She released amulet fire through Jasal's diamond, striking Ken'nar after Ken'nar, using an inordinate amount of strength to keep the broken beams of deadly light from turning on the amulets of her companions. So many wore the heraldics of the provinces, she could not tell friend from foe until they moved to strike. Her Healing Aspect rose at the pain and injury around her, the pain and injury caused by her, superseding her Defending Aspect now. It threatened to overwhelm her with catastrophic discord.

This was her home. Deren, the impenetrable fortress. The citadel that could withstand any onslaught. And it was dying.

Tetric Garis. She could have stopped him. For sevendays, months, she rode alongside him. She never even considered he could have been the Dark Trine until it was too late.

The learning hall now loomed ahead of her. Mirana forced its gates open, hammering at them with the Aspects, Teague's strong arm around her as he sat behind her in the saddle. Morgan, Binthe, and Sido surged through behind her without stopping their charge.

She lifted her head as they rode across the courtyard and looked toward her room. High above on the fifth floor, the windows to her small bedroom had been shattered. The wind drove in the rain, soaking the tapestry covering. A woman's body hung partway over the embrasure. One of her mother's seers. Had she run to the room, thinking Mirana was there? Had she come to defend the daughter of her prime?

Higher still rose Jasal's Keep, a hard, menacing spire lashed by rain and wind, a watchtower that would mean both her victory and her doom.

She and the others raced through the courtyard. Two Fal'kin came out from behind a portico column, blades drawn. All four horses screamed. Teague pulled back hard on Bankin's reins to avoid the pair.

"Mirana?"

Rabb Plout held his stained long knives in front of him as Timir Sadhi gripped both his citrine amulet and his sword. Both men were covered in blood, some of it their own. For a moment, no one said anything.

"You're real! Not harvested!" Mirana slid from Bankin's saddle and ran over to the men, embracing them. At least something of the provinces survived.

"Thank the Aspects!" Rabb quickly sheathed his blades and returned her hug.

"We weren't sure what became of you." Timir paused. "After everything."

"Where is he? Where is Tetric?" Bodies and ash were strewn across the courtyard. She swallowed back her sickness and her guilt. Rabb gestured behind him to the keep. The others quickly dismounted.

"We can't stay here out in the open," Morgan said.

The Tash-Hamari defender nodded, his sword remaining in his hand. "Most of the Ken'nar have gone. He must have ordered them to go out into the city. We took care of as many as we could, but there were so many. He has others still with him. I see you captured his second." Timir nodded at Sido.

"I hate to disappoint you, Defender Second Sadhi, but we are now allies. Which means you have to be nice to me," Sido replied with an anything-but-nice smile.

The two seconds looked at Mirana. "*Ai*," she said. "I'll explain later. The keep. I have to get to the top." She searched the keep's pinnacle but was forced to turn away as lightning flared.

The Sün-Kasalan seer placed a hand on her shoulder, holding her back. "He knows you are here."

Timir squinted up at the watchtower. "We should leave. He thinks he's won because he sits in the learning hall. We can try to regroup our forces then make some sort of concerted effort to take it back."

She shook her head. "I must get to the top. Jasal used the keep to save Deren once. I intend to use the keep now to save Deren again." She held up the half diamond in her palm. She turned to the others. "Go. Do what you can for Deren." She glanced up again at the keep's pinnacle. "My fight is here."

Teague held her arms. "I'm never leaving you again—"

"Teague—"

"—even if that means I die beside you."

Binthe put her hand on Mirana's shoulder. "He speaks for all of us, *siba*."

She couldn't ask this of them. Not this. "You will die."

"Probably," Morgan said, "but you are our Light Trine. You are willing to give your life for Kinderra. And we are willing to give our lives for you."

"And him?" Morgan indicated Sido.

Mirana frowned. Deflecting a blow from a sword was easy; deflecting prejudice was proving much more difficult. "He comes, too."

"I think I have a better idea," Sido said. He scanned the courtyard. "I'll stay here and guard the keep doors."

She shook her head. "It's too dangerous by yourself. Even for you."

"There might still be some Ken'nar who don't know I've— well, whom I can command. I'll order them to posts outside of the learning hall." A feral light glimmered within his amulet, within his eyes. "Tetric's face. When he loses it all. I *need* to see that, Mirana. Give me that. Please."

"If I can." She embraced him warmly. "Be careful, *Ëi cara*."

Mirana and the others ran across the courtyard. With a swift wave of her hand, the tower door flew open, banging against its hinges. The Fal'kin flew up the steep stairs of the keep, but Teague held her arm, keeping her back. "You said that Jasal's amulet was the lock and the key to his keep. But it's not, is it? It's the one who wields it that gives it power." He gathered her into his arms. She saw the muscles in his chest tighten as he swallowed, fighting back tears. "I told you I understood. And I do. All of it. Even the parts you didn't speak of. You must choose all the amulets in Jasal's Keep. And it will take all of you to do it."

She gave him a brief but fierce kiss. "Thank the Aspects Above for you, Teague Beltran." Together, they entered the keep.

The penetrating darkness swallowed the light from torches lining the interior, the gloom never allowing the glow to reach beyond the flames themselves. Lightning flickered through the tiny half-moon window in the pinnacle's roof far, far above her, briefly illuminating the stairs before plunging them into darkness again.

No longer solid and comforting, the spiraling interior had become a tomb swathed in heavy, claustrophobic shadows, threatening to collapse on top of her. She stumbled and fell before a set of doors.

The Quorum chamber.

The ravaged silence of death and the oppressive, suffocating *end-ness* hit her with full force. The finality of the sensation pulled the breath from her lungs. Silent screams echoed from those who had been murdered, begging to be avenged. Life itself had been wrenched from the living, flayed from the soul only to be perverted into an instrument of death.

Teague and the Fal'kin stopped. He knelt. "Miri?"

She could not speak. The smothering silence of death overwhelmed all three of her Aspects.

"Mirana, don't go in there," Binthe whispered, her voice strained. "There's nothing we can do for them now."

"We can do something, Binthe," Morgan snarled. "We can find the dark bastard and kill him."

Teague helped her to her feet. "Come. Let us finish this."

She ignored him and placed her hand on one of the doors. Her Healing Aspect exploded within her, lighting the amulet she wore. She groaned as that precious power pulled her toward all the death yet pleaded in bitter agony for being unable to heal. She pushed a door open. A cry caught in her throat.

The Quorum chamber had been turned into a charnel house.

The horror of what had taken place held her captive. The great round table was cracked in two. Blood spattered the walls. The acrid odor of burned flesh clung in the room. Ash swirled in dark eddies as the air rushed in through the open door. Ash piled in corners, darkened chairs. Ash smeared the faces of corpses. Ash drifted through the air. She could smell it, taste it.

A few bodies lay strewn on the floor, contorted by violence, mouths frozen wide in silent screams.

Her mother.

"Your ivory dress. You look so beautiful, *Maithe.*" Mirana had played dress-up in it as a child, pretending she was a prime presiding over a Quorumtide dance. Her *maithe* made it more beautiful when she wore it, her presence shining golden like her amulet. Mirana wanted to touch her mother's face, the brocade fabric, but if she did her mother's death would become real. For this one moment, she needed to pretend it was not.

Maithe's blood was made more vivid against the pale fabric, a stark contrast to the dark-armored corpses that lay near her.

She sank to her knees onto the blood-soaked floor. She reached out to touch her mother's hair. She had wound it up in a braided gilt coil at the nape of her neck. She had always worn it that way when she wanted to appear strong, as if ready for battle.

Maithe's music was gone. Gone. It had always been there. Always. Mirana had known her mother's life music before she knew her own. Since the first moment the Aspects Above called her into being, the life of who and what her mother was had been with her, an inseparable, indivisible harmony to her own life's melody. How could it be gone? Silent? Her mother's living essence was as assured, as reassuring as the dawn. Her mouth could not form her mother's name, her lungs had no power to speak it.

Mirana didn't recognize him at first. *Paithe* had fallen on his back, his body partially covering her mother. Her father's face shone ghastly white in the dim light of the room. Blood flowed from his mouth. Her Healer's Aspect told her that a lung had been punctured. Three arrows, her eyes saw. Her Seeing Aspect and her Defending Aspect burned an afterimage of an immediate-past skein of time in her mind of his murder. A long sword had impaled him through the abdomen. She knew that long sword. She tried to lift her hand to close his eyes, her mother's eyes, but she could not move.

The wounds on *Paithe's* chest still oozed in pathetic pulses. It was in his blood that she knelt. The sickeningly sweet, coppery stench of it filled her lungs as she tried to breathe. His amulet, as red as his blood, glowed with her nearness.

Mirana heard the others speaking to her, shouting, but her mind could no longer make sense of the words. Her Defending Aspect whispered a warning to her. She ignored it. Her body began to shake as if trying to rid itself of the violations to her Aspects. With trembling fingers, she reached over his heart.

A note.

"Father?"

Another note, a distant echo of what his life's music had once been. It was faint, indistinct. But present.

"Father? *Paithe?*"

She placed both her hands over his heart, flooding him with healing, desperate to close the wounds that stole his life from him. Another note, and another, and another.

"*Paithe!*"

Kaarl's eyelids fluttered. He looked at her through their slits, too weak to open them any farther. "Mirana." It was more of a death's rattled exhale than an utterance.

"*Paithe,* it's me. I'm here. I heard you. I heard your call. There is nothing to forgive. I should be the one to beg your forgiveness. I love you and *Maithe* so much. I am sorry. I am so, so sorry. You tried to save my life. I know that now." Her words tumbled out, tripping over each other in their haste to reach her father's ears before he could no longer hear them.

"Mirana, stop."

"I love you. I love you and I can heal you both, *Paithe.* You and *Maithe* both. I am a healer. I am a Trine. I can—"

"Stop, Miri. *Maithe* is safe. No one else can hurt her now."

"But *Paithe*—"

"Tetric—" Blood and saliva dribbled from the corner of his mouth as his attempt to speak forced air from his ruined lungs. Whatever time her Aspects had bought him, it was ending. "Tetric waits for you. He will kill you."

Her body heaved in great sobs, her tears falling from her face to her father's. "Not unless I wake the keep first. Jasal's amulet." She wiped her tears and his blood from his face. "I will save Kinderra. And I will save you."

"You are the Thrice-Blessed. We always knew. We never gave up hope." His abdomen rose with the effort to give air to lungs that had all but stopped working. "You are the Light Trine. Our Trine. My tiny—"

A single note faded into silence.

"Father? *Paithe? Paithe!*"

She pulled her father's body into her arms, rocking it, holding it fiercely against her as if her sheer will could call him back across the boundary of death. Anguish wracked her body, the depth of her sorrow unable to be voiced by mere frail tears.

Her Defending Aspect rose in earnest. She no longer cared. Her parents were dead. Tetric waited for her now. He would kill Teague and her friends. He would take the amulet. And he would kill her. She had been right all along. She had failed before she had even begun. Kinderra was already lost.

Jasal's amulet pressed against her breastbone, against Teague's precious mica-and-blossom pendant, as she held her father's body to her chest. Her father's death would be in vain, all of theirs would be.

If she turned back from her destiny.

"We are taking losses," Binthe said, urgency and fear tingeing her soft voice. "Sün-Kasal and your mother's troops cannot hold the Ken'nar line." The seer woman's verdant amulet glowed deep emerald in the dim light of the chamber. "We must leave now."

Mirana's Defending Aspect spiked with a warning.

She held her father's body a moment longer, then gently laid him down next to her mother. She kissed her *maithe*, then her *paithe*. … *I will not fail … I will save Kinderra … For all of us …*

Binthe gasped beside her. Mirana turned to the chamber entrance.

A dozen Ken'nar streamed into the room.

CHAPTER 25

*"I could no easier ignore the need than I could ignore
my beloved Antiri's call."*
                              —The Codex of Jasal the Great

The Ken'nar flowed into the Quorum chamber. Teague
and the Fal'kin drew their weapons as they were surrounded.

"That Ken'nar seer bastard double-crossed us," Morgan
snarled.

Mirana shook her head. "He wouldn't have sold us out."

Teague shrugged and hefted his broadsword, preparing for
the coming onslaught. "We could have gotten lucky for once,
and maybe Sido was killed."

"Teague," Mirana said, and grabbed her amulet.

"I was only kidding—"

"Teague!" Mirana screamed as Ken'nar amulet fire lit up
the chamber like a lethal rainbow.

He ducked a swipe that should have taken his head from his shoulders. Bringing up his blade, he blocked the Ken'nar backstroke. "Missed!" His assailant snarled something unintelligible and grabbed his amulet.

Uh oh.

During his sword training with Morgan, the defender had told him that the Aspected needed a moment—but *just* a moment—to concentrate power before releasing amulet fire. Teague didn't think but acted, and immediately thrust his sword under the Ken'nar's helmet into the unprotected slit of space by the throat. The defender went down with a gurgled cry as a deadly wash of fire shot up to the ceiling.

Teague brought up his arm to protect his eyes from the brilliant light and spun away—directly into the crossfire of Timir's and another Ken'nar's amulets. He screamed and bent over as the skin on his shoulder was singed.

"Down!" Morgan screamed and loosed more purple fire from his amethyst at one attacker. The il'Kin defender launched his hand, throwing another dark warrior. The Ken'nar dropped to the stone floor as orange amulet fire drilled through him from Timir Sadhi's citrine amulet.

Another Ken'nar circled behind Mirana as she battled two opponents. "Miri!" Teague threw his weight against a heavy stone chair, tripping the dark-armored defender at Mirana's back. He dispatched her fallen antagonist with a blade thrust between the rib plates while Mirana sent arcane flame at the chest of the remaining fighter, turning him into fire and ash.

Teague recovered his stance only to be knocked off-balance again when the Ken'nar fighting Binthe stumbled into him. The seer woman took the advantage of her opponent's distraction and kicked. The Ken'nar—a woman, by the shapely cut of the armor—fell to the floor, her sword clattering away.

Teague pinned her to the floor with a foot on her chest, the tip of his blade at her throat.

"We shall die together, Fal'kin," the Ken'nar hissed. Teague dove to the floor, avoiding immolation, and rolled to put out the flame on a shirt sleeve.

"Teague!" Mirana cried.

"I'm all right!" That was too close. He sprang to his feet and tried to give himself room to fight in the space already cramped with combat.

Rabb and Timir had cut an opening through the Ken'nar at the chamber's entrance. "Mirana! Go! Now!" The Sün-Kasalan seer motioned to her with a blood-soaked long knife. They wouldn't be able to hold an opening for long.

"Mirana, hurry." Binthe pulled one of her long knives from the back of a Ken'nar's neck. Two more Ken'nar immediately took up position between the Fal'kin seer and their fallen comrade.

"Get to the keep." Teague lunged for one of the Ken'nar attacking Binthe. "We'll hold them here. Go!"

She started toward him. "Teague."

"Go!" He ducked a Ken'nar blade meant for his throat.

"But—"

"I can't do anything for you at the keep," he replied, looking everywhere at once for an approaching dark warrior, "but I can do something to help you here." He kissed her passionately. "Now, go!"

She nodded, an entire conversation of love and gratitude in her eyes, then ran for the stairs.

Teague watched Mirana leave a bit too long. A Ken'nar crept up next to him and made a vicious swing at his head. He shouted, startled, and ducked.

This one had chains on his epaulets. A commander. Four chains. A high-ranking commander.

"Morgan! Timir!" Teague shouted. "A little help here!"

He gritted his teeth and made an upper cut with his stolen Ken'nar broadsword against his assailant's thick blade. Morgan, Binthe, and the seconds were busy fighting for their lives. If he was going to live, he would have to save himself.

His attacker brought his blade down hard, cutting Teague's arm. He screamed in pain and staggered back as the Ken'nar commander pressed him with a series of moves, each one intended to kill him.

He blocked the Ken'nar's onslaught as best he could, but he was not a swordsman. It was only due to Morgan's teaching, and probably a healthy amount of dumb luck, that he was still alive.

A heavy blow brought him to his knees. Stunned, he was slow in blocking another strike. The warrior drew a deep wound across Teague's chest. He hissed in pain, clutching at his torn tunic, his blood seeping over his hand. The warrior towered over him, laughing.

"Get up, maggot!" the commander sneered. "This is the most fun I've had all day."

He was going to be killed by a Ken'nar with a terrible sense of humor. How nice. Teague climbed unsteadily to his feet. The Ken'nar bade him to attack. "Yeah, yeah." A terrible sense of humor and hopefully stupid.

Teague brought up his broadsword but stopped mid-motion. He gasped and pointed. "Look out!" The Ken'nar spun around and cringed from a strike that never came. Teague swung his blade and brought it down on his assailant's shoulder.

The Ken'nar hissed and snarled. "So the Sightless mongrel actually has fangs." He laughed and pressed him back with a flashing blade. Apparently, the alloyed armor was tougher than it looked if hit straight on.

Teague fended off the Ken'nar's attack, but without an Aspected's augmented stamina and with the constant drain of his own vitality from the Ken'nar's Power from Without, he was tiring. The dark-armored warrior continued to come at him in bursts, feinting, toying with him, and advanced again.

He was in trouble. "Morgan?!"

The Fal'kin defender took a glancing blow from an assailant. "Morgan!" Teague shouted. He tried to evade his attacker to help his friend, but the Ken'nar defender commander was far too quick and blocked him.

Teague ducked his opponent's blade again. The grynwen whore's son was *enjoying* this. His assailant could incinerate him any time he chose; he was merely playing with Teague, like a cat with a mouse. When the Ken'nar grew tired of the game, he would simply turn him into dust. If Teague couldn't take the Ken'nar down with his sword, he'd have to find another way.

The Ken'nar's beryl amulet glowed in the chamber's torchlight, an angry, red serpent's eye guiding its master where to sink its steely bite. Teague leaned back from a swipe at his neck by the warrior's sword. He spun away and hammered down with his broadsword. The move was supposed to drive his attacker's blade into the stone pavers. At the last moment, the defender slid his sword away from the move and thrust again, nicking Teague's upper arm.

"Even defenders have some Sight. Unlike you," the Ken'nar sneered. He thrust again, forcing Teague to bring his blade up. The swords crossed in front of his face, his panting breaths fogging the steel. There was something familiar about this Ken'nar, but before he had time to make the connection, his assailant gave a hard shove with his body and his Aspect, slamming him into the stone wall.

Teague staggered and shrugged off the blow.

He had to remove the Ken'nar's amulet. That was the only way he'd survive. Without an amulet, the warrior would still be plenty dangerous, but at least he wouldn't be able to light up Teague or his friends like a Quorumtide bonfire. To get the amulet, though, he'd have to get in close.

Teague held his heavy Ken'nar broad sword in front of him and the Ken'nar commander answered him with a searing combination of blows.

"Get down!" Morgan advanced, amulet in hand, but the Ken'nar lashed out with his boot. He caught the defender in the stomach and sent him sprawling to the floor. Immediately, another warrior leaped upon the Fal'kin.

Teague moved in, trying for some advantage. The Ken'nar hammered the hilt of his sword down hard on Teague's wounded arm, and his sword clattered to the stone floor.

The Ken'nar defender pressed the tip of his blade at Teague's throat, forcing him back against the wall. "I want to hear you scream like a little girl and beg for death."

The sharp point scratched the hollow of Teague's throat as he swallowed. The Ken'nar's voice. Only now did he recognize it. "Khorr?" It was the same Ken'nar commander who had nearly gutted him like a fish when Healer Prime Belessa Tir died.

"Good memory, boy. And I remember *you* for making me look like a fool," Khorr growled.

The Ken'nar had it out for him personally. Great.

Khorr was right about one thing: defenders did have a preternatural sense of situational awareness akin to the Seeing Aspect. But if Teague could keep the quatra commander gloating for one moment more—

"Naw. You do that pretty well on your own."

"You little *penilare masticár*—"

Teague lunged and grabbed the chain of the Ken'nar's amulet.

"Teague!" Morgan surged toward him as Teague dragged the Ken'nar down to the pavers with his fall.

Khorr fired his amulet, but the beam shot at an oblique angle, melting the chain—and singeing Teague's fingertips. The Ken'nar surged to his feet only to scream in abject desolation as the amulet fell from his neck.

"I will kill you!" Khorr brought down his blade just as Morgan hammered his sword down on the Ken'nar's wrist.

Teague rolled away from the blow and stumbled to his feet, weariness dragging his movements.

Suddenly, everything slowed.

Khorr side-stepped Morgan's blade and pivoted toward Teague. The Ken'nar thrust his sword deep between his ribs. Teague groaned and collapsed as air and blood spurted from his side.

"*Teague!*" Binthe spun away from the amulet fire of her opponent.

Rabb pulled his long knife from under the chin of another Ken'nar. Timir fired his amulet at Khorr, but once again, the dark-armored commander evaded the blast.

The Ken'nar hurled chairs at the Fal'kin, throwing off their counterattacks. He dashed through the chamber entrance and slammed the doors behind him.

"Teague!" Binthe raced over to hold him.

"Go," Morgan said to Timir and Rabb. "Stop him."

"No," Teague shouted. Well, he meant it to be a shout. All he could do was exhale the words. He moved his mouth again, attempting to tell his friends that Mirana needed their help more, but pain stole away any air he had to speak.

Binthe held him in her arms. "Morgan, he's hurt."

"It's not that bad." He tried to smile. "See, it's hardly wider than four fingers across." The deep burning in his side made his whole body ache. "Morgan, let him go. Mirana—" He gritted his teeth. Wasn't shock or something supposed to stop the pain and make everything around him surreal? He had never been more aware of *feeling* in his life.

The seer woman's hands felt cold against Teague's cheek. Everything felt cold. "Teague's right. Mirana needs us. Let the Ken'nar go."

Teague smiled. Or sort of. Smiling hurt. Everything hurt. "He can't—" He took a breath. "—do much without this." He held up Khorr's amulet. It seemed heavier than it should be. His arm, too. The beryl amulet slipped from his bloody fingers to the pavers.

"He's going to wish he were dead." Morgan brought the heel of his boot down on the crystal with such force, it shattered into several shards.

Timir knelt by a blue sapphire in a pile of ash. "You are with the Aspects Above, *Ëi Patrua.*" He raised his head, tears making clean lines through the soot and blood on the young defender second's face. Closing his eyes for a moment, he pulled the amulet from the remains and tucked it into his belt pouch.

"Morgan, help me." Binthe motioned him over. "He needs a bandage." She pointed to the scorched and tattered standard of Kin-Deren province.

Rabb held the dark quartz amulet of Sahm Klai reverently in both hands like the relic it was. He turned to Timir. "We will mourn them proudly, *Ëi cara.* I promise you."

"Help me up," Teague wheezed. "We're running out of time." He was almost successful in holding back a groan of pain as the seer woman assisted him to his feet.

He was running out of time.

CHAPTER 26

"That is why I, and I alone, shall bear the burden."
—The Codex of Jasal the Great

Mirana pushed the deaths of her parents and the peril of Teague and her friends from her mind. She raced up the stairs, not stopping until she at last burst through the door that led out onto the keep's pinnacle landing. She stood still, searching with her senses and Aspects alike. No presences were near, but she'd be overwhelmed with blood lust and death if she opened herself any further.

Thick drops of rain mixed with ice pelted down from the angry evening sky, dark clouds revealing themselves between intermittent flashes of lightning. The howling wind drove the sleet into her face, stinging her skin like shards of glass. The pinnacle of the keep rose twenty more feet above her.

She blinked back the rain. She had to awaken the keep, but how? Some clue, some sign, directions, glyphs, something must be here to let her know how to connect with amulets inside the tower's stone walls. Her panicked frustration rose, a partner to her Aspects.

… Jasal, tell me what to do … It might have been a prayer or a call. It was utterly ridiculous either way.

"You needn't bother to ask him."

Mirana spun around.

Tetric Garis.

He stood with six Ken'nar. These were no mindless slaves. These had freely chosen the Power from Without and would die protecting their Ain Magne.

"Mirana, it is over." His voice was quiet, gentle. Menacing.

She held the amulet of Jasal Pinal. "*Ai.* It is. Call off your men, Tetric. Stand aside."

His obsidian eyes bored into her. "I do not want to fight you."

She returned his gaze. "I do not want to fight you, either. Kinderra was never meant to have a sole ruler. The people of this land have always been free. I intend to keep it that way."

He drew his long sword, the ringing scrape of the metal against its sheath singing like a death song. "You think I lied to you."

She took a step back. "You did. You lied to me and everyone else." She pulled her own blade from its scabbard. It felt heavy and unwieldy in her hand.

"Did I not tell you Fal'kin lives that would have been lost had been spared by my harvesting? Did I not tell you that if the Quorum of Light named me Primus Magne, I would end this war?" He stepped closer. "Did I not tell you that you were destined for something magnificent and not to die a coward's death by your own hand? How are those lies?"

She stiffened at the memory. "No life has been spared by being left a breathing husk of a person. The war would end through your subjugation of Kinderra as an overlord. And neither of us realized my destiny would be to stop you. You have made your choice, *Ëi patrua*. And I have made mine." She couldn't risk moving her eyes away from him to search for a way to connect with the keep. She would never look away.

"All of this, child," he spread his arms wide, indicating the embattled armies inside and outside of the citadel, "all of this could have been prevented had you given me the amulet in Trak-Calan. Your mother and father. They died because of you."

Guilt, like a lance, drove itself through her heart. He spoke the truth. She could have prevented the deaths of her parents, of the primes, had she given him Jasal's amulet. It was the truth, and yet it was so far from being right.

"Mirana." He stepped closer. She brought her sword up, ready, wary. He stopped and held out his empty hand. "You cannot win here. You sacrificed your parents' lives needlessly. For what? For your pride? Your misguided faith in a power that is such a paltry expression of what the Aspects Above would have us become? Are you going to needlessly sacrifice Kinderra as well?"

Her sword wavered. It seemed heavier than she remembered. Again, he spoke the truth. All the lives lost she now felt, deafening in their screams through her Healing Aspect. They died because of her. Fal'kin and Unaspected. Men, women. Children. And Ken'nar.

She could stop the war. Instantly. If she gave Tetric the amulet. *Ai*, the war would end, but so would freedom. "No. I am going to save Kinderra."

"How, *Ëi biraena?*" He laughed sadly. "You cannot possibly choose all the amulets in this keep. You are not strong enough. Even I would not be strong enough with just my Aspects alone. *Ai*, you made your choice to use only the Light from Within. That is where you will fail. The keep can only be chosen with the Power from Without. You have failed, Mirana, before you have even begun."

Doubt, guilt, and rage built up within her. Where her powers had once been wild and without focus, she now had an amulet with which to channel her Aspects. Its heat burned her skin as it lay against her palm.

She was doomed to die no matter what she did. But that didn't mean Kinderra had to fall in her wake.

"Maybe I have already failed, but I will make certain you will not succeed."

Mirana released her Aspects through the diamond crystal, hurling them at the Dark Trine. A single tendril licked him, the others fractioned to curl back on themselves toward the keep pinnacle.

Tetric blocked her white fire with a wall of silver-tinged black flame. He laughed in pity. "The pathetic power you wield from Within does little more than sting. The amulet you hold on to so tightly cannot protect you. It is meant for the keep. Not for you. Give it to me." Bolts of light hurled in her direction from the Ken'nar. She bent her amulet fire from the Dark Trine and deflected the flames. Spinning away from the attack, she brought up her sword.

The Ken'nar surged forward to defend their master. "No!" he snarled, holding them at bay with his hand. "She is mine. Guard the door. They will come." He moved closer, nearly within reach of his sword. ... *I have the power to save your life ... Or take it … I will give you one last chance … Give me the amulet … Or die … It is your choice …*

Mirana held her ground. "You have the same choice. You can stop your armies regardless of what I do. You could have spared the primes and my parents regardless of whether they supported you or not. You have the choice to truly become the man you almost are. But you have chosen instead to accept weakness and denial and abdication of responsibility of your powers instead of the Light from Within. You will never have this amulet."

The diamond crystal seared her palm. The Dark Trine towered over her, framed in the fierce lightning arcing overhead, his will threatening to crush her. All expression bled from his face. Bitter tears ran and merged with raindrops on her own. She once sought to save Tetric Garis's life. That man had always been the illusion. His truth was now revealed. The being, the monstrosity standing before her, was the reality.

… So be it …

The Dark Trine swung at Mirana with his long sword, and she answered him with her own blade.

*   *   *

Teague fell again, hard. His teeth snapped together as his chin hit the step ahead of him. He didn't feel the fall. That was probably a bad thing. He didn't feel much of anything. That wasn't exactly true. The burning, crushing agony in his side. *That* he felt.

"Teague." Rabb helped him rest against the wall, concern written on his face. "The bandage has come loose."

He looked down. The torchlight was not bright enough to illuminate colors. A dark, palm-sized patch bloomed across his shirt. "Oh." At some point, Binthe had torn some cloth from a flag and tied it around his chest. Wasn't it Binthe? Maybe it was Morgan? Binthe would have made a good healer. He shook his head to clear it.

Binthe knelt beside him. "Morgan, go with the others. I'll stay here with him."

"He needs a defender to guard him," Timir said. "His mother was Tash-Hamari. I owe it to her."

"No." Teague coughed lightly and grunted against the pain. A coppery sweetness washed over his tongue. "No. Mirana will need all of you. I'm slowing you down. Go." Lightning flickered through the tiny half-moon window high above him. "I'll catch up. There are four hundred and thirty-eight steps to the pinnacle of the keep tower. We only have a hundred and two more to go."

Morgan knelt. "How do you know?"

"We used to run these stairs." He pulled a breath. "And tag the lintel stone on the door at the top." He drew another ragged inhale. "A game. We used to. To play." He tried for another breath, but it didn't quite come. "Only the Quorum. Is allowed. In here. We never got caught." He forced a smile. "Almost never."

"You have the bravery of a thousand defenders." In the dim light, the corners of Morgan's eyes glinted.

Teague twitched his shoulders in a spare shrug. "Maybe nine hundred." He squeezed his eyes shut against another wave of pain threatening to drive him to unconsciousness. He needed to say this. It was important. "If I were ever to have a brother, I'd want him to be you, Morgan. Binthe—" He forced a ragged inhale, tasting more rust. "*Ëi siba.*"

She kissed him on the forehead. "We will be back. With Mirana."

He watched the Fal'kin until they were lost to the darkness above him, and their footsteps grew faint.

Four hundred and thirty-eight steps. One hundred and two more to go.

He hauled himself to his feet, gripping the wall for support. He lifted a foot. It dragged at his leg like the dead weight of a corpse attached to his ankle.

"One."

CHAPTER 27

"For not only am I the Lock, I am the Key."
—The Codex of Jasal the Great

Mirana slid her sword out from under Tetric's blade and curled it over to strike at the shoulder of his sword arm. He hissed in pain and swung at her neck. She backed away but caught the tip as it scraped the skin across her throat.

"You little fool!" he spat. "End this senseless charade. What do you hope to gain by fighting me? My army controls Deren and will soon control all of Kinderra. Those you love are dead. You cannot win. No hope remains. Give me the amulet."

"There is always hope." She released her power through the amulet. Again, the beam parted into wildly coruscating streaks; she couldn't spare the energy to merge them back together. It could stall his counterattack at least, even if it couldn't incinerate him. He answered with his own amulet, blocking her white light.

Warning. Presences. Near.

She did not look at the keep's doorway. She refused to take her eyes from the Dark Trine.

Morgan Jord, Binthe Lima, Timir Sadhi, and Rabb Plout emerged through the entrance, their weapons drawn.

"Hurry, Mirana! Take the keep!" Morgan shouted.

"Kill them!" Tetric screamed to his Ken'nar. The dark warriors surged forward to meet the Fal'kin, swords clashing, amulets lighting. "I gave you everything I had. You made yourself my enemy. An enemy to the Aspects Above themselves."

His face contorted with grief and rage. He struck his blade at her with such intensity, the blow drove her to her knees. She blocked his blade with her slim sword. He'd pulled his arm back for another blow when she surged upward and rammed her shoulder into his abdomen. He staggered back. She called to her Healing Aspect and sought his sword arm.

Muscles contract. Nerves fire.

He dropped his sword as his arm contracted involuntarily. He growled in pain and fury. He thrust out his hand, sending her flying into the side of the keep. She crashed against it, dropping her weapon and cracking her head against the stone bricks.

Stunned, she fell to the pavement, sprawled on her stomach. He drew closer. She fought the urge to call her weapon to her hand, but not just yet. One moment more. Tetric's Power from Without pulled at her. She pushed herself up and released amulet fire, fingers of light **arcing** through the air, before he could kill her. He stepped back from her attack, pouring out his Aspects through his dark amulet. She poured more of her will into the brilliant white fire, pulling separate strands together. The energies of their amulets fought to repel each other, a column of white and black, as each sought a weakness, fighting for supremacy. She gasped from the exertion, the amulet fire from the half diamond ceasing.

… Ëi biraena … You are just not strong enough to win against me … Please … Stop this insanity … The Dark Trine's words rang in her mind.

Mirana called to her sword and sent it flying toward the Dark Trine. He moved out of its way, stepping closer to her, not farther, and the blade meant to kill him only raked across his shoulder. It fell, skittering across the icy stone pavers. Startled by his advance, she faltered and stepped back closer to the keep.

She reached out to her Seeing Aspect to anticipate his next move. The Healing Aspect surged within her instead, not at her calling. The discord of injury grew closer, louder, more needful, taking precedence over her other Aspects. A living-but-fading essence now wove itself through the healing prescience.

"No."

Teague was dying.

*   *   *

Eighty-three.

Teague had long since given up counting aloud. He slipped again. For a moment, even the gloom of the keep's interior faded. No. He would not leave Mirana. Not just yet. He had to make some sort of distraction, anything, to give her whatever advantage he could to take control of Jasal's Keep. He had one chance to do what he needed to do, but for that, he needed to be alive. Or mostly alive, at least.

The fall where he'd clocked his chin was giving him a most irritating headache. Why that pain rose above that of his other wounds, he didn't know—or care, really—but at least it cleared his head. His sorry plan would only give Mirana a moment, but it was all he could give her. Maybe, just maybe, it would be enough.

Footsteps came up the stairs behind him. He craned his neck over his shoulder. The rangy silhouette of a man, sword in hand, appeared in the torchlight.

Dammit. Couldn't the Aspects Above have given him just a few more seconds before they took his life?

Sido Rendel limped up the stairs and collapsed next to Teague. "They left you behind? You need to get better friends."

He shook his head and dragged in a breath. "Told them to go." He struggled to turn from his side to face the seer. He didn't want to look like he'd died a coward when they found his body. "Hurry up and kill me then."

"I am *not* going to kill you. Haven't you figured that out already, you dolt?"

Teague struggled in the darkness to see Sido's expression. "But those twelve Ken'nar? Khorr? You let them through."

"Do I look like I let them through?" He pointed to his thigh. A dark, wet patch had soaked through a makeshift bandage. "I'm good, believe me, but twelve-against-one are not odds I like. I knew I wouldn't make it if I kept fighting on one leg, so I took a dive and played opossum."

"You—" Teague laughed, well, wheezed a humorous exhale. "You pretended you were dead?"

"That, and more than a little seer's ruse helped. Defenders in a full lather from fighting aren't especially clever. They're more—"

Teague rubbed a bruise on his temple from having been thrown into a stone wall. "—reactionary."

"*Ai.*"

"And Khorr? He didn't skewer you to make sure you were dead?"

"No." Now Sido laughed. "What did the Fal'kin do to him? He ran out the courtyard screaming like a little girl."

"I stole—" Teague's chest heaved in a breath. "—his amulet."

"Impressive," the seer replied. "I never thought I'd feel sorry for Khorr. Most Aspected would rather kill themselves than live without their amulets."

Sido tilted his head to look up the spiraling staircase. "I did try to hold them back, you know." He shifted, hissing at the pain in his leg. "Is Mirana—?"

"Fine. At the moment."

The seer nodded.

"Sido, why are you doing this? Really. You hate us. You hate me."

The seer remained silent for a long time. "I hate you, *ai*, but I don't hate Mirana," he answered at last. "I matter to her. Not because of what I can give her, or my sword, or knowledge from my Seeing Aspect. She cares about *me*. For some reason, that's enough for her to try so hard." He laughed again, but this time, it sounded more sad than happy. "I'm just not sure whether I'm trying to prove her efforts are wrong. Or right."

The seer would never know just how similarly Teague felt. "And Garis?"

"The Underworld is too good of a place for his ashes to rot in. But it's the best option we have. And I will do whatever I can to help Mirana make that happen."

The seer reached over and adjusted Teague's chest bandage. "Furthermore, I'm not about to give that silver-eyed sylph the satisfaction of hating me the rest of her life if I let you die on me and become a martyr."

Teague laughed and choked on something thick and metallic-tasting as a small rush of air fought its way up from his ruined lung.

So long ago, it seemed like another lifetime, Mirana had left him to prevent this very moment. What she did not know at the time, what he himself hadn't known, was that this moment needed to be. Everything was exactly as it should be. She needed this moment—him—to work her miracle. Was that not the ultimate act of a healer? To give one's life so another could live? For Mirana, he would willingly give his life every day if it meant she would live. That was the easiest choice he could ever make.

"So do you have a plan?" the seer asked.

Teague shook his head. "Not really. Do you?"

Sido shrugged. "Not really."

Teague frowned. "Ass. Just when I need your devious self."

The former Ken'nar snorted a laugh.

"We have to make some sort of distraction." Sido's amulet winked in the faint light. Amulets. The man was a seer—he couldn't make amulet fire. And with a wounded leg, he'd be hard-pressed in a physical fight. Oddly, Sido's injury reminded him of Binthe's trauma sustained during the Battle of Edara.

And of Binthe's courageous actions with the Seeing Aspect that saved their lives that night.

He smiled.

Sido groaned. "You're not serious? That's a terrible plan." He must have heard his thoughts.

Teague nodded. "*Ai.*"

"I'll call your bid and raise you. I have an idea of how to make your bad idea even worse." He cradled his amulet with both hands against his heart. "Here." He lifted the peridot relic over his head and handed to Teague.

"Are you sure?"

"Of course not," the seer replied, "but we don't have a lot of other choices." His voice already sounded strained.

Teague fumbled with the amulet. His arm wouldn't lift high enough to place it over his head. The stairwell was too dark to see Sido's expression, but the frustrated growl the seer gave was expression enough. He looped the amulet around Teague's neck.

"Now, on your feet, herbsboy." The seer hauled him up, and they both groaned in pain with the effort.

Sido surely had suffered some blood loss, not to mention the seer must be in as much pain as he was. Teague clenched his teeth. Would it interfere with what they would attempt to do?

They struggled up the stairs. "I'm going to have to use you, you know," the seer said.

Teague nodded. "I know."

"She isn't going to be very happy with either one of us."

He smiled. "I know that, too."

CHAPTER 28

"And I will choose it!"
—The Codex of Jasal the Great

Mirana poured all her strength into her Defending Aspect, as her friends fought beside her against the Ain Magne's lieutenants. The half-diamond amulet belched white fire, its separate beams pulled back together by the force of her will, as deadly brilliance and blade bore down on the Dark Trine. He cried out in pain and collapsed to his knees under her onslaught. Exhausted and breathless from the sustained outpouring of her Aspects, she broke off the attack and stumbled back from Tetric. Her former mentor's weakness, however, was a feint, one she caught too late. He lifted his hand and wrenched vitality from her, driving out what was left of her breath. Mirana repulsed his grip on her life force and retreated a few steps to give herself more room to fight.

Presences.

Out of the shadows of the stairwell came Sido Rendel. With his arm around Teague's throat.

"Sido!" Mirana cried. "What—?"

For a moment, the fighting around them stopped.

"Mirana, give the amulet to our Lord Trine, or your herbsboy dies," the Ken'nar seer said.

She shook her head slowly, horrified. "No. Sido. Please don't do this."

Tetric laughed, a hacking noise like ax chops. "Do you honestly think, seer, I would ever take you into my confidence again?"

Sido edged nearer to the Dark Trine. "I never left it, my lord. I had to do something to make her trust me so she would never suspect my loyalty to you. *Ai*, I disobeyed your orders to stay away from her—because I saw she would never make it across the glacier. I know how dear she is to you. Even now."

Mirana scowled in indecision then in disbelief. Wait. Sido moved closer to Tetric. Not her. Her friend wasn't trying to kill her or Teague at all. He was trying to— "Sido, I know this isn't you!"

"Mirana," Teague breathed, "don't listen to him. Choose the keep." Sido tightened his hold on him, drawing a stifled cry of pain.

"Teague." Mirana shook her head in panic. If she couldn't help make Sido's ruse believable, they were all dead. "Let him go. Please."

Tetric tightened the grip on his sword as his amulet brightened. "I made you who you are, boy. I know your mind."

"And I know yours," the young seer replied. "You desire Kinderra above all else. Even Mirana. Controlling the keep will give you everything. I have always given you my Aspect in service to that."

Binthe, Morgan, and the other Fal'kin now pressed their attackers to reach her, but the Ken'nar would not yield.

"Stay back," Tetric ordered the Ken'nar. "This is *my* fight."

"*Our* fight." Mirana advanced toward the Trine, sword in one hand, amulet held by the other. "Call off your Ken'nar and let Teague and the others go. He's wounded." No, he was dying. And there was absolutely nothing she could do now to save him.

"Lord, you know she loves this Sightless maggot above everything," Sido said. "She would do anything to save his life."

"As I would do for her, you rackin' Ken'nar bastard, Teague hissed. "Mirana. Choose the keep." He struggled weakly in the seer's grip, trying to wrest the Ken'nar's arm from his neck.

Mirana's eyes flicked between Teague and her oppressor. Maybe Teague was a better actor than her *or* Sido.

Something, some current, whispered from within the Aspects. It was so subtle Mirana couldn't discern from which of her three it came. She advanced again toward the seer and her beloved. "I know I broke your heart, Sido, but I thought you were still my friend. Despite everything, I trusted you. I trust you now." She hoped the seer understood she was aware of his plan. If she gave any hint of it through the Aspects, Tetric would know.

Sido, pale and sweaty from his wounds and the effort to remain conscious, made a half-hearted smile and a strained laugh. "You trust me the way I trust grynwen."

Before she could acknowledge him in their subterfuge, Tetric dragged Teague from his second with a lightning-fast move and brought his long sword down on his servant's arm. Sido doubled over in pain, dropping his blade. "I do not suffer enemies." He flung Teague from him into the wall of the keep's pinnacle entrance. Teague slumped to the stone pavers and lay still.

"Teague!" Mirana rushed toward him but slid to a halt as Tetric's sword barred the way.

The tall Trine lashed out with a boot at the seer and caught him in his wounded thigh. Sido's leg collapsed and he fell to the stone, crying out in pain. "I suffer traitors even less."

Amulet fire, like the edge of a shadow, exploded from the Dark Trine's amulet, striking his former second. Sido screamed and writhed in agony, the flesh across his chest blackened, blistered, and bleeding. "I know your mind *and* your heart." Tetric continued to release muddy silver fire, unrelenting, into the young seer. "You will die by your own Aspects, traitor."

"Sido!" Mirana dove in front of the flame and deflected it with white amulet fire. Tendrils of white-hot flame shot out in all directions, some curling back to the keep tower. She poured more of her will into the crystal to reunite the branches of fire, but the effort exhausted her. Flickers of flame snapped around Tetric like embers. She hadn't stopped him, only slowed his defense. It wouldn't be enough. She had to connect with the keep. Somehow.

Mirana gasped from exertion. Fire crackled and arched around Jasal's amulet in her hand. "Call off your army." She gulped a hurried breath. "If you do not, every single Ken'nar warrior will die. If you truly want peace for Kinderra, you will."

His dark eyes bored into hers as he grasped his amulet. "It is you who stands in the way of peace." She readied herself for the flare of his amulet, but none came.

Instead, he lunged forward, pulling the beautiful ebony-and-pearl stiletto from his waist as he closed in on her. Shock and fatigue weakened her defenses, leaving her unable to ward off the slim blade as it plunged into her stomach. She dropped her own weapon with a choking groan and collapsed against Tetric. He raked the stiletto across her abdomen, and his betrayal stabbed just as deeply.

The desperate struggle of her friends receded as pain and despair engulfed her.

Tetric held her to him, her chin on his shoulder, his blade sunk in her body. … *Give me the amulet, Ëi biraena … It is time … You know this was always meant to be …*

Through some distant knowing of her Seeing Aspect, she saw the Fal'kin attempt to surge forward to her, only to have the Ken'nar beat them back. Her heart hammered in her chest, mirrored in an excruciating throb through her abdomen. This moment was the skein of time she had seen for most of her life. The *when* she had given everything to avoid.

… Ai … You have seen this before … You have seen your own death … Your own failure … But it does not have to be … Tetric's mind's voice was as soft as it was sinister. *… You are the Aspects Above alive on Kinderra to me … Please give me the amulet …*

Pain flared with each beat of her heart. She pushed herself out of his embrace and off his stiletto to stagger back and collapse to her hands and knees. The gravel of the stone paving under her palms dug into her flesh. A loop of something grayish pink pushed out from between layers of rent muscle and bleeding skin. Ice pelted the back of her neck, burning with cold. Blood gushed thick and hot over her hand as she tried to hold the wound closed. It ran over her fingers and down her side, steaming in the chill air.

"The Power from Without can never bring peace." The words bled from her lips. "You do not give. You take. That is the truth you could never believe, Tetric, the truth you could never accept."

Beyond her pain, beyond Sido's pain and the injuries her friends sustained on her behalf, Mirana heard the fading wail of near-death. Unlike the awesome polyphony of life, death was the dissolution of life's music. Note by note, the song of a life unraveled.

Teague.

… Ai … I hear it, too …

Tetric stalked to the pinnacle entrance and remained facing her with his sword leveled. He hauled Teague up by the throat.

"Teague!" she cried. "Let him go. Please. I beg of you!"

… He is dying … I can give him his life back … If you give me the amulet …

Indecision held her captive as her blood dripped onto the paving. The downpour created little pink rivulets in the grout, her blood running away in the channels. Sacrifice Teague for Kinderra. Kinderra for Teague.

The world slowed around her as her vision tunneled. Out of the corner of her eye, she saw Sido drag himself, bit by bit, closer to Tetric and Teague.

… Think, Mirana … the Dark Trine intoned through her mind. *… Is his life worth your mindless adherence to a flawed philosophy? … Is Kinderra? …* "Give me the amulet."

Teague.

She sat back on her heels and tried to heal herself to give herself more time but no longer had the strength to direct her Aspect. Pain wracked her body, her heart, her mind, her spirit beaten. Her hand fell away from her wound.

Teague fought in the Dark Trine's grip. "Don't give it to him."

All around her, the death and destruction of Deren cried out to her. Buildings burned from naphtha fires, unquenchable despite the driving rain. Cries of the dying, so numerous before, now grew fainter as they succumbed to their ends. The searing agony of the amulet-fire burns Sido had sustained trying to save her would not abate. Her friends fought so hard for so long to give her the chance to save Kinderra and she'd failed them. They would die. Her parents were dead. Teague would die.

Kinderra was lost.

Teague's life had always been a part of hers since she drew her first breath. Even in this very place where they had played as children, racing up the steps to leap and tag the carved indentation on the doorway's lintel. He was as much a part of her as her Aspects were. And she had failed them all.

She could not heal him—or Kinderra—like this.

"Let him live. Please."

"My child." Tetric sobbed with relief. He tossed Teague aside like a ragdoll, her beloved's body making a wet slap as he fell.

"Miri," Teague said. He collapsed and lay still.

"Teague." Sido groaned and inched closer to the fallen herbsman. "*Ëi cara.*"

The Dark Trine crossed behind her. He gently brushed back the long hair from her neck, his fingertips as cold as ice. Her breath now came in ragged pulls as her life leaked out from her. Cold fingers grasped the heavy chain of the amulet. The amulet glowed from her Aspects, from Tetric's Aspects.

She raised her eyes to the pinnacle door where Sido and Teague had emerged. When she and Teague were children, that door was the goal of their tagging game. Sometimes, Teague would win. He was taller. Sometimes, she would win. She was faster. In the pouring rain, her fading eyesight caught the faint indentation in the doorway lintel.

"*Ëi ama,*" Mirana sobbed.

The impression in the lintel. It was cut in the shape of the amulet she wore.

Teague. Aspects. The tagging game. Aspects. Lintel. Aspects. Jasal.

She gasped in understanding. *I am the Lock and the Key.*

The lock. The amulet. The key.

Teague suddenly surged to his knees, Sido's hand on his arm. "I have the blood of defenders and healers and seers in my veins!"

Tetric snapped his head around toward the pair.

Teague held an amulet out in front of him. "You will not have the keep!"

The pale-green gem flared to life, sending a jet of flame toward the Dark Trine. He screamed and spun away, shielding his face with his arms to defend himself against the amulet fire that engulfed him. He called his fallen long sword back to his hand. His body, however, was left unscathed. For a moment, just a moment, he hesitated in shock.

Mirana's Aspects erupted within her. She flew to her feet and raced toward the pinnacle door, pulling Jasal's amulet out of the Dark Trine's grasp as she passed. She leaped up to tag the lintel with the half diamond in her hand.

"No!" The heavy wooden door swung shut at Tetric's call. He hurled his sword at her.

Her fingertips around the amulet touched the stone of the lintel block. Excruciating agony exploded through her back. Blood welling up from her lungs drowned out her cry of pain. Sensation disappeared from her legs, her feet. She slumped forward against the door, the wood pressing against her cheek. Her body hung suspended off the pavers, the long sword impaling her to the keep. She clung to the amulet with numb fingers.

"Why did you make me do this? Why?" Tetric Garis cried in mortal torment.

The cacophony of her pain now overwhelmed the other minds reeling in horror. Half her body seized in agony, the other dangled limply, paralyzed, lifeless.

With the lucidity of coming death, she now understood. The choice to succeed or to fail, to be good or evil, lay within oneself. She could give in to despair and it would steal her strength to act, and she would fail. It would drown her determination, her need to make right all the wrongs that Tetric had caused, that she had caused.

She could have chosen to turn back from the quest for the keep passages. Yet she did not. She could have chosen to remain bound to the Power from Without. Yet she did not. She could have chosen not to accept Teague's sacrifice and let the Dark Trine take the amulet and the keep. She could choose to hold on to her victory, her goodness—her Lightness—as easily as she could choose her Darkness, her evil, and her failure.

… My destiny is upon me! … And I will choose it! …

Mirana reached higher with the amulet in her grip as the Dark Trine's blade cut deeper into her body. Her lifeblood rushed out of her, taking the notes of her own life's music with it. She placed the half diamond into the depression carved in the lintel.

Buried under summers of age and dirt lay the naked face of another amulet. Her diamond touched the other crystal, and she poured out her Aspects through her amulet. Light flared within the gem it touched, a topaz bursting in sun-yellow luminescence. Its light caressed another amulet, its crystal calling to her, accepting her as she accepted it. Blue light from a sapphire long embedded within the mortar of Jasal's Keep reached to another amulet, an emerald, then a garnet.

A strange and wonderful sound permeated her mind. A note. A life note. Then another. And another. Colors burst forth one by one, adding to each other, blending, building. The notes grew stronger. A chord. A harmony. Her own life's music amplified, augmented, multiplied. A symphony began to build around her, within her, surrounding her in a rhapsody of life. Amulet after amulet answered her call as she poured out her life's music into the crystals. She gave to the amulets all that she was, her Aspects choosing them, allowing their harmony to add to her own life's music.

The Aspects merged as one, pure and total, into tangible insolubility that swirled around her, through her. Sight, Defense, Healing—and her fourth Aspect, Love, championed by Teague's pendant—emanated from her. They became her and she became them. No division, no end or beginning. Beyond love, beyond light, she was a being transformed, embodying the rapturous creation of the Light of the Aspects Above themselves.

At last, her Aspects beheld the other diamond shard, the mate of the one she held. Like a new sun bursting to life, the pinnacle of Jasal's Keep erupted in blinding light, all the colors of the amulets housed within merging into pure brilliance. She was complete at last.

Mirana lifted her face to the sky and smiled as white light enveloped her.

CHAPTER 29

"This is the one purpose for which I have come unto the world."
—The Codex of Jasal the Great

Tetric Garis, the Prime of Dar-Azûl, the Ain Magne, the Dark Trine, cried out in anguish. The world around him grew painfully bright, as if the light of a thousand suns dawned above him.

Jasal's Keep was *his*! His to control, his to use in shepherding Kinderra into a new age. He was the only true Trine, neither denying nor accepting one path to the power of the Aspects over the other. The Power from Without and the Light from Within joined in union within him. The Aspects Above had given to him the fullness of their expression and he accepted it, willingly.

He had given everything he was, all that he had ever been destined to be, in service to the Aspects Above. He gave over his second, a living tool he had forged at his own hands. He had sacrificed those he loved and faced death time and time again. He accepted the terrible and awesome path of the Soul Harvest to serve the creation of the Aspect Above.

He sacrificed to the Aspects Above the one he loved as a daughter.

What more did they want from him? What more could he give them that he had not already sacrificed? The keep was his birthright.

His.

"Damn thee, thou Aspects Above! The keep is mine!"

Tetric braved the unrelenting brilliance and ran toward the keep. The ruined shell of Mirana's body fell to the storm-battered stone pavers when he pulled the sword from her. Stepping over her, he ripped his hematite amulet from his neck and tore the diamond from the keep's lintel stone. He thrust his own crystal into the depression and forced his three Aspects through his amulet. The crack that bifurcated the hematite's face spread wider.

And was repulsed back.

Tetric worked his mouth in shock and fury. "What?"

He could not choose the other amulets. *She* would not let him. She refused to allow his Aspects admittance to the keep's amulets. They now answered to her and her alone.

He screamed out in wrath. It couldn't be. He was the Trine of Kinderra. His Seeing Aspect had always told him so. He may be the most feared defender on the continent, the most accomplished and accursed healer, but it was his Seeing Aspect he cherished above all else.

He gripped his dark amulet. Wrenching life from around him, he fueled his Power from Without, pulling in the very light of the keep to him. … *This power is mine, Mirana Pinal! … Kinderra is—* …

Visions assailed his mind's eye.

Mirana Pinal. Hailed as a savior. Standing proud. A blonde girl with smiling silver eyes. Other babes with silver eyes. Mirana Pinal struggles. Accused by those who once lauded her. Hated by those who once loved her. The Aspected, once heroes, are now hunted. Jasal's Keep explodes in light.

Mirana had been right. So wrong, yet still right. Jasal's Keep would destroy them both. And she—she *would* destroy all she loved.

… Ëi Biraena Trinus … Release the keep … If you do not, you will lose more than you can imagine … Release the keep, biraena … You have not saved Kinderra and all you love … You have condemned it …

A column of pure white light arched and flowed down from the sky, washing over him. Incomprehensible pain and rapturous release became one within him, indivisible from the light that surrounded him.

Tetric Garis perceived a single note of the universal life song that no mortal sense could ever possibly define, until it, too, faded into silence.

CHAPTER 30

"At last, my destiny is upon me."
	—The Codex of Jasal the Great

Teague squinted his eyes against the painfully bright light in the keep. Where Tetric Garis stood a moment ago, now lay a dark amulet without an owner, man and Aspects transformed into ash. Some of the detritus stained Mirana's pale, scarred hand where she now lay sprawled, unmoving, on the pavers. Her eyes remained open to the light as it gleamed and pulsed far above her.

The agony of losing her bled out of him in a cry as his blood ran from the mortal wound on his side. The light took her from him, as he had known it would. She was never his to begin with. She belonged to Kinderra.

"The keep," Morgan whispered in awe. "Mirana has reawakened the keep."

His friend's strong arms held him as Binthe's gentle hands tried to staunch the gash in his flank. Rabb and Timir stood over Sido, their swords drawn against the two remaining Ken'nar poised to attack their former seer second.

The Ken'nar surged forward, preparing to strike them down, when a finger of light peeled off from the brilliant column and touched them. The luminescence instantly immolated them. Ash turned into silt and washed away in the wind-driven rain.

Rabb and Timir carried Sido back to the others. He shuddered against the pain of his burns and bleeding wounds. "I saw her survive this. She can't be dead. She can't be. I saw it." He grabbed Rabb's arm. "You are a seer, too. Please tell me you see her live. Please."

Rabb shook his head and gave the young seer a weak smile. "I didn't have a chance to look."

The former Ken'nar closed his eyes. "Let me go."

"Look!" Timir pointed out over the battlefield.

Teague blinked against the light flaring wildly above him. He must be hallucinating. Dozens, hundreds, thousands of fingers of light separated from the brilliant white column.

"Lift me," he breathed. "I need to see."

Binthe brushed the rain-soaked hair from his eyes. "Teague."

"Please. It's Mirana. I need to see her."

Morgan and the seer woman gently lifted him. When he and Mirana were children, this vista would take his breath away. Now he had almost no breath to take.

"Mirana."

Countless tendrils of earthbound lightning struck the Ken'nar below, killing them, but leaving the Unaspected and the Fal'kin untouched.

"The Ken'nar call the Aspects to them from Without, bringing the strongest life, the strongest power to themselves," Binthe said, transfixed in awe. "The Fal'kin touch the Aspects from Within. The Unaspected breathe the breath of the Aspects Above alone."

"The stupid bastards," Sido said with a rasping laugh.

Teague wept and laughed at the seer's words, at the miraculous fingers of light. Tears quickly overcame the joy. The perfect logic of Jasal Pinal's design had saved Kinderra but could not save Mirana. His knees buckled as the last of his strength left him. Morgan and Binthe lowered him down.

"Bring her to me," Teague said as he lay against Binthe. "I want. Hold her. One last time."

Morgan hurried over to where Mirana lay. He cradled her half-diamond amulet reverently and gently lifted her body from the wet pavers. He laid her in Teague's arms and placed the amulet back around her neck. Rabb and Timir knelt beside him, holding Sido.

Teague brushed his fingertips over her lips. "I loved her. I loved her more than life itself."

"*Ëi siba.*" Binthe wiped the blood and the rain from Mirana's pale face. "Teague, *Ëi sibe*, you shall be with her in the Aspects soon. You will be with her forever." She lowered her head and wept.

A tendril of light cleaved from the keep and slowly reached down toward them. Teague held Mirana to him. He steeled himself for the light's fiery touch to hasten his death. Instead, it washed over his body, as gentle as a lover's caress. A sensation of love and life flooded through him, filling him. It swirled around him, concentrating on his side. The pain receded. His wound slowly faded then disappeared altogether. He could breathe once more.

The light flowed from him to Sido, his ruined flesh made whole, leaving the faintest traces of scars. It enveloped Binthe, its brilliance concentrated on the still-healing wound on her thigh she had received in the killing fields of Edara. The brilliance left her to surround the others, undoing the work of the Ken'nar's cruel weapons.

At last, the light in the keep settled like a shroud over Mirana. Teague sat up out of the seer woman's arms and cradled Mirana in an unbreakable embrace of love. "Don't take her from me. Please don't take her from me. She is the one who deserves life, not I. She is the Light Trine."

He buried his head against Mirana's chest, clutching her to him. If the Aspects Above were going to take her, they would have to take him, too.

… You forget, Son of Healers … Am I not a healer as well? …

The voice resounded in his mind, words not spoken, but pure concept making its intention known. He knew that voice, the sense of it. He knew it as intimately as he knew his own.

The wondrous column of light flared once more and collapsed in upon itself. All was still. Even the battlefield below stood hushed. The broken, miraculous, perfectly imperfect diamond at his beloved's chest radiated with light then softened to a glow.

Mirana gasped in his arms as her eyes snapped open.

"Mirana?" Teague loosened his embrace on her as her chest rose and fell once. Twice. "Mirana?" He placed his hand on her chest. A rhythmic vibration pulsed against his palm. "Mirana!"

She smiled up at him. "I tagged the lintel first. And I won."

Teague kissed her, his desolation turned to unsurpassed joy. The Fal'kin embraced them, wrapping them in the light of their own Aspects.

CHAPTER 31

"Hope shall remain."
                    —The Book of Kinderra

Peace.

Peace surrounded Mirana, the sensation all-encompassing.

But the skin on her belly itched.

She scowled. An itch seemed to be a terribly odd feeling for one to experience when one was no longer part of the physical realm. So was scowling.

She shifted, intending to scratch her stomach, but the movement brought a wave of pain. No, not pain, but the discomfort felt after being in severe pain for a long time. Sore from being sore.

Then the memories came back to her.

The siege of Deren. Her parents' ruined, lifeless bodies. Tetric Garis's unrelenting attack. Her friends in peril. Teague's impending death. The pain. The light. The awesome, all-consuming, all-giving light. Tetric's warning, a desperate plea, and a dark victory. And the light.

She moaned, a true, physical sensation in her throat.

"She's waking up. Oh, Light Above! She's waking up. Mirana! Mirana, can you hear me?"

Teague.

Mirana awoke with a start. She lay on a cot in a tent. Dawn painted a deep orange hue on the canvas walls, as if the light from her mother's yellow topaz amulet and her father's red garnet amulet had blended around her. Something warm rested on her chest.

She opened her eyes. He was alive. Teague was alive!

"Teague," she whispered. Breathing, let alone speaking, seemed as odd as itching—half-forgotten functions she only now remembered.

His hand remained on her chest. "I wanted to feel your heartbeat." He swallowed and curled in his top lip for a moment to capture some tears. "I didn't know if you would stay." He laughed and cried at the same time. "You're here. Alive."

"*Ama.*" She traced the features of his face with her fingertips, brushing at the tears streaming down his cheeks, not believing he was real, not believing she was.

With a finger, he tenderly pushed aside her amulet to reveal the peda blossom pendant. "After all you've been through, you still have this sad little thing?"

"It is more precious to me than a thousand amulets." All at once, she sat up and threw her arms around him.

He held her close to him. "You died, Mirana. You gave your life for us."

"No, I didn't." She brought a hand to her chest and touched the half-diamond amulet that lay there. "I don't know if I'll ever fully understand what happened, but what I experienced was not death. It was life. I was more alive than I've ever been."

He brushed her lips with his once more. "I didn't think I'd ever kiss you again."

"You almost didn't. Just what were you and Sido thinking with that stunt you pulled?"

"Well, it did go a little more awry than we had planned," he replied, a sheepish grin on his face.

She smiled in bewilderment. "And you never thought either of you could be thrown or incinerated?"

Teague laughed and shrugged. "In our defense, we were bleeding to death, so…"

Mirana shook her head. "Where is Sido? I remember—" She scowled. "Remember" wasn't the right word, but it was as close as she could come to explaining the knowledge. "He was wounded. Then healed."

Teague glanced at the others and back to her. "After he saw you were breathing on your own, that it wasn't some temporary state, he left."

She bit her lip and nodded. "I wanted to speak with him." To assure herself he had indeed been healed. To apologize. Again. For so many things. To thank him for his bravery, not only for his willingness to give up his life for her despite everything but his bravery in redeeming himself.

Fingers brushed the hair on her forehead. She turned. Gemma.

She returned the herbswoman's smile. Tears filled the dark eyes of the Jad-Anünan woman, who had long since become accustomed to injury and death.

"Sweetling." Gemma cupped Mirana's cheek with a warm hand. "Don't you dare scare us like that again."

"Is she all right?" Teague asked.

"*Ai*, I'm fine," Mirana replied before the herbswoman could respond. "I'm just…" What? Weak, *ai*. And hungry. More than that. Much more. Whole? Complete? No.

Changed.

Ai, she had changed. She was no longer what she had been, but someone, *something* different. She shook her head and smiled. "I'm fine."

"Binthe?" Teague called. "Binthe! Morgan! She's awake!"

The flap to the tent parted, and her dear friends entered, hand in hand. Rabb Plout and Timir Sadhi filed in behind them, followed by the lumbering figure of Quartermaster Haarlen Lasen.

Binthe's face broke into a stunning smile. "*Ëi siba!*" She ran over to embrace her.

"Tiny but tough." Haarlen chuckled, a deep, reassuring basso. "We thought you left us, *biraena*."

There would be time to understand later. "How? How did you survive?" Mirana asked Haarlen and Gemma, looking from one to the other.

The quartermaster shrugged his brawny shoulders. His cheeks were not as hale pink as they normally were, but his smile was just as broad. "I've lost count of how many chicken necks I've wrung. It doesn't take much more effort on a Ken'nar."

Gemma tucked an unruly lock of graying black hair into her headcloth. "I don't have anything like this brute's strength, but I was trying to dispose of some oil that had gone bad when I spilled it. All over the stairs. In front of a dozen Ken'nar." She grinned. "Clumsy me."

A presence.

The life essence came softly to her mind. A certain haughtiness, coupled with curiosity and an abstract longing. A quiet, trilling sound preceded a whiskered cinnamon and cream-colored head.

She laughed. "Cider!"

Her tomcat leaped upon the cot and butted her face with his own. His body vibrated against hers in a loud purr as he kneaded her with his paws. "Well, it's nice to know I rate somewhere close to his interest in mice."

She picked him up and nuzzled the soft fur between his ears. The rain had left his coat spiky with dampness, and patches of fur had been singed, but her Healing Aspect told her he was otherwise healthy. If only Ashtar could be here. That beautiful, brave beast. She swallowed against tears of her own. Her cat. In her arms. Her selfish, aloof, brave, precious ball of fur. This small life had survived against the greatest evil Kinderra had ever faced. And he lived. Like her.

If her cat survived, maybe Deren—

"I need to see it. I need to see Deren."

Teague kissed her tenderly. "Come."

He lifted her in his arms and carried her out of the tent. Once outside, he set her down. Droplets on the rain-soaked grass reflected the sun like the facets of amulets. The air was cool and fresh, and the light of early morning shone down on the citadel.

She brought her hands to her mouth. The walls crumbled and homes smoldered, an invalid struggling to remain on its feet, but it stood.

People worked on repairing what they could, already striving to erase the destruction the Ken'nar had wrought. Others tended to the injured in tents, still others comforted children, elders, and each other. Farmers, homesteaders, shopkeepers, young and old, rich and poor, they had survived. Many, many perished. Even now her Healing Aspect could hear the retreating echoes of the dying. But many, many more still lived. The people lived.

By the Light, they lived!

She turned to her friends. "I owe you all so much."

Morgan clasped her hand in his own. "You owe us nothing."

A defender came forward and kneeled. "My Lady Trine." Behind him stood dozens of other men and women bearing amulets against eagles, horses, bulls, capricorns, leopards, and lions on their chests. The Fal'kinnen.

"Niall Corran. Thank the Aspects Above." Her mother's provincial defender second. No. Dav Koehl was dead. Niall would be defender commander now. With a shock, she realized he was *her* defender commander. Was she prime of Kin-Deren province? Good Light! What was she?

Later.

Mirana reached down and lifted him with a hand on his elbow. His pain—physical, emotional, spiritual—drew her Healing Aspect close. His formal dress tunic was torn and stained. She bit her lip. He wasn't in uniform but in festival finery, or what was left of it. She needed no Sight from her Aspect. If he hadn't been with the provincial forces near the Garnath River, it was because he was still recovering from injuries. Two Rivers Ford? Edara? It didn't matter. He had fought anyway.

"You're hurt."

"*Ëo anaíle; Ëo aspece.*" His gaze drifted to Gemma and a trace of a smile crossed his lips. The herbswoman grinned even brighter. "I will heal."

Interesting. Mirana arched an eyebrow. How long had that been going on? She smiled. Why should she be surprised? She and Teague were a living testament to how the most unlikely of people could stand against anything when joined by love. "I didn't dare to hope your life had been spared. All the Ken'nar could not have perished."

Niall Corran shook his head. "They did not, my lady. Some of us did what we could in the city." He gestured over his shoulder to other Fal'kin in tattered, bloody formalwear and glittering amulets. "Our vanguard along with Sün-Kasal forces and noble Unaspected harried toward the Garnath River what handfuls of Ken'nar were left after"—he paused, swallowing—"after the light."

Rabb Plout held his ruddy brown topaz. "My Sight has told me they will run into a very small but very angry reconnaissance group from Varn-Erdal."

Timir Sadhi nodded. "I would very much like to be with her—erm, *them*."

Teague took out an amulet from his belt pouch. "Now we can truly have a chance for peace." He held a fractured silvery-black crystal encased in a crude, scorched setting.

She took the amulet from him.

Tetric.

He could have been a good man. He could have been Kinderra's savior. If he had only chosen to be. She tucked the hematite amulet inside the folds of her shirt.

A youth about her age rushed over. "My lady. It's true. We saw it. We saw your light in the keep."

"Maark Bedane?" When she had last seen him, he'd had stitches on his arm. Now his arm bore a scar and a long bow. She laughed and embraced him warmly.

The people, by the hundreds, thousands, with the Aspects, without the Aspects, lifted their voices into the bright morning air, a battle cry of victory. Of survival. Of hope. Teague kissed her ardently, then touched his lips to each one of her scarred, perfectly imperfect hands. At last, tears came freely and spilled over her lashes to run down her cheeks.

"It is I who should be hailing you," Mirana cried out above the celebratory din. "It is you who saved Kinderra with your courage, with your lives." She smiled at Teague. "With your love." She turned to the gathering once more. "We will rebuild Kinderra. Together."

The people cheered once more.

Off in the distance, a young man stood in the shadows formed by a damaged wall. A cowl obscured his face. He had some height to him, but not so much as to be imposing. He was thin with a sort of feral grace to his bearing. Around his neck hung a pale-green peridot. Now he drew back the curtain on his presence.

… Sido … Mirana called.

… I told you I was right … You are standing, victorious, in Deren, Kinderra at your feet … I guess you were right, too … My vantage point was indeed wrong … Ben íre … He nodded and turned to leave, then paused *… E Gratas Oë …*

… Stay … she returned, hopeful. He shook his head. He had made a choice not to go back to what he once was but now had to choose how to go forward. Oh, the agony of that particular dilemma. The answer could only be found by oneself. *… You are a good man …*

… No … I'm a bad man who occasionally does good things … But maybe I might become good … Someday …

Sido Rendel turned and left, disappearing into the broken, striving city.

She took Tetric Garis's amulet from the folds of her shirt and studied its dark, metallic, and fractured face once more. In those final moments, she had seen what he saw, heard the mind-words he spoke to her. It seemed like something of a dream. Or recalling someone else's memory. That vision had been filled with so much joy. And so much more pain.

Had it been the Dark Trine's last, desperate attempt to get her to cede control of the keep over to him? A final ploy? Except she had sensed no duplicity from the man—or whatever he was at that moment.

Tetric Garis's whole life had been a lie, even if he chose not to see it. That was the ocean of difference between them; she acknowledged her lies, mistakes, and denial. And she chose to spend the rest of her life always reaching for honesty and selflessness, to become the best version of herself she could possibly be.

Mirana slipped the bifurcated amulet back within her shirt.

Somewhere above her, a songbird gave its morning call. A hammer pounded on stone and a saw scraped against wood. Farther still, a woman sang, and children laughed. Life.

She smiled.

Hope remained. And always would.

The Saga Continues…

**TRINE GUARDIAN
THE KINDERRA SAGA: BOOK 4**

TRINE REVELATION
The Kinderra Saga: Book 3

Dramatis Personae

Kin-Deren—1ˢᵗ Hall. Standard: gold field with red eagle

ANTIRI il'Amil Pinal (2094–2127): Seer. Joined in union with Jasal Pinal. Son, Jasan (b. 2122). Born in Tash-Hamar province. Amulet: blue-green aquamarine.

ATAN Robaar (3350–): Fal'kin scholaire Defender. Chooses early to support the Battle of Two Rivers Ford. Amulet: red ruby.

DAV Koehl (3319–): Defender. Defender Commander of Kin-Deren provincial Fal'kin forces. Amulet: blue sapphire.

DESDE il'Kellis Pinal (3319–): Seer. Prime of Kin-Deren. Served as il'Kin battle seer before elevation as Prime's Second. Joined in union with Kaarl Pinal. Mother of Mirana Pinal. Amulet: yellow topaz.

GANNAH Tesabe (3345–3367): Defender. Member of the il'Kin. Born to Jad-Anüna Province. Killed in a grynwen ambush in Kana-Akün forest in 3367. Amulet: yellow sapphire.

GEMMA il'Lakumbe Piaar (3318–): Unaspected. Senior herbswoman at the Healing Hostel of Kin-Deren. Born in Jad-Anüna province. Husband Baden Piaar (deceased). Mother to five children (three sons, two daughters) killed in a Ken'nar raid in 3350.

HAARLEN Lasen (3312–): Unaspected. Quartermaster of the Learning Hall of Kin-Deren province.

ILRIK Maldaar (2089–2122): Defender. Ken Defender of the Dark Triumvirate. Also known as "Ilrik the Black." Amulet: deep red-purple garnet.

ISEL, Wend (3317–): Defender. Horsemaster of Kin-Deren province. Oversees the stables in Deren and the province's warhorse herd. Amulet: yellow zircon.

JASAL Pinal (2092–2122): Trine. Primus Magne and Prime of Kin-Deren. Amulet: diamond.

KAARL Pinal (3314–): Defender. Defender Commander of the il'Kin. Named Steward of the Quorum of Light after the death of Toban Kellis. Joined in union with Desde il'Kellis Pinal. Father of Mirana Pinal. Amulet: red garnet.

MAARK Bedane (3352–): Unaspected. Orphaned when his parents were killed in a Ken'nar raid of their homestead and farm in 3365.

MIRANA Pinal (3351–): Fal'kin scholaira, training as a seer. Daughter of Kaarl and Desde Pinal.

MORGAN Jord (3334–): Defender. Commander's Second of the il'Kin. Amulet: purple amethyst.

NIAH il'Sahli Beltran (3325–): Healer. Priora of Healing Hostel of Kin-Deren. Born in Tash-Hamar province. Joined in union with Tennen Beltran. Mother of Teague Beltran. Amulet: rose quartz.

NIALL Corran (3318–): Defender. Commander's Second of the Kin-Deren provincial Fal'kin forces. Amulet: red beryl.

TADDIE (Taddeus) Egen (3362–): Fal'kin scholaire Seer. Apprenticed under Defender Wend Isel as a stable hand.

TARN Salka (3315–3365): Defender. Member of the il'Kin. Killed in a Ken'nar skirmish near Thyre's Crossing in the Trak-Calan highlands in 3365. Amulet: blue zircon.

TAUL Brandt (3320–): Unaspected. Magistrate of Deren.

TEAGUE Beltran (3351–): Unaspected. Son of Healers Tennen and Niah Beltran. Apprenticed as an herbsman in the Healing Hostel.

TENNEN Beltran (3322–): Healer. Priore of Healing Hostel of Kin-Deren. Joined in union with Niah il'Sahli Beltran. Father of Teague Beltran. Amulet: light-purple sapphire.

TOBAN Kellis (3272–3367): Seer. Former Prime of Kin-Deren, Steward of the Quorum of Light. Father of Desde il'Kellis Pinal. Amulet: light-yellow beryl.

YENIRA Irasda (3349–): Fal'kin scholaira Seer. Chooses early to support the Battle of Two Rivers Ford. Amulet: blue topaz.

Trak-Calan—2ⁿᵈ Hall. Standard: gold field with green tiger

HINSAH Parn (3348–): Defender. Commander's Second of Trak-Calan provincial Fal'kin forces. Amulet: medium-green peridot.

KOBEN Ryotan (3314–): Seer. Prime of Trak-Calan. Raised as a foster brother to Tetric Garis. Amulet: dark-orange garnet.

SHALAS Yutan (3245–3330): Seer. Prime of Trak-Calan. Foster father and patrua mentor of Tetric Garis. Amulet: golden topaz.

Rün-Taran—3rd Hall. Standard: white field with blue capricorn

BINTHE Lima (3343–): Seer. Battle seer of the il'Kin. Granddaughter of Eshe and Lindar Pashcot. Amulet: green emerald.

ESHE il'Bahane Pashcot (3270–): Seer. Prime of Rün-Taran. Joined in union with Lindar Pashcot (deceased). Grandmother to Binthe Lima. Amulet: pale-blue zircon.

LINDAR Pashcot (3268–3330): Defender. Defender Commander of Rün-Taran provincial Fal'kin forces and Prime's Second. Joined in union with Eshe il'Bahane Pashcot. Grandfather to Binthe Lima. Amulet: red-orange carnelian.

SYNE Develan (3289–): Defender. Defender Commander of Rün-Taran provincial Fal'kin forces and Prime's Second. Amulet: orange citrine.

Tash-Hamar—4th Hall. Standard: purple field with red leopard

AMAHL Khabarh (2079–2143): Defender. Prime of Tash-Hamar during Jasal Pinal's lifetime. Offered aid to Antiri il'Amil Pinal and her newborn son after Jasal's death. Amulet: blue-violet iolite.

FALANNAH il'Aldi Sadhi (3308–3350): Seer. Served as a battle seer in the Tash-Hamari provincial Fal'kin forces. Mother of Timir Sadhi. Sister of Fasen Aldi. Amulet: pink morganite.

FASEN Aldi (3303–): Defender. Prime of Tash-Hamar. Uncle of Timir Sadhi. Brother to Falannah il'Aldi Sadhi. Amulet: blue sapphire.

TIMIR Sadhi (3333–): Defender. Defender Commander of Tash-Hamari Fal'kin provincial forces and Prime's Second. Nephew of Fasen Aldi. Amulet: deep-orange citrine.

Kana-Akün—5th Hall. Standard: green field with gold hart

BELESSA il'Isofar Tir (3279–3367): Healer. Prime of Kana-Akün. Presumed killed in the Battle of Falantir, winter 3367. Amulet: green tourmaline.

THIEER Pannen (3321–3367): Seer. Ranking Seer, served as a battle seer and Prime's Second of Kana-Akün. Presumed killed in the Battle of Falantir, winter 3367. Amulet: yellow apatite.

Varn-Erdal—6ᵗʰ Hall. Standard: white field with red horse

CLARIENNE il'Hadten Jord (3336–3359): Unaspected. Shepherd and homesteader. Wife of Morgan Jord. Died with infant son, Pieter, in a Ken'nar raid in the Varn-Erdal plains in 3359.

DREI Carada (3348–3365): Defender. Son of Trein Carada and Marienne Tans. Attacked by Ken'nar, winter 3365, presumed dead. Amulet: deep-magenta rhodolite.

ERAN Talz (3315–): Unaspected. Horsemaster of Varn-Erdal province. Oversees the stables in Edara and the province's warhorse herd.

GRENNE Fadern (3325–): Seer. Ranking Seer, elevated to Prime's Second of Varn-Erdal before the Battle of Edara. Two sons (deceased), one daughter (deceased) by Trein Carada. Previously coupled with Trein Carada until his death. Coupled with Liaonne Edaran. Amulet: deep-pink tourmaline.

ILLENNE Talz (3349–): Unaspected. Horse herd mistress and archer. Daughter of Eran Talz.

LIAONNE Edaran (3342–): Defender. Prime of Varn-Erdal, elevated after the Battle of Two Rivers Ford. Daughter of Vallia Edaran. Amulet: yellow topaz.

MARIENNE Tans (3318–): Unaspected. Learning hall attendant and laundress. Mother of Drei Carada. Coupled with Trein Carada until his death. Bore five other children (three sons, two daughters), all defenders, deceased.

NATHEN Keldir (3298–): Defender. Senior defender on Prime's Council. Father of Liaonne Edaran. Amulet: amber citrine.

PALEN Clar (3298–): Unaspected. Senior learning hall herbsman.

PIETER Jord (3358–3359, d. 6 months): Unaspected. Son of Morgan and Clarienne Jord. Died in a Ken'nar raid in Varn-Erdal plains.

PIOL Lidan (3295–): Defender. Senior defender on Prime's Council. Amulet: green chrysoberyl.

TREIN Carada (3317–3365): Defender. Attacked by Ken'nar, winter 3365, presumed dead. Amulet: blue apatite.

WESAL Pettan (3293–): Defender. Senior defender on Prime's Council. Amulet: dark-pink zircon.

VALLIA Edaran (3317–3368): Defender. Prime of Varn-Erdal. Perished in an ambush during the Battle of Two Rivers Ford. Amulet: red ruby.

Jad-Anüna—7th Hall. Standard: blue field with gold lion

ABER Hebari (3328–): Defender. Defender Commander of Jad-Anünan Fal'kin provincial forces and Prime's Second. Amulet: green spinel.

NAMBRE Dinir (3302–): Defender. Prime of Jad-Anüna. Amulet: red-brown andalusite.

TILENATETE Nasta (2835–2867): Trine. Prime of Jad-Anüna. Elevated to Primus Magne during the Red Plague of

2864–2866. Killed by Ken'nar when she tried to offer aid during the pandemic. Amulet: pale-green chrysoberyl.

Sün-Kasal—8th Hall. Standard: red field with white bull

BYSTRA il'Tari Klai (3312–3350): Defender. Joined in union with Sahm Klai. Two sons (deceased), one daughter (deceased). Amulet: blue-gray cordierite.

RABB Plout (3328–): Seer. Ranking Seer and Prime's Second. Amulet: red-brown topaz.

SAHM Klai (3308–): Defender. Prime of Sün-Kasal. Joined in union with Bystra il'Tari Klai (deceased). Two sons (deceased), one daughter (deceased) with Bystra il'Tari. Amulet: smoky-brown quartz.

Dar-Azûl—9th Hall. Standard: black field with argent silver griffin

BHRECHT, Jass (3335-): Defender. Born to Sün-Kasal province. Amulet: green emerald.

KHORR, Lyer (3320-): Defender. Quarta Commander (4 silver chains) of the Ken'nar forces. Born to Kana-Akün province. Amulet: red beryl.

SIDO Rendel (3345–): Seer. Serves as commander of Dar-Azûlan Fal'kin provincial forces and Prime's Second. Born to Kana-Akün province. Amulet: light-green peridot.

STAINE, Kev (3325–): Defender. Warlord Commander (5 silver chains) of the Ken'nar forces. Born to Kin-Deren province. Amulet: medium-blue kyanite.

TETRIC Garis (3313–): Trine. Prime of Dar-Azûl. Amulet: hematite.

TRINE REVELATION
The Kinderra Saga: Book 3

Glossary of Terms and Words

-á..past perfect tense; joined to the word it modifies. Example: had created = creará.

a ....to

a nehíl ....(you are) welcome; literally "a nothing;" not to be confused with a greeting "Ben ve" as in "good coming."

accepte, acceptem..............accept, acceptance

ad..at

adam, adamé, adamá ....forget, forgot, forgotten

agen....................................again

ai..yes

ain......................................one, whole, complete, only

aire....................................air

alainne................................beautiful

alta....................................above, high

ama....................................love

amausar ....steward, stewardship, manage; literally "loving use"

amula ....amulet; Amulets allow an Aspected to further focus and use their innate Aspects, especially outside of themselves. An Aspected's life force harmonics will resonate with one specific crystal, except in the case of a Trine. Because they possess all three Aspects, Trines have the innate ability to modulate their life harmonics to adapt to any amulet.

amulets ....The sacred tool and relic containing a gemstone used by the Aspected to manifest their powers outside of themselves. While all Aspected have certain abilities without an amulet (e.g., telekinesis, telepathy), to produce major actions with their Aspects requires the use of an amulet. Typically, when they've reached 18 summers old, Aspected choose a single amulet for life through a mystical union of life harmonics matching the natural harmonics within the gemstone's crystal structure. The connection is unique and indelible. The loss or destruction of an amulet causes untold anguish to the Aspected individual, most committing suicide. Only Trines, those with all three Aspects, can choose more than one amulet. (see Aspects, Aspected, Choosing Ceremony, Trine)

an .... an

anaíl, anaíle .... breath, breathe

anelies .... another

animale .... animal

Anqa Lingua .... literally "old tongue"; the ancient language of Kinderra

aonta .... union

aquete, aqueté .... water, watered

aquila .... eagle

ár .... on, upon

as .... as

aspeca .... life

aspecaem..soul, spirit

aspece, aspecae ....live, alive

Aspecta('e)...Aspect(s)

Aspecta'e Alta....................................Aspects Above; This is the trinity-like deity that Kinderrans believe created the universe and all living things. They are the source of life and the powers of the Aspects.

Aspected...Generic term for one who possesses the powers of the Aspects. In the culture and beliefs of Kinderra, the Unaspected were the first peoples created by the Aspects Above. Some of these were chosen by the Aspects Above and touched with fingers of lightning, bestowing upon them the powers of the Aspects to become the Aspected, stewards and protectors of all of Kinderra. The expression of Aspect powers occurs in about one of every 1,000 births.

Aspects, Powers of the..................The powers of the Aspects occur in three types:

Defending, conferring extraordinary reflexes, speed, strength, and situational awareness, as well as the ability to manifest amulet fire from one's amulet; Seeing, conferring the ability to see into the past, present, and future; and Healing, conferring the ability to stimulate the healing of injury and illness thousands of times faster than normal. Major expressions of the Aspects require the focus of an amulet. For example, while it is possible for a healer without an amulet to suppress pain in another to a degree, to set a broken bone would require an amulet to focus the Healing Aspect. All Aspected have certain innate abilities that do not require an amulet, including telekinesis, telepathy, and some ability to shunt away pain and enhance endurance.

aste .... star

atuda .... together

aud, audé .... hear, heard

avera ....long for, want

ban...white

bath...both

bé ....by

ben..good, kind

Ben dië...good morning, good day

Ben iré..farewell, goodbye; literally
                                                    "good leaving"

Ben kin; B'kin ....hello, hi (informal); literally
                                                    "good light"

Ben nöc...good night

benedicta, benedictaé,
benedictan ....bless, blessed, blessing

besa...kiss

bhéth; bhéth en aonta.....................join; join in union (marry)

bia ....before

bir..bring

biraen, biraena, biraen'e ....child/son, daughter,
                                                    children; often used as a term
                                                    of endearment

biran ....birth; literally "bring forth"

Book of Kinderra, The..................Historical reference of
                                                    Kinderra written before the
                                                    Sundering by Aspected and

Unaspected scholars.
Considered one of the two
revered books of the Fal'kin
along with the Ora
Fal'kinnen.

braith, braith ár .... depend/rely, depend/rely on

brea .... great, most (quantity); (see
also magne)

bremaithe .... grandmother; also, term of
respect for female elders

brepaithe .... grandfather; also, term of
respect for male elder

buai... win

caela .... sky

call.. telepathic communication
("He called a warning to her
mind."); also, the act of
telekinesis ("He called a cup
into his waiting hand.")

calora, calorae.................................... warm, warming

cara, caran; Ëi cara('e) .... friend, friendship; my
friend(s)

cëos; cëosan....................................... choose; chosen

cerebus... brain, mind

Choosing Ceremony .... The sacrament where
Aspected *scholaire'e* choose

their gemstone amulets through the mystical union of their life harmonics with the harmonics of a gemstone's crystal. The ceremony is held annually for those who have reached 18 summers old.

chosant...protect

cin ....with

cinen..within

cinstandan..withstand

clae..sword, weapon

Codex of Jasal the Great, The.......The journal of Jasal Pinal. Written between 2117 and 2132. There have been several attempts throughout history to destroy the work, but none have succeeded.

com..like (similar to)

comé...what

compre...know

comprende, comprendea ....understand, understanding

confian ....trust

consente...agree; Example: I agree, okay = Ëo consente corem .... face

covrir (v.) .... cover

crear, crearé, creará .... create(s), make; created, had created

il'Crearae (The Creation) .... The creation psalm from the Ora Fal'kinnen. Also, creation or a euphemism for Kinderra or the universe

culpa; Ëo ad culpa .... fault; "I'm sorry" (literally, "I am at fault")

cunaré (slang) .... derogatory term for female genitalia

daingaen .... stable, solid

dam .... give

dar .... mountain

defecta, defectim .... fail, failure

defende, defendeä, defendeo .... defend, fight, protect; defender; defense, protection

defender .... An Aspected individual who possesses the Defending Aspect

Defender Commander .... Highest-ranking officer in a Fal'kin provincial army; (see Second)

Defender's Second....................Second-in-command of a
                                   Fal'kin provincial army; (see
                                   Second)

derra ....earth, land, world

derranen..............................foundation; based on the
                                   root word for "land"

dhái....................................past

dici.....................................speak, say

dië ....dawn, day, morning

digita..................................finger

diu......................................long (length)

doma..................................home, house

dúa ....between

-'e ....plural suffix (pronounced
                                   'eh'); joined to word it
                                   modifies. Example:
                                   friend/friends = cara/cara'e.

-é ....past tense suffix; joined to
                                   the word it modifies.
                                   Example: created = crearé.

e...and (pronounced 'ee')

Ëa..me

Ëam ....mine

Ëi ....my

elies .... other

ëllenas .... fill(s)

empe, a'empe.................................... begin, had begun

emplecti.. embrace, hug

en.. in

engre (n.), engren (v.)...................... anger

enigma .... puzzle, riddle

Ëo.. I, I am

Ëo anaíle; Ëo aspece .... "I breathe; I live." A
defender's adage.

Ëome .... us

Ëomus .... we, we are

et... there

eta(n) .... there was/were

etim .... still

etís .... there is/are

expel.. Punishment for a capital
crime among the Fal'kin
where the condemned is
forced to leave Fal'kin
society and his/her province.
In the most extreme
circumstances, a Fal'kin's
amulet is taken. Most Fal'kin

would prefer death to be kept from their calling to the Aspects, their amulets, and their province.

il' Exultantae (The Rejoice) ....A psalm of praise from the Ora Fal'kinnen

exulte...exult, exalt, praise

fal...follow

Fal'kin; Fal'kinnen............................"They who follow the Light;" the whole body of the Fal'kin. These Aspected people believe in the philosophy of the Light from Within. They use their innate powers of the Aspects within themselves as their sole source of power. To draw in life forces to augment one's power is considered the most extreme crime one could commit. Fal'kin caught using the Power from Without are relieved of their amulets and expelled from the province.

fár...for

fárdam, fárdamen;
Ëo fárdam Oë.................................forgive, forgiven; "I forgive you"

fhí, fhíagn, a fhí ....weave, weaving, to weave filam .... thread

fin .... at last, end, finished

fissura... crack, fissure, split

forma .... form

forte .... fort, keep (building), strong

fos... yet

fuádain .... fleeting

gainem .... sand (n.)

gemma .... crystal, jewel

gente, -n, -na..................................... people, man, woman

gháinn, gháinn'e .... grain, grains

gloria, gloriae, gloriaé .... glory, glorify, glorified

Gratas, Gratas Oë............................. thanks; thank you

grynwen.. Massive, wolflike carnivores known for their pupilless red eyes and their viciousness. It is believed they use some type of primitive Aspect-like senses to hunt.

gryphus.. griffin

hac... here

hale.. holy

har .... hill healer...An Aspected individual who possesses the Healing Aspect

i' ....of; joined to word it modifies

-í...future tense suffix, joined to word it modifies; Example: will create = crearí.

id (m.), ida (f.) ....it(s)

Iëa, Iëam Iëas....................................she, her, hers

Ië, Iëm, Iës ....he, him, his

il'-...of the; joined to word it modifies. Often used as a prefix in formal surnames, especially matrilineal names.

il'Kin..The Fal'kin strike force comprised of defenders and battle seers from all nine provinces. The il'Kin is a special operations unit serving all of Kinderra and augments provincial forces in times of need. It is under the direction of the Steward of the Quorum of Light and led by a defender commander. Historically, the il'Kin has served Kinderra in the absence of a Trine's provincial forces. Only the most highly accomplished

Fal'kin are invited to join its ranks.

imbecilae, -t...................................ignorance, stupidity; ignorant, stupid

impatientia ....impatience

inaspeca (n.)...................................free will, will

incendio..burn

infera...below, under

inimica ....enemy

íre..go, leave, journey

ísi(é)..are, be, is; was (preposition); (see pronouns)

íuven; íuven sibe/siba....................young; younger ("little") brother/sister

ken...power

Ken'nar; Ken'narren ...."They who use the Power;" The whole body of the Ken'nar. Ken'nar believe in the philosophy of the Power from Without. They use their innate Aspects and their amulets only to pull in the life forces around them and pour out that power back through their amulets, providing a seemingly limitless supply of power. They believe the use of the Aspects should not be limited by one's innate powers.

Ken'nar ranks ....Ken'nar military leadership is denoted by chains on armor epaulets.

5 gold chains: Ken Lord. The supreme leader of the entire Ken'narren, akin to a Fal'kin prime or even Ain Magne.

1 gold chain: The Second (Defender, Seer, or rarely, Healer), or second-in-command of the entire Ken'narren.

5 silver chains: Warlord Commander, top-ranking officer, second only the Second. Equivalent to a five-star general.

4 silver chains: Quatra Commander, commands a quarter of the full Ken'nar army; 3 silver chains, Trina Commander, commands a third of each Quarte legion; 2 silver chains, Seconda Commander, commands half of each Trina legion; 1 silver chain, Unis Commander,

commands half of a Seconda legion.

kin...light

Kin ísi Oëa.......................................Light be yours; a formal greeting. The reply is "E Oë" (And you).

kinema ....lightning

len..gentle, soft

leten..allow, let

locarae...location, place

luve...rain

luveclae..storm, tempest; literally "rain sword"

ma, maís ....may, may be, maybe

maent...meant

magistrate...the highest-ranking government official of a province's Unaspected, akin to a Fal'kin prime

magne ....great (honorable); (see also brea)

maithe..mother; has the connotation of "mommy"

manë ....hand

marca..brand

matrua ....aunt; also, can mean "godmother," "teacher," or "mentor"

mer..sea, ocean

mercare, mercaré.............................buy, bought

minia...little, small, tiny

mista...mist

morte, mortea, mortean,
mortes ....dead, death, die

mor..more

nome ....name, call; also, a telepathic call of communication

necesit ....must

nefas, nefas'e....................................sin, sins

nehíl..nothing

nöc..night

nubla...cloud

numbers, 1-10
(cardinal, quantity)..........................primus, seconda, trina, quatra, quinta, sexta, septa, octa, nonta, decema (see also "ain")

nun .... nor

nunqa .... never

-ó .... present perfect tense; joined to the word it modifies. Example: have created = crearó

o.. or

obsca; Obsca Oëa osa.................... close, shut; "Close your mouth" ("shut up")

Oë... you

Oëa... your, yours

Oëma .... who, whom

Oëme... they

Oëmea .... those

Oëmus.. them, their

onoír .... honor

Ora Fal'kinnen .... Literally "Prayer of the Fal'kin." The major religious work of the Fal'kin, detailing their relationship with the Aspects Above, the powers of the Aspects, and Kinderra. Considered one of the great books of the Fal'kin along with The Book of Kinderra.

osa...mouth

oscuil, oscuil'e................................eye, eyes

pace...peace

palibre ....word

passenae (n.), passen (v.)................passage, hallway (n.); pass (v.)

paithe...father; has the connotation
                                                of "daddy"

patientia ....patience

patrua ....uncle; also "godfather,"
                                                "teacher" or "mentor"

pecta ....breast, chest

penilaré (slang)................................derogatory term for male
                                                genitalia

per..but

periclaem ....fear

pericul, periculus ....danger, dangerous

pián..pain, suffering

placre...please (v.)

potest...possible

pon, pone ....lay/lay down, lies/rests

potem...after

Prime .... The Aspected leader of a province's Fal'kin

Prime's Second................................. The Aspected next in line for primeship (see Second)

Primus .... Anqa Linqua for "prime;" used as a formal reference

Primus Magne .... A dictator-like role elevated from among the Aspected to lead the entire continent's Fal'kin. This role is enacted during times of extreme duress in Kinderra, such as a pandemic or other widespread calamity.

priore (m.), priora (f.),
priore'e (pl.) .... The head of a healing hostel or infirmary, something akin to the chief of staff

pronouns.. are capitalized; Ëo (I), Oë (you), Ëomus (we), etc.; state of being implied. Example: I am here = Ëo hac.

proxi... against, close, near

qua.. which

quen .... when

quet, quetís.................................... where, where is

quis... some

quistempre('e) ....sometime(s)

quod ....because

Quorum of Light............................The council comprised of all the primes and seconds from the nine provinces of Kinderra. The Quorum discusses the state of affairs in Kinderra and sets policy and laws affecting the Fal'kin of every province.

Quorumtide...........................The major holiday time in Kinderra, marked by feasting and celebration, and often fewer military actions due to impending winter weather. It coincides with the Quorum meeting, which occurs in Deren for one sevenday each Reckoning in Fifthmonth.

reace ....reach

Reckoning...........................The literal number of the year. Example: Mirana Pinal was born in the Reckoning of 3352.

rememore ....remember

Rememore Kin en Forte.............Remember the Light in the Keep

Rememore Kin e Forte.................. Remember the Light and the
Keep

responara.. answer

requa .... require

revelar... reveal

risa... rise

rith... run

robare.. steal

runh... secret, hide

sana .... health

Sana e Kin a Oë.............................. Health and Light to You; a
formal greeting

sanare, sanarente, sanareä.............. heal, healing, healer

sculpte... sculpt, shape

scinane, scinané, scinaneá.............. shine, shined, shone

scholaire (m.), scholaira (f.),
scholaire'e (pl.) .... Aspected students learning
how to use their powers.

Second.. The second-in-command of
a province's Fal'kin (Prime's
Second) or Fal'kin army
(Commander's Second). This
is an extremely influential
and pivotal role, requiring
much vetting and

interviewing, and provides an immediate and seamless transition of power upon a prime's or defender commander's death or incapacitation. Final approval for either role rests with a province's prime, although in the case of a Commander's Second, the Defender Commander's choice strongly influences the decision.

Seconde...See Second

seer...An Aspected individual who possesses the Seeing Aspect

seer's ruse ....A seer technique for projecting visions through an amulet to be viewed by others. (see also Visi Externa)

servad..servant

settan ....set

siba, Ëi siba ....sister, my sister

sibe, Ëi sibe ....brother, my brother

siber (n.), sibere (v.) ....sieve (n.), sift (v.)

siniúint ....destiny skene .... skein

solis .... alone, apart, separate

staíonnae, staíonne .... need (n.), need (v.)

statam .... now

standan .... stand

Steward of the Quorum of Light . The influential facilitator of the Quorum of Light is elected by the primes and seconds of the Quorum. The steward has no vote for his/her province but can cast a single vote by proxy for another province unable to attend Quorum meetings as well as cast a tie-breaking vote in the rare instance when it occurs.

straitéis .... strategy, plan

summer .... Euphemism for a calendar year, especially in reference to age (I am sixteen summers old; the man has seen thirty summers); also, the literal summer season. (see also Reckoning)

ta .... to

talus('e) .... claw(s), talon(s) te ....from

tempre ....time

ten ....has, have

testus; Ëo testus ....swear (an oath); I swear

tha ....than

the ....then

thet ....that

toucha ....touch

todhái ....future

traiseh ....treasure

tré ....through

treor ....command, guide

trevia ....direction, way; (see also íre, passenae)

tuda ....all

tudempre ....always, eternal, forever; literally "all time"

tudsa ....also

tuil, tuilé ....earn, earned

u'- ....not, un-; joined to word it modifies. Example: u'kin meaning dark or "not light."

u'ai .... no

u'ben .... evil; literally "not good"

u'bendicta .... curse; literally "un-blessing"

u'cin .... without

u'gen, u'gente .... none, no one

u'kin .... dark; literally "not light"

u'len .... hard

U'Nehíl .... Literally "false nothing." The practice of masking one's presence from within the Aspects by manipulating one's Aspects to mimic or reflect the "life force" noise in the general vicinity.

u'pace .... battle, war; literally "not peace"

u'verdas .... falsehood, lie

u'vide .... blind, sightless, often derogatory; "u'vide vermihn" meaning "sightless maggot" as someone without the Aspects.

u'vide excra (slang) .... Unaspected; literally "sightless shit"

Unaspected .... those without the Aspects upacaem .... destruction; based on the root word for "war"

usar .... use

ve .... come(s)

verda, verdas .... true, truth

vermihn .... maggot, worm, or any vermin or disgusting creature; often used as an insult

vide, vidé, Videä, Vidë .... look/see, looked/saw, Seer, Sight

virtú .... bravery, courage

visi .... vision

Visi Externa .... A seer technique for projecting visions through an amulet to be viewed by others; also known as a seer's ruse

voide .... void

year .... see Reckoning; see summer

ABOUT THE AUTHOR

While other kids read comic books under the covers with a flashlight at bedtime, C.K. DONNELLY wrote fan fiction and fantasy stories.

She used her love of writing to pursue a career in journalism and was honored with several press awards for business and economic reporting. She has also held careers in healthcare, and currently runs her own freelance writing and marketing support firm.

The self-described "unsuccessful quitter" resides in Arizona with her oh-so-patient husband and her little black dog (who is equally patient). She no longer writes under the covers by flashlight. Usually.

www.ingramcontent.com/pod-product-compliance
Lightning Source LLC
Chambersburg PA
CBHW051200190726
48288CB00006B/1736